SPECIAL MESSAGE TO READERS

THE ULVERSCROFT FOUNDATION
(registered UK charity number 264873)
was established in 1972 to provide funds for
research, diagnosis and treatment of eye diseases.
Examples of major projects funded by
the Ulverscroft Foundation are:-

- The Children's Eye Unit at Moorfields Eye Hospital, London
- The Ulverscroft Children's Eye Unit at Great Ormond Street Hospital for Sick Children
- Funding research into eye diseases and treatment at the Department of Ophthalmology, University of Leicester
- The Ulverscroft Vision Research Group, Institute of Child Health
- Twin operating theatres at the Western Ophthalmic Hospital, London
- The Chair of Ophthalmology at the Royal Australian College of Ophthalmologists

You can help further the work of the Foundation
by making a donation or leaving a legacy.
Every contribution is gratefully received. If you
would like to help support the Foundation or
require further information, please contact:

THE ULVERSCROFT FOUNDATION
The Green, Bradgate Road, Anstey
Leicester LE7 7FU, England
Tel: (0116) 236 4325

website: www.foundation.ulverscroft.com

Christopher Ransom is the author of three international bestselling novels. After studying literature at Colorado State University and managing an international business importing exotic reptiles, he worked at *Entertainment Weekly* magazine in New York, various now deceased technology firms in Los Angeles, and as a copywriter at Famous Footwear in Madison, Wisconsin. Christopher now lives near his hometown of Boulder, Colorado.

Keep up with Christopher online at:

www.ransomesque.com
www.facebook.com/ChristopherRansomAuthor

THE FADING

Since childhood, Noel Shaker has been able to disappear, without warning or explanation. But his gift leaves him alone and afraid — and the more he tries to control it, the nearer he comes to madness. When Noel learns that some people can see him — and that his power has unleashed an otherworldly evil — he must descend into darkness and confront a relentless killer to discover the true source of his 'fading'.

Books by Christopher Ransom
Published by The House of Ulverscroft:

THE PEOPLE NEXT DOOR

CHRISTOPHER RANSOM

THE FADING

Complete and Unabridged

CHARNWOOD
Leicester

First published in Great Britain in 2012 by
Sphere
An imprint of Little, Brown Book Group
London

First Charnwood Edition
published 2013
by arrangement with
Little, Brown Book Group
London

Lyrics from 'Feel Us Shaking' with kind permission
of Sean Kelly and The Samples. Copyright Sean
Kelly and The Samples. All rights reserved.

A catalogue record for this book is available
from the British Library.

ISBN 978–1–4448–1555–9

Published by
F. A. Thorpe (Publishing)
Anstey, Leicestershire

Set by Words & Graphics Ltd.
Anstey, Leicestershire
Printed and bound in Great Britain by
T. J. International Ltd., Padstow, Cornwall

This book is printed on acid-free paper

For Sally
True friend, celestial soul sister,
mother luminescent

gentle thoughts meander through the sand
as the ship made currents reach the land
the omniscient sun paving through the sky
and when it's done all the seabirds fly

I'd like to stay but I couldn't stay with you
I have to go, I have a lot I want to do
pleasures be waiting by the sea
with a smile for all the world to see

diamond waves through sunglass days go by
so beautiful to be here and alive
though I've built sometimes so hard
did I survive?
feel us shaking

THE SAMPLES

The true mystery of the world is the
visible, not the invisible.

OSCAR WILDE,
The Picture of Dorian Gray

1

He was still a soft floating consciousness in his mother's womb when the nameless thing that would destroy his ability to lead a normal life, even as it allowed him to thrive in darkness and secrets, first reached out and blanketed him. Sheltered and growing at a rate deemed natural and healthy, the fetus was in his twenty-seventh week, a period known for rapid brain development and the lids' first shutterings over newly formed eyes. The shroud fell upon him in less time than is required for light from a lamp to cross a room and touch the window, lasted 2.45639 seconds, and retreated as quickly as it had arrived.

He registered nothing physically or mentally. It was as though a star had been eclipsed by a strange moon in a planetary system ten thousand galaxies away, the frictionless vacuum of blackout unobserved and silent, except that here the eclipsed object was the child and the universe was his mother. There wasn't much to it that first time. He simply vanished in the absolute absence of light while sleeping in total darkness, and five heartbeats later was revealed, still sleeping in total darkness.

His mother, who was napping on the couch while the end credits and depressing chords of *Days of Our Lives* played from the console Zenith, also felt nothing. The shroud left no trace, scar, impairment or disability. No medical test could detect it. Ultrasound sonograms were not standard at the time, but even if Rebecca Shaker had undergone one at the precise moment her unborn child disappeared, the sound waves would have painted a normal picture of the life she carried. Sound was sound, after all, and light was light. One could bounce off what the other could not illuminate.

His change, if it could be called such, happened and unhappened too quickly for the human eye to record. The in-between was a silent aberration. And so it was that, for lack of a witness to the event, no one would ever know it had found him so young.

Or that it was only beginning to form an attachment to him.

2

The next incident did not occur until 29 February 1976, a leap day, just fourteen minutes before he began his descent into the birth canal. He was veiled for a little more than nine seconds, as if the child or forces interested in him were unsure of his place in the world. Not even Dr Roose, a sober man overseeing his one hundred and eighty-eighth delivery, happened to see the child depart from and return to the humanly visible spectrum. The mother felt nothing other than the usual contractions and agony.

The leapling crowned. His shoulders made Rebecca Shaker scream through the final release. The boy slid forth into Dr Roose's large gentle hands. The cord was cut. The child took well to breathing. Becky and her husband John, who were young and in love and could not know their child would lead such an extraordinary life, cried with joy. At seven pounds six ounces, the Shaker baby — who was named Noel, in honor of a son Becky's grandmother had lost in his infancy, but whom the grandmother from then on regarded as her angel of grace and strength — was pronounced intact and lovely by the senior nurse, his head of black hair most impressive.

A second, younger nurse, who was always anxious during deliveries, noted the cold assessing regard in the baby's eyes as they roved around the room with unnatural alertness. He looked lost, searching, as if he had been expecting to find someone or something else waiting for him upon his arrival. During the weighing, he fixated on one corner of the ceiling, the darkest point in the room, above the drapes and the cold black pane of glass. His tiny mouth fell open and his breath seemed to catch before he scrunched his eyes and craned away in apparent genuine revulsion.

The young nurse, whose name was Onnika — a Scandinavian word for light — had inherited her parents' superstitions about unnatural darkness and dim rooms. Onnika became momentarily hypnotized by the darkly recessed corner, as the child had been, and moments later she was blinded. Losing all vision in an instant, Onnika cried out and ran from the delivery room, colliding with the door and a linen basket on wheels in the hall before fumbling her way to another, empty room, where she fell to the floor sobbing in distress. After several minutes of frantic praying, her vision was restored.

Onnika did not share the cause of her panic or its blinding effect with Dr Roose or the Shaker parents. She was reprimanded, but she convincingly explained she had only been tired and overcome with emotion. She was sent home early, but had difficulty sleeping and required a reading lamp to be left on at her bedside at all hours for several weeks. She did not know what the child had seen, but feared it was a demon that had followed her home and was waiting above her bed each night, preparing to take her

4

while she slept. Onnika's greatest fear was that the demon would occupy her soul and command her to kill herself, extinguishing the light and life she had been blessed with.

Her fear lessened some months later when she met a nice man named Ian, pronounced like the oxygen-taking gesture which precipitates sleep, who was visiting Colorado as a member of the Norwegian national ski team. Ian came to the emergency room with a broken ankle and chapped lips, to which Onnika administered plaster and emollients. Riding the gurney between floors, Ian told her a joke in Swedish. Onnika stayed past her shift to bring Ian cocoa with freeze-dried marshmallows. He returned to Norway but wrote her letters weekly, often on the backs of post-cards featuring grainy photos of the fjords. Onnika fell asleep reading Ian's letters in her bed.

Their courtship, no less intense for its glacial inertia, reminded Onnika she had much to live for, replacing her superstitions about good and evil, demons and light, with superstitions about love. After Onnika mailed Ian a pair of her white nurse stockings, he agreed to move to the United States. Onnika birthed two boys and a girl. Ian broke his lower back skiing and retired from the international circuit to launch a line of après ski apparel, which proved so successful he was able to stay home with his family more often. For much of the remainder of her life Onnika and her children were quite happy, almost never staring strangely into rooms without lamps, or peering for too long up into ceiling corners beyond light's reach.

3

When Noel was seven months and ten days old, his mother awoke to the sound of his cries making their way down the hall. Rebecca exited her bed in one smooth rise that did not disturb her husband and, still half asleep, shambled blindly into the spare bedroom. As if appeased by the comforting sound of his mother's approach, Noel ceased his bawling by the time she reached the threshold. John had painted the walls blue with silver and gold moons that now looked too real, as though their home was open and balanced on the edge of the solar system. The bare wood floorboards were cold against Becky's soles. Swaying, she steadied herself in the doorway a moment.

Eight feet away, on the other side of his room, a blurry white shape filled the four-square window above his birch crib. The shape was of a small man, from the waist up, wearing a white suit and matching rounded top hat. His features were as indistinct as hers in the darkness, the face a smeared oval with dark sockets and a reddish ring around the unsmiling mouth.

Becky gasped and thrust herself into the room to protect her child. Within her first two steps the figure in the window retreated and was replaced by her own hazy reflection, bringing her to a halt. Absurd though she knew it to be, she reached up and patted her hair, half expecting and hoping to find that she had pinned up her hair in a bun or some other nest which might suggest the shape she had seen in the window. But her hair was down, hanging around her chin and barely protecting her bare shoulders from the draft now seeping through the window frame.

Her heart slowed its frantic beating as she gazed down at Noel. He was staring up at her, face bunching with a fresh round of squalls. She checked his diaper and found it dry. His forehead wasn't hot. His chest was not clammy. He was hungry, that was all.

She settled into the reading chair beside the small table and lowered the right strap of her nightgown. He began to feed at once, pulling at her with resentment. She touched his eyebrows and wiped something that had dried at his nose, then folded the hem of her gown up around his legs and torso. Oh God, she was tired. Everyone said motherhood stretched you thin, but no one came right out and told you just how utterly flattened the daily cycle of caring for an infant left you. She didn't want to fall asleep in here again, waking with a sore neck, but she couldn't help closing her eyes for just a moment. Soon she began to doze.

Outside the tiny bedroom, a winter wind rolled down from the Rockies and crooned against the frozen gutters and brittle window panes. Becky's mind swirled with dream-state images of their first family Christmas to come, gathering candles and strings of light and the cookies she would bake into a cozy tableau, and with the next gust abandoned these thoughts as instinct warned her to wake up, check the baby, make sure he's all right.

But of course he's all right.

In a minute . . . I'm so tired I could sleep for a month.

Eyes closed, she could feel him there, suckling, the small but growing weight of him in the basket of her arms.

But that shape in the window . . .

Groggily she glanced down to see if his eyes were narrowing with the fulfillment of his midnight meal.

He wasn't there.

Her thickened nipple stood glistening in the moonlight, still warm from his mouth as a single drop of milk fell slowly into the air over her lap and was absorbed into . . . nothing. Her arms were empty, but her panic was still a distant thing, slowed by the dreamy unreality of the vision and lessened by her crushing fatigue.

What a strange dream. My boy is gone and my body has turned to gold.

Against her will her eyes closed again. She must have gotten up, set him back in his crib and sat back down, too tired to return to bed. This had happened before, on those nights when she didn't want to leave him. Not out of fear, but the love of watching him sleep. She would drift off in the chair, sometimes reading a mystery novel that always wound up face down in her lap, and wake just before the sun began to cast its morning blue into the room.

The wet pressure at her nipple, which had

ceased some time ago, grew more insistent. The weight in her tired arms became real, as real as the whetted smack of his lips, as real as the hardening edge of his gums clinging to her.

Becky found the lamp switch and clicked soft yellow light into the room. Her eyes scrunched in reflex against the glare, but not before she once more glimpsed the emptiness in her arms and the glossy bud of her breast still shining with saliva and the fine beads of milk he had left encircling the darker ring where his mouth should have been. She forced her eyes open wide and snapped forward in the chair.

He's gone, he's gone . . .

Noel was there, of course. His mottled blushing forehead, the tiny squib of his nose, his narrow chest and his hot plump belly within the mint-green terrycloth jumper. He was here. *Here.* For a moment her mind raced with the knowledge that something was wrong. Something had happened to him, to them, and it wasn't normal. Something had come between them while she dozed, taking him away, only now he was back.

She arched from the chair and turned toward the window, where she had seen the little man in the white suit and top hat. The window was dark, closed and latched, empty but for the outline of their backyard.

But something was here. It came inside and took Noel away.

But that was silly because . . . what could it be? What could have happened to make her think her child was here, then not here, then here

9

again? Either she had, sleepwalking, put him back in his crib and then fetched him again. Or she was simply confused, half asleep, letting her imagination run away from her.

The phrase *sleep deprivation* came back to her. Dr Roose had warned her about this common symptom of early motherhood. That's all it was, that's all it could be. She was tired. Her mind had slipped, the way it had slipped a few days ago when she went to unload the dishwasher and put half of the cups and plates away before realizing they were still dried with mashed potatoes and apple juice.

Noel continued to rap at the food source with one bunched fist. His color was robust, his eyes drooping. She felt his forehead again, then her own. No, there was nothing wrong with him. As for her, she needed another six hours of real sleep.

'Don't you do that, Noel-baby,' she whispered. 'Don't you try to get away from Mommy ever again.'

She stayed with her son until almost five a.m. In the morning he was fine and she was relieved. Her protective nature had pulled one over on her sleepy mind. After a month or so, she had forgotten what she had seen (the face in the window) and not seen (her son where he was supposed to be). Noel was growing, changing, becoming more of a handful every day. There were a lot of sleepless nights. A lot of strange dreams, but none featuring a small man in a white suit and top hat.

There would be more episodes in the months

and years to come. Some as short as twenty seconds, others as long as sixteen minutes, and many which happened in the middle of the night. But by luck or fate or perhaps even his parents' need to deny the barely glimpsed and totally unexplainable phenomena, almost three years of his life would pass before anyone noticed the arrival or departure of Noel's fleeting affliction.

This first eyewitnessed account was also the moment in Noel Shaker's life when, with some regularity, terrible things began to happen.

4

Becky was washing dishes in the kitchen inside the house on 7th Street, her back to the breakfast table where Noel sat spearing cold scraps of toasted oven waffles drowned in syrup. John had left for work half an hour ago, so it was probably 9.15. She was tired, but not unhappily so. She was a dutiful and doting young mother but never resented the nature of her fragmented days, the diapering, cooking, laundry, cleaning, crying, colds and flus, naps, tantrums, readings, baths and, very rarely, time alone with her husband. Without John's or her own parents nearby, she was alone in her motherhood but never felt lonely. She had Noel.

Their house, nestled between North Boulder Park and the first ridge of the foothills in Boulder, Colorado, was a warm green cocoon. Nine hundred square feet with two small bedrooms and a sun porch shaded by a weeping willow, the cherry tree back by Noel's sandbox yielding its stony fruit for the first time this summer. The great expanse of grass and baseball diamonds and playground of North Boulder Park was half a block from her front door and she took him strolling there for hours.

Between nine a.m. and four p.m. traffic was almost nonexistent. A decent amateur photo of the block taken at sunset would serve nicely in the dictionary beside the word bucolic.

Sometimes she drove Noel to Crossroads Mall and browsed for an hour without buying anything, except for that giant stuffed frog he threw a tantrum over in Nuestetter's and would not let go of. That stupid beautiful frog was larger than her son and had cost more than any dress she owned, but he wasn't spoiled, rarely clamored for new things. When he wanted something he wanted it badly, squalling in a wounded manner that convinced her he had made a deep personal connection to the object, and so she had caved in and bought the frog.

She felt safe here. Her life was gentle and she had no aspirations toward career, volunteerism or social status. They were becoming more of a family every day, their solidarity strengthening with the comfort of routine, her and John's unspoken but deepening appreciation of their lot.

That John worked no fewer than seventy and sometimes as many as ninety hours per week moving the store from its current eleven thousand square foot space on Arapahoe to the new forty thousand super footprint in the Village Shopping Centre was not a source of stress, but a comfort to her. He had his role and she had hers.

With the mountains so close, Boulderites could not get enough ski poles, fishing rods, climbing rope, running shoes, metal canoes and cycling gear. Richardson Bros Sporting Goods was family-owned and took good care of its managers. With his overtime, John was making engineer money. He walked the floor, helped customers, was head buyer for new product, handled human resources. He was the sixth employee in a store that would soon have a hundred. People drove in from Wyoming and Nebraska to buy Finnish skis and let their sons and daughters choose from more than sixty baseball mitts. He had promised that when he got his bonus for helping make the grand opening on schedule, they would take a five-day vacation to Yellowstone. Becky wanted to sleep in a tent with her son and husband. John wanted to have a campfire and teach Noel to fish. Noel wanted to feed the bears donuts.

'Mommy, guess what!' he cried from the table.

'What's what?' She knew what was coming and smiled despite herself.

'But guess what!' He liked to warm up to it, never said it on the first try.

'What?'

'Chicken butt!'

'You're very funny today, aren't you?' She adjusted the water from hot to warm (to keep her cuticles from splitting) and added more detergent to the swamp of plates and forks and Noel's favorite tractor, which had gotten dirty yesterday. He liked it shiny red and wheels polished before each play session.

'Yep.'

'Are you going to tell jokes like that next year at preschool?' She turned and raised one of her dark eyebrows at him. The boy could look so serious for a two-and-a-half-year-old. Was he contemplating the question, or the prospect of pre-school?

'I prolly will, Mom,' he said, nodding thoughtfully.

Becky burst out laughing. He stared, admiring her, she thought, or maybe admiring his ability to make her happy. His plate was as empty as it was going to get. Becky walked over, soap bubbles dripping from her left hand, and ate the last bite of his blueberry Eggo. She flipped a drop of foam onto his nose and he covered his face, scolding her. She took his plate and the rubber fork to the sink.

He giggled again, differently, as if gripped by a fine surprise.

She heard the chair legs squeak along the vinyl flooring and then felt Noel's little hands dragging across the backs of her legs as the sound of his sneakers pattered out of the kitchen. She hoped he was going to try the potty again on his own, but his determination to go like a big boy seemed to alternate weeks, so she never knew.

'Where you off to, Noeller Coaster?'

'Closet!' his voice came back from the hall.

Becky gazed into the backyard, rinsing the last of the plates, pulling the plug. A robin danced in the grass, bobbing for worms. Closet could be for clothes, but he was already dressed and wearing his shoes. Probably he had stashed a toy in there. Or was inviting her to play hide and seek. The gray water made a sucking sound down into the drain, the mounds of suds dissolving to reveal his tractor. She ran a sponge around the chunky tires and white metal rims, rinsed it and set it on the dish rack to dry.

How many seconds or minutes of silence will pass before an attentive mother senses her child is testing the leash, has gotten into something he shouldn't be into? For Becky the answer was usually no more than a minute, but it was morning and the front screen door was locked and she would have seen him in the back, so perhaps two or three minutes passed before she noticed the stillness that had settled in his absence.

'Noel?'

He didn't answer.

'Noel?' Louder, but with no real edge.

This time he answered. 'Hi, Mommy!'

He sounded far away, in another room or outside. Had she left the back door open? Maybe John had gone out to fetch a tool from the small shed this morning and forgot to shut it. She wiped her hands and walked, not hurrying, into the hallway beside the kitchen. To the left was the only bathroom, a wide alcove that contained the washing machine and dryer, and then the two steps down to the mud room. The door to the backyard was closed.

Becky hurried to the front door, detouring briefly — Noel wasn't in his room, his bed was still made, and he wasn't hiding in his closet — and found it shut and locked, too. She leaned against the front window to scan the yard anyway. The mailman, Dave Linderman — who played softball with John and seemed to think hand-delivering a package constituted a license to flirt with her — was walking by and two steps later disappeared behind Mrs Ryeberger's unruly towering hedge. Dave would have stopped if he had seen Noel playing alone in the yard, but better safe than sorry.

Becky stepped out, pacing the lawn, checking the sides of the house, peering north and south along 7th Street. The sun was bright on Mr Millward's parked red Dodge truck a ways down. Directly across the street, the Elkinsons' bay window was black with shade from their massive weeping willow. Noel had left his trike (it was a yellow plastic motorcycle with a six-volt battery under the black rubber seat and four wheels as well as manual pedals, but Becky called it his trike) halfway up the narrow sidewalk, but he wasn't sitting on it. He wasn't out here. Couldn't be. She'd just heard his voice calling to her from inside the house.

She went back inside, stopped in the living room and turned in a circle, chewing her lower lip.

'Okay, enough!' she barked, surprising herself. She turned and walked back into the kitchen. A little softer. 'Where are you, hon? Noel? Noel?'

He didn't answer this time, but she thought he might have giggled. She heard someone giggle. It came to her faintly, from behind a wall. Hide and seek. Great. Why had she taught him this game? What was so fun about it? Her fear lessened somewhat, but its aftertaste left her in no mood to play games.

'I know you're in here,' she said, and her voice rang hollow.

She looked in her closet, but there were no little legs protruding from behind the rows of her dresses, nor were his blue and orange rubber-toed shoes standing among her sandals and hiking boots.

'Noel. Come on out, now. Mommy's not in the mood . . . ' her voice trailed off as confusion, then mild shock, then outright terror blossomed up through her throat. She had wandered back into the hall, to the front of the house, and taken another look through the screen door's upper pane of glass. Noel's yellow trike was not on the sidewalk. It had been there less than two minutes before. Now it was gone.

From the north side of the house, filling the morning air with a beastly rumble, came the sound of a car engine. A large car or truck, revving and shifting through the gears, gaining speed as it moved down 7th, toward her house.

Becky shoved the screen door and stumbled diagonally across the lawn.

★   ★   ★

His body didn't feel different, but now everything was different. One second he was wiping bubbles from his nose and the next he couldn't see his hand. The smell of syrup was at his fingers, but there was nothing there, here, not even the usual blur that was the tip of his nose. He watched the place in the air where it felt like his hand was, and down, down, until he felt his fingers fall on his leg . . . except that his leg was gone too. Both legs, and his swinging feet. The sheer crazy surprise of it made him dizzy. He could see right through to the chair and he felt like he was floating.

Noel squirmed forward and to his delight his feet stopped him from falling. He stumbled back, his butt sliding the chair across the floor. He ran toward Mommy, thinking, *Look, look what happened! I hiding, I hiding!* but something made his voice stop inside him. He sensed already there were two ways to go with this new thing. He could tell her, or use this time (it wouldn't last long, he sensed) to play hide and seek. Mommy was always good at finding him, even though he knew sometimes she pretended it was hard, but this time would be different.

He couldn't help teasing her, though, brushing his hands against her legs as he ran by. It was a dare, a clue, but she didn't turn around.

'Where you off to, Noeller Coaster?' she said.

'Closet!' he answered, running into the hall, but he was going to trick her. She would think he was in the closet, but this time he would hide in Mommy and Daddy's bedroom, behind the curtains. He could probably hide right in the middle of the room if he wanted, but somehow that didn't seem like much of a game. He swirled into the heavy blue drapes, the dry smell of dust and sun-warmed cloth tickling his nose. A few minutes passed before she called out again.

He couldn't remember the last time this had happened, but he knew it *had* happened before. It didn't feel as strange as it should. It felt like a dream, or like Uncle Charlie visiting. It was something that you never thought about until it happened again, and then it was a neat surprise that changed everything. He wondered why he couldn't do it more often, and he guessed it was just one of those things like learning to walk or remembering to use the potty. It took some practice and maybe someday, when he was a big boy, he would be able to do it whenever he wanted.

He could hear her searching his bedroom now and he shivered with excitement. When she got close and he yelled *Boo!* she would be so surprised. Time seemed to stretch on and on, his whole world slowed.

In the vague but instinctual way children grab at complex thoughts, Noel wondered how come he never saw Mommy or Daddy this way, changing, disappearing. They never talked about it and he didn't think they had a name for it. Maybe the very thing this *was*, whatever it was, also happened to be the reason he never saw Mommy or Daddy doing it — because there was nothing to see. People were either there or not there, in the room or in the other room. Probably there were lots of times Mommy and Daddy did it in front of him and he didn't even know.

She entered the room. He held his breath and forced himself calm. He could see her outline on the other side of the curtains, her tall curving body as she paused, looking around, looking right at him. He wanted to yell *Boo!* now but he also wanted to make it last as long as possible, because, once she knew, the game would end. And maybe he resisted showing her because there was something thrillingly powerful when he was like this. For the first time he could remember, he had an advantage on Mommy, a trick that would help him win the game.

Mommy was in her closet now, pushing her dresses around. The hangers were sliding and tinkling, and she was huffing and puffing around the room, right past the curtains and the window light warm on his back, the sun shining through his back, inside him in a way that made no sense but made him feel light and free.

By the time he decided to follow her and give up because he sensed she didn't want to play the game any more, she was opening the front door and there was his trike on the sidewalk and that was a whole new idea. The outside, the open freedom. The screen door swung back and he turned sideways and skipped out behind her just in time, watching his steps. He didn't find it strange that his shoes and the rest of his clothes were hidden like he was. His clothes were just a part of him and, whatever this was, it was powerful enough to cover everything.

He came to a halt on the sidewalk and blinked in the bright morning light, waiting for her to see, and something about being outside made it more real than before. The way Mommy was playing along, her face changing as if she were about to scream — it was almost too much for him to watch.

The trike! He would ride it and she would see it and then she would know he really was here! Mommy would be amazed at what he could do, and then she would lift him up and laugh, kissing him, and probably by then he would be back, all normal again. He lifted one leg over the seat and got his feet on the pedals. But when he looked back, Mommy was inside and the screen door was latching.

Now he was outside. Alone.

Noel knew this was bad, something Mommy and Daddy told him he was *never ever ever* allowed to do. But it wasn't his fault, really. And he knew better than to play in the street, where the cars were. He wouldn't do that. He just wanted to show her the trick using the trike, so he pressed the button under the rubber handles and the yellow motorbike jerked to life and began to hum, pulling him down the sidewalk.

He turned right, where the sidewalk split both ways, so he could look back at the front window and see Mommy inside. Watching the ground unspool as the engine tugged him along. Careful not to steer into the grass. And when he looked up from the handlebars and front wheels, Dimples was waiting for him. Dimples was back, playing outside, too! He was waving at Noel from just a little ways up ahead, smiling, laughing without making a sound and clapping his hands without making a sound, and Noel knew that Dimples was proud of him for doing something good, and he forgot all about Mommy right then.

Noel didn't know if Dimples was really Dimples's name. But he looked a lot like Dimples on *Dimples's Fun Party Club*, with the white face and red mouth and big round red nose and even the neat top hat Dimples always wore when he was in the Fun Party Club House where he lived on TV. This Dimples was wearing the same kind of suit, but black instead of white like the one he wore on TV, with his bright yellow suspenders.

Something else was different about this Dimples, though. Maybe he was Dimples's baby brother or son or something, because he was a lot smaller than the Dimples on TV. This Dimples was like a miniature Dimples, about as tall as Troy, who lived on the other side of the park and rode a big kids' bike with cool wheels. Troy was eight. Eight seemed old enough to do lots of things Noel couldn't do yet. Like riding a real bike and running faster and playing by himself in the park.

But even though he was about the same size as Troy, this Dimples seemed older, like Dimples on TV. He sometimes had a real serious face, like Daddy after a very long day at the store. Noel hadn't seen Dimples since his Turning Two birthday party, when Dimples was on TV singing to all the other kids whose birthday was the same day, but also right there in the living room beside Noel, too. That had been strange, because Noel hadn't seen Dimples step out of the TV (and the other, really tall Dimples was *still* in the TV, even after this Dimples was in the living room, standing in the corner watching Noel play dinosaurs on the floor while Mommy napped on the couch before the party), so he guessed it couldn't really be the same Dimples.

Just like today on the street, Dimples hadn't made any noise on Noel's birthday, but he put a finger to his lips and made the shushing sign before pointing to Mommy on the couch, reminding Noel not to say anything or else they would wake Mommy up and Mommy needed her sleep. Noel remembered all the funny hand signs Dimples had done on his birthday, pointing at Noel right before he covered his eyes. Playing Peek-A-Boo, the way Noel played it with Mommy, and finally he realized what Dimples was trying to show him that day on his birthday.

That Noel had done it again, he had disappeared.

He'd looked down and saw Dimples was right. He couldn't see his legs or his arms or the new green shirt and matching green pants Mommy had gotten him for his birthday party. His clothes and shoes had vanished, and when he looked up in surprise Dimples was no longer standing in the corner.

He had moved across the living room faster than a blink and now he was standing right in front of Noel and holding his finger over his lips. He was still smiling with lots of yellow teeth, but his eyes were scared, wide and shaking and red inside his white chalky face as he stared down at Noel, warning him not to wake up Mommy. Noel got scared then, afraid *he* was the reason Dimples was sad and scared. Noel wished he could make Dimples happy again, the way he sometimes made Mommy happy for no reason at all, because when Mommy or Dimples was sad, Noel was sad, too.

Noel couldn't remember how long it lasted on his birthday. He only remembered being fascinated by Dimples's red eyes and his strange huge smile. He must have fallen asleep on the floor, because, the next thing he knew, Mommy was shaking him awake and Daddy was home from work early with a gigantic wrapped present with a red bow, which when he opened it after eating cake turned out to be his trike.

The trike he was riding down the sidewalk now. Dimples was about one house ahead of him, laughing and rubbing his belly and waving for Noel to follow. The small old clown's mouth moved and, when Noel concentrated hard enough, he understood every word, even though his friend wasn't making a sound.

Hurry, Noel, hurry on this way, my little buddy! You can do it! Let's show Mommy what a big boy you are!

This seemed to be making Dimples very happy, the way Noel was riding the trike farther and farther down the street, following Dimples as he tugged at his suspenders and danced a little dance into the middle of the road. Noel steered the trike to the edge of the sidewalk and the front left wheel rolled over the curb, hanging in thin air for a moment, and Noel's tummy fluttered as he realized he was about to crash. He yanked the handlebars the other way just in time, keeping the trike upright. A little farther along there was a dip at the end of Mrs Fryeberger's driveway. Noel aimed for it, understanding that if he used that dip he wouldn't fall over sideways.

He would gain speed and coast right out to where Dimples was standing in the middle of the road.

★　★　★

Becky was halfway across her lawn when the disgustingly long sedan, its dirty metal grill angled up, its cream vinyl top sloping back and low, roared in from the left corner of her peripheral view and blurred past her property. She caught the wind made in its wake and ran three more steps before the shriek of the monstrous thing's brakes slapped her to a terrified standstill.

5

Anthony Sobretti II, who was also called
Anthony Sobretti Sr or Poppa S or sometimes
just The Old Man now that he was a
grandfather of eight, was just about goddamned
fed up with the tidy little man who had taken
over the Speedway Repair Shop inside the
Mobil station down on Broadway. The tidy little
man, who appeared one day without warning
and announced he'd bought the place from
Deke Penrose, was of what Poppa S thought of
as the Asian Persuasion. He might have been
Chinese, Japanese, Korean, or some mongrel
mix of the above whose portions were irrelevant
to Poppa S, but whatever he was, he was
definitely of the Asian Persuasion.

Poppa S had just gotten off the phone with the
Asian Persuasion and now he was going to pay
the sly little prick a surprise visit. The Oriental
had been trying to explain in his soft nervous
Asian Persuasion voice why he was justified
in charging Poppa S forty-two-fifty for a new
muffler, even though Poppa S had the JC
Whitney catalogue right there in his lap and
could see with his own polished glasses that the
exact muffler cost just twenty-eight even. Poppa
S pointed this fact out and the Asian Persuasion
— who had the nerve to wear a name patch on
his mechanic's shirt that said Ronald, as if he
were born in the US of A and related to the

goddamned hamburger pitchman, even though Poppa S knew a G-BOB (get back on the boat) when he saw one — began to tell a cute little story about how the Caddy's pipes were so rotted out with rust and the mounts were so stripped, he had no choice but to 'salvage them' (as if Poppa S's entire vehicle were a rolling pile of scrap metal) with a weld job that ran nearly two hours. It was Poppa S's fault he refused to pay for all-new exhaust pipes, but, now the job was done, you couldn't unweld welded pipes, and, even if you could, the muffler couldn't be returned, so Poppa S owed Ronald The Dirty Jap Oriental Asian Persuasion Bastard forty-two-fifty . . .

That's when Poppa S had slammed down the phone and stormed out of the living room, ramming the spare keys into his wife's Caddy, and reversed out of the driveway seeing bloody slant red. Far down deep at the back of his mind was a foggy memory of himself standing in the Speedway's office, telling Mitch, the Asian Persuasion's college flunky assistant, *sure, go ahead, do the repair, the goddamn car smokes and makes so much noise I can't go anywhere without looking like a jerkoff, so get on it, tiger lily.*

But that memory was nothing but a postcard buried in the sand on a speck of fleashit Pacific island, old old news, not nearly as important as the World War II movie Poppa S had starred in on that same island, in 1942, when he'd watched the Dirty Jap Bastards come out of the jungle like a swarm of yellow ants and drill

28

Anthony Sobretti's platoon brothers in a haze of red mist and spiders and crotch rot. And then had come the bayonets, the sluice-gutting banzai screams . . .

Poppa S felt better the second he shifted the Caddy from R to D, running the wheel under the heel of his palm as he straightened out onto 7th Street and gave the pedal all kinds of brick-stomp hell. He was not so much seeing slant red now as he was bug-eyed with happy hot horny fucking glee as he imagined the pleasure that would be, in less than five minutes, his honking and screeching arrival at the Speedway station on the other side of the park, just three blocks down Alpine, and the look on the Asian Persuasion's face when Poppa S put a tire iron through the nip's brand new fancy-schmancy Bubble-Up machine and maybe just maybe the goddamn cash register, too.

Because, honey, this is what you got when you fucked with the wrong greaseball.

He was driving too goddamn fast, no doubt about that. But though he was sixty-one and a grandfather of eight, Poppa S was no old goat. He had the reflexes of a panther and the balls of a bull moose and he could maneuver a piece of Detroit iron like Steve McQueen with an Ali MacGraw hard-on. The street was plain old fuckin' empty this time of the morning anyway, so he laid it on, taking down about half a gallon of go-go juice at thirty-six cents a gallon. He didn't need to check the speedo to know he was pushing sixty by the time he crossed Cedar. The houses began to blur but The Old Man wasn't looking at the houses. He was staring straight ahead, knuckles white, eyes on the road, and the fuckin' road was clear. No cars backing out, no kittens crossing, not even a tumbling leaf. Another four blocks and he'd shoot the S-turn over to Alpine, and then Ronald McDonald Bruce Lee, he of the Asian Persuasion, would be in for the surprise of his short goddamn li —

There was a boy standing in the middle of the road. A little bitty pecker no more than four. And he didn't come runnin' and he didn't pop out from behind a parked car. There was no before and after, no lost baseball of a warning, no movement on the kid's part. It was like someone had spliced a single extra frame into a film strip. The road was empty and then faster than a blink (and by bloody shitting Christ Poppa S knew he *hadn't* blinked, his eyes were too busy bulging out of their sockets with erect violence) the kid was standing in the middle of it, whole, all at once, perfectly still and staring right through the windshield at Poppa S with no expression at all.

In the split-split-second before he stood on the Caddy's brakes, Poppa S's eyes locked with the kid's. They held each other across no more than twenty feet of asphalt and morning sunlight, and Poppa S saw the kid wasn't one bit afraid. He looked, Poppa S thought, like he had nothing to worry about because this wasn't real, it was an illusion, and what was about to happen couldn't hurt him at all. And maybe that was true. Maybe this wasn't really happening, maybe by Holy Fucking Christ I'm Going to Kill A Little Baby Boy it was a freak hallucination.

30

But to be sure, Poppa S, whose real name was Anthony Sobretti II, yanked the wheel anyway. Yanked it just about as hard as any old greaseball could.

* * *

Becky couldn't see the street beyond Mrs Fryeberger's hedge and she couldn't make her feet go one step more. The tires shrieked for a horribly drawn out moment — in which she closed her eyes — and then the shrieking became a heavy sliding sound, the sound of rubber being ground down dully against the road. A big double whump . . . another eternity of silence . . . and then a horrendous crunch and shattering sounds as the big car collided with something of equal or greater mass but which, to her ears, stood only thirty-nine inches and weighed just thirty-four pounds.

In the ringing silence, Becky wailed and went careening into the street. Noel's trike was lying on its side, in the gutter not fifty feet from her. He was not there with it. He was not on the sidewalk or in the other yards.

He was half a block down, standing in the middle of the street. In his yellow striped shirt and knee shorts and tiny sneakers. He was turned in profile to her, his thin body as haloed as an angel glowing on the mantle, staring numbly at the big brown car that was now an accordion of metal and vinyl and glass pressed into the fully mature weeping willow at the center of the Elkinsons' front lawn. Two parallel

31

strips of clean dirt lay exposed where the tires had peeled sod from the earth. Steam rose from inside the lacy sagging branches while dozens of blade-shaped leaves dipped and spun lazily to the ground.

'Nooooooooel!' she screamed deep from her stomach.

He turned slowly and stared at her with a numb no-look on his face.

Unharmed, her boy was unharmed. She knew this but kept running and screaming to him anyway. She scooped him from the road and she was full of rage, not at her son but at the driver. The nasty sonofabitch who had come blowing down her street hell bent for —

'It's okay, sweetie, it's okay, Mommy's got you,' she said into his ear, clutching him against her breast as she danced back onto the sidewalk. Noel was shivering, face buried in her neck and hair.

The old woman, Mrs Fryeberger, emerged from her house, slippers flapping under her sensible blue polyester pants as she trampled out parallel to her hedge, hands on her hips, some kind of hideous pink and green kerchief tied around the clouds of her blue hair. Alice Fryeberger was the last woman on the block Becky would call a friend, but she became one now with the first words out of her mouth.

'Reckless endangerment! That was Tony-Anthony's boy and I guarantee you he's drunk! Speeding! I saw the whole damn thing and you ought to sue that whole family upside down. I'll testify, you bet I will!'

Becky could only nod and seethe as the shock ran out of her. She kept glancing at the crumpled Cadillac, expecting the driver to stagger out and enter an argument with her. But no one had gotten out. The door probably wouldn't even open, she realized as her ears stopped buzzing. Becky was grateful for Alice Fryeberger's bold defense, but after another minute she couldn't help feeling at least a pang of concern for the driver, whoever he was.

'Your boy okay,' Mrs Fryeberger said, more of a statement than a question.

'Yes.' She searched him again for scratches or scrapes but knew there weren't any. If the massive car had so much as grazed him, he would be sprawled in the street right now, broken in five places. 'He's in shock. It was just so scary and I didn't — '

Becky's throat locked up. She didn't want to cry but the tears and choked sobs came anyway.

Alice Fryeberger spat on the road and marched over to the smashed vehicle, parting the curtains of willow branches, right up along the driver's door. She leaned sideways to peer inside. She scooted further along, closer to the hood. She lifted her chin as if inspecting fruit at the grocery store, nodded at something, and walked back, wrists folded against her bony hips.

'Well, that's not Tony-Anthony, the little one,' Mrs Fryeberger said. 'It's his old man, the father. Anthony Sobretti Sr. Went to elementary school with him and used to be friends with his wife Stefana, bless her heart.'

Becky squinted, holding her son tighter. Alice

Fryeberger didn't seem upset, so maybe it wasn't as bad as it looked.

'Ambulance,' Becky said, but her tongue felt swollen and it didn't come out right.

The old woman flapped her blouse at the chest, cooling some heat that had arisen there. 'Oh, honey. He went out the windshield. His head opened up pretty good on that tree. Terrible mess. He's a goner and he ain't coming back.'

Becky cried, and the boy cried with her.

★   ★   ★

Noel Shaker, age two years and seven months, did not understand what had just happened. All he knew was that he had played the game wrong and done a very bad thing. There was no way he could explain to Mommy now, no way to show her the thing. It was a bad thing and he was afraid of it. He promised himself, in whatever ways such young children are capable of, that he would never do it again. He cried inside this early taste of guilt, inside his promise, and stared tiredly through his tears over his mother's shoulder, up the street.

There was no sign of Dimples. He had vanished just as quickly as Noel Shaker had been restored.

6

Few events altered the playground hierarchy like the appearance of a brand new Nerf football. Kids who barely knew one another, and others who possessed no speed or passing skills, suddenly flocked to the colorful foam beacon like stray dogs to a restaurant steak the chef has lobbed into the alley. Class divisions crumbled. Sworn enemies who had come to blows over stolen candy at Halloween found themselves backslapping one another after the completion of a mondo huck down the leaf-strewn sidelines. Shoelaces got tied in double knots. At least one tomboy crossed over from the rope-skippers to play safety. It was a mystery, the power this cheap toy commanded.

But not a very deep mystery. It was an inviting ovoid, meant to be shared. The pebbled grippy fruit skin gave form to a soft missile that promised to chafe noses without bleeding them. In its simplicity and forgiveness, the Nerf suggested they were all worthy of touching it, running with it, savoring the fresh bike-tire scent of it whistling under their chins. It made their little hands feel as big and strong as Terry Bradshaw's.

Didn't matter if the kid who brought it was the budding athletic star or the wall-eyed pencil neck with a down parka feather stuck to the corner of his chapped lips. The child whose mother had shelled out $4.99 for a navy blue or canary yellow or classic orange Nerf essentially crowned her kid king of the playground.

Such Nerffound status, however, like the ball itself, never lasted more than a few days — and its chrysalis lifespan was precisely what made it so precious, a currency that knighted its owner. As the rubber coating began to crack and peel like a sunburned shoulder, as the laces stiffened and the ball found its way into a mud puddle, waterlogged, dried hard and devolved into a dog toy, so too did the adoration of its owner dwindle and fade.

By age nine, Noel Shaker needed a Nerf football day. When pressed to fill a guest list for his birthday party, he could rustle up three or four names, but none were guaranteed to show. It wasn't that he didn't fit in with the sprouting jocks, the math whizzes and eager bookworms, the troublemakers from the low-income families or the nascent band of preppies who lately seemed to spend most of their lunch breaks posing and gossiping with actual girls. It was that no one clique desired his membership, and as a result he had become a master of tagging along. Or simply keeping out of trouble by keeping to himself.

Among his teachers, the running suspicion was that Noel Shaker was on the fence and soon would fall (or jump) to one side or the other. Good kid, bad kid. Smart kid, wasting his potential kid. Unusually quiet and attentive kid, spacey and weird and sometimes downright creepy kid. There were a lot of fences, even in the fourth grade, and Noel Shaker straddled most of them.

He hardly ever missed a day of school, his parents sent him into battle groomed and dressed decently, and looks-wise he was perched somewhere between a little awkward and androgynously striking. He was pulling mostly Bs with one A (language arts) and one unsettling D (science). Nothing much to be alarmed about. But for reasons unknown, Noel had become the kind of boy teachers and students approached with oven mitts on both hands. Though he had never turned violent, there was something in his tense posture and bracing brown eyes that suggested one push in the wrong direction and he would blow.

Only thing was, as his gym teacher Mr Coach Kanasaki put it one morning in the teachers' lounge, 'You don't know if he's gonna blow like a house full of oven gas or like an electrical fuse. You know, where something tiny inside just goes *click* and the turn signals never work right again.'

Mrs McGinnis, who taught music, had been married three times, and wore shawls her sister loomed for Christmas presents, unleashed a funnel of Winston Gold smoke over Coach's head and nodded in grave agreement.

'It's his fiber,' she croaked. 'The boy lacks fiber. He does just enough. He's like the second house in *The Three Little Pigs*. He's not going to be the easiest to knock down, but when he goes, there'll be a lot more than a pile of straw to clean up.'

Waving a hand to clear the haze of Rosalyn

McGinnis's two cents, Coach K said, 'I don't know if the father is too hard on him or if he's maybe just stitched a little too tight at the seams, but he's a thinker. He's living too deep for a kid that age.'

'I've met the mother,' Mrs McGinnis said. 'I'm not sure I cared for the way she was keeping herself.'

'Mrs Shaker is a dedicated mother,' Coach K said. 'I don't see a problem on her end — '

'You wouldn't,' Mrs McGinnis said, further browning her teeth with a swig of lounge decaf.

Coach K frowned. 'Okay, I don't know what that means, but my point is, if Noel can hang on till middle school and Bud Jarvis over at Centennial can get him on a team, a lot of that pent-up energy can be converted into points on the board. He has good legs. He should be running. Best thing for anxiety — '

'Sports,' Mrs McGinnis said. 'It all comes back to sports with you.'

'Then why don't you teach him to play the guitar, Rosalyn?' The phys-ed teacher slapped the table where a decimated box of Dunkin' Donuts Munchkins sat seeping grease onto copies of the latest *Cougar Courier*. Coach K thought the cartoon cougar on the masthead of the school's newsletter and Rosalyn McGinnis were beginning to bear a suspicious resemblance to one another. 'Do you really think the piccolo is going to unlock the passion in their souls?'

'It's called the recorder, you tone-deaf ape.'

As it happened, Noel wasn't able to hang on till middle school, or much past today. Which

38

was a shame because the morning had gotten off to a promising start. He rode to school avoiding his mother's eyes from the passenger seat of their rattling loud microbus, but he knew without looking that hers were circled in darkness, watery, her nose red at the tip. She'd been crying again, last night while his dad worked late again. When they pulled up, seven minutes past last bell according to Noel's rubber Timex, he shouldered the door open but his mom stopped him, pulling on his sleeve.

'Wait a sec, hon. I forgot to give you this last night.'

She dug into the clutter between the seats, cast aside a small pink umbrella, and bobbed up holding a two-tone maroon over black Nerf football. For a moment it sat there between them like some imaginary bird's lost egg, belonging to neither mother nor son, and Noel didn't know what to say.

'Where'd you get that?' he finally managed, his Carnation Instant Breakfast turning thick in his belly.

'Where do you think, silly? Don't you want it?'

'Did Dad bring it home?' He regretted this as soon as it escaped his lips. He could feel his mom tense, saw her uneven fingernails threatening to puncture the Nerf's delicate packaging.

'No, Noel, he didn't. I'm sorry. I know you asked him months ago, but he's busy and he forgot. Your dad forgets a lot of things these days. I stopped by the store yesterday and I stole it, okay? Now, please, have a good day.'

She thrust the ball into his limp arms and

leaned over to kiss his cheek. She smelled like cherry cough drops. He secured the Nerf in his backpack.

'Thanks, Mom.'

'Noel?'

'Huh?'

She pinched his chin, steering his eyes to hers. 'Don't lose it.'

'I won't.'

The day only got better. During math, he ran through fractions with what felt like magical ease. He scored nineteen out of twenty on his spelling pre-test. And then filing down the hall alphabetically toward the cafeteria he could smell his favorite hot lunch being served before he turned the corner. Baked cheese and tomato soup and probably green beans, which meant, all in all, life was pretty good for a Tuesday in April.

Concealing the Nerf in his backpack, he sat with Ryan Argento and Trevor Malcolm during lunch. He wasn't close with either boy, but Ryan had invited him over to play Intellivision on Christmas break, once, and Trevor sometimes rode his bike through Noel's neighborhood, so it didn't feel like a weird choice.

Ryan pressed his steel-framed glasses against his nose and studied Noel. 'What's in the bag, Shaker?'

'Hm? Nothin'.'

'Then why you carrying your pack in the lunch room, dingus?' Trevor said.

Noel shrugged. They waited, staring at him. He unzipped his pack and aimed the mouth so they could see inside.

40

'Issat a Nerf? Sweet!' Ryan was already diving for it, but Noel swatted his hand.

'Outside,' he said.

Trevor was staring at Noel like he was crazy. 'Whatta we been sittin' here for? Come on, man! Let's chuck that thing.'

They bolted from their chairs and Noel felt out of control as he trailed onto the playground. 'Just us, okay? Seriously, guys.'

They found a corner in the gravel soccer lot, away from the higher trafficked asphalt sections of the playground, and unwrapped the prize. They took turns squeezing it, massaging it, mashing it between their palms and slapping the belly of it, as if it needed to be brought to life before it could take flight. Noel found himself grinning at their excitement, their unusual envy of him. He waved Trevor back a few paces and graciously tossed the Nerf, a good portion of his trust departing with it.

Trevor caught the ball, admired the packed feel of it, then dropped back a few steps and fired to Ryan. Ryan broke toward an imaginary end zone and snagged it on the run. Pivoting, he completed the circuit back to Noel, who stumbled but caught the ball low, fingers inches from the pea gravel. The triangle stretched as the ball yearned for more distance and their arms warmed with new blood. Soon their chatter subsided and it was just the soothing quiet of the deep red and black blur arcing through a forty-five-degree day under silver clouds, their breath free in their chests, legs alive, snouts happily panting between the punctuation of the

41

deep smack landings. The spirals tightened. Their feet grew wings. Noel forgot about the rest of his life. He forgot about himself. He forgot he was even at school. A kind of love for these two almost-friends swelled inside him and sprang free in the form of laughter, hoots, applause when they made a good catch.

Maybe things would be different from now on.

They could have gone on this way for hours, each boy piecing together a highlight reel in his imagination, but within minutes a group of eight or nine other kids, led by Dean Boettcher, who was officially king shit of their rivals, Mrs Baird's fourth grade class, began to circle like buzzards. You could only ignore them for so long. A request to share or just hand it over was imminent.

Throwing the ball to Dean would probably result in Dean and his band of studs taking control of it until the bell rang. Refusing Dean outright, without a counteroffer, would most likely result in a brawl or total chaos in the form of an impromptu and mean-spirited session of smear the queer. The only sane choice was to beat Dean to the punch and suggest a fair game with some kind of rules. Maybe Noel would get to be a captain. It was, after all, his ball. Shouldn't he be able to dictate the terms?

Except, something had already been ruined. Noel didn't want to share his ball with sixteen other kids, half of whom probably didn't even know his name. He especially didn't want Dean Boettcher mugging and throwing nasty blocks at the rest of them. Dean was loud and felt the need to touch everybody, always slapping and shoving and bear-hugging kids he barely even knew. And, despite owning four or five of those trendy corduroy ballcaps with the patches from the top ski resorts like Aspen and Vail and Steamboat, and a brand new Redline that Noel had seen in *BMX Plus!* for $350, Dean strutted around school as if he deserved a piece of every other kid's business. He didn't beat kids up, just made them miserable enough to give it up. Dean was not so much a bully as a barger. He barged in on whatever he wanted whenever he wanted. And no one could be bothered to stop him.

The buzzards had stopped circling and now were standing hunched in a half-circle, wings folded at their sides, sniffing and hopping closer to Noel and his friends. For a moment Noel wished his mom hadn't given him the Nerf at all. Or stolen it, if that's what she had really done. Maybe the stupid thing was cursed.

For the first time he could remember, Noel wished that the thing that sometimes happened to him would happen right now. He wanted to be beamed away, to anyplace but here. But of course that would be disastrous. If it happened in front of his friends or the playground monitor, there would be holy hell to explain and he would forever be marked as a freak. The discovery of his secret would set off a chain of torturous events. Teachers would get back to his mom. He would be forced to leave school. He would be taken away . . . somewhere, where they put deformed mental cases like him.

Noel didn't understand a lot about the thing

that visited him once in a while, but he knew it wasn't normal. *He* wasn't normal. Kinda how Jesse Lubbens wasn't normal. Last year in third grade, Noel's class had been outside playing kickball for PE, and Jesse Lubbens was up at bat. When the fat red ball came bouncing to the plate, Jesse kicked it real good, over the second baseman's head (because, as Tod Shrine said afterwards, retards have superhuman strength and Jesse Lubbens's musta been confined to her leg) and into the outfield. She ran three-quarters of the way to first base and then froze, her whole body stiffening. She began dancing in a tight circle, skittering off the baseline until her eyes rolled back and spit dripped all over her Esprit sweatshirt and Coach Kanasaki had to stop the game to take her to the nurse's office.

Jesse came back to school about nine days later and at first she seemed fixed. But only three periods in, during US History, she smacked her hands on her desk and bucked out of her chair and pitched another fit on the carpet. Some of the other girls screamed. Two of the boys laughed. Jesse's pink jeans took on a dark stain around the crotch as her heels beat against the carpet. Principal Lawrence Morgan, who let the kids call him Lare-Mo, came running in with a handful of wooden sticks.

That had been the last of Jesse Lubbens any of them saw at Crest View Elementary. Rumor was, she had been sent away to a special farm in Florida where everybody sat outside in the grass, weaving straw hats and drinking grape juice.

Noel wanted to get away, but not like Jesse Lubbens got away.

'Hey, anus-face, I said whose ball is that?' Dean Boettcher said to Trevor, his eyes gliding over to Noel as if he knew the answer and wanted to screw with them first.

'Shaker's,' Trevor said, tossing a duck to the owner, eager to be rid of it.

Trevor's pass bounced off Noel's knuckles and bob-bled at his feet. He smirked, chased it a few steps and scooped it up. He glanced at Ryan and saw neither fear nor support in his eyes. Ryan had entered a zone of detached curiosity. *What are you going to do, Noel? You got us into this, how are you going to get us out?*

Noel sighed and turned to face Dean and the other boys, all ten or twelve of them. Dean clapped his hands loudly and put them up, smiling. *Over here*, he didn't need to say. *Throw that ball to me now.*

Noel did not throw the ball.

Dean clapped his hands again, harder, and now he was no longer smiling.

'Can't,' Noel said softly.

Dean snorted in disbelief. 'Why not?'

Noel shrugged.

'Throw me the damn ball, Shaker.'

Noel shook his head once each way.

One of Dean's buddies, an apple-faced boy named Avery who had gained his bully status primarily through the consumption of donuts and who wore a Boy Scout shirt stretched so tight his shirt buttons could be heard pleading for their lives, whistled in an amused tone that

45

forgot to bring sarcasm with it.

Dean scowled at Avery. 'Shut your face, tuba boy.' He turned back to Noel. 'What's the freakin' problem?'

Noel pushed a hill of pea gravel with his sneaker, graded it flat. 'Nah.'

Dean took a few steps and some of his friends took their cue to close ranks. 'What? You afraid I'm going to steal it?'

'Not really,' Noel said, and this was true. He wasn't afraid of anything right now. He simply didn't want to share, or even be here. He felt empty, hollow, lost.

Dean moved a few steps closer. 'It's a football, you dumbshit. What'd you bring it out here for if you don't want to play? Come on, let's get a game going. Eight on eight. Five on five. Whatever, let's just scrimmage.'

Noel felt himself caving in. He looked up from the ball and his mouth opened to say *fine*, but no words came out. His breathing stopped. He was staring past Dean, between the impatient shoulders of the other boys, whose faces had become mere blurs as the thing far behind them came into sharp focus.

Someone was standing on the other side of the fence on the west side of the playground, about a hundred feet away. It wasn't a boy. It was a man, but not a grown man, and maybe not even a real man, just a strange short person in black pants and a black jacket that were like the suits Noel's dad sometimes wore to funerals or the store Christmas party. But this suit was shabbier, the shoulders rumpled and loose, as if the jacket had

46

been made to fit someone twice the size. On either side of the blurry face, its fingers were laced through the chain link.

'What's wrong with him?' Dean Boettcher's voice was a distant jumble, of no concern to Noel. 'Do you guys want to play ball or not?'

'Up to him,' Ryan or Trevor answered.

Behind them, the figure shook the chain link separating them and while no one turned to see what all the fuss was about, Noel could hear the ring and rattle of it as if it were happening inside a pair of stereo headphones.

Dimples. Or what Dimples has become this time.

No, not here, please. Anywhere but here.

The figure seemed to read his fear, and he seemed to like it. Dimples magnified by ten, telescoping back to Noel with flat white eyes the color of chalk set deep within their sockets, sunken as if there were no brain inside the head. The cheeks once painted white and rosy were now the dirty no-color of chewed gum. Noel could see teeth inside the thin but widening lips, and they were not fangs or made of metal like that scary guy in the James Bond movies — just the opposite. They were tiny and flat and there seemed to be about seventy of them. Noel's legs felt like they were made of butter and soon he would melt, but that would be bad, because what he needed to do right now was run.

The grinning thing in the suit raised his hands higher, too high on arms that seemed to stretch like desperate inch worms, and gripped the top of the fence. With one slight bend it bounced up, hovering high before tucking its knees to its chest and landing on the other side, inside with them. Arms coiled back to normal size, hands smoothing the jacket, it began to walk toward them.

Less than a minute before, Noel was still willing to believe that maybe he was just overreacting, that maybe this was a stranger, a parent or some creep interested in the events that had been unfolding on the playground. But there could be no doubt now. He hadn't come to Noel in over a year, and now he was changing again. This Dimples looked stronger than he had summer before last, when Noel had been riding his bike on the path by the 19th Street park.

His feet had been hot and sweaty from pedaling across town on what was a ninety-some-degree day, so he stopped to soak his feet in Farmer's Ditch. He had dumped his bike on the bank, rolled up his jean cuffs, and let the cold water rise to his calves. He'd been sitting there with his eyes closed for a few minutes, enjoying the smooth stones under his arches, and when he opened his eyes again his feet weren't in the water. He could still feel the cold flowing around his skin, but his legs were gone. His pants were gone. He was gone.

And Dimples was sitting on the opposite bank, about twenty feet to Noel's right, soaking his feet too, his suit pants rolled up to his knees. Dimples's legs were covered with dark fur, and through the water's refracted light his feet looked cut short, more horse hooves than the human kind with ten toes. That was the first time

Dimples appeared without any of his clown costume, and his plain white face softening in the heat like oven cheese. Noel felt sick, and as if ashamed Dimples looked away from him. He stood and began to walk away, his ankles hidden beneath coarse wet hair, his feet blending into the ground as he moved down the grassy bank of Farmer's Ditch toward the big slope of 19th Street, where he turned onto the sidewalk and disappeared up the hill.

'Noel? Noel? Hey, are you okay, man?' Trevor was saying.

Noel came back to them, remembered where he was and what was about to happen. It was seconds away, he was sure.

Think of something, his mind cried. *Get out of here now! Its going to ruin everything! They can't see you, they can't see it happen!*

The thing that used to be Dimples was less than fifty feet away now. Walking faster, pulling at the folds of his jacket, yanking the cloth straight as his eyes got larger and larger. Its stumpy black dress shoes were shiny against the gravel but made no sound and left no divots in the gravel.

Don't lose it.

That's what his mom had said when she handed him the ball this morning. And that was his answer now. He knew what to do.

The thing that used to be Dimples was perhaps twenty feet away.

'I'll tell you what,' he barked at all of them. 'We'll play a game of five hundred. But we're going to play it one time and one throw only. I'm

49

gonna chuck it, and the one who catches this ball gets to keep it. Now line up!'

At least half of them did not believe him and just stood there, scowling. But when Noel trotted back a few paces, the other half of them guessed he was serious enough and took off running right at Dimples, who stopped, shifted right, then left, confused in the flurry of running boys. But by then Noel wasn't watching them, he was running, looping out of the pocket.

He ran backwards, almost daring the sad face to come after him. When he could wait no more, he came to a gravel-plowing halt, found the puffy laces, cocked his arm, and with every fiber of muscle he could summon launched the ball into the sky. Every single boy, the ones who were playing and the ones who were just bored, the ones who wanted so badly to be the new owner of this new Nerf football and the ones who just wanted to stand back and watch as the fight broke out, turned their faces to watch the Nerf fly at a forty-five-degree angle. It was a prize now, not just a game, and Noel was no longer a part of it.

He was free.

The Nerf sailed high and true, shrinking to a pill as it traced a fine arc some fifty yards downfield. If Coach K had been there to see it, he would have placed a phone call to his friend Bud Jarvis over at Centennial Middle and told him he had a prodigy quarterback coming his way in two years.

The ball was still spiraling tightly when Noel turned his back on them and ran in the opposite direction, toward the bike racks near the front of the school. He ran as hard and as fast as he could. His lungs throbbed and his thighs burned. He dared not look back, because whatever happened next he did not want to know. He ran and ran, the only sounds his chuffing breath and the intermittent crunch of his feet in the gravel. He counted five and then five more huge strides before chancing a look down. Below his scissoring vanished legs the gravel continued to crunch and spread in clean little pots, but the boy who reshaped the ground as he ran was no longer here.

Far behind him came the shouts and cries of boys clamoring for a ball. And somewhere between where they played and where Noel Shaker was headed, from something much older than all of them, something ageless and corrupt, came the howl of a jackal with an empty belly.

7

He slowed in the teachers' parking lot as a cramp (probably from the extra baked cheese sandwich) turned vicious under his ribs. Looking back to make sure no one was following him (and, really, how could they? but he had to look anyway), he slipped between a blue Mustang and a battered white Jeep with a black cloth top. He crouched, peering through car windows to make sure the oddly changing version of Dimples hadn't tracked him. So far the coast was clear, but he couldn't stay here for ever. He needed a plan, but it was hard to plan anything when you didn't know when and where you would blink back into existence.

Most of the other episodes had ranged from thirty seconds to ten minutes. But it was hard to be sure, because the time he spent missing was so distorted by fear and confusion that each minute felt like an hour. Noel wished he had kept notes. There was no schedule he could follow, but on the whole they seemed to be lasting longer. Maybe the older he got, the longer they would last.

If that were true, this one might last anywhere from twenty minutes to an hour. He thought again of the multiplication tables he had learned this year, the way small numbers bounced off each other and grew frighteningly fast into big numbers. What if his problem was like that?

Twenty seconds tripling into a minute, three minutes, nine, nine times nine was eighty-one minutes, and some day maybe eighty-one minutes times eighty-one minutes . . . but he didn't want to carry the math that far right now. He didn't want to think about how one of these times it might never let him go.

He couldn't go back to class today. He never wanted to go to school again. He wanted to go home and lock himself in his room. But what would he tell his parents? What if someone in the school was calling them right now? Maybe he would just run away. From school. From home. From everything and everyone. Visions of an adult life filled his head. He would take a cab downtown, to the mall, order a steak with fries for dinner, check into a fancy hotel. He would stay up till ten, go to the arcade for hours, then skip school tomorrow and the next day and . . .

Money. If he was going to have to survive on his own, he would need lots of it. Suddenly the myriad ways in which money seemed like the thing that would save him were too vast to count. Where could he find some money right now?

Actually . . . close. Closer than he'd ever realized.

He raised himself up from between the cars and, still feeling a little nauseated, headed back toward the school.

★ ★ ★

Mr Hendren's School Supply & Toy Shoppe wasn't a real store, only a closet in Mr

53

Hendren's sixth-grader classroom with a fold-up counter, its door decorated and shelves stocked to look like a store. For sale to all students who came during store hours (10 a.m.-noon, closed for lunch, 1-3 p.m.), with their teachers' permission in the form of a yellow hall pass, were all kinds of useful things: pencils (both regular and mechanical, with lead refills), erasable pens that most of the other teachers had banned, rulers, notebook paper, Elmer's glue, twenty-four-count boxes of crayons, and other school supplies ranging from ten cents to a buck fifty. There was even a little toy cash register with working buttons and number signs that popped up inside the glass cover and a spring-loaded drawer.

Mr Hendren had created the store to teach his students about math, retail inventory, customer service and a few other basic business concepts. As the store thrived and his students began to jockey for the envious role of store sales clerk, Mr Hendren expanded his inventory to include a few simple toys to be given out as rewards for excellent scores on tests, best behaved student of the week, and eventually for general sale to any kid who wanted them, further boosting his profits (all of which were rolled into a kitty for the end of the school year pizza and soda party).

Noel had been here on various missions to replace a broken pencil or refill his Trapper-Keeper, but, strangely, the sight of all the toys did not stir his interest the way they had so many times before, when he couldn't afford them. He saw now that most were trinkets, the kind of junk you got out of the gumball machines at the grocery store. Plastic finger puppets, cheap yo-yos, miniature NFL football helmets, crappy rings and necklaces for the girls, all stuff Noel had somehow outgrown this year.

There's only a few minutes of recess left. Grab the money and go, hurry!

Only now, staring at the little cash register, did he realize he had nowhere to hide the money. He couldn't carry it . . . or could he? The truth was he didn't know what would happen because he'd never tried taking something with him into one of his spells.

The closest he'd ever come was two summers ago in his backyard tree house, where he'd hoarded his Hot Wheels and a good length of track. He'd built a ramp down, across the yard, to launch his cars into the sandbox where he had dug a pit and filled it with water for the alligators which would chew the imaginary driver to pieces. He'd been sitting Indian style at the top of the ramp, the purple Corvette with orange flames running up the hood resting on his palm, when he blinked out. The 'Vette was suspended in the tree house's hot and faintly sour wood summer air. He'd picked up another Hot Wheels, and then another, gliding them, hypnotized by his ability to make the cars fly. By the time he remembered to put one in his pocket and see if it too disappeared, it was too late. The five- or six-minute spell had elapsed.

Nor had it occurred to Noel that day, at age seven, to ask how the thing that changed him changed his clothes, too. Only a few weeks later, watching Grover on Sesame Street change into Super Grover, with his cape and metal helmet, did he consider the ways in which a costume changed you. Like how the cape and helmet seemed to be all Grover needed to become Super Grover.

Since then, the closest he'd come to understanding his rare and unpredictable visitor was to think of it as a kind of bubble that concealed everything it contained. The question now was a simple but baffling one: how large was the bubble?

And as crucial — how much could it hide?

Large enough to hide a Nerf football? No, that wouldn't have worked. The Nerf was too big to fit in your pocket. But what about something smaller? Say, for instance, a folded wad of dollar bills and a handful of change? After all, his jeans pockets were hidden inside his jeans, and now his jeans were hidden inside the bubble with him.

Mr Hendren and his class would be back any minute, as soon as the bell rang. This was his big chance. The lights were off and even if he had been normal, no one would see him do it. The toy cash register had a broken drawer. Noel knew this because he had seen it and because there was a thick rubber band holding it closed now. He unsnapped the band and the spring-loaded drawer banged out at him like a square tongue. Inside the drawer was a cigar box with a smiling woman in a slim blue dress on the lid. Under her was a nice sheaf of paper money. Ones and fives mostly, but at least half an inch of them, plus about thirty quarters and some smaller coins. No time to count it, but it looked like at least thirty bucks, maybe forty. A fortune.

Noel reached for the drawer as if it were one of the bright red coils on his mom's electric stove. For a moment he was disoriented by the darkened classroom and the clumsiness that came with not being able to visually orient his hands and arms in relation to physical objects. Then his fingers grazed the bills and his tummy fluttered and his face flushed with hot shame.

It's stealing.

When he'd been hiding in the teachers' parking lot, the idea of raiding Mr Hendren's School Supply & Toy Shoppe hadn't seem like stealing at all. He deserved a way out of this mess and the whole school seemed to be standing against him. But now, on the verge of doing it, he felt like Dean and his parents and Principal Lare-Mo and all of them were watching over his shoulder.

But. *So what if it's stealing? Wasn't there something in the Bible about how it was okay to steal bread if you were starving? Didn't Jesus want you to steal if it meant saving you from dying? Well, I may not be starving after eating those two baked cheese sandwiches, but I need help and there's no one here who can help me.*

I need help. I need help so bad . . .

'Somehow I knew you'd find your way in here,' a scratchy old voice said, managing to come from behind him and from within the closet at the same time. 'Just like I found my way into you.'

Noel backed into a box of supplies and cried out as he stumbled to the floor. He whined in fear of the punishment he would now receive and a few hot drops of urine leaked into his underwear. When a minute passed in quiet, Noel got up and took two tentative steps out of the closet, his eyes darting across the rows of empty desks and dusty chalkboards. The darkened classroom was empty.

'You have a problem,' the scratchy voice continued, from nowhere and everywhere. 'You can't use a phone to call a cab, not to mention pay the driver. Whattya think the suckhead's gonna do when an invisible boy hops in and tells him to beat it to North Boulder Park?'

Noel's lips began to tremble. That weird person in the playground might have been Dimples, but this wasn't Dimples's voice. He didn't know who this voice belonged to, even though it did sound a little familiar, kind of like it belonged to a thug on TV. Fresh hot tears burned down both cheeks.

'Aw, now, don't be a baby,' the man said, and there was a creak, as if he had just sat down on one of the desks. Noel looked to Mr Hendren's chair and he was pretty sure it was leaning back now in a way it hadn't been before. Also, the air around the chair was darker, as if a special shadow was hanging all over it. 'We can find a way out of this, Noelski. You did the right thing getting away when yous did. They wouldn't understand your powers. Know why? Because they ain't special like you. They ain't got no powers and they're frickin' dumb as stumps, 'cause they can't do the things you and I can do or see the things you and I see. Ya see?'

Noel was a long way from being able to respond, but his tears stopped when the speaker said the word 'powers'. Noel had never thought of it that way, like something a superhero owned, and it sounded a lot better than a bubble or a freak condition.

The shadows were fuller now, with the suggestion of big belly, thick chest. Above the wide shoulders, the outline of a smaller head sitting next to, or part of, a larger head made Noel think of Mr Potato Head and maybe his little brother.

His visitor sighed. 'You don't remember me, do you, kid?'

'No.'

'No, you wouldn't. You were just knee-high to a god-damned grasshopper when you walked out in that road.' A pair of dark but still blurry shoes propped on Mr Hendren's desk. Behind them, pants, and now a white t-shirt with dark blotches of something on it. 'Ah, hell, it wasn't your fault, I guess. Wasn't even Ronald Lee's fault, I see that now. If I was to blame anyone, it should be that fucking willow tree. If that hadn't a-stopped me, I mighta plowed into that fucking house and eaten the sofa . . . well, your mom remembers me, I'll bet. Pretty little gal, she was. But she can't help you anymore than she helped me, kiddo. That's the sad fuckin' truth.'

'I love my parents,' Noel said, defensive but scared. He didn't understand who this man was or what he wanted.

'I know you do, Noel. Your parents are good yolks. But they ain't here now, so it's all up to you today, isn't that about the tits?'

'I guess so.'

'But you're not alone in this. No, sir, my friend. Because Anthony Sobretti, the Italian Torpedo from Toledo, is here and he understands everything.'

Noel wiped his nose and stepped out of the closet. A smear of small white teeth smiled at him from the shadow at the desk. 'You do?'

'Of course I do,' Mr Sobretti continued, the smaller, darker potato on his shoulder wobbling a bit. 'Been in a few jams myself, just like this one you find yourself in today. Now, are we in agreement that you need to get out of here before the clock strikes twelve fifty-five and all the boys and girls come back inside?'

'Yeah.'

'And we understand now that a taxi cab, while a nice idea for someone in a pinch, isn't going to do jack-squat for you?'

'I know. It was a stupid idea.'

'Not at all. In fact, you got it half right! The taxi is a no-go, but the money. The *money*, Noel. That was brilliant. Long green is my specialty, see? Money won't fix everything, at least not today, but you would be surprised at the things money can buy once you're all grown up out there in the world. Money is always nice. So, grab what you can and let's hit the fuckin' bricks.'

Noel turned back for the money but, as before, his hand stopped a few inches above the bills and he felt a quiver of sickness inside.

'What's the matter? Don't you want it?'

'But if I can't take a taxi . . . or check into a hotel or go to the arcade, what do I need it for? Why do I have to take it?'

Mr Sobretti chuckled. 'My friend, you don't have to take a friggin' thing. You don't have to do anything you don't want to do, *capiche?*'

Relieved, he began to shuffle away from the closet.

'Hold your horses, shortstack.' Mr Sobretti leaned forward in the chair. 'I am afraid you're looking at this situation the wrong way.'

'What do you mean?'

'I mean, just because you can't do anything with the money now, while you are hidden away from the rest of the world in your special bubble — excuse me, inside your special powers — that doesn't mean you won't be able to use it later, does it?'

Noel blinked a few times.

'Think of it this way,' Mr Sobretti said, and shot out from his chair until he was standing at the edge of the desk just a few feet away. It wasn't a Mr Potato Head. It was part of his broken head and it made Noel look down in shame and revulsion. 'The things you are able to do with your powers can make your life so much the better when you *don't* have your powers. Today's money, which is really just some extra change from the bottom of a few purses, doled out by impatient mothers for children who chew too many pencils, could be tomorrow's new Nerf football. After all, they — ' and here Mr Sobretti jerked his thumb toward the windows, beyond which was the playground, ' — took your football away and your mother might be, excuse me, A BIT FUCKIN' PEEVED IF YOU DON'T REPLACE IT! Now, am I right or am I white?'

She stole it in the first place, Noel thought but did not say. From my dad's store.

'But who needs a Nerf football? What if some day, some day in the very near future, you need a new bike? What if you want a new pair of hi-tops, like Dean Boettcher has? Wouldn't it be nice to go to the movies anytime you wanted? And candy bars and sodas from the 7-Eleven on the way home from school? What if when you grow up you turn out to be an ugly old greaseball like Poppa S and the girls, they don't like you so much, see, and maybe you wanna go out and get yourself a real nice hoor? No? Okay, look. It doesn't matter what you decide to do with the coin. My point is that winter is coming and you are still a young squirrel. If you don't start saving some acorns for when the weather turns nasty — and it *is* going to turn nasty, I assure you, Noel, because our secret can't and won't stay a secret forever — you might find yourself shut out in the cold. Alone. Starving down to your ribs and veins. With no mom and no dad and no friends to help you. When that happens, you will look back on today, on this moment, and you will be very sorry you didn't prepare yourself.'

Noel was too frightened by this vision of the future to speak. He wanted to say no, no, please, it won't be like that. He wanted to make Mr Sobretti tell him things would get better, not worse. He opened his mouth as two pools of tears filled his eyes — and the lunch bell went *bbbbbrrrrraaaannnnnggggg!* shattering the quiet of Mr Hendren's classroom.

Mr Sobretti stared at Noel and Noel stared at the old man's separated head shapes. No words were spoken but it felt like Mr Sobretti was shouting at him. And then he did shout, but it was only one word, spoken under the bell's quieting echo.

'HURRY!'

Noel turned and raked the cigar box clean.

★ ★ ★

'Noel? Noel. Wake up, pumpkin.'

His body was stiff, his stomach hollow. His mom was patting his leg. He sat up on his elbows, confused. Full dark outside his bedroom window. He barely remembered coming home. Crawling into bed to hide. Missing dinner, his dad at work, his mom somewhere else, the house silent until he had fallen asleep as the sun set. He couldn't remember leaving the bubble, but he saw by the look in her eyes — that she could see him at all — he was normal again. It must have lasted six hours or more . . .

She looked stunned by something. Her eyes were unfocused and she smelled like apple cider, her clothes like smoke. She must have gotten a call from the school.

'I'm sorry,' he said.

'You have nothing to be sorry for, sweetie. Don't ever apologize for things like today. It's not your fault. Don't you know that by now?'

When he didn't answer, she looked to his window, as if she were trying to see something hidden there.

'Do you think your momma's crazy?' she said, not meeting his eyes.

'No. Course not.'

'Can I tell you a secret, Noeller Coaster?'

'Okay.'

'Your daddy thinks I am. Maybe not all the way, but enough.'

'Why?'

Her eyes focused. She was seeing all the way into him. He was sure she knew all about the money he'd stolen and he was almost relieved. Her voice was careful and hushed with frightened wonder.

'Where do you go? Hm, my boy? Where do you go? What do you do?'

'Nowhere,' he said, embarrassed and afraid.

'Yeeeessss. Always going away. Where no one can find you.'

'I'm here.' Noel swallowed, closing his eyes. 'You just can't see me when it happens. No one can.'

'I know. Oh, how I know.' She sighed. 'Is it scary for you? That's been my worry. Ever since you were a baby. I get so scared for you, Noel, you can't imagine.'

'No. It's okay, Mom. I promise.' A tear rolled down his face and fell in silence to his blanket.

She reached out and touched his cheek,

rubbing below his eye with her cold thumb. 'You're a miracle. A beautiful miracle boy. Don't you ever forget that.'

Noel swallowed and nodded.

She closed her eyes and patted her chest. 'I can't help you, can I? There's nothing I can do about it. I know that now. So many nights I tried to think of a way to stop . . . not like there's someone to call . . . they would ruin us.' But she couldn't finish, only shook her head. 'I'm so sorry, baby. I wish I could take it away. I wish I could go back . . . ' She covered her mouth, unable to speak.

'What should I do, Mom?' He sat up, scooting toward her. 'What am I supposed to do?'

'Don't let them catch you!' she whispered, clutching him fiercely. 'Never give in and let them win. When you find yourself alone, in trouble, you do whatever it takes to protect yourself. You fight. There are no rules in that time. You are the only thing that matters. Whatever happens, whatever you have to do, I will never blame you or be mad at you. I will always be your mommy, no matter what. Understand?'

He nodded, fascinated. All this time he assumed she didn't know.

'And don't tell anybody, Noel. Nobody can know, not ever. It will be our secret, no one else's. You can't trust anybody with it. Police. Teachers. Not girls when you are older. Not even your best friend. There's monsters out there.' She placed her hand over her chest. 'And in here too.'

'But how I am supposed to — '

'We just have to get by,' she cut him off. 'One day at a time.'

'Do I have to go back to school?' he said.

His mom studied him, then laughed. 'Do you want to?'

'I hate it.'

'Then you can stay home with me. I will teach you and we'll have more fun, won't we?'

He smiled at how easy this was, then frowned. 'But what about Dad?'

'You let me worry about your father. He's a man, and like lots of men he deals with things by pretending they aren't there. He's not as strong as you or me and he's afraid of what will happen if he sees the truth. He doesn't understand, but maybe . . . maybe someday he will. And if he doesn't, that's his problem, not ours, okay?'

Noel nodded, but he didn't think she understood how serious it was.

His mother leaned across the bed and held him tight. 'I love you so much. So so much.'

'I love you too, Mom.'

She rose unsteadily from his bed. At the door, when she paused and looked back at him, he did not like the way she was grinning. Like an enchanted girl in a fairy tale, not any way a mom was supposed to look.

'What's it like, Noel? What's it like to disappear?'

He couldn't find the words, so instead he slipped off his bed and reached under the frame. He pulled a shoe-box out and opened the lid. Inside was a leather pouch for his marbles. He emptied it of the money and held up the rolled bills and coins, an offering and a confession.

His mom's eyes went wide. 'Where did you — '

'I took it from the store. In Mr Hendren's class.'

'Where they sell the pencils and stuff?' She was staring at the money, not him.

He nodded.

'Why?'

'Mr Sobretti told me to. He said I might need it.'

Noel's mother jerked back a step. She looked at him quickly, then away, as if she were embarrassed, or afraid. Her hand was at her chin, scratching her throat.

'Keep it,' she said, backing away. 'You deserve it. You deserve the whole world, baby. And I'm so sorry I can't give it to you.'

She closed the door and padded quickly away.

Noel leaned back on his pillows, thinking about how Mr Sobretti had been right. His parents couldn't help him. He was going to have to be careful, and smart, and take what he could so that one day in the future when things got hard and he was on his own, he would be able to survive.

He fell asleep to the gentle murmur of her crying sounds reaching through the walls, long after he'd given up waiting for the heavy chime of his father's key ring dropping on the table by the front door.

8

Noel was in the garage looking for something more to pawn when he noticed the gasoline can by the lawnmower and decided to burn his father's house down. The can was only about a third full but there was enough to soak a good patch of carpet. The fumes would fill a room and he could use one of the matchbooks piled high in the oversized wine glass on the hearth — apparently Happy John and his new fiancée Lisa had been to a lot of bars and restaurants and hotels and fancy places in the past few years — and there'd be a helluva boom.

Noel had come to the house in Westminster eight weekdays in a row and there was nothing left for him. He'd eaten all the good food. He'd emptied the change jar on the dresser of its silver. The checkbooks were of no use beyond ordering a couple pizzas, but last time he did that the Domino's guy had scoffed. He couldn't pass them at a bank and there was no real money hidden in the house. After the power tools and the antique radio and the box of cheap jewelry, there was nothing more he could steal, at least not by carrying it home strapped to the back of his motorcycle.

The Honda was parked two blocks away at the clubhouse, chained to a fence post. Someone in the homeowners' association might remember that, but Noel doubted it. You wouldn't automatically connect a motorcycle with a fourteen-year-old kid, even if that kid was, as his last family counselor had said to Rebecca, fourteen going on eighteen. And anyway, who cared if he got caught? What would his dad do? Send him to juvie hall? Military school? None of those places could keep him.

He carried the metal can back into the kitchen and set it on the counter. He was thinking rags, he was thinking Molotov. He looked under the sink. There was a green bucket with rubber gloves, a tile brush, sponges — and some scraps of Happy John's discarded t-shirts. Noel placed a handful beside the fuel. He unscrewed the steel nozzle and bunched a scrap of rag into the hole, but it fell through, into the gas.

'Shit.'

'What are you doing?'

Noel turned. A girl was standing on the other side of the kitchen, near the hall with the coat rack. She looked younger than him, which meant they were probably close to the same age. She was short and thin with black hair bobbed like half the girls wore it at the last school Noel had attended before giving up again. The strap of her book bag cut diagonally across her chest, between the slightest of dual rises. The bag was Army Surplus but the rest of her was name brand, and she looked like the kind of girl who could evolve either way. Punk, prep, rat, rocker, athletically sexless. He couldn't help staring at her, morphing her through costumes, his own leanings still undefined. Her eyes shone with a fearless frigid intensity.

69

'It's cool,' he said. 'My dad lives here.'

'I know, but what are you doing?' She took a couple of steps into the kitchen and set her hands on her hips.

'What?' He was a child denying the obvious.

Her eyes went to the gas can and widened: *that's what*.

'Who are you?' he said.

'Julie.'

'Julie?'

'Uh, Wagner? My mom lives with your dad? Which means I do, too.'

He'd known Lisa had a daughter, not that she'd been imported. 'Where's your room?'

'The basement. I keep it locked, so you better not have even.'

'Oh.' He didn't know there was a basement, hadn't found the door on his first rounds. She was new here, probably felt like an alien in the new school, the new life. This was comforting to believe.

'So, what the hell are you doing?'

'Just cleaning up.' Noel screwed the nozzle back on and carried the gas can back to the garage, set it against the wall near the lawnmower, and returned to the kitchen. He washed his hands at the sink, reminded himself to breathe normally while feeling the stab of her disbelieving eyes at his back.

'When did you guys move in?' he said over his shoulder.

'You're not supposed to be here.' Julie's footsteps pattered across the floor, and the sound of collapsing books came as she slung her bag into a dining room chair. She appeared on the other side of the breakfast bar, a fence between them.

'Why not?' Noel smiled in challenge. 'He's not my dad any more?'

'I don't know,' she said, chewing the inside of her cheek. 'You just aren't.'

'Are you going to tell on me?'

'That depends.'

'On what?'

'On what you were doing with the gas can.'

Noel laughed. 'I rode my bike. It ran out of gas.'

'Bikes don't use gas.'

'What grade are you in?'

Julie's upper lip curled. 'Ninth, but I skipped fifth. Why, what grade are you in?'

'I'm not in a grade, Julie. I don't go to regular school, which you probably heard. And my bike is a motorcycle, so, yes, it does run on gas.'

'You're not old enough,' she said. 'You don't even have a license.'

'So?'

She crossed her arms. 'You're totally lying.'

'Why do you care? Where did you come from?'

She wouldn't let it go. 'But why did you have to come all the way here for gas?'

He dried his hands and sighed. 'I guess I didn't.'

They stared at each other. He could see that she knew the real reason, or some bullshit school counselor version of it. He could hear his dad talking to her and Lisa at the dinner table. *Noel is a troubled boy. He's very fragile. He's not to*

71

be in the house without supervision. He shrugged and looked away. He couldn't look at her too long or else she would know he was already thinking things about her.

'It's okay if you miss your dad,' she said.

Noel laughed and went to the fridge. He needed a Coke or something, then he was getting the fuck out of here. 'Why would I miss an asshole like John?'

'He's not an asshole,' Julie said.

'Really? What is he, then?'

'He's really nice. And sometimes nice is enough. That's what my mom says.'

'And what do you say?'

'We lived in Florida. My mom came here first, for her job. Then my dad sent me to visit and I decided not to go back.'

'Good for you.' Noel slammed the fridge. 'Tell your mom to buy some Coke.'

'You're the one who's been eating all the food.'

He glared at her.

'They thought it was me for the first few days, as if I would eat frozen egg rolls and bean burritos.'

'They know I've been here?'

'Well, duh. Who else would it be?'

'Shit. I gotta go.' He headed toward the front door.

'I won't tell,' Julie said behind him.

'Like I give a crap!' He slammed the door. Outside, walking to the clubhouse, he felt like a jerk. But then again, screw her. Some little spoiled brat moves in, acts like she owns the place. Didn't buy his story about the gas.

72

Probably'd tell her mom as soon as Happy John's new trophy wife got home. Although, really, Noel had seen Lisa and she wasn't much of a trophy. She had that nutty permed hair and a serious butt.

Julie, though. Not bad at all. Why hadn't he seen her before today? Home from school early? He looked at the Swatch he'd absorbed at the mall the week before he turned thirteen. It was five minutes till three. Stupid. He must have gotten distracted in the garage. Julie the Princess Eighth Grader now had major leverage over him.

Whatever. He'd find another way to fuck with Happy John, from a distance.

★   ★   ★

He went back again the next day. Told himself it was to look for more money. His stomach was queasy during the ride out to Highway 36. Told himself it was because he didn't eat breakfast. He rode up and down the street, to see if anything was different. The shitheel hadn't called his mom last night, so maybe the brat had kept her word. He locked the Honda up near the pool and took his time walking back to the house. The neighborhood was all gray. Gray three-story town houses with sharp angles, with a line of yellow and blue flags lining the streets, like this was a yacht club. In the middle of Colorado. Yuppieville.

On her way out the door for work this morning, his mom had asked him what he was going to do today.

'Same thing I do every day,' he said from the bathroom, into the mirror. He had a new pimple in the small cluster that liked to form at the left corner of his mouth. He needed a haircut. 'Read some books and do the exercises.'

Three years ago, when he had turned eleven, Rebecca took him to Boulder Bookstore on the Pearl Street Mall and bought him $300 worth of books. She started him on *Jonathan Livingston Seagull* and *The Adventures of Huckleberry Finn* and *The White Mountains*, gradually led him into *Johnny Got His Gun, Gatsby, 1984*. 'I knew it,' she told him midway through the first year, after administering a standardized test one of his former teachers gave her. 'You're reading at the eleventh-grade level.'

After he got a taste for it, losing himself in the safe and simple bubble that was reading for pleasure, his mom let him wander his way through the Beat writers. *On the Road, Howl, Naked Lunch*. Reading pacified him at first, giving him an excuse to stay in bed all day, hiding from all those eyes. The blink, as he had come to think of it, came now and then, but he was safe at home and stopped worrying about it so much. At times it was like a private shame, taking him when he was alone. In the shower. When his mom was at work, masturbating to old copies of *Playboy* he'd stolen from his dad.

Once, during that first year, he found himself so engrossed he did not even pause his reading when the hands holding *Deliverance* vanished and the warped paperback hung suspended over him, its pages turning themselves, as if the Word was being handed down to him from a divine source, saturating his brain with poetic and terrifying survival images that seeped into his dreams, waking him only after the book fell on his belly, which had reappeared as he slumbered away the rainy afternoon. He was in love with books, the frail lives and unmasked adults inside, the adventure and wickedness and heroism (and the cruel costs of all these things).

After he was hooked, her quizzes began. Sometimes Rebecca read the books in parallel, assigning him reports on topics she chose from the texts. He spent most of his twelfth year in biographies and, as a reward, crime novels. Aging boxers. Felons. Women who liked knives. Last year he'd trudged through a seemingly endless historical phase. *Shogun*, *Exodus*, and more Michener than any boy should have to endure. Sometimes he lay in bed and stared up at the book titles on his shelves and imagined them as courses he would never get to take at a real college, filling in the discussions and lectures with imaginary professors and midterms, moccasin-wearing classmates and cute rich girls of his own choosing. His geography and history and science were *Centennial*, *Hawaii*, *Poland*, *Space*. His friends were Malcolm X, The Old Man and that boy on the Sea, George and Lenny, the Animals on the Farm, and Charlie, the little girl who could start fires.

Rebecca employed New Age weirdos to entice him into philosophy, which only left him tired and frustrated.

Zen and the Art of Motorcycle Maintenance,

with its strangely inviting lavender cover, its quiet angry dad and troubled kid, was a puzzling exception. He read it twice and then carried it everywhere for a few months, dipping into its looping metaphysical passages while his mom dragged him around on her errands. Though he didn't understand a lot of it, it made his brain hurt in a good way, serving as a sort of Jungle Gym for the mind, and gave him the idea to buy the Honda.

Maybe it was being cooped up in his room for three years. Maybe it was puberty. Whatever the reason, he was now sick of books and wanted to be around real people. He'd seen a good deal of the world without hardly ever leaving the house. He craved experience.

'How's it going?' his mom said, rummaging in her purse, cursing lost keys. She was always running late, forgetting something, coming back two or three times before the Corolla was safely away. 'I'm sorry I haven't been much help lately.'

'It's fine. A little more math and I can take the GED and get it over with.' He walked into the kitchen to look for some breakfast. 'We're out of waffles,' he said.

'I'll go to the store tonight.' She pulled on a dirty purple windbreaker one of her boyfriends had left behind and he didn't understand why she kept wearing it. It was too big for her and made her look like the people they had seen in line for food stamps. 'Anything else you need?'

'Milk, cereal, bread, lunch meat, Cheetos, bacon, Rice-A-Roni, some steaks — '

'Okay, Noel, I'm doing the best I can. Jesus.'

76

He came out of the kitchen which, in their apartment off Kalmia, was only about four steps from the front door. 'Do you need some money?' he asked her.

'No. Absolutely not.'

'Right.' He dug into his jeans and handed her two crumpled twenties he'd taken from the open cash register at the grocery store last week. He hadn't been in the bubble, but being in the bubble had taught him the value of opportunity, and the ease with which the common blindness of others presented it.

She hesitated, but not for long. 'This isn't right.'

'Have a good day at the restaurant,' he said, and kissed her on the cheek.

'I promise someday — ' Rebecca started.

'I know, I know.'

'For such a tall drink of water, you're a good kid,' she said. 'Stay out of trouble.'

'Uh-huh.'

Tico's was Boulder's busiest Mexican restaurant. With her tips it was almost enough, but also, in another way, it was not even close to enough.

★ ★ ★

The TV was on, so he didn't hear Julie come through the front door. Of course, he hadn't heard her come in yesterday, either, so maybe she was just really quiet. He'd been telling himself he would leave by one. Then one thirty. Then two. But every time he got up to leave he wound up pacing the kitchen, checking the cupboards, as if hidden in one of them was the answer to the question: if he really wanted to fuck with Happy John, what was he doing here? He could have ridden to the store — the new Richardson Sporting Goods mega-store at 88th and Wadsworth — and slashed his dad's tires. He was eating the last Oreo when the sound of her book bag crashing onto a dining room chair startled him.

'What a surprise,' Julie said.

He wiped black crumbs from his lips, thinking of his pimples. Her lips were shiny with some kind of pink gloss and she was wearing designer jeans, a plain white shirt buttoned to her throat, and a gold chain with a cross. She planted her hands on her hips again, stepping back into her bossy role. He swallowed, licked his teeth.

'Well?' she said.

'What?'

'Exactly. What do you want?'

'Why didn't you tell on me?' he said.

'Maybe I did.'

He smiled. 'Nope.'

'What's your problem anyway? What did you do?'

'No idea what you're talking about,' Noel said.

'Your dad said you got kicked out of school. You had to go to family counseling. Then you went away for a while.'

Noel went to the fridge and drank milk, watching her over the carton his nose was stuck in. He guzzled for effect.

'Really?' she said. 'You really have to do that?'

Noel belched.

Julie made a horrible face. 'You filthy pig. No wonder they locked you up.'

'They didn't lock me up. I went into an exile of my own choosing. And Happy John's the one who went away, remember?'

'How should I know? I wasn't here.'

'Right. You were in Florida, with the alligators.'

'What's that supposed to mean?'

'Think about it,' he said.

She took a bottle of sparkling water from the fridge and left the kitchen with as much drama as she could muster. He followed her into the living room where she plopped down on the couch and used the TV as an excuse to avoid eye contact.

'So, what was it? You steal John's car or try to kill yourself or something?'

Noel sprawled over a reading chair in the far corner. 'I refused to go to school.'

'And?'

'And that's it. One day I just refused to go. My dad freaked out. He and my mom fought a lot. About their own bullshit, mostly, and me. Then my dad left.'

'There has to be more to it than that.'

Noel shrugged.

'Come on. Seriously, tell me.'

'First tell me something you did.' He smiled at her and winked.

She faced him, aghast. 'I didn't do anything.'

'Never?'

'Stop looking at me! You're freaking me out.'

'Yeah,' he said, laughing. 'You did something.'

Julie chewed the inside of her cheek. They watched a talk show, then she changed it to *The People's Court*. The plaintiff was suing for $847.00 because the defendant had ruined her couch and broke the TV.

After a couple minutes Julie said, 'You should go soon.'

'Show me your room first.'

She glared at him. Her neck turned spotty pink.

'Please?'

'No way, you pervert.'

'I bet you have a doll collection. Like a hundred of them, don't you?'

'Oh, my God, you are such a loser. Go away.'

'Can I come back tomorrow?'

She ignored him. The bailiff, an old man who was always grinning slyly, carried a folder from the plaintiff to the judge. Photos of the ruined couch spilled out. The broken TV. The judge whistled and the bailiff's belt of cuffs and gun holster jiggled with mirth.

Noel stared at her, waiting, but she wouldn't give in. The cross on her necklace was crooked over the smooth pad of her left breast. He imagined her ribs underneath, her tiny belly button, her bony hips. His heart felt like it was dangling on a string.

He spoke slower and quieter than he planned to. 'I have a medical problem, all right? It makes me do strange things. It's like I'm not here, even when I am. When it happens I can't, like, interact with things or people. I'm just gone. It only lasts a few hours, but it kinda messes up my whole life. It creates problems. For everyone.'

She looked at him with neither sympathy nor warmth. 'I don't get it. What, like schizophrenia?'

'It's just a change that comes over me.'

''A change that comes over you?' Dude. That sounds a little psycho.'

'Hey. I've never hurt anybody.'

She was frowning. 'Does it have a name?'

'No.'

'I don't get it,' Julie said. 'Is it mental or physical or what?'

'Forget it. It's not a big deal.'

'How long has it been? Since the last one?'

'It happened about five or six times right around the time John decided to move out, but then it stopped for about a year and a half. The last one was right around spring break before last. And maybe once in summer, but not for a while now.'

'Well.' She twirled her hair around two fingers. 'Maybe you're cured.'

He smiled, doubting it was so, but appreciating her effort. 'Maybe.'

'Why hasn't your dad ever said — '

'Don't tell him!' Noel all but leaped from the chair. Julie froze and he knew she thought she was in the house with a crazy person. 'Sorry, just. He doesn't understand. He doesn't want to know anything about me and it caused a lot of problems between him and my mom. So please, don't bring it up around him.'

'Okay, I won't.'

Could he trust her? Too late for that. 'I gotta

go.' He headed for the door.

She changed the channel just before the verdict was announced. 'It's not my house either,' she called after him.

When he figured out what that was in response to, he smiled the rest of the way home. He came back next day, and the next, until their afternoon routine spanned sixteen days, skipping the weekends. He didn't know yet that he was falling in love, or that his fall was about to destroy what remained of his family, though it was unlikely knowing these things would have kept him away.

9

Noel began arriving and staying later, after Julie told him her mom didn't come home until at least five. She watched a lot of TV but sometimes did a bit of homework. They weren't family, but one day they might be, if John and Lisa were married. And yet he felt the way he felt. He'd never spent this much time around one girl, just the two of them. Beyond his attraction to her, he was fascinated with the mere presence of the other gender, one his age. He was taking a new class, Girl 101.

On the fifth day she made macaroni and cheese. She set it out on the dining room table, on wicker place mats with napkins. The formal setting seemed to put her in charge, allow her to open up. She talked about Florida, missing her best friend, Bailey, who was supposedly rich but didn't flaunt it. Julie's dad, whose name was apparently Big, was a real estate person. He lived in a condominium development and threw lots of parties for people who lived there or who he wanted to move there. He sounded cool, but Julie liked her mom better and her dad hadn't fought her decision to move. Julie called his casual indifference 'the clincher' to the actual decision. Lisa hated Florida, the humidity and the heat, and after she met Noel's dad at a sporting goods expo in Orlando they started having long conversations by phone. Lisa was a traveling sales rep for Spalding and as long as she sold enough stuff they didn't care where she lived, so it was easy to move to Colorado.

Julie didn't mind school, she said. It was easy for her, Noel sensed, the work as well as the structure, the rules, the brutal cliques. She wasn't popular but had made a few friends. But mostly she simply went to class, paid attention, did her homework at lunch, and came home to veg out until she was eighteen, when she planned to go to college somewhere she could 'study art and business and then hopefully combine the two so I can travel a lot and live in London'.

Noel realized she was probably really smart; she didn't have a rebellious bone in her body. She was getting along just about as well as Andy and Opie in fucking Mayberry, adapting to the changes in her life with seemingly no discomfort, and he envied her. He wanted to know her secret. His initial jealousy was turning to respect, but he wished he could find something wrong with her so that they wouldn't be so different. The cross resting at her chest convinced him she was a virgin in all things. He wondered if she had ever kissed or smoked or had a drink, but didn't know how to ask without sounding dumb and he realized the answers weren't that important. He hadn't done any of these things, either, but he had done other things that set them apart.

It was the middle of October and Colorado was experiencing an Indian summer with almost no rain, but the nights were getting cooler and soon he wouldn't be able to ride his motorcycle to see her. It was almost fifteen miles each way.

Was there a bus he could take? It probably didn't stop near here. He grew antsy, quieter each day.

'Why'd you want to see my room?' Julie asked him on the last day. He hadn't asked since that second day and was surprised she remembered. The fact that she brought it up now made him nervous. Like she had stored his request somewhere, to be used when it was to her advantage.

'I don't know.' Noel was sitting in the living room, flipping through an issue of *Sports Illustrated*. 'Probably because you keep the door locked.'

'Did you try to get in?' she said.

'I didn't even know there was a basement.'

She laughed. 'I can't decide if you're really smart or totally dense.'

'Maybe I'm so smart I'm dense.'

'No, I think you're just dense.' Julie pulled her hair back and let it fall. She curled her lip again the way she often did, as if she were disgusted by something unidentifiable in her presence. 'Do you still want to see it?'

He dropped the magazine and walked over to her, feeling like a beast. He was more than a head taller than her. Slowly she looked up at him and her expression, for once, was bare. She was frightened and adorable and he had a crazy urge to lean down, tuck the thick hedge of her black hair around her tiny pink ear and lick it.

Julie hiccup-laughed. 'You're like my step-brother, right?'

He realized she needed to square it as such. Not in some kinky way, only so that it wouldn't be weird for him to enter her room.

'Sure,' he said. 'Close enough, I guess.'

She frowned and turned away. He followed her down the stairs. He had imagined a cold empty space, concrete floors, paint cans and a big ugly furnace, but of course Lisa wouldn't allow her daughter to be housed in a dungeon, and Happy John was all about keeping his new sex wife lady happy.

The basement was entirely furnished, with thick white carpet that was, if anything, nicer than the carpet upstairs. There was a whole 'nother couch and TV set up down here. An aquarium with plants and a school of small red and blue fish. Julie had her own bathroom, with two sinks and bulbs that went all the way around the mirror. The counter was a mess of teen magazines, make-up, nail polish, perfumes, bright purple and pink bottles. A damp waft of locker room, sweet fruit and chemically brisk hair-product girlness nearly smothered him. Being inside it was like being trapped in her pillowcase, under her armpit. On the floor beneath the vanity lay one of her bras, white and flat across the carpet as if it had been ironed there. It looked so formless as to be unnecessary, a five-year-old's swimsuit top, but the sight of it made his feet clumsy.

'In here, dummy,' she said, and unlocked the door to her room.

Crossing over, the inner sanctum. He felt more of a trespasser now than he ever had in his dad's house. Immediately his gaze was drawn above her bed — a silver silk-quilted queen with thick black pillows stacked against the black lacquer headboard — to an expensive poster framed under track lights.

It was a mounted cloth tapestry of some four feet by four feet, featuring a guy who looked like a skinnier, stranger and far sadder version of Elvis sitting on a bar stool underneath black letters that were either the name of a band or a movie. He wore a dress shirt open at the collar and was smoking with beautiful royal disdain for the entire world. Pouting lips. A woman trapped in a handsome man's body. He was a new twist on a familiar type: the rebel, the stray cat, the crooning bad boy, but he had taken it all to new extremes of who cares. His large presence in her room, placed so prominently over her bed, no less, filled Noel with aspirations and heartsick envy. This was what *she* wanted. This was the object of her dreamy longings, her innocent pillow-grinding two a.m. sweats. He had no idea who the man was, but the iconic pose and leering sad eyes and sideburns immediately rooted him in Noel's consciousness as an evolutionary marker to be reached as soon as possible. Julie was in love with this creature, he had no doubt, and she should be. Noel fell in love with the man, too, in the way of a boy who wants so badly to be more than a boy, who falls in love with Superman or Evel Knievel or his fireman father, his idolized future self.

Sometime during this fugue, Julie stopped talking, her warm curiosity turning to concern. Her big round eyes. Her pale cheeks. Her glossy hair. Her reality becoming more real with every heartbeat. What was he supposed to do? What would that guy lounging above her bed do? You think a guy like that cares what anyone else thinks of him? You think he's afraid to walk into a girl's bedroom?

It was like stepping off a bridge unable to see the water below. He leaned down to kiss Julie on her lips, hesitated less than an inch away, waiting for the slightest tension in her body to tell him this was what she wanted, or didn't want, or maybe didn't know until it happened. But she only stood in slack paralysis, and for a moment everything blurred, he wasn't touching her but the air between them firmed and pushed back and just this, this being so close, locked into the almostness with her, allowed him to soar.

Until she broke the trance and pressed her face to his neck, her warm breath coming in fierce little blasts at the hollow of his throat. Her arms encircled his waist and she squeezed him, all pent up with lonely from her mom not being there the way she used to be when it was just us two girls, her dad not giving a damn whether she was in Florida or Colorado or in outer space. A hug. What she really wanted was for him to comfort her, be here. She was as terrified as he was, and this was a relief and a disappointment.

He was disappointed he didn't get to kiss her but he liked the feel of her small body against his. He held her, looking down the slope of her shiny black hair. It was so straight and perfect, all he could think to do was settle his moist palm over the back of her skull and gently let it slide down, drawing the heat from beneath the silken layers, knowing that when his hand got to the end of the hair he would be a failure, the boy who didn't kiss her when he had the chance. Already sinking in regret, he tried to make it last, wanting nothing more than to feel her pampered strands gliding at his wrist for an hour. But too soon he had reached the bottom and his hand fell to the back of her neck, corded and hot as pavement, and it was the end of something that could never be gotten back and he felt a piece of his life fading away, going with time, vanishing for good.

'What are you thinking about?' Julie said into his shirt. She shifted her weight and hugged him again.

Noel breathed in her citrus hairspray and the faint catch of natural oil beneath that, and looked up again to the tapestry. He was about to ask what The Smiths meant when the man in the poster turned his head and looked directly at Noel. His pouting lips spread into a smile and his puppy dog eyes widened in recognition. His entire lean frame slithered from the barstool as he stepped down, out of the black-and-white poster and onto Julie's bed. His body and clothes and high forehead retained their granulated black-and-whiteness as he entered the three-dimensional world of color. He reached back into the smooth plane of art and, with impossibly long maestro fingers, retrieved a burning cigarette from the bar. He took a drag, squinting, and held the cigarette out to Noel, clamped between his thumb and first finger, the nails of which were painted fuzzy newsprint black.

Smoke and its raw sick tint roiled at Noel, the snaking tendrils swirling in the space between them. He lost whatever inertia he had gathered from Julie, slumping as he watched the smoke curl and settle into a gray reef roaring with the silence of hallucination, revealing black holes and edge-scapes dense with dark amoebic life forms, glass fish and electric eels that darted and burrowed in knots of darkness.

'Don't you think it's time we show her? I do,' the man said, his gray sickle moon face rising through the smoke reef. His voice was nasal and British, swerving from falsetto to baritone with the stilted affect of lounge singer lyrics. 'I think she can handle this, I think she can handle every little fish, boy-o, how about yoooooooouuuuu?'

'No,' he managed, barely audible. 'Please . . . '

'What's wrong?' Julie said, releasing him. 'Did I do something wrong?'

'No.'

Julie followed his eyes to the wall, the bed. 'What are you staring at?'

The man twigged to the sound of her voice, springing from the bed with a cold sharp laugh. Of course Julie couldn't see him, the old Him who kept changing disguises. He floated for a moment, hanging in the air, his battered brown boots above the white carpet, and then his heels landed without a sound and he loomed with a hysterical grin right up in Noel's face.

'I know, I know, it's seriiiii-eeee-oooouuusssss,' he sang, and Noel's teeth clicked on the edge of his tongue, drawing blood.

Backing away from him, looking over her

90

shoulder, Julie said, 'Hey, what? What was . . . where did you go?'

The Smiths man was humming deliriously, and Julie's words scared him more than if she had started screaming bloody murder.

'Noel? Seriously, this isn't funny. You're scaring me.'

Noel closed his eyes but it did no good. He could see through the lids, through the hands he covered them with, through the bones and flesh of his windmilling panic, and he had no choice but to witness all that followed.

10

He didn't know if it was the sound of his footsteps or his breathing that alerted Julie to the impossible fact that he was still here but no longer visible. He hadn't dropped in so long, he forgot the basic commandments.

Don't speak. Don't move. Don't breathe.

As far as anyone with you at the moment of change is concerned, you simply weren't where they thought you were. They didn't see anything because there is nothing to see. A person is either here or not here, but there is no 'vanishing' to witness. They will chalk it up to a mental lapse, a blink or distraction that lasted too long, but only if you let them. If you shatter the safety of their logic-hungry delusion with the reality of your invisible presence, you will only create chaos and harm, and the hell will come down on you again.

After her first sharp intake of breath, Julie twirled, confused, half-formed words dying on the lips he had almost kissed. Trying to reclaim what was already lost, Noel forgot himself and said, 'I'm sorry.'

Julie yelped, his voice too close, emanating from nowhere. Her face paled and she backed into the wall. He should not have confessed to her earlier, let himself get attached to her, for something in the way they had bonded now allowed him to think he could explain. The

Smiths man was grinning at him from her bed, hopping up and down, humming a new disturbing melody.

Noel tried again. 'It's okay, don't be afraid, wait, just listen to me — '

Julie jumped away, his fingers grazing her arm.

She flinched, her eyes wild. 'What's going on? How are you doing that? What are you doing to me?'

Above them the house echoed with the slamming of the front door.

Julie began to shake. 'Oh, my God, my mom's home . . . '

Noel's heart tightened like a fist and then opened with a sharp rush as she bolted for the door. 'Wait, Julie, don't do that!'

He threw himself across the room, trapping her just before she collided with him. She screamed and jumped back, twisting and wheeling her arms as if she were being swarmed by hornets.

'Julie, stop! Stop!'

Julie screamed again.

Upstairs, muffled, her mother might have said, 'Julie? Is that you? What's wrong?'

'Mommy!' Julie ran toward the door.

Noel couldn't help reaching for her. 'Julie — '

But her screams cut him off, froze him. She spun away, colliding with the door, wrenched it open and slipped into the basement living room. He sought to minimize the damage before she ran crying into Lisa's arms and they shut him in down here. If that happened, he would be trapped and his dad would know and his mom

93

would be in trouble and they would send him away.

Noel caught her on the run at the foot of the stairs. He gripped her arm and with his free hand cupped her mouth, silencing her. Julie slipped and they fell together, back and hips banging onto stairs. She fought and he rolled off but did not let go. Above them Lisa called out, heels clicking across the main floor.

'It's okay!' Noel hissed at Julie. 'It's just me, this is what I was trying to expla — '

Julie bit the fingers she felt but could not see, grinding his knuckles. Noel yelled and tore his hand away, opening the way for her screams. She wrestled from under him and up the stairs, stumbling to her feet. Now there was only escape. The basement contained no exits. There was no salvaging anything. His entire existence funneled down to a hot bolt of self-preservation.

Noel shoved himself off the floor and stormed the stairs, passing Julie on the landing, pulling himself up and dancing past her with the handrail.

Three steps from the top, the doorknob retreated from Noel's falling hand. The door flew wide and the kitchen's brightness hit him a moment before Lisa filled the doorway. He saw Lisa, a terrified mother, seeing through him the commotion of her daughter scrambling up the stairs, and she gasped in confusion.

'Mommy! Help!' Julie wailed, and Lisa lunged forward.

Noel dodged to her right and it would have been so much better if he had simply collided

94

with her, knocking her to the kitchen floor, even giving her a concussion. But he slipped between her and the doorway and dove. Something heavy struck his ankle with a thud. Julie screamed again and breath was knocked from one of them as he hit the kitchen floor, tripping as he had tripped Lisa. A chaotic rumble shook the stairs, followed by a sickening silence, then a final slam into the wall. A strained moan issued from one of them, rising in pitch to a gulping, desperate choke. And died.

The house fell quiet but for Julie's sobbing.

Noel got to his feet. He went toward the front door, but when no one chased after him he stopped. He turned and stared at the orange digits of the stove clock, the clean counters, the red leather purse Lisa had set next to the toaster. There was a mother and daughter here. Julie was her daughter and Lisa was her mother and they were a family with or without his dad. Happy John loved them and somehow the duo that they were, not even his family yet, made it all unbearable. He wanted again to burn the house down, not out of anger but to erase the whole stage where this had happened. And if they weren't here, he could do that and sit inside, letting the flames turn his invisible bones to ash.

A minute passed. Julie didn't come to the top of the stairs. Lisa didn't come to the top of the stairs.

He was the only one who could help them. He walked to the top of the stairs.

Julie was crouched two steps above her mother, looking down, huddled in a ball, knees at her chin. She gave no indication she knew he was here.

Lisa lay on her back. One of her brown leather heels was standing on the third from bottom stair, upright as if on display. The other shoe hung by the toe of her left foot. Beside it, the right foot seemed more naked than naked in its brown stocking with the white toe pad. Her legs were extended in a straight slide down to the landing where the upper half of her body rested flat. Her chin was dug into her chest from the wall that stopped her descent at the back of her head. Blood threaded from one ear down to her chin where it was pushing a stain into her blouse. She could not see him because of who he was and what he had become. She could not see him because she was knocked unconscious or dead.

Her eyes saw him, though. The shiny black rings of them between strands of her messed black hair were watching him and seeing everything he had done, everything he had become.

He turned and ran.

★   ★   ★

The drivers in the cars on 88th, the people walking out of the bank and the kids at the bus stop could not see him because he did not exist to them. He was glass. He was air. He was a phantom with no place to rest. He had run from his father's house until he could run no more. Now he was numb, walking aimlessly, beyond tired. He was hungry inside, but not for food. He needed something to make him feel the body he could not see, to take away this emptiness, to mark him in the nothingness of his own life.

Dusk settled over Westminster as he crossed the parking lot to the mall. There was another fall day not so long ago his mother had brought him here to pick out school clothes, but he did not remember that now. He stood in the corner of the lot and watched as a long black sedan parked in a vacant space far away from the rest of the cars. The door opened and a man stretched his way up and out of it, his black suit and stovepipe pant legs unfurling on a warm autumn breeze. The man's back was to Noel as he faced the mall, but Noel knew who it was. The set of the shoulders and the glossy black shoes, maybe. The unhurried alley cat stride, for sure.

Noel followed.

On their way to the bank of doors, the stylish man paused and looked over his shoulder, offering a sad smile. He cocked his chin — *this way, my little bloke, we have to go this way and make the best of it.* Noel moved on instinct. This guy. This man. This confident dude would show him the way.

Noel felt no stress at all as he approached the doors and the other shoppers filed past him, unaware. He moved into the bright lights and food court smells, the shopping center warm and alive with the splashing of the coin fountain and the voices everywhere, the filtered music playing loud enough to mask his footsteps. The man from Julie's poster, who Noel had come to think of simply as Smith, was only about a hundred feet ahead and disappearing around a corner.

Noel hurried, afraid of losing his guide, passing a hair salon, a toy store, racks of shoes, a record store, Orange Julius with its ferris wheel of oil-beaded hot dogs and whirring blenders. Voices like radio waves, garbled and pushing into his ears one moment, retreating in a wash of white noise the next. There he was. Smith was waiting at the base of the escalator. Seeing Noel, he stepped on and up.

Noel eased into the foot traffic and rode in a soothing glide until the steel stairs delivered him at the top. There was no sign of Smith, only a wooden oval booth with a security sign and two husky men standing together, badges and gold buttons on their white shirts. Noel caught a glimpse of a black jacket entering The Gap. He moved faster, crossing the mezzanine and flowing into the circle mazes of sweaters and dress shirts, veering away from the dressing-room cages with the legs below kicking into jeans, clacking plastic hangers, and, just as quickly out, back onto the polished wooden promenade. Smith wasn't in The Gap. It was beneath him.

Where did he go? Noel scanned the promenade and walked on, searching. Cookie booth. Watch store. Stationery. Candles. He reached the far end of the mall and stopped outside the last department store, gazing up at the lifeless alabaster mannequins posed in purple and green dresses, raincoats, rainbow leggings. A white glow snagged at the corner of his right eye, a twinkle slightly behind him. He turned.

Smith was leaning against an onyx pillar, smoking, even though smoking was not allowed in the mall. He nodded *that* *way*. ZALES JEWELERS, the sign announced, with a neon-tubed diamond beside it. Smith put the cigarette out on the back of his hand, flicked it away and ambled inside.

The terror and numbness vented from him in seconds. Noel's mind thrummed with an electric buzz that spread in all directions like lightning, dimming him before the world, securing him in its blinding eye. A nearly sexual hunger welling up inside him, confident and demanding to be fed, Noel felt like a boy who has located the X on the treasure map and has just been handed the shovel.

11

The store was small and cut diagonally with the corners cut again, like the face of a gem, with rows of glass cabinets filled with bright light that bounced off the precious things. A tall woman with straight white-blonde hair falling to the waist of her red dress was standing behind a display. Between attempts to lure pedestrians with her promising eyes, she fussed with a T-stand looped with necklaces. She had a huge smile with horse teeth and her hands seemed large enough to grind the necklace stones to powder. She looked directly at Noel from less than six paces and her gaze passed through him like a warm wind.

There were only three customers in the entire store. Two employees. The tall blonde and a shorter, older woman, who reminded Noel of Weezy on *The Jeffersons*, if the matriarch of the titular family had been white instead of black. Her posture kept her leaning forward and her butt followed her like parade balloons. Weezy whispered something in the tall blonde's ear, patted her shoulder and went into the back room.

Smith sat on one of the glass cases, his smile gone, his eyes darker, serious. *Be patient*, the nasal British voice came to him again, even though Smith didn't so much as open his mouth. *Observe. Be smart, but not afraid. They can't touch us in here. Use the people, young chap. They, not the bubble, are your real camouflage.*

Noel walked to the far end of the front counter, away from the others, and gazed into a cabinet filled with thick watches of gold and silver. Massive polished dials for men, slimmer ones for women. Then bracelets made of silver and gold, with gems of red and blue and green, displayed in clusters according to color. After the necklaces, rings. Everything from tiny bands with diamonds the size of sand grains to thick, zig-zagging bands that interlocked and held rectangular blocks of diamond thrust up in their metal teeth. Noel became dizzy, but it was not an unpleasant feeling.

He watched the tall blonde. She wore a lot of jewelry and he guessed she made a lot of money working here. She came forward to greet a young couple who had entered the store. They were dressed in jean jackets and cowboy boots and were laughing, holding hands, practically falling into each other as they pointed at different rings. Noel suspected they were drunk, but not too drunk, just enough to make a little party of their shopping. He was happy for them, and knew he could use them.

Smith yawned, tapped another cigarette against his wrist, stared at Noel expectantly.

The blonde saleswoman removed a green rubber spiral bracelet from her forearm. A number of keys were attached to it. She used one to open a door on her side of the displays and extracted a felt panel with at least twenty rings sunken into it. The young couple made pleasure

101

sounds and caressed the rings, then the man pointed and said, 'That one, darlin'. That's the honey right there.'

The girl tried it on, held it up to the lights. The tall blonde put the panel back into the case and Noel knew it was because she wasn't supposed to leave too many out on the table at one time.

While the three of them were talking, Weezy came out of the back room. She was heavily made up, with high curls of reddish brown hair that fairly screamed off her lemon yellow pantsuit. She leaned into the tall blonde again, and the blonde nodded before slipping the rubber bracelet of keys from her forearm and handed it to Weezy, who Noel knew was her boss.

His eyes followed the green rubber spiral as Weezy pushed between two small black saloon doors, into the back room. Noel walked to the end of the display cases at the far corner of the store where a waist-high kennel door stood. He pushed against it, but it was locked. He planted one hand on the top edge and the other on the glass counter, and hopped over, thinking of a cat as he landed. The tall blonde was still talking to the young couple, and he knew she would be stuck with them for at least another few minutes because they were having too much fun to decide quickly.

He passed Smith, who sighed with boredom as Noel ducked below the saloon doors, rising up inside a shallow space that extended about fifty feet in either direction, with rows of steel shelves and drawers filled with paper bags and folded gift boxes. He had expected rows and rows of jewelry but realized now that was stupid. Of course they wouldn't keep piles of diamonds and gold and all those rings lying around like Aladdin's cave on that one *Bugs Bunny* episode where Daffy unleashes the angry genie Hassan from the magic kettle. It was all probably in a safe, a huge safe he could not get into, so what was the point of this adventure?

Weezy's voice came from Noel's right, at the end of the shelves. He walked toward her, not understanding the terms she used. She was talking about weights and carrots and clarity. At the end of the row a black door stood halfway open, revealing a cramped office. Noel moved closer and saw her propped rigid in a leather chair on wheels, talking on the phone. Her back was turned. She sounded very serious, almost angry. Beside her elbow, lying on the desk's smooth surface, was the rubber key ring.

Noel stepped forward, leaned in, and reached . . . but couldn't get there.

Weezy sat forward and said, 'That's all really impressive, David, but I'm going to be out of stock before Christmas, so what are you going to do for me? South Africa I don't want to hear about.'

Noel swallowed hard, took another half-step. His fingers touched the rubber spiral. He pinched and lifted it carefully so that the keys did not scrape or jingle against the desk. He backed away, walked calmly and ducked under the saloon doors, into the brightness of the store.

Several more people had entered and the tall blonde in her red dress was hurrying back and forth to greet them without losing her conversation with the young cowboy couple, who were now kissing.

He crouched. Duck-walking to the other end of the employee lane, he tried the last lock first. The key didn't fit. He tried another. It fit but wouldn't turn. Another. Another. And on the sixth key, the lock clicked and the key twisted to the right. Noel slid the door open until the metal lock fell from its sawtooth tab and thunked at his feet. He looked down, then up quickly, peeking over the counter, but no one had heard it land on the carpet.

On the felt stump neck, a thick gold necklace with a large gold music symbol shone at up him. The music symbol was lined with at least thirty diamonds. He removed it and held it suspended in the air at his side where Red Dress would see it if she wanted to, and then he plucked six more necklaces from their beige felt stumps. His head swam and his entire body went loose.

Beside the necklaces stood a horizontal arm of black felt ringed with bracelets of varying thickness. Silver and platinum, some bare and clean, others dotted with blue gems. He dragged a dozen of them to the end of the arm, clutching them in a bundle at his waist, as if this might still hide them. The cluster was as thick and heavy as a handful of cooked spaghetti. Noel hurried to the end of the row and dropped his haul over the low door, onto the floor at the edge of the carpet.

He was trembling badly and sweating, and there was no sign of Smith. He had to force himself not to breathe loudly as he turned back and tried the keys in another lock. He did not even bother to look up this time. He couldn't stand the sight of any of them, the customers or the employees. He was in a tunnel, as blind to them as they were to him. He fumbled the keys and almost dropped them, then managed to work through three before finding another that slid into the lock. It turned on the first try and Noel began plucking rings with green and blue stones shaped like hearts, circles, squares, something ugly brown-yellow, and then a dozen or more bare gold rings fat as caramels, into the basket he made of his shirt.

On the way back to the stash he glimpsed stacks of black plastic bags tucked into shelves built into the wall. He drew a medium-sized one out and quietly dumped his loot inside. Better. But the bag would still be a problem. He carried it to the end of the row and stepped over the waist-high door, scraping the inside of his thigh as his foot landed on the other side. His hair was tingling. His chest heaved and the air blew through his nose in a hard whistling rhythm that seemed louder than anything else in the store.

He bent, scooping the pile of necklaces and bracelets into the bag. The bag was nearly full, a black bulging square of reality hovering three feet in the air. He couldn't hide it. He had to find a way out right now, before he lost his composure and started screaming.

Noel looked both ways down the mall. Dozens

of people were walking toward him, away from him, talking and smiling and looking in all directions.

'The eyes, Noel. Look at their eyes,' the Englishman crooned inside his head. 'Put it where their eyes don't go.'

Noel studied the passers-by, eliminating his options. Up high? Level with the store windows? Lower? Maybe he could fling them behind a bench, then a trash can?

The floor.

Smith said, 'Brilliant, lad. Now take your time and don't go cocking it all up.'

Noel set the black plastic Zales bag on the floor. If anyone saw it, it would look like a bag, maybe a piece of trash, something any shopper might have set down for a moment. He nudged it with his foot, closer to the wall. If anyone came after it, he could simply walk away. Or scare them. But no one looked at it. They just walked along, lost in their browsing.

Sweating, terrified but more excited than he had ever been about anything in his entire life, Noel sidestepped along the wall, keeping his back against the storefronts. He edged away from Zales and passed another store, which through him and through the window display shoppers could see an assortment of novelty items and gag gifts, magic sets, rubber monster masks and lamps burbling blue and purple lava. The plastic hissed and twice he had to stop to bend over and repack some rings and a bracelet that spilled out, but no one saw the bag.

You can't see me or my bag, he thought with

106

vehement force. *You can't see anything around me. Not my hair, not my clothes, not my jewels, not my shoes . . .*

He rounded the corner into a different wing of the mall. To his left, past half a dozen more shops and benches and tree planters where at least twenty people strolled, there stood a bank of glass doors with glowing green exit signs above them.

Freedom had never looked so far away, and it was very tempting to scoop up the bag and run, damn the consequences. But more than the thrill of his stolen treasure, he was riding the high of outsmarting them, the people inside the jewelry store, the other shoppers, the maintenance man socking a new bag into the trash can, everyone walking by with no clue what he could do, what he had done, what he was.

Go ahead and look, he wanted to shout. *I'm too good for you!*

Eight long minutes later he crouched, took the bag in both hands, and put his shoulder down. He hit the doors with a barely repressed scream and fled into the October night.

* * *

Seven and a half hours after the bubble took him, he parked the Honda behind the building on Kalmia, chained it to a small tree and let himself into the apartment. He was thinking of clothes he could fit into his backpack and the two or three books he would take with him, but his mother was waiting for him on the couch.

She was smoking, staring at the front door the moment he stepped through.

'He's home,' she said into the phone, her eyes rooting him where he stood. 'Not now. I'll call you later. I can't tell you that because I don't know. He's still your son, John.' She slammed the handset to the cradle.

They stared at each other. Noel hugged the backpack. She didn't ask him why or how. She did not leap up to hug him or assure him everything would be all right.

Instead she said, 'The doctors said her mother won't be able to walk for a long time. Maybe ever again.'

Noel said nothing.

'Of all the places, you had to go there? How could you? How could you think that was even remotely a good . . . ' She shook her head, unable to finish. Her eyes were blackened with streaked mascara and her skin was an ill shade of gray.

Noel moved a few steps into the living room. He unzipped his pack and turned it upside down. He shook it until the entire contents spilled out on the carpet.

Rebecca covered her mouth. The enchanted girl was gone. In her place was a steam-ironed mother who'd just been told her son was dead.

'We can run away,' he said. 'There's enough here to last a long time. I counted the tags. It's over two hundred thousand — '

'Stop it!' she screamed.

He let the pack fall onto the pile.

'I can't protect you,' she said. 'I love you but I

can't protect you. Not from the rest of the world. Not from yourself. Not even from me.'

She cupped her face in her hands, and he knew she couldn't stand to look at him.

'I did it for you,' he said.

'I didn't ask for this!' she screamed. 'I don't want it! I can't live like this! Do you understand me? I can't live with you!'

Rebecca hurried from the room and her bedroom door slammed.

Noel sank to his knees and set his hands on the pile of jewelry, thinking of nothing, nothing at all but how beautiful they looked slipping through his hands, hands that seemed capable of almost anything.

12

At the age of nineteen, having reached his full height of six feet two inches but weighing only one hundred and fifty-five pounds, black hair unfashionably long and stiff, his spine bracketed to the rake of constant anxiety planted in his life, weary of sunlight and solid human beings, Noel had become a pale scarecrow of a man without a Dorothy.

Food held little interest, but he forced himself to hoard extra stores between his spells (when acquiring food and having an appetite was nearly impossible), sometimes binging for weeks without ever filling out his lean frame, his facial features made severe by hollow cheeks and a steep forehead. He barbered himself only every six months or so — once while in the blink, watching it reappear in the sink twenty-seven minutes after he cut it, and re-emerging four hours later deciding it wasn't a bad job for a blind man.

He lived alone in a one-bedroom apartment on Canyon Boulevard in downtown Boulder, in the kind of anonymous building that exists one rung above squalor and conceals bland people living marginal lives. He did not have a job or attend college, but he always managed to pay his rent on time. He owned a used Toyota 4-Runner purchased with funds from the fenced jewelry, but he preferred to walk on his errands to minimize the risks of driving. He had never had a meaningful relationship with any woman beyond his mother, whom he had spoken to only a handful of times in the past five years.

After her nervous breakdown, Rebecca voluntarily entered a psychiatric hospital in Colorado Springs, her stay paid for by her ex-husband. John lived in Calabasas, California, with Lisa and her parents, who funded her care. When John wasn't lifting her in and out of bed, Lisa relied on a wheelchair to get around, though last Noel had heard she could stand for short periods of time. Julie had been exported with them, and Noel had not spoken to any of them since the accident. John had forbidden his son to come to the hospital. Noel had penned sincere and extensive letters of apology to John, Lisa and Julie, but when a bundle of fourteen was returned unopened, he stopped writing to them.

Four months after her admission, Rebecca was deemed healthy enough to be released into her own care but stayed at a women's co-op in Colorado Springs for another year. If she was diagnosed with something that would explain her belief that her son became a walking, talking ghost every few months, no one told Noel.

For the first year, Noel continued to stay at the apartment on Kalmia. It took the state nine additional months to catch onto the Shaker situation — the father out of state, the mother hospitalized before going into self-imposed hiding, her fifteen-year-old son living alone — and, when they finally sent a social worker to the apartment, Noel ran away for three weeks, living off dumpster scraps from the restaurants downtown or stealing his meals from the grocery store, sleeping in parks at night until it was safe to come home. When he was sixteen, he retained legal counsel and petitioned the state for emancipation from his parents, and his petition was not contested.

Rebecca answered his first few letters warmly, assuring him she was better now and would be home soon. But as the one-year anniversary of her release neared he realized she wasn't coming home, that living with him would send her back to the hospital, or worse.

Since his nearly seven-hour episode at age fourteen, the one that ended in the paralyzation of Julie's mother and the final destruction of his family, Noel had dropped out of the spectrum twenty-two times. The stairway tragedy seemed to have in some way satisfied the beast or cleaned his cursed soul, for it spared him for thirteen months in the wake of Lisa's multiple and unsuccessful spinal surgeries.

But on Thanksgiving of his fifteenth year, it came back with a vengeance, claiming him from wake-up till three a.m. He rode the bus for hours, until it began to fill near rush hour, then skipped off at the downtown station, where he followed a homeless man in a railroad engineer's cap all day, telling himself he was studying the lifestyle in case things got really bad. He reappeared as the choo-choo man finished a quart of Lucky Lager he'd bought at Liquor Mart, at which time the choo-choo man screamed and Noel ran home.

The next three hit in rapid succession, scrambling his entire perception of the visiting curse as something with an even remotely predictable timetable. He dropped in two days before Christmas and stayed two minutes shy of twenty-six hours, in the midst of a major snowstorm. Determined to burst through the shell, he bundled himself inside enough clothes to stay warm in Antarctica, but the blink claimed every single layer of hat, gloves, scarf, sweater, long underwear, and both parkas, the Sorel boots. He went outside anyway and spent hours throwing snowballs at cars on Broadway, causing two accidents, one of which required an ambulance, before tiring of the game.

The third of that winter series was actually a string of forty or fifty episodes, but they came and went so quickly, Noel counted them as one horrific day at the carnival. Maybe it had something to do with the drinking. On 1 February, at three in the afternoon, he discovered a stash of liquor Rebecca had been keeping in the linen closet. Large bottles of cheap vodka for the most part, plus one odd smaller bottle of Wild Turkey he suspected one of her old boyfriends had left behind. He dropped out at the first slug of Tvarski. The timing frightened him, so he put the bottle back on the shelf until the blink gave him back to the world just seven minutes later.

Enjoying the warm glow filling his limbs and making his head swirl, the fumes turning his thoughts loose, he took another belt. As before, he disappeared within seconds of the vodka's slide into his empty stomach. It was exciting. He believed he had finally found the ON/OFF switch he had been searching for all along. Something about the clear burning liquid seemed to be the perfect catalyst for his condition, erasing his image and restoring it as the vodka's effect lessened. In and out, on and off. The shots went in and the bubbles rolled over him and away like a tide, dragging him out to the sea of inebriation and numbness and braying fits of donkey laughter.

With three-quarters of a bottle down, he stripped naked and watched himself in the mirror, rolling in and out of existence with each shot. Sometimes minutes passed, other times mere seconds. Eventually the bottle was empty and he fell down, emerging from the flickering bout to find himself wrapped in a blanket on the bathroom floor. He felt so awful he took another shot, flashed out and returned while vomiting. The watery bilge he brought up splashed in the toilet bowl, reappearing on its way down. He spent the night on the couch, head spinning as his hands and legs blinked in synchronization with his shivers and he came very close to calling 9-1-1, consequences be damned.

But he wasn't too drunk to forget that if his secret was exposed he would spend the rest of his life in one form of prison or another. Hospitals at first. Then in science labs, government facilities, places where men in green fatigues or radiation suits injected him with colored dyes and cut him open in a thousand places to find what could not be found. The answer, the trigger, the secret.

After the vodka, he resolved to stay sober and not break any laws, as if bargaining with whatever cruel god was in charge of his karma and the cloak. His parole from the bubble-cell lasted ten weeks. A spring thaw was on and he felt better than he had in years. He made a to-do list. Cleaned the apartment. Ventured out for longer periods of time. He was pushing a loaded grocery cart down the pasta and sauce aisle at three in the afternoon when a single erasure swooped down from whatever cloud held his reserve stock and made checking out impossible. He abandoned his cart and walked home, where he spent the next thirty-seven hours, his longest episode to date, watching the one thing he could focus on besides himself — television.

The weeks and months and intermittent episodes of his life became a blur. The strain of constantly waiting for it to hit ruined any chance of living a life outside of the thing. He felt starved: for downtime, for social interactions, for money, for food, for a reason. He couldn't hold a job or pursue any goal that required planning, consistent effort, commitments. He was forced to take what he could not earn.

But stealing had its drawbacks for the simple fact there were limits to what he could take. Sure, he could walk into a bank vault this afternoon, if he followed the right employee. But he couldn't hide two duffel bags filled with a million dollars on the way out. As soon as someone saw the bricks of cash floating across the room, the party would be over. The bubble

115

seemed capable of harboring nothing larger than what he could stuff in his pockets. As a thief, he was a petty one, if for no other reason than he lacked the ambition and imagination to concoct the big score.

He stole money from open cash registers and purses when backs were turned. He stole small valuables while in the void to pawn for cash when out. He grew to hate and fear the solids, his term for normal people.

Even with his ability to move undetected, sustaining a decent living was an endless process of foraging for scraps. Large quantities of money simply did not appear before you, invisible or not. Most of the time he lived as a man who collects two thousand aluminum cans and plastic bottles to redeem, only to find himself with barely enough money to cover a few days' worth of expenses.

He entertained a phase of breaking into Boulder's large but not overly fortified suburban homes, taking during the day, but always he returned to the problem of transportation. How to get the goods out. How to get to and from the site of the score. How to transform the stolen property into usable funds. His residential burglary phase came to an end one summer morning when he slipped, invisibly, through the unlocked patio door of what he was sure was a vacant house, only to find himself confronted by a hundred and twenty pounds of slobbering Rottweiler. It did not matter whether the dog could see him. Its fat black muzzle scented him in an instant and charged, driving him against the dining room table and putting three puncture wounds the size of bullet holes in his calf muscle. He beat the dog back with a silver candlestick holder and escaped before it relaunched for his throat.

Dragging himself back across town, leaving a trail of red drops over the sidewalks and vacant dirt lots, hospitals and doctors and even a regular pharmacy out of the question until the bubble released him, the predicament of his mortality and the reality of how quickly he might perish without access to basic human services hit him full force. What if it hadn't been a dog but a stay-at-home grandpa who was also a member of the NRA? What if he was digging through someone's jewelry box and took two rounds in the back, shattering ribs and collapsing a lung? After the dog bite, after walking almost three miles home before he was able to clean and bandage the wound with Dawn dish soap and paper towels and duct tape, after spending another seventeen hours waiting to become whole and worrying about rabies, he swore off home invasion.

It was an ironic discovery, then, to realize that stealing brazenly, while a regular visible young man, was easier. He dressed in delivery man clothes bought at the Army Surplus Store. He carried a clipboard and pen. Sometimes he just fucking took what he needed and ran. Three times he had run from security guards and police, dumping the merchandise (a basket of steaks, a Walkman, stacks of video games, a floor model 20-inch TV) but so far he had not been caught.

The guilt took its toll, of course. He felt like slime. A sub-human spider living in the shadows and fringes. With no one to talk to, no trusted ally who might offer counsel, he experienced deep valleys of depression between manic summits of glee. He lived in his own head, drove himself to misery with introspection.

His next birthday was two months in the rearview before he realized he had turned twenty. It was something of sucker punch for the fact that 29 February only really happened once every four years and he'd missed it. The next time he would be able to celebrate his actual birthday wouldn't come for another four years. He'd be twenty-four. He didn't like to imagine what his life would be like then.

Most of his early teenage rage bled and thinned into something more disturbing. A detached amusement at first, then a loss of all guilt and concern. He didn't feel much. He almost wanted to get caught. He cried himself to sleep at night the way most people brush their teeth before bed. By twenty he felt old. Time had become a cruel god, torturing him with empty days that never ended.

He carried with him at all times a bubble that was worse than the bubble that hid him from the world. This other bubble was the prison cell that living with the real affliction had constructed around his life. To make friends, to reach out for help, to form attachments, was forbidden by his very real fear of discovery.

And then one day this too evaporated, his fear of so many possible bad outcomes. He gave up trying, worrying. He lost himself in the drudgery of getting by and, as if responding to his lack of stress, woke up one morning to realize the bubble had not taken him in over six months. He was alarmed by its absence, and his progress reversed. He had squandered six months waiting for it to happen, time that could have been spent living like a normal person, working a job, making friends.

But the thought of another spell filled him with such dull dread, such insistent malaise, that waiting for it became worse than the event itself. The when and where and how long this time of it all consumed his thoughts. Then all at once his ability to care about it, himself, all consequences, leaked from him mind and body and he found that he had nothing to live for or against.

One morning soon after this, he woke in a solid state, got out of bed, urinated and walked into the kitchen to make himself a fresh pot of coffee. Watching the black brew drip he grew listless, unable to reach up and pull a mug down from the cupboard. Time seemed to stretch, the coffee taking an eternity to reach the four-ounce fill line. Drip drip drip. His whole life dripping away, being filtered by this abominable curse. He looked at his sad set of four bowls and four plates and four silverware and realized he had never entertained a single guest in his apartment, let alone used the entire set at once. In the utensil drawer, under a masher his mother once used to make his favorite dish, fried mashed potato pancakes with maple syrup, he found a heavy dull chef's knife.

He tested the blade on his forearm and found it too blunt too cut the black hair growing there. He became frustrated that he could not even scrape a few hairs with this knife, then fascinated by the dry powdery scrape of his skin. This skin, pale pink and pliable. How could it disappear? Where did it go? Why did it hate him so much? Or was it the world his skin hated? The world his skin?

There had to be more to it.

This skin.

The world.

The secret to his secret.

Soon he was sawing back and forth across his forearm in long patient strokes. He didn't see the blood until he felt it spattering onto his bare feet. The pain was real but far away, stinging but tolerable. He was more interested in the layers of tissue and muscle he had opened up above his wrist, on top of his forearm, and this was interesting until the white edge of bone appeared, stopping his progress.

He rolled his arm over and examined the network of green-blue veins there, the undulating cords of tendon that slid like puppet strings when he wiggled his fingers, the soft smooth white skin holding it all together. He wanted to see inside, autopsy this prop, delve into his own self. He brought the knife around and, pressing hard to make the dull blade do its stupid job, sliced a clean line halfway up to his elbow. The blood began to pour and Noel began to laugh at the mess he was making.

Behind him the coffeemaker beeped that it

was done. He turned and stared at the full pot, his feet sliding in the puddle forming on the floor. He felt light-headed and his vision magnified sharply before growing fuzzy with black and red clouds at the corners of the room.

This was beautiful. Why hadn't he thought of this before? All along he had been trapped, but here was his key to the cell door, right here inside him. The blood, his blood, was his key and if he let enough of it to flow from his disgusting body, his spirit would go with it. He turned the knife over using both hands to get the handle in his dry right fist, so that the blade was angled down, as if he were going to stab someone, and then began to stab himself.

The first try his aim was off and he jabbed bone under his thumb. On the second swing the point pierced his skin where the buckle of his watch would have been and he shuddered with hot ecstatic searing pain. He was screaming, but the voice belonged to the prisoner in the cell and he ignored it. He raised the knife a third time and saw its dim reflection in the glossy black control panel of the stove, and halted.

Beside the knife's long shadow was a silhouette of a man in black clothes. Noel turned, slipped again on the wet floor, and saw Dimples standing in the living room. He had let himself in, sneaking up on Noel while he was busy with this messy task. How interesting. Had his visitor come back to witness Noel's final vanishing act?

The only problem was, this wasn't really Dimples.

This man wore none of the clown make-up from the early years. And besides, his face was all wrong. Dimples's face had always been blurred, doughy, the eyes deep black holes of non-flesh. This man's face was as clear as a photograph, as rosy and concerned as the face of a preacher on television, and his eyes were liquid green. No, this wasn't Dimples, unless Dimples had stolen a more familiar likeness to present himself this time around. He was a little older and fleshier than Noel remembered, but in all other ways the visitor was the spitting image of John Shaker, his father.

13

Noel rode in the passenger seat of John's rented Taurus, head against the cold glass separating his cheek from the bracing February air as his dad drove them into a neighborhood somewhere in south-east Boulder. His left arm was securely bandaged from elbow to palm, concealing the one hundred and thirty-seven stitches he had acquired in the aftermath of his failed — not that he was ready to accept it as such — suicide attempt. His mind was still dulled by the sedatives and painkillers they had given him at Boulder Community Hospital, where he had spent the past two and a half days, but he had presence enough to wonder if John was going to install him in one of these places where men in white clothes watch over you, and he realized he didn't much care so long as there was a warm bed.

'What now?' Noel had asked this morning while waiting to be discharged.

'I thought we'd stop for breakfast. You could use a real meal.' John was sitting in a chair beside a window overlooking North Boulder Park, just three blocks from the house Noel had been born into. 'Lost a lot of blood there, kiddo.'

'Not really hungry,' Noel said.

'Well, can't hurt to try.'

John did not seem uncomfortable or gravely sad or ashamed of the situation, of his son. He was clear-eyed and composed, dressed in the relaxed, semi-professional slacks and sweater of the early retired. His hair was combed, his cheeks aglow with West Coast sun. He had conferred with the doctors and nurses but had not relayed much of the discussion to the object of these findings.

'Doctor says the stitches will itch, but you'll be back to have them out in ten days. Do you want some coffee? You're allowed to eat and drink anything you feel like.'

'Why aren't you in California?'

John blinked several times. 'I wanted to make sure you got through this.'

'No,' Noel said. 'I mean, how did you happen to be there right when . . . '

'Oh. Yes.' John smoothed a hand over his mouth. 'I guess you didn't get my messages. I called you four times to let you know I would be visiting.'

'Messages? What messages?'

'On your machine. Just a few days ago.'

A dim light began to blink in Noel's brain. He did and did not remember this. He wasn't used to getting phone calls, so he rarely checked his machine. But a vague memory of his father's voice babbling on returned now and Noel was dumbstruck as to how he'd walled off an event as significant as his father's arrival, even factoring in the depression he'd sunken into. Had he been drinking before things got so bad? Maybe.

'I'm sorry,' Noel said. 'I guess I was a little lost in . . . ' he trailed off, meaning to add, what?

124

Lost in my own thoughts? My life?

'I was in town to check on Julie, actually,' John said, avoiding the implication of Noel's admission. 'It was Lisa's idea for me to stop by and see you. She's forgiven you, which means I guess I have, too. I got your address from your mother, but I haven't spoken to her since . . . I didn't want to upset her with this.'

Noel was thinking, *Julie? Julie's in Boulder? Why? How? For what? What does she look like now?*

'We thought maybe you'd seen her, but I guess you didn't know,' John said. 'Julie enrolled at CU the fall before last. But we haven't spoken to her in, well, maybe it's been a few months now. Thanksgiving break was her last call home. Lisa's worried, but obviously she can't travel comfortably. I flew out Sunday. Was hoping to catch her at the house she's been renting with those two other girls, but her roommates haven't seen her.' His father paused. 'I don't suppose she's been in touch with you?'

Noel swallowed, his throat thick with dried layers of something unpleasant. He sucked ice from a cup. 'I haven't seen or heard from Julie since I was fourteen.'

John nodded. 'Well, I'm sure she'll turn up. Anyway. I'm glad I stopped by when I did.' *Just in time. Before you bled out.*

During the silence that stretched between them, his father regarding him as if he were a glass that might shatter under too penetrating a gaze, Noel entertained the alarming possibility that he had, at least subconsciously, known

125

exactly when his dad was due to arrive and — was such a thing possible? if so, how pathetic was this? — that he had cut himself not so much to end everything as to scream for help.

He groaned in disgust with himself.

John cleared his throat. 'How's the pain?'

'You don't have to stay,' Noel said.

'Stop. I want to be here.'

Before checkout, John handed Noel a clean t-shirt and a large green parka, the tags still attached. Woolrich, marked down 50 per cent from $199.99. Big as a fireman's coat, only heavier. Noel reluctantly pulled the parka over his shoulders. He refused the wheelchair ride out.

At The Village Coffee Shop, Noel's appetite sat up and begged like a dog. The tiny greasy spoon was so busy, the air so tantalizingly heavy with the aroma of sausage gravy and pancakes and frying bacon, to decline breakfast would have brought the place to a screeching halt as all eyes turned to the young man who really must be dead. John had two over easy with links, coffee, dry toast. Noel ate every last bite of his breakfast burrito smothered in hot green chili, plus hash browns, four pieces of toast with grape jelly, and three cups of heavily creamed terrible coffee.

Now he felt full and lucid but tired, not at all in the mood for whatever father-and-son talk John had planned as he pulled into a parking lot and turned off the Ford. Ahead of them was a winding strip of frosted dead grass and a formation of rocks that struck Noel as something constructed for a film set, vaguely familiar and not quite real.

'I won't do it again, if that's what you're worried about,' Noel said. 'I appreciate your help and I feel better now.'

'Come out here a minute,' John said. 'I want to show you something.'

The February chill drove his balled fists into his pockets. His jeans were still stained and one of his dirty white hi-tops was streaked with more blood gone brown. John stood before the few hundred small boulders, stacked and piled together to create dozens of tunnels, holes, entrances and exits and open spaces to look out over the park. Noel remembered now. He had played here as a child. Inside was a series of caves and chutes for children to crawl through, climb up, burrow into. Memories of himself on his hands and knees, wiggling his way through sharp-edged walls and the cool damp sand at its floor, playing pirate. How old had he been when Rebecca brought him here? Five? Seven? She had called it the Rock Park, and back then it had seemed almost infinite, a magic castle where ogres and dragons had made their home.

Now it looked like a dirty frozen lawsuit waiting to happen, far too small to admit anyone over three feet and fifty pounds. The entire edifice stank of mud and mildew, the scallop of playground sand around its borders dotted with frozen cat shit.

'You remember this place?' John said.

Noel nodded, folding the parka's collar up to his ears.

'You used to beg your mom to bring you here, but she didn't like it. She didn't like it at all. Do you know why?'

Noel sighed. So here it was. Punishment for trying to off himself — we're going to talk about The Family. As if there still was one. As if there had ever been. He kept quiet and stared at the rocks.

'She was convinced that one of these days you'd crawl into that heap of rocks and never come out. She thought you were going to vanish inside and even if they tore the entire thing apart, they would never find you.'

Noel snorted.

'The truth is, your mother had a severe case of the mental apron strings. She had a paralyzing fear of losing you, her one and only child. It started in your infancy. She used to come to bed at night after nursing you sometimes, crying because she was convinced something had tried to snatch you from her arms. Soon as you learned to crawl, she worried constantly you would just up and disappear, beamed away like one of those spacemen on that dumb TV show. Didn't take long for me to figure out this was not your typical motherhood fear. She became pathological with it and, frankly, I don't think she ever got over it.'

This sounded unsurprising to Noel, but hearing his father say it aroused his interest. What did John know? How much had she told him?

'She was delusional, of course,' John continued. 'By the time you were three, she was no longer worried about you disappearing. She was convinced you *had* been disappearing. Many times. In your bedroom. In the yard. From pre-school, once you started attending Bixby out there on 30th. She couldn't stand to be away from you. Took you out of school in fourth grade. Said she was trying to protect you, but she couldn't take care of herself without you. She believed — and I can't stress enough how literally she believed this, believed it the way I believe it's cold today — that some diabolical power had attached itself to you and was hell-bent on using you, stealing your likeness. Does this sound familiar? Some of it must.'

Noel nodded. All of it did, just not the thrust: *your mother was crazy, that's all.*

'I suppose a lot of it's my fault,' John said, squatting to pull some grass from the tundra at their feet. 'I wasn't a nurturing father like these young guys nowadays. I know that now. Hell, back then your job was to bring home a paycheck, put a roof overhead, food on the table. Let your mother handle the rest. A lot of dads aren't really interactive on any kind of emotional level with their offspring until the kid starts talking, walking, playing. That's not an excuse, and I'm sorry I wasn't there more. I worked seventy, eighty, sometimes a hundred hours a week when the store was expanding. I was what they call nowadays a workaholic, diseased. Back then it was a virtue.

'But please understand, by the time I could afford to have a relationship with you, your mother and I were already deep into our own

129

problems. We fought too much. We avoided each other. She had her own issues, repressed memories and traumas I had no idea how to cope with, even if she had wanted to, which she didn't. She used you to validate her fears and be her security blanket. Took me a while to understand it wasn't just stress, but real mental illness. Delusions, psychotic episodes. Total breaks from reality. And also, I think, what they call Munchausen's syndrome.

'By her own actions and fears, she made you think you were sick, different, at risk, so that she could keep you with her as much as possible. So that the two of you would be special and draw the attention I wasn't giving. She pushed me away, and sure, okay, I let her. I thought maybe if I wasn't around, if we made that decision, there would be less conflict. But it only got worse. When you got older, she believed you were afflicted with . . . well, something a mother should never think.'

Noel said, 'What?'

John shook his head.

'Go on.' Noel had a vision of himself striking his father.

John looked at him. 'A demon. She said it was a demon.'

Noel almost laughed, but something angry inside him hissed and writhed like a snake on fire. Again he imagined bloodying John's nose, standing over him and kicking him in the ribs.

John walked to him and rested a hand on his shoulder. His eyes were red. Red and tired from crying last night or this morning, red with regret.

The slashes of gray in his hair weren't handsome or dignified, only reminded Noel that his father was aging. Soon to be old and sad with what had happened to his women. First madness, then paralysis. Both because of Noel.

'She was very sick,' John said, his voice breaking. 'Demons. Talk of spirits capable of erasing our son from the world, claiming his soul, stealing his image for their own wicked purposes. For God's sake. It's disgusting the way she filled the house with that trash talk. I can handle a lot of things, Noel, but your mother's ranting, raving irrationality. Her faith in metaphysical crap. That's when she truly lost me. 'What's so bad about our world?' I used to ask her. 'What's wrong with this life? With you and me and our family? Why isn't this good enough for you?'

'She threw me out when I accused her of mental abuse. That sounds harsh, perhaps, but considering all you've been through . . . she infected you worse than I ever knew, my son. She abused you. She made her sickness your sickness. Do you understand what I'm saying? Do you see how we got here?'

Was John really suggesting, after all this time, after all Noel had been through, that his bubble was not really real? That it was nothing more than another form of mental illness?

Well, pardon me, motherfucker. I've seen and done too much to swallow that.

'I don't have an answer for what went wrong with your mother,' John went on, closing in, setting a hand on Noel's shoulder. 'But I know you have to see the past in order to have a future. I know it hurts to look at your whole life with a new pair of glasses, but it won't always. All of this can get better, if you want it to, Noel. But we've got to fix you up with a new pair of glasses. You need to see yourself in a different light.'

Can the fucking talk show patter, Dad. Memories of Julie floated up, a piece of evidence in his scattered defense.

'Julie saw it,' Noel said, backing away. John's hand slid from his shoulder and a dazed expression came over him.

'Saw what?'

'It. She saw it happen.' Noel felt a hot rush of vindication building within. 'The day of the accident. When Lisa fell on the stairs. It happened in Julie's bedroom. I disappeared. There's no other word for it. I was there, then I was gone, and Julie saw it. I was talking to her and she couldn't find me. It scared her. Scared her bad.'

John's face reddened. 'Is that right, Noel? Tell me, how does a fourteen-year-old kid disappear? Was it magic? How did you do it?'

'I don't know how it works. But it fucking works.'

'Can you do it now? Help me understand. Show me how you disappear, for Christ's sake — '

'Stop pretending you don't know! It's real! It's the reason Mom lost her mind. It's the reason you left us. It's the reason Lisa's wearing a diaper and the reason I woke up in a hospital today. You arrogant asshole. Think you know

132

everything. You can't see it, and so you don't believe it. But whether you want it to be or not, it's real, a separate entity, a medical problem or disease as real as Lisa's broken back.'

'All right!' John shouted. 'Since you brought it up, fine. Let's talk about that day. You let yourself into our home without permission. You would have been welcome there anytime, but you had to break in and steal things that didn't belong to you. And then you got mixed up with Julie. You charmed her with this bad boy bullshit, and then you got cozy, and then minutes before the accident you forced yourself on her. Forced yourself on Julie. Her words, Noel. 'He tried to kiss me. He attacked me. He grabbed me on the stairs and covered my face and blinded me!' That's what she told me, her mother, and the police. She allowed you to stay a few days and tried to be your friend, and what did you do? What did you do? You attacked my daughter — '

'She wasn't your daughter then,' Noel said softly, cutting his father off. 'But I was still your son.'

'Splitting hairs,' John said. 'Those girls were my family as much as you are today. You know what you did, you ran away and didn't care who you stepped on, and it ruined an innocent woman's life.'

'I didn't do anything, John,' Noel said, seething with calm. 'I can't control it. It controls me.'

John stomped off, barking at the gray sky. 'Do you hear what you're saying? You're talking about science fiction! Comic book horseshit!

You're not Spiderman, Noel, and most kids know that by the time they turn five. Please. I brought you here today to tell you about your mother. You're a young man. You don't have to live your life like she did. But you have to be stronger. You have to choose which way to go. And if you don't think there's a choice to be made, today, right goddamn now, you are worse off than she ever was.'

'Yeah, Dad? And what's my choice? What choice do I have?'

'You can choose to believe in demons and magical powers that absolve you from responsibility, that take you away from the real world with all its challenges and problems. And with it, your ability to lead a normal life, your sanity — gone. If you go that way, you will forfeit everything in favor of a sick childish fantasy and it will ruin you, I promise it will.'

Oh, take me now, you stupid blink. Let's show him the sick fantasy. Let's surprise the ever-loving shit out of him and give him a massive heart attack.

John continued on, trying to show him the light. 'Or you can choose to face up to your mistakes and accept the damage your mother has done. You can choose to be honest with yourself, get some therapy, work hard, earn a living, have lasting friendships, and maybe one day make a family of your own. It's not easy but it's real. It's real. You have more brains than me or your mother. You can do anything you want. Anything, and I will help you if you let me. It's your choice, but there's only one of these ways that allows you to find love, Noel. Only one that allows you to find peace inside that head of yours. Inside your heart.'

Noel hated his father at this moment. Hated him for popping back into his life after leaving them alone for so many years. For saying these things about his mother. Hated him for the possible truth in his words and what it meant for him.

'What do you want?' John said, quieter, wrung out. 'You want to wind up in a hospital, drugged to the gills? Isn't some life better than that life? Don't you want to have good things in your life? I don't think you need a hospital. I think you are stronger than she ever was and all you need to do is choose to be your own man. Hell, you've managed to get this far on your own and that is admirable, but this is a wake-up call. No more, Noel. No more.'

Noel couldn't respond. He was crying and he didn't trust his voice. John came back and reached for him. Noel backed away and John surprised him by lunging, stopping them both, clutching Noel tight against him.

'No. Don't hide. Let me help you. Please let me help.'

Noel resisted but his father was stronger. He gave up, wrapped his arms around John's ribs. The skin along his left arm felt tight, prickly and burning in fine lines.

'I know you think I don't understand,' John said. 'But I promise you I do.'

'Okay,' was all Noel could manage.

'Okay?'

His father's pleading, frightened tone broke the impasse.

'I'll get some help,' Noel said. 'I'll do whatever it takes.'

They separated and looked at each other.

John cleared his throat. 'Okay, then let's get the hell out of here before we freeze our balls off. What do you say?'

They went a few steps, stamping the cold away, finding their legs again.

'The Flash,' Noel said.

'Hm?'

'Fuck Spiderman. I always wanted to be the Flash.'

John laughed.

In the warmth of the rental car, Noel's thoughts returned to Julie. He hadn't forced himself on her, he knew that. They had shared something good, for a moment. There was always something good, for a moment, before the veil descended.

Noel hoped his father would be leaving soon, before something bad happened to him, too.

14

That evening, father and son dined at Boulder's finest steakhouse, The Cork. The low, unassuming, adobe-type building was located in North Boulder, its darkened interior lit with wall torches and a large gas fireplace, where men in sport coats and women in cocktail dresses gathered for a classier, we're-not-really-drunks version of happy hour. Cozy groups of four or five tables were tucked into various rooms, with throne chairs of fine leather strapping. The dinner menu was no longer inscribed on both faces of a large, dulled meat cleaver — as it had once been in the days when the place was still called The Cork & Cleaver and featured a cow's face on the sign out front — but many of the dishes Noel remembered from those very rare special occasions during childhood were still on offer.

Attractive waitresses with pinned-up hair and masculine dress shirts tucked into dark skirts conspired with a wandering sommelier who seemed to know half the patrons by name. He wormed his eyebrows and offered Noel the wine list as if keen to sniff out a young man deserving of a drink and one more way to gouge the old man.

'Have whatever you like,' John said, jovial from all they had accomplished in one day. After delivering the heavy speech in the park, John had spent the rest of the day cleaning Noel's apartment and doing laundry while Noel napped.

Noel had woken around three, apologizing for not helping.

'Don't mention it,' John had said. 'How's the arm?'

'Stiff, hurts. But not too bad.'

Noel showered, holding his arm in a newspaper baggie outside of the spray, and then John took him shopping for a plethora of household supplies — trash cans, toilet paper, cleaning products, shaving cream and a high-end razor with sleek disposable heads, a pack of athletic socks, honest plaid boxer shorts, a new microwave oven and, what the hell, a new 32-inch Zenith color television.

John unloaded everything while Noel sat at his kitchen island feeling like a child invalid, then wrote a check for $2000 and told him to buy some good groceries, start eating better. Splurge on a girl, he said, and, not knowing what his father's estimation of his social situation might be, Noel wondered if the plea was to find a date or hire a prostitute.

'You don't have to do all this,' Noel said. 'I have my own money.'

'Overdue,' John said. 'I still collect a pension from Richardson's, plus the stock. The chain went public two years ago. We're in Brazil and Japan now.'

'Awesome.' Noel folded the check into his shirt pocket.

John strongly insinuated there would be more

checks of this nature if Noel kept his doctor's appointments and stayed out of the emergency room. He made Noel promise to call every day. It was exhausting having a parent in his midst, but also comforting. He was grudgingly surprised and a little hurt, then, when at dinner John informed him that he was booked on an eleven o'clock flight that night. What if Noel hadn't been able to come home from the hospital? What if he had been a drooling idiot who couldn't stop screaming?

'May I suggest a heartbreaking Malbec,' the sommelier said to Noel. 'Drop-shipped this week from Luigi Bosca's eighty-five private reserve, with delicate notes of grass and anise. It pairs exquisitely with our famous teriyaki filet.'

'That sounds rad,' Noel said. 'But a Coke sounds better.'

'Low blood, low blood sugar,' John said, and laughed a bit too heartily. 'I'll have the house red and some more butter to go with these rolls.'

The sommelier nodded mournfully and left to plead his case at another table.

They ordered the teriyaki filets, pilaf, spring greens. Beside them, a girl of twelve was celebrating her birthday with her parents and a slice of mud pie that stood at least seven inches high and must have weighed two pounds.

'Save room for one of those,' John said.

Halfway through their meal, a stabbing pain lanced its way through Noel's stomach and lower, into his bowels. He broke out sweating and his arm tingled hotly. A dog-whistle ringing he knew no one else could hear bored into his ears. The gas fireplace glowed at his face like a small sun. The room spun and he knew he was either going to throw up, shit himself or pass out.

'Excuse me, Dad,' he said, sliding back his chair.

'Everything all right?' John looked up, his steak knife sawing to a halt.

'It's great,' Noel said. 'Be right back.'

He hurried through a corridor of textured plaster walls and shoved the door open. He was disappointed to find the men's room occupied by a hand-towel and mint-dealing servant standing at the center of the back wall, facing the double-sink vanity layout. The short, plump Hispanic man looked like an implant from the 1930s, with his lard-matted hair parted down the middle, a push-broom mustache, placid unseeing eyes and a white towel draped over his left forearm in horizontal salute. He did not so much as nod or blink as Noel careened past, locking himself in the far stall.

Noel fell against the wall, closing his eyes. It wasn't a nature call. His entire body was trembling. The sweat on his face and back had turned to ice. He placed his right hand over his tripping heart. What was this?

Nerves, exhaustion, a reaction to the stress of trying to present himself well in front of a man he hadn't seen in a decade and who happened to be his father. It would all be over soon, this day, this night. Then he could go home and sleep for twenty hours. He concentrated on the restaurant sounds coming through the walls, clinking plates in the kitchen, the murmuring guests, the lone

140

peel of raucous laughter from the now-inebriated bar crowd.

The door banged open. The restaurant's speakeasy din pierced the tiled room and just as quickly ceased as the door shut. Someone else was in the bathroom now, and somehow Noel knew he had been followed.

Two or three footsteps moved slowly toward him, business heels clacking on the floor, and there was a judgmental intake of breath: *tsk-tsk-tsk* . . . like somebody's grandmother catching a child in the act of stealing a cookie. Noel didn't know how he knew, but was sure the admonishment was coming from the butler attendant with the towel draped over his arm.

'Evening, Carlos,' a man with a helium voice said. 'How the patrons treating you tonight?'

Carlos, if that was the attendant's name, did not answer. The crackle of a urine stream melting bar ice echoed off porcelain and filled the room.

The interloper sighed. 'Whattsa matter, hombre, *el gato* got your tongue?'

Noel raised the back of his head from the wall and opened his eyes, as if staring at the inside of the stall would allow him to better hear the exchange.

A disgusted string of muted Spanish issued forth.

'What was that?' the high voice said, testy and daring. 'Wha'd you say to me, you dirty little kumquat?'

'*Voy a chupar la polla por cincuenta centavos.*'

Whatever this was, it earned a round of

141

high-pitched laughter. 'Is that right? Maybe I'll suck *your* cock for fifty cents. How'd you like that, shortstack? Talk to Bobby about getting you a raise, but first you take care of *el chorizo*, eh?'

'*Chenga a tu madre, bastardo,*' Carlos hissed.

The urinal flushed. More slow footsteps crossing the room. A strained silence, followed by a single smack of flesh, very like a palm slapping a cheek. Carlos grunted. The high-voiced man tittered, released another sigh of pleasure.

Then . . . nothing. A minute passed. No one spoke or moved.

Noel leaned down and peered under the stall. Carlos the bathroom attendant's feet were in the same spot as when Noel entered, and another pair of shoes — polished black and white spats draped with cuffed charcoal trousers — were standing nearly toe to toe with them. What the hell were they doing? Kissing, he thought, until the whispering began.

Easy, easy. We're not alone, Carlos said, his Spanish-accented English as careful as it was quiet. *He's in there.*

Who, the kid? his tormentor turned conspirator said.

Si, papi.

Well, what are you waiting for? You want to stand here all night with a face like that? We have places to go.

Let him be for now, Carlos whispered. *Can't you see he's been through enough? I have seen this before. He is broken.*

Oh, dear God. They were talking about him?

Noel covered his mouth and could feel their heads turning to watch the stall.

I want my face, the high-pitched man said. *Tell him I need my face!*

If you push him now, you will kill him. The others feel we should allow him to grow stronger.

And then what? the high-pitched man whined. *How am I supposed to go around looking like this?*

You have waited a long time. Waiting a little more won't kill you, Carlos said. *When he is well, we will all grow stronger with him. There is no question he will learn to fade, and when he does he will open doors for us. Many, many doors.*

This was madness. He had to get out of here. Noel reached for the metal tab locking him in, but just then a series of slapping footsteps came racing at him and a great weight slammed into the partition, shaking the entire stall.

'What the fuck!' Noel cried, backing into the toilet.

Fists pounded the wall as another stream of profanity-laced Spanish poured out, berating him, accusing him of something he couldn't understand.

Noel choked on the word 'Help!'

The pummeling stopped. The verbal assault stopped.

The toes of two small polished black work shoes protruded beneath the stall.

Noel slid along the wall and saw a single shining black eye peering at him through the crack between the door and its frame, all pupil, twitching side to side.

'What are you doing?' high-pitch said. 'You said leave him alone.'

'I jess want to see him,' Carlos said. 'I wan' him to know how much pain I am in.'

The door lock jiggled. The Carlos eye continued to track him. Noel covered his mouth to keep from screaming.

'Don't forget about me,' Carlos whispered. 'Don't listen to your father, Noel Shaker boy. You are not loco. You must be brave now. You must be brave for all of us.'

'Leave me alone,' Noel said. 'I didn't do anything to you.'

'I did my job!' high-pitch shrieked, joining Carlos to rattle the door with renewed violence. 'Now you must do yours! Do you hear me, Shaker? I want my face! Gimme back my beautiful face!'

'Stop it!' Carlos said to his friend. Then more softly to Noel, 'We believe very strongly in your potential, and it would be a shame if all that potential went to waste because your father filled your head with such cruel things about your kind and loving mother. You are not mentally ill — '

The other man's footsteps raced away from the stall. 'Smoke! I smell smoke!'

Carlos said, 'Don't listen to him!'

High-pitch careened around the bathroom. 'Please! Don't leave me in here! I don't want to die!'

Within seconds Noel smelled smoke. Heavy, black, lung-smothering smoke that burned his eyes and tasted like chemical death. And then the heat. The room becoming an oven. The walls rattled and the roof roared as flames erupted all around him. The bathroom was at once consumed with flame and the screams of dying men.

Noel coughed and fell to his knees, clawing blindly at the stall and bathroom walls behind him. Ceiling panels melted and dripped like wax. Globs of charred insulation rained down smoldering on him, burning his hair and through the back of his shirt. The room thrummed and light bulbs popped, and then the walls exploded.

Noel covered his head and wished himself away, willing his bubble to shelter him from the fire. He imagined it carrying him off, not just erasing him but transporting him home, across town, to France, anywhere but here. The fire's consuming roar reached a pinnacle of violence and there was a suction wind pulling him from every direction at once, and then only silence.

Noel blinked. He was still here. There was no fire. The eye in the door seam was gone. The polished black shoes were gone. The room felt hollower than before. Noel coughed twice more but already his lungs were clearing and he breathed easily, though a sour taste lingered on his tongue.

He exited the stall, inspecting his clothes for burn marks. There weren't any.

No one was standing at the urinals or at the sinks sunken into the vanity. He reached for the door but his hands were blackened with soot. Greasy and smudging his cuffs. He wanted it off, now. He turned back to the vanity and ran the water, careful not to splash onto the bandaging, using the pink liquid soap and lathering thoroughly before rinsing. He tore a brown paper towel from the dispenser and looked up, into the mirror.

Carlos the bathroom butler was standing against the wall and his face was gone. He stood perfectly still staring at Noel from ash eyes sunk inside a blackened skull, the face and nose scorched and flame-eroded beyond recognition. White teeth exposed to the roots stood out from blackened gums. The larded hair was singed into bleeding tufts. The hand attached to the arm holding the white towel was a deformed knob of burned flesh and pink bones. It was a corpse, Carlos's charred remains standing calmly in the pristine white jacket, black trousers and polished black work shoes.

Noel spun around, but Carlos was gone. In his place there was only a chrome-plated trash bin set into the clean white tiled wall and, beside that, the push-button hand dryer. Once again Noel was alone.

Except that he knew he wasn't alone. Noel knew that when he turned and looked in the mirror again, the butler with the charred face and hideous ruined lips and broiled eyes would be standing right where he was a moment ago, watching him.

There was a fire here, he thought. Years ago. Maybe decades ago. And the ones who died in the blaze are still here. They wanted me. They are waiting for me to blink out again. And it's going to happen again, soon. I see the dead when I am about to drop, or have already gone inside. But why? What does it do for them? What do they want me to do?

Noel turned to the mirror slowly, but before he could face it the bathroom door opened and John was there. He looked at his son, concern transforming into a gentle smile of relief.

'Hey, sport. Everything working all right in here?'

Demons. You mother actually believed a demon had attached itself to you and wanted to take you away.

Was that what Noel had seen in the mirror? Is that what the men were, the apparitions who'd been whispering about him before the fire took them away? Demons?

'I don't believe in demons,' Noel thought, then realized he'd spoken aloud.

'I should hope not,' John said. 'Is that why you came in here? To convince yourself?'

'I had a stomach ache.'

'Better now? Do you want to go home?'

Noel looked into the mirror again. His own reflection was staring back at him, none other. In minutes, a few hours at most, that would disappear, too. He could almost feel it building inside him, a storm front of pressure in his cells. He did not want to fight it. Better that his father see for himself. See what was wrong with his son.

'No, I'm ready for that dessert.'

⋆ ⋆ ⋆

147

On the way home, in John's rental car, Noel remembered a question he had been wanting to ask one or both of his parents for years.

'What happened to Dimples?'

His father sat up a little straighter in his seat. 'Who?'

'Remember Dimples? That clown who used to be on Channel Two. He did the birthday show every morning. He always had that same huge yellow cake, like seven layers high. I always wondered what that tasted like until one day I realized it was a cardboard prop they wheeled out for each show.'

'Oh, yep,' John said. 'Sad story. What made you think of him?'

'I don't know,' Noel lied. *The dead men in the bathroom, perhaps.* 'He went off the air a long time ago, right?'

John nodded. 'Your mother wanted to get you on that show, as a matter of fact. She wanted to take you down the studio in Denver for, oh, I guess it would have been your first or second birthday. She was really sad when it didn't work out. You were so young. I'm surprised you remember that now.'

'Why didn't it work out?'

'Well, I forget what it was, but it was sort of a tragedy. Dimples — the old guy who played him on TV, I think his name was Hal something. Lichtman, Luckenbach, I don't know. Anyway, yeah, he died on air. It was in the news, parents were all messed up about it.'

'Are you kidding me?' Noel's arm began to tingle again.

148

'I don't know if it was standard procedure, but the day it happened they were taping the show live. The poor old guy had a heart attack or a stroke, something severe. He keeled over during one of the musical numbers, right there in front of the parents and kids in the audience. And apparently the cameraman or producer was sleeping off a dose of NyQuil or some damn thing, because they didn't cut away for almost two full minutes. Dimples died on live Colorado TV.'

'Jesus.'

'Yeah, that was the end of that show.'

'That's . . . disturbing.'

'But you didn't see it,' his father added. 'I know because I asked your mom if she'd left you in front of the TV that day and she swore up and down she didn't. Good thing. No two-year-old needs to see something like that, though of course a bunch did.'

Noel didn't ask any more questions until they got home.

★   ★   ★

'Oh, I almost forgot,' John said as they walked to Noel's front door. 'Good news. Lisa called this afternoon while you were napping. She spoke with Julie this morning.'

Noel fished in his coat for the apartment keys. 'Oh?'

'Turns out she was in Vail for the weekend, skiing with friends. Lisa said she sounded fine. I wish I had more time, but Lisa has therapy

149

tomorrow and her parents are due in Santa Barbara for the week. I'd feel a lot better if I had been able to visit Julie in person while I was here, but maybe that wasn't the real point of this trip.' He glanced sideways at Noel.

'Glad she's okay,' Noel said.

'That's the thing with you kids. Who knows, right? And I don't remember Julie skiing. You see what I'm getting at.'

What did he want Noel to say? 'She was always very smart. I'm sure she's fine.'

John eyed him warily at the door, both father and son aware there was something sad and wrong about him leaving tonight, but each grateful for the other's excusing of this awkwardness. Today had been more family drama than either had bargained for and they both wanted a break. Noel could see John waiting for him to offer some final reassurance that everything would be okay.

Noel smiled. 'Don't worry, Pop. I'll take the meds. I'll eat the food. I'll call you every night.'

'A new beginning,' John said with such earnest good cheer it made Noel's heart sink. 'For both of us, I hope.'

'Yes. Definitely.'

John lingered, squirming.

'What?' Noel said.

'If you hear anything about Julie, if you should run into her. I mean, if you know anybody who knows her, maybe you could ask around? See what she's doing, who she's running with? Keep me in the loop? Lisa would kill me if anything happened to her.'

'I doubt I know any of her friends,' Noel said. 'But I'll keep my ears open.'

'Good man.'

'Thanks for everything,' Noel said.

'I love you, son.'

Noel nodded and looked at his shoes. When he looked up again, his father was gone. The same could not be said of his demons, nor of the power that drew them to his dimmed presence like hounds before the moon.

15

In the morning it was a relief not to have to look at his arm.

The night his father left, Noel fell into bed and stayed there for almost sixteen hours. He woke up alone and saw under the hollow tent of his bedding that it had taken him while he slept.

Maybe it was all he had been through in the past few days. Maybe it was seeing two ghosts or demons or his own split personalities in the restaurant bathroom. Maybe it was seeing his father. But whatever it was, for the first time in his life, Noel did not despair over how long it would last, or what the cause might be. He was who he was, and if that sounded like surrender, so be it. He'd tried hiding from it, railing against it, crying over it, killing it. None of his reactions had changed a damn thing. None had helped *him*.

Maybe some day he would find a cure. Maybe some day it would just stop. Maybe it would take him and never let him go. But right now, starting today, he needed some semblance of a life. He decided that it was okay if this life turned out to be something he didn't ask for — whose didn't? If he was doomed to live as a man who blinked in and out of visible existence at the whim of higher powers (or even his own damaged psyche), then like a prisoner who is granted a walk in the sun only now and then, he would find a way to carve a little happiness from his bizarre life sentence.

He showered, shaved and changed the bandages on his arm as the nurse had shown him. He didn't know how badly the wounds needed redressing until he discarded yesterday's bandages and saw them reappear, blood-stained and dirty, in the bathroom trash can some ten minutes later. He swabbed the stitched cuts as a blind man reads Braille, with wads of cotton and Betadine solution. The purple-brown antiseptic liquid turned yellow against his transparent skin just before the bubble took it away, then he wrapped the invisible limb in fresh gauze, which also vanished by the time he finished pulling on clean clothes, which similarly were absorbed in a micro-blink of an eye.

A bowl of Golden Grahams went into a hole, milk dripping from his clear-as-air chin, down a hollow tube, and came to pool in his grateful fish-bowl stomach. He knew from previous experience that the food and beverages took to hiding within him, within the bubble, as soon as he closed his mouth and swallowed, but he still resisted the impulse to lift up his shirt and peer down at his belly organs just in case the rules suddenly changed.

Embracing his condition, he returned again to ways he might capitalize on it. Aside from being a thief, there were a hundred other roles he could, in theory, play.

The hero rescuing kittens from trees, but to whom would the victims and near-victims be grateful? He could play the voyeur, pervert, stalker, spy, but he had been observing from the outside for so much of his life, more than ever he craved intimacy, not artificial thrills taken from a distance. His unfulfilled moment with Julie, and the damage his longing had caused, had scared him off women, and in the years since, the other half of the species had become too painful to contemplate, let alone torture oneself with by following into gym shower bays.

He had come close to playing the seething monster, destroying property and inflicting harm simply because no one had to know it was him. Sometimes he dreamed of setting fire to anonymous buildings, smashing clothing store windows, stealing a Mercedes for a few hours of joyriding before launching it into Sunshine Canyon. But always there was the fear of emerging from the blink in the midst of such hijinks. There was no telling when he would come back, in front of witnesses, and he didn't want to wind up in prison, waiting for his next episode to make his escape.

Contrary to the books and movies that exploited his condition, opportunities did not flower before him. He didn't need excitement. The simple life would do, if only he had someone to share it with. He was like a blind and deaf man, a schizophrenic or an epileptic like his former classmate Jesse Lubbens. Hostage to his sickness, his ON/OFF switch. He was a young man unique in his particular ailment and yet, in all other respects, shared so many of the challenges and needs of any other disabled person.

What he really needed was a partner — in the simplest definition of the word. Someone to share the burden, and help him grow to manage it on his own. Someone who could fill the role of caretaker, mentor, trusted confidant, coach and friend. Someone who accepted him for what he was, and who would be there during the long climb out. A partner, and some kind of job.

Noel was slopping the last of the cereal into his mouth, staring out the patio window, watching as a guy layered in winter work clothes shoveled the courtyard, Walkman headphones clamped over his knit Broncos cap. He was bobbing and weaving as he cleared a path in the last of the white crust, scattering rock salt the way a farmer feeds his chickens. Mindless labor. Simple work.

There appeared to be some pleasure in this until a tall older man in a dark suit and long wool overcoat approached the snow-shoveler. He was long in the legs and trunk, a big loping dullard of a guy with chapped lips and, when he removed the beige Isotoner gloves, obscenely large raw fingers. Wiggling pink bananas, flexing and clapping together as he attempted to warm them. The shoveling dude removed his head-phones, blew a wad of phlegm into the nearest snow bank, and cocked an ear.

They chatted for a minute, but the exchange was not a happy or casual one. They were standing too close and their lips hardly moved. Noel did not figure them for family or friends. Maybe employer and employee, but he'd never seen either on the apartment grounds before now and he'd lived here over two years. Something linked them, something he could not name but could almost taste.

Well, their sunglasses for starters. Hard to be sure from here, some thirty feet away, but they seemed to be wearing identical Ray-Bans. The classic Wayfarer design, square at the top, round below. Popular sunglasses ever since that movie star wore them in that huge comedy hit a couple years back. But still a curious coincidence, the two men being of such obviously different social strata.

And why did they look so frustrated with one another? The older man, who might have been an All-American basketball player in his youth, like that loose cannon in the Rabbit novels Noel had read when he was fifteen, was now playing the role of the coach. Stabbing his obscene fingers into the shoveler's sweatshirt. What the hell — it wasn't like the guy had been doing a poor job. The entire courtyard's concrete and flagstone square was immaculate, clear of all snow and ice . . .

That was it. The patio had been clear all morning and, Noel was almost certain, yesterday morning, too. He remembered looking at it when he and John went to the store and again when they left for dinner. He had been watching every step because he felt so weak from his stay in the hospital. Also, it hadn't snowed last night.

So why was the dude shoveling the same patch over and over, pushing little spilled piles of the stuff back into the banks lining the perimeter?

'Because it's bullshit,' Noel said, walking to

156

the glass sliding door. The shovel job was just cover for something else.

As if they had heard him speak, both men turned their heads. He was standing in plain view behind the glass, but of course they couldn't see him. The veil still had him, but that didn't change how it felt. Two sets of dull eyes in their pinkish cold faces, staring right at him.

'Go fuck yourselves,' Noel said.

They didn't react, simply returned to their conversation. Were they just a bit calmer now? Less animated? Trying to look ordinary, as if this were just a property manager rattling off a to-do list to his hired hand? Maybe.

Or maybe the shoveler had been hired to watch Noel's apartment. To watch him. Maybe they knew he was in here, invisible or not, and were waiting for him to venture out again. Maybe some shady people or some organization had caught onto his activities. Maybe this was CIA shit creeping around his home, about to get up in his business. There could be surveillance mikes up on the roofs, aimed at his sorry pad, recording every word and flush of the toilet.

'I am coming for you tonight,' he said to the window. 'I will find you in your homes and pee in your Apple Jacks.'

The men did not look at him.

More likely he was being paranoid. But if anyone had a right to be paranoid, wasn't that person him? He hadn't broken any major laws. But what he was . . . what he could do . . . It was only a matter of time before someone with deep resources and big plans caught wind of that, wasn't it?

The shoveler was talking now, his apparent superior nodding along. Noel swore he could feel them resisting the temptation to look at his door again, but they didn't. The big boss in his tweed overcoat patted his man on the shoulder and the two of them walked to the end of the courtyard, out of Noel's view.

He thought about walking out, coming up behind them screaming, 'Hey, assholes, I'm right here! How about it? You want some?'

But he didn't do that. He pulled the louver blinds, and went back to the kitchen, pacing, hovering around his island, drank a glass of water. He sat on the couch, couldn't concentrate. He flipped on the TV, got up, checked the courtyard again. Neither of them had come back.

The afternoon sun came and went with impatience, and before he knew it he had wasted another day.

★ ★ ★

He was in the kitchen microwaving one of the premium-brand TV dinners John had bought for him when the phone rang, making him jump. He hadn't gotten a phone call in months and the ringing seemed ridiculously ominous. Then he remembered he was supposed to call his dad and report that he was still alive. This must be John, calling at almost ten p.m. California time.

Noel picked up on the seventh ring. 'Hello?'

158

'Noel, it's your dad.'

'Hey, how are you?'

'Just fine. How are you holdin' up, bud?'

'All good here,' Noel said.

'Yeah?'

'Yeah, Dad.'

'What've you been up to the past two days? Was hoping I'd hear from you last night.'

Last two days? Hadn't his dad just left last night? Did he expect Noel to call him in the middle of the night, after his plane ride home? Or had he slept all night, through the day and another night? Jesus . . .

'Sorry about that. I meant to.'

'No big deal, just so long as you're feeling better.'

'I am. Looking for a job, eating a lot. Healing.'

'You clean the arm with the stuff they gave you?'

'Makes a hell of a mess, but yep. Looks real clean.'

'Did you schedule an appointment with, what was his name, the therapist?'

'Dr Albe. Next Tuesday, eleven a.m.,' Noel lied, though actually telling the lie almost made him want to make it come true.

'That's good, son. I think a few sessions down that road will make you feel a lot better.'

Make *you* feel a lot better, Noel thought.

John took up the slack. 'Listen, I hate to bother you when you should be resting, but I have a favor to ask and we don't know anyone else out there. I'd come back and do it myself but I can't leave Lisa now. Her parents are still up in Santa Barbara for an extended fundraiser for Hugh's largest charity. It's absurd the amount of money these people . . . never mind all that. We haven't heard from Julie in a few days and Lisa's getting worried.'

'About . . . ?'

'Thing is, the more she told me about Julie's last phone call, the more skeptical I am that she's holding up her, uh, responsibilities out there. All I've got is her address and phone number, and between you and me, I think her roommates are shining me. Maybe Julie asked them to cover for her.'

'What do you want me to do?' Noel said. 'Call them?'

'Actually, you're just down the street. A mile or two at most. House up on the Hill, next to campus. You know the Hill?'

The Hill was a nickname for the University Hill neighborhood, but really just the three or four blocks of 13th Street where it split off Broadway near campus, a sort of informal mall with a barbershop, head shop, a few bars, a pool hall, late-night taco joints, record stores, the old Fox Theater that used to be a movie palace but was now a venue for up-and-coming bands and Disco Inferno throwback parties. Noel thought of the Hill as a poseur playground, a place where the trust fund babies and skate rats kicked around, trading dope for $5.00 concert tickets and Ralph Lauren socks. If you wanted drugs of any kind, he guessed the Hill was the place to find them.

'Of course I know it,' he said. 'I grew up in

160

Boulder, remember?'

'I'm aware of that,' John said. 'What I meant is, how well do you know it? The people, the scene?'

'Oh. Not very. It's not my thing.'

'Well, we're worried it might have become a bit too much of Julie's scene.' John paused, clearing his throat in that way he always had done when he wanted to impart the seriousness of the matter. 'I was thinking maybe you could take a walk by her place. See what you see. Shit, that sounds awfully creepy. We don't need be dishonest about this. We're just concerned. Just knock on the door, introduce yourself to the roommates — the one I spoke to is a Sarah? Sarah or Sasha. If you can find Julie and get a look at her, see for yourself how she's doing, that'd help Lisa calm down a good bit.'

'And you're worried she's, what? An addict now? No offense, I just want to understand what I'm walking into.'

John sounded relieved someone was asking straight questions. 'I don't know, but yes, maybe. There was an incident a couple years ago, when she was in high school. Pot. A few pills. We didn't think it that unusual for an eighteen-year-old, and her grades were still top-flight. But she's been going through a lot of money this semester and her grades have tanked. Her emergency credit card is maxed out. Can you take a walk for me, Noel?'

'I guess so. Yeah.'

John caught the hesitation in his voice. 'But what?'

How should he word this? 'Well, last time I saw her, she wasn't exactly . . . I mean, it's a little weird me showing up out of nowhere now, isn't it?'

'I hear you. But time has passed. Lisa and I agree it wasn't all your fault. I think the two of you were young and impressionable. Got your hormones mixed up, all right?'

'That's not how you felt two days ago.'

'I was angry, Noel. We were talking about things I thought we agreed were not helpful.'

'So you don't think I forced myself on her? I just want to be clear.'

John sighed for the third or fourth time. 'Whatever happened, it was an accident. We know that. Julie knows that. And my sense was, aside from the scare she had, I think she liked you just fine. You're a good guy. I can count on you to do the right thing and avoid any, ah, decisions that might upset her, right?'

'Of course,' Noel said. 'I'll see what I can find out.'

'Today?'

'What?'

'Can you go by tonight?' John said. 'Lisa's starting to panic, so the sooner the better. Call me back collect.'

'It's gonna be midnight by the time I get there,' Noel said.

'Is it that late? Even so, might be the right time to have a peek, nothing more if the lights are off. But if there's a party, you see what I mean?'

'Okay,' Noel said. 'I'll do a walk-by tonight, see if the place is Animal House. If not, I'll go

162

back tomorrow morning and knock on the door.'

John gave him the address on 10th Street, one block off College. Noel started to write it on his palm, but the ink became disappearing ink and he had to start over on the back of the frozen dinner box.

'Got it.'

'Thanks, Noel. Keep warm out there. We saw on the weather you got yourself some new snow.'

'Not yet, but probably soon.'

'Let me know.'

Before Noel could answer, John hung up.

Noel went upstairs and dressed warmly, knowing he couldn't take the 4-Runner. Two days he'd been under. How was he going to contact Julie in this state, the same state he had been in when he nearly killed her mother? Maybe it would release him tomorrow. Tonight he would just have a look, see what he could see while no one could see him. If she was up to no good, his current condition might even prove to be an asset.

At just a few minutes past midnight, Noel stepped out to find that his father had been right. The sky had formed a blanket of deep gray and was now releasing a slowly descending storm of snowflakes. He would have to be careful. Soon there would be enough for him to leave footprints. He shouldn't be doing this. But being outdoors and walking in the cold felt good, woke him up and made him feel alive in ways he hadn't felt in months.

He found the Boulder Creek path and trekked past Boulder High, across the now white football field, then cut up Broadway, which at this hour and in this weather was mostly deserted. The university came into view, and then the Hill proper, with its loud bars and coffee-shop urchins and rowdy students trying to make snowballs while they smoked on the sidewalks. After the Hill he moved into the residential streets, circling until he found 10th and College.

He followed the addresses, and double-checked the torn piece of TV dinner carton in his pocket to make sure he'd gotten it right. 1024 College. But here was 1016, 1020, and past this out-of-control stand of pine trees, 1028.

No 1024.

He went around the same block three times, checking both sides of the street, but he couldn't find the house. It wasn't where it was supposed to be. He continued on, circling, checking numbers, certain he had it wrong. Her house had to be here somewhere. But it wasn't. Julie had lied about her address. Which meant she was probably lying about much more than her address.

Noel found himself roaming in a broadening spiral, further and further from home, deeper into the old bungalows and Victorians and brick Colonials that had been divided for student living. He strolled past fraternity and sorority houses. He watched the windows and covered front porches and alleyways for signs of life, and the more he walked the less tired he became.

The trees turned white, and the streets brightened under twilight as the storm settled in. Snowflakes fell on his shoulders and eyelashes and whether they melted upon impact or were absorbed by his mighty shield against the world, he could not say.

Midnight turned to one, and one blurred past two in the morning. The sky became one great big shredded down pillow of a storm. Noel walked on, looking for a sign, lost and searching for the only girl he had ever opened his heart to and who, for a few sweet days that seemed a lifetime ago, had opened her heart to him.

16

After canvassing most of the Hill, up to the cemetery at 9th, he had navigated the south side of campus, around the student housing towers behind The Dark Horse Tavern and the old Wheels Roller Rink (now a health club, dormant at this hour), then cut back through campus, as if Julie might choose the middle of the night during a snowstorm to join a game of disc golf. Feeling like the most extreme case of foreign exchange student as he gazed up at the departmental buildings with their rows of darkened classroom windows, at nearly three in the morning, he began retracing his original route back toward home.

The snow had stopped falling, but it was everywhere and thick. Noel was tired and his feet, even clad in two pairs of socks and his heavy Sorels, were numb. His thighs were weak from trudging and slipping through the storm. The twin churning tunnels made by his weevil-burrowing feet were the only signatures of his passage through the eight inches of fresh powder.

He got within two blocks of his apartment, but the thought of calling his father with no update was too depressing, so he continued east, then south, cutting back up to Folsom Stadium, the GU football field, and further east until he was within spitting distance of the Foothills Parkway, scraping Boulder's fringes.

Boulder had close to a hundred thousand residents, thirty or forty thousand of them students. The citizenry were a haystack buried under a snowstorm and Julie was a needle with a fake address. He didn't know any of her friends. He didn't know anybody. What the hell had he been thinking? He was useless. He was dizzy, hungry, having left his frozen TV dinner in his new microwave. If he was really worried about Julie, he would go home now and call his dad, tell him about the mistaken address, tell John it was past time to call campus security or the local police. Someone who could actually do something about a missing girl.

The shortest route home led back through campus, and he lost his sense of direction, cutting through more buildings and courtyard commons, running into a wall of pine trees. The trees were planted ten or twenty feet apart but the lower rungs of their branches fanned into each other like gears, making his passage through them a gauntlet of spiked turnstiles springing into his thighs and chest, hurling snow at his face.

When he got out of that mess, he saw that he was now back on the Hill, right across Broadway, only two or three blocks from his original destination. Delirious and beyond tired, he started to laugh and before he knew it he was standing at the corner of 11th and College again. He went toward the mountains, turned onto 10th, and slowed, watching every mailbox, every driveway, more trees, this goddamned town was nothing but trees, and nearly tripped over somebody's frozen newspaper — wait a minute.

Those trees.

Noel backed up ten, then twenty paces, wiping snow from his eyes.

1016 College.

1020 College.

And now a long, wide stand of pines, just like the ones he had hacked through minutes ago. This border was similar, and he went a few more steps, peering around the wide snow-laden branches. There was a driveway here, a very narrow path made of parallel sidewalks, most of it grown over. Noel shoved his way through and popped out on a small lawn in front of a house that was set maybe a dozen paces deeper on its lot than the neighboring houses were on theirs.

'Dumb dumb dumb . . . '

He'd walked a good six, maybe ten miles tonight and it had been here all along.

1024.

The address was painted on the middle of six concrete steps leading to the covered front porch of a brown-trimmed, deep purple brick bungalow. All the lights were off. The driveway was empty, but who would bother parking back here when they had to drive through a Christmas tree lot to do so? There were no mountain bikes or lawn chairs, no candles on the window sills, no hammocks or beer bottles, nothing that said *here there be students*. The porch's front barrier wall of brick was bulging, the concrete seams crumbled and missing in many places. One good kick, he could topple that wall into the yard.

168

Safety hazard, landlord headache. Though the house was less than three blocks from the Hill's nightlife, the street was so quiet and the house so solemn it may as well have been ten miles from the town center.

He thought of those old ladies, the holdovers, the real bone and liver spot warriors on a walker, ninety-year-old crazies who refuse to sell even when the neighbors are raining beer bottles down on the roof and some developer or pregnant yuppie couple was offering half a million to just please go away and die already.

Noel climbed the steps, trailing little worms of snow from his boot soles onto the clean dry porch. More disrepair: two of the three front windows were cracked, none had blinds or curtains. The third was broken, a few triangular glass teeth dangling by the last of the putty, allowing the cold air to flow directly into the living room.

The front door was thick with many semesters of paint, the latest coat a yellowing cue ball white with a dirty brass mail slot. At the top of the door, in lurid orange streaks, someone had painted FUNHOUSE. The doorknob was missing, only the stripped bolt jutting forth. Noel pressed his nose to the left window and saw a narrow closet door and a mess of styrofoam peanuts spilled across the wood floor. A small bedroom was his guess; vacant not a guess at all. The window on the other side of the door gave him a view into the living room. A white stone fireplace streaked with soot, more bare floorboards, leaves blown into one corner, and a single cable antenna extended from the wall like a crooked twig.

If anyone lived in this house, they were squatters, derelicts.

But already he knew that no one lived here.

Just to be sure, Noel removed his right glove, sticky with pine sap, and reached through the broken pane, up to his shoulder, and waved his hand in the empty air. No heat. If such thing were possible, the living room was colder than the air outside. Outside the temperature was probably no more than twenty-five degrees, but to his naked hand the air inside the house felt like a deep freezer in someone's garage. He withdrew his arm and turned, looking at the trees, the tops of the other houses beyond, recalling the rest of the block, the neighborhood.

This was strange in a number of ways. The house was prime real estate. These houses, so close to campus and the action on the Hill, were never vacant. Three to six students usually chipped in, splitting rent of a couple thousand dollars. Demand was high. The other houses within sight, and the tall white apartment building at the corner, looked occupied. Cars, bikes, lights on in at least some of the windows, kids studying, pulling an all-nighter.

Why not this house? What was wrong with it?

It was February, which meant the spring semester had only recently begun, which meant Julie probably hadn't moved in and left so soon, which meant one way or another she was lying to her parents and had been for some time. Even if you're on a downward spiral, it takes more than a few weeks of a new semester to get kicked out. John had mentioned roommates. They all got kicked out? Not likely.

So, no one had lived here for a while. The landlord was losing maybe twenty-five hundred a month. Noel hadn't seen a FOR SALE or FOR RENT sign in the window, or out on the sidewalk. Why wasn't it on the market?

During his inspection, the healing lines of stitched flesh along Noel's left arm had begun to itch. They were burning now. Despite having stopped walking almost ten minutes ago, he was sweating inside his new parka and jeans and the two pairs of socks he'd pulled on before stepping into his boots. And he didn't feel like he was catching a cold. This wasn't a fever.

Something was wrong here. He was starting to feel nauseated the way he had in The Cork two (or was it three?) nights ago.

Something inside the house was affecting him. It wanted him to enter. He was being called to it, the way he had been called to the restaurant's men's room from his dinner table. He looked at the door again. FUNHOUSE. The cracked and broken windows. The house was dark and cold and, hell no, he did not want to go inside and have a look around.

But his arm was crawling with trails of fire ants. The cuts themselves felt alive. Noel's body, this strange vessel that moved with its own mysterious cloak, was responding to whatever was in here. Which convinced him that whatever was inside this house, however benign or malignant it might prove to be, had something to do with Julie, or with his own peculiar condition. He had not walked all night and been drawn back here to chicken out. Julie was in some kind of trouble, and the clues to her situation (or his own) were only steps away. He was sure of this.

Noel took hold of the threaded peg where the knob used to be, jabbed it forward with the heel of his gloved palm, heard it clang and roll on the wood floor. He jabbed again and the door cracked free, swinging into the house as a small rain of dried paint crumbled at his invisible feet.

'Hello,' he called out, knowing no one would answer, but needing to do it anyway. 'I'm coming in. No harm here, I'm just looking for a friend.'

But he was wrong, quite wrong, for he had gone no more than a dozen steps through the living room and was angling toward the kitchen when someone did answer.

17

What was that? No, seriously. What in the name of Christ was that sound?

The sound, or words, if that's what they were, had come from the back of the kitchen and Noel didn't really want to turn his back on whatever had made them. He stood in the living room, waiting for it to come again, to say something else, but the minutes wore on and nothing happened.

I want to go home.

That's what it had sounded like. A genderless voice, soft and tired. Only, it wasn't normal human speech. It was as if someone had said, 'I want to go home' through a mouthful of wooden toothpicks. And then it came again, in more of a slur of word-sounds, as if the speaker were slipping under the rubber nitrous mask before a brief but painful medical procedure from which it might never wake up.

Eye-ont-oo-O-home.

Followed by two minutes of silence.

Behind him was the first, empty bedroom he had glimpsed on the left side of the house. Closer to where he now stood, also on the left, was a closed door. Another small bedroom, he assumed, but the sound hadn't come from this direction.

Directly in front of him, to the right of the kitchen, was a bathroom. This door was open, and he could see the side lip of a bathtub, the protruding flare of the toilet bowl. The bathroom was empty (of course it was empty, the whole house was empty, except for that splintered voice) and, besides, the voice sounded like it had come through the arched entrance to the kitchen.

The fire-itching burn along the cuts in his left arm wasn't so bad now that he was inside. The maddening ant-crawling had ceased. Now there was only a mild warmth, soothing, like ointment. This did not make him feel better about being here.

'Oh God, please,' the voice came again, more strained but not as garbled. 'I can't breathe in here.'

'What's wrong?' Noel said, surprising himself. 'Where are you?'

The voice did not answer.

He walked quickly into the kitchen. A sink, an old blue or aqua green refrigerator, a brown electrical stove. Appliances that had been new and stylish in the sixties or seventies. The floor was tacky, stained with grease and dirt. On the back wall, hanging over a little breakfast table, was a warped paper calendar turned to the month of May. Noel moved closer. The picture above the date boxes was of a man on a ladder, painting the exterior of a house. His blond hair was perfectly parted and his painting attire consisted of trousers, dress shoes and a button-down shirt. *Kwal Paint Turns a House into a Home!* read the jaunty tagline above the man's head. The year was 1964. Almost thirty years ago. Long time to leave a calendar hanging on a wall.

'I'm going to miss you all so much.'

There it was again. The wounded voice, clarifying with every new complaint. Noel thought it was coming from the kitchen closet, but the voice sounded farther away than right behind this door.

'Who's there?' he said to the door. His arm was pleasingly cool now, and the coolness was spreading up his shoulder, into his neck and chest and down his back. He liked it. 'Who are you?'

Another minute passed before a response was given:

'Can you hear me? Somebody there? Can you hear me?'

'I can hear you,' Noel said.

'Oh, thank God. Please don't leave me here.'

'Where are you?' Noel walked deeper into the kitchen toward a step leading to what might have been a sun porch before the backyard.

'In here,' the voice replied, muffled as before. This was turning into a game of Marco Polo, hotter and colder, and apparently Noel had chosen the wrong direction.

'Where?'

'In my room.' The voice losing urgency, fading, tiring. 'Help. Help me.'

Noel walked back through the kitchen, into the living room, and stopped outside the open bathroom. To the right of it was the other closed door.

'I'm in the living room,' Noel said. He

swallowed dryly, staring at the doorknob, waiting for it to open. 'I don't know what to do.'

'Don't go,' the voice said, and Noel was sure now that it belonged to a young man. Strained, feminine, but male all the same. 'Can you see me yet?'

'No.' Noel was less than five feet from the door. One more step and he could reach the knob. 'Do you want to open the door for me?'

The young man cried softly for a moment, then fell silent. Some time passed. Noel's brain was sinking with fatigue into tar-pit fear.

'I can't,' the young man said. 'I need *your* help.'

Jesus. The energy between his body and this door was magnetic. Whatever it was, it was pulling him, tugging through his clothes. Okay, okay. Enough of this. Open the fucking door and see what the problem is.

Noel took two fast steps, gripped the cold knob and pushed. The door creaked in its frame but wouldn't budge. He turned the knob side to side. It wasn't locked. Why wouldn't the door open? He shoved again. Nothing.

On the other side of the door there arose a gasping sound, a drowning man breaking the surface of a lake.

Noel looked up at the door frame, seeing no trim on his side. Then he understood. The door opened into the living room, toward him, not into whatever lay behind it.

He turned the knob as he pulled and the door swung open.

The room was dark, but the windows were

bare and enough snow-moonlight was reflected in for him to see a small bed, a small desk with a chair turned sideways to it and a short bookshelf.

Next to the bed, sprawled on the floor, was a writhing body. Lying on its side, the legs tucked up and cycling in slow, pained movements. The arms were limp and the head was thrown back, as if the eyes were trying to see something behind it. Noel thought of a bird that had flown into the side of a glasshouse before falling to the ground.

Thin to the point of emaciation, he might have been Noel's age and wore the clothes of a studious young man. Dress khakis, brown loafers, a blue Oxford shirt tucked in and belted. His hands were curled into claws. The body went rigid and the head came forward as the face strained to look up at the door, at Noel. Seeing the face, Noel thought he had been mistaken. This was not a young man at all, but an old one, drawn, wrinkled and decaying yellow. The eyes, which were sunken and surrounded by puffed, blackened flesh, lingered everywhere but settled on nothing. Crusts of blood were dried at the mouth, with more fresh and leaking from between purple bloated lips.

No, it wasn't an old man. Innocence lurked beneath the mask that had ruined the once handsome face. And the spirit inside the body, this Noel could feel like his own. It was tormented, struggling and so very tired of struggling. It wanted out. Out of this room, out of this house, out of this body.

But even as he watched the old-boy staring up at him, speechless, the body began to writhe again, an animal in its terrible final agony. The knees retracted nearly to the chest. His left arm was pinned at his side but the right kept reaching, grasping at something out of range. The bony chest was heaving in buzzing fits as the deformed mouth opened and closed. At last the throat emitted what Noel had never heard or seen but could only think of as a death rattle. A final, cackling plunge of stale air seemed to go out with godawful effort, and then the entire body went slack, silent, still.

Unable to move, Noel thought two things: whoever this kid was, he just died.

And he wanted me to watch him die.

As soon as this realization formed, the boy curled into a ball, covered his face with both hands and, moving with a newfound grace, reached up to the bed and pulled himself to his feet. Arms loose at his sides, he stood at a height nearly matching Noel's, and though he was far too thin, he presented a posture of youthful health.

He was normal again — or normal in the way Noel would have imagined it before this thing that killed him had a chance to transform him and age him so. Now he was clean-faced, with no wrinkles or blackened puffiness around his eyes, and his lips were pink, smiling stiffly. Green eyes alight but never once blinking, the dead student began to walk toward Noel.

Noel backed into the door frame.

The dead student reached for him, the thin fingers curling.

'No,' was all Noel could manage before staggering into the living room. He caught a heel and lost his balance, toppling backward, falling as the dead student continued after him. Noel's butt and elbows took most of the impact and he was afraid to turn his back on this thing. It was leaning down at him, the eyes widening.

'Stop!' Noel cried, and to his surprise the dead student obeyed.

Noel was panting, kicking his legs as if to drive his pursuer away while simultaneously trying to get a foothold to stand, but when the dead kid tilted his head and crouched, Noel sat still.

'Thank you,' the young man said with no emotion, only the flat, lifeless tone and cadence of . . . there was no equivalency or context for it. It was neither a caricature nor an echo from the grave. It was merely the monotone of a dead man.

When Noel failed to respond, the same inanimate voice produced the words, 'Can't imagine how long I waited for someone to help me.'

'I . . . ' But what had he done? He didn't understand anything.

'You saw me,' the boy answered. 'You didn't leave me to go alone.'

Noel got to his feet and backed up a few more steps, but the dead student did not attempt to follow him. 'How — ' *long have you been dead?* But Noel worried his question would come off as an insult. ' — long have you been in here?'

The kid stared a moment before answering, 'In their time twenty-seven years. In this one forever.'

Noel thought of the calendar in the kitchen. This wasn't purgatory. It was a hell.

'You look like my older brother, Mark,' the dead kid said. His facial muscles did not seem to be working properly. 'I missed them all so much. I missed all the people. I'm sorry about what happened to you, but it's nice to have a friend over here.'

That the conversation was even happening was too much for Noel to absorb. So it took him another moment to extract the meaning of this observation.

'A friend?'

'Bryan,' he said, the words still coming slowly. 'Bryan Simms. I'm from Pennsylvania but came here to study astrophysics. Do you think they still teach that?'

'I don't know,' Noel said, unable to entertain the idea of the boy returning to school. 'Not friends. It's not . . . '

'Why shouldn't we be friends?' Bryan Simms took another step toward him, his eyes full of need. 'We are the same, aren't we? You and me. Aren't we the same?'

18

Noel turned and ran from the house. He slipped on the front steps and fell onto the snowy sidewalk, bare hands plunging into snow to meet with rough concrete. He leaped to his feet and rushed toward the trees blocking the driveway, only to find Bryan Simms standing in the snow, blocking his escape. Noel barked something short of a scream. The dead student watched him with the same flat expression, only now it felt like curiosity and possibly mild amusement.

'Are you all right?' Bryan Simms said. He wore the same Oxford shirt and plain khaki pants, nothing more, but he did not shiver and his word-breath produced no clouds of steam in the four a.m. chill.

'We're not the same,' Noel said, wiping snow from his stinging hands, hands he could see no better than his invisible green parka. He could see Bryan, and Bryan could see him, but he couldn't see himself. Could Bryan see himself, or were they conversing on some plane of half-death, half-life where perception did not extend to the self? It hurt Noel's brain to consider such things.

Bryan's eyes seemed to deepen with concern. 'Are you sure?'

'I'm not — ' Noel began, then swallowed to catch his breath and amend the statement. 'What

181

happened to you, that never happened to me. Nothing like it.'

Bryan Simms said, 'I didn't know at first. But if yours was recent, your denial would be understandable. I believe I spent most of my first six months in that room trying to convince myself I was just paralyzed or brain damaged. But it doesn't have to be that way for you. I can help you make peace with it.'

'Get out of my way,' Noel said.

Bryan looked down at his loafers and stepped to one side. 'I'm not trying to stop you. I just wanted to help.'

'I don't need your help.'

Bryan Simms glanced over Noel's shoulder. 'You came to the house for something. Not me.'

Julie. In all of this, he had more or less forgotten the purpose of his journey. 'I'm looking for someone. She's supposed to live here.'

'What's her name?' Bryan Simms said.

'Why does it matter to you?'

'We can't always see them, and they almost never see us. Maybe she's still . . . around.'

Noel did not bother to sort out the 'us' and 'them', only said, 'Not likely.'

Bryan studied him a moment. 'You're young and you don't look sick, so it must have been an accident. I'm sorry for your loss.'

Noel opened his mouth and shut it. He was rubbing his arm, he realized. His stitched cuts were starting to itch again. The cut marks. No. No, it couldn't be. He'd attempted to kill himself, the key word being *attempted*. He'd been in the hospital. Gotten stitches, a prescription. Spent the day with his dad. Walked around town. Left tracks in the snow. He wasn't dead.

Noel looked at the recent trail of prints leading up to the porch and back. 'There,' he said, pointing. 'I made those. You don't have any.'

Bryan Simms stared at the ground, where there were no tracks leading to or away from his feet. He looked to Noel.

'I'm cold,' Noel said. 'It's freezing out here, but you can't even feel it, can you?'

They both knew this was true. Bryan Simms rubbed his arms anyway, then pressed his palms over his Oxford shirt and shrugged.

'This is strange,' Bryan said. 'None of the others could see me, but you did. How did you do that?'

'I don't know,' Noel said. 'But I didn't do anything. And what others?'

'The people who live there.' Bryan nodded toward the house. 'The people who've come and gone. Years ago there was a gas leak. Carbon monoxide from the malfunctioning water heater in the basement. It's silent and odorless. I was napping in the afternoon, after studying all night. My roommates were already gone for the weekend. It was almost three days before anyone found me. Ever since, these students come and go, living in my room, walking right past me in their ridiculous clothes, taking their drugs, having intercourse in my bed. Years and years. And then you come along. Who are you? What makes you special?'

Noel stuffed his hands back into his gloves. 'I

can't explain it. You wouldn't believe me anyway.'

Bryan Simms stared at him.

Noel almost laughed at the absurdity of his statement. 'For starters, I'm not dead. I disappear. For periods of time. Like the invisible man, only it's not my body, or not only that. My clothes go, too. I think of it like a bubble, a thing that comes down on me and takes me in. I have no control of it. It's an affliction. I don't understand it, but it's been happening since I was a baby. It drove my mother insane. No one believes it's real because there's nothing to see. Get it?'

Bryan hesitated only a moment. 'I can see you.'

'You can. No one else can, not right now. Trust me. I've been out of the visible world for going on three days now. And it's happened dozens of times, maybe hundreds. It's ruined my life on more than one occasion.'

Bryan could not express his interest, but Noel felt it anyway. 'Is there some kind of cloaking technology in this time I am not aware of? Something that bends or refracts light even as it reflects your surroundings?'

'Technology? No. It doesn't exist. I've read up on it, believe me. It's not man-made. It's not anything you can explain with your physics.'

'What about time?' Bryan said.

'What about it?'

If it was possible for the dead student to become animated while still presenting as a speaking corpse, Bryan Simms did so now.

'Well, it's either light or time. The manipulation of light or time. Nothing else would make invisibility possible. Either light doesn't behave around you like it should, for certain periods of time, thus rendering you invisible. Or time is not the same with you as it is for others. Maybe during these periods you are moving along a different path in the continuum.'

'I'm not a time traveler,' Noel said. 'They don't have that technology either. When I disappear, I am still here, watching people, knocking shit over, making a mess, being in the here and now. They just can't see me.'

Bryan was shaking his head.

'What?' Noel said.

'Sorry, no. It must be one or the other. Light or time. There is no other explanation.'

'What about this?' Noel said.

'What about what?'

'You and me, here, now. This isn't normal. You're a . . . '

'A ghost?' Bryan answered for him. 'Maybe. But there's got to be a scientific explanation for ghosts, hasn't there? Perception, mind, hauntings, the soul. What could be behind these things if not psychology, cells, synaptic pulses, light? If I exist here with you, there must be rules and some kind of natural explanation for us.'

'This isn't natural,' Noel said.

'What is not natural?' Bryan said. 'The supernatural? Fine, let us turn to anthropology. In ancient times of drought, the rain was a gift from the gods. A Kodak camera is an instrument of supernatural power to primitive peoples who

185

do not have experience with or any foundation in technology. To them it is magic. Just because we can't explain it or don't understand something now doesn't mean it's not real or that there is no science that can be applied to it.'

Noel didn't know whether to be frustrated or hopeful at this reminder. It was better than thinking he had succeeded in killing himself and was now walking around like some purgatorial version of Bryan, but not much better. He shivered, more from the cold than the conversation.

'What's the girl's name?' Bryan Simms asked.

'Why do you want to know?'

'Maybe I've seen her. Or heard her name.'

'She's not here,' Noel said. 'I hate to tell you, Bryan, because I know you've been lonely for a long time. But whoever lived here, they're gone. That house is empty.'

'Is it?' Bryan was almost smirking.

'Yes.'

'A bubble, you said? That's what it feels like?'

'Sometimes. I don't know. Why?'

'I'm just thinking,' Bryan said. 'Maybe there's more going on here than what you can see when you are in your bubble. Maybe when you disappear, you see some things, like me, that no one else can see.'

'You're not the first,' Noel said. 'Others have followed me. Others like you.'

Bryan nodded. 'But what if sometimes, when you are so close to my kind, in this level of things, you don't always see what else is going on? What if there's another world going on all around us, and by helping me, by immersing yourself in this bubble, you've blinded yourself to the rest of the world?'

'What the hell does that mean?' Noel said. 'This is the world. Trees, snow, houses. The only thing out of place here is you. And, in another way, me.'

Bryan Simms walked to one of the pine trees and reached out for the branch, as if to shake the snow from it. His hand disappeared, or ceased to exist, as it moved through the branch and the snow was left undisturbed.

He looked back at Noel. 'I don't know the answer. I know that I felt you coming, before you ever set foot in that house, and I think you felt me, too. Somehow, between whatever state I am in and whatever reality this affliction of yours put you in, we were able to meet in a place that is neither here nor there, not quite then and not yet now, but a little bit of all these things. And I think the best thing now, for both of us, is that I leave. I need to see my family one more time, or what's left of them, and then I am moving on. But I think you should stay awhile, Noel. Stay here and look for your girlfriend. Because if what I suspect is true, or close to true, finding her might be a lot easier once I'm gone.'

'She's not my girlfriend,' Noel said.

'Oh? Who is she?'

'She's just . . . ' He almost said 'sister' but that didn't feel right either.

'Someone important,' Bryan Simms said.

'Yes.'

'Then don't give up,' Bryan said. 'This is a

popular house and things tend to look different when you're not dead.'

Was that a joke? Noel didn't know what to say to any of this.

'Thank you for helping me, Noel,' Bryan said, gesturing at Noel's arm as if he could see through the parka. And come to think of it, how did he know his name? That was the second time he'd used it and Noel did not remember providing it. 'Whatever this thing of yours is, it is rare and it helped me, so it can't be all bad.'

'It's not good,' Noel said.

'To me it's the most beautiful thing that ever happened. It's all a matter of perspective. Or maybe a perspective of matter. Or anti-matter. Or something. Anyway. Good luck, Noel.'

Bryan started to walk away, then paused and looked back.

'Oh, please don't worry. I won't tell anybody.'

'About what?'

'What you did for me. If word gets out, if this bubble of yours keeps following you, you could become a very popular guy in ways you probably don't want to be.'

Noel's skin crawled at the thought. Bryan started off again.

'Bryan?'

The student paused again. 'Yes?'

'Aren't you scared of what comes next?'

For the first time, Bryan did smile. It was not a handsome smile, but it was a smile. 'I don't know what comes next. But I do know one thing.'

Noel waited.

'There is pain in life, but life's worth a hundred years of what I went through. And there's pain in dying, but that's not so bad unless you go alone. It's being stuck that hurts most, Noel. Moving on, accepting who you are, there's no pain in that.'

Bryan Simms walked into the pine trees. The branches did not bend and the snow did not fall.

Behind Noel, a light began to glow and music began to play. Voices, alive and filled with laughter permeated the cold winter night. The sound of raucous conversation echoed from the other side of the house. The music gradually got louder, a slow melody carrying a balmy island breeze of marijuana smoke on a steel drum beat.

A girl hollered, 'Goodnight, Pamela! Be careful!' and a few seconds later walked past Noel, throwing a fluffy pink scarf over the shoulder of her brown corduroy jacket and the spill of her blonde hair. He watched her hips sway drunkenly, knowing without seeing her face that she was real enough, alive, but not Julie. She pushed through the branches audibly, sending snow down in clumps, and reappeared a moment later walking down the sidewalk on the other side.

Noel turned back toward the house and saw the porch light on, a mountain bike chained to a pillar, half a dozen plastic beer cups aligned along the rebuilt retaining wall, and the bodies of late-night revelers moving inside as the party — a party that had been happening all along inside 1024 — began to wind down with a modicum of respect for the coming dawn.

Noel approached the porch steps one more time, wondering if Julie still lived in the house and, if so, in how many ways she, too, had become haunted.

19

If Noel had been hoping his accidental good deed in freeing Bryan Simms would restore him to the visible world just in time to mingle at the party, he should have known better. He was reminded of his status when he reached the porch and a hefty bearded burnout bedecked in a bright yellow Colorado Buffaloes sweatshirt and matching pajamas careened through the doorway and trotted barefoot down the stairs to regurgitate beer foam into the snow. He panted a minute, wiped his mouth and returned at a much slower pace. He looked right through Noel on his way back inside, made a U-turn into the small front bedroom, and bellowed, 'The fuck outta my room!' at two girls who had been conversing in there and collapsed onto his unmade bed.

The girls — one a butch blonde with a nose hoop, the other a diminutive but fierce-looking brunette in a navy peacoat and Fidel Castro lid — moved into the living room, which was dark but for a few candles and the lights from the stereo system where Peter Tosh was singing about chasing down vampires in Buckingham Palace, took one last forlorn look around, and left the party without so much as a glance at the specter loitering on the porch.

More evidence of the bubble's expanding power: the front door was painted a dull shade of gray now instead of cream, yet still bore the legend FUNHOUSE (in red instead of orange), as if every tenant since 1964 had found the moniker too irresistible to remove. He peered in the front windows, noting none were cracked or broken now. Only two people remained in the living room, a couple or one-night-stand in the making judging by their moist embrace of one another. The rest (couch, love seat, coffee table, stereo system, rock posters, etc.) looked as if a hurricane of cigarette butts, beer cups and pizza had recently passed through it.

Noel entered, watching his step but not worrying much about his audible signatures. The music wasn't as loud as it had seemed a moment ago (now that the shock of it being here at all had worn off), but it masked any trace of his entrance. Even with the front door open, the house was warm inside. Somewhere a furnace was working overtime. Stepping around an overweight black Labrador snoozing on a nest of jackets and pilfered couch cushions, Noel wondered how he had navigated this mess the last time around. How had he not tripped, or bumped into somebody, heard the music or felt the heat? It made no sense and did not fit the pattern and rules of his usual episodes, where the real world remained the same for others as it did for him and only his appearance was altered.

It's either light or time, Bryan had said. *The manipulation of light or time. Nothing else would make invisibility possible.*

Noel had never given the concept of a time-shift much thought; he'd never had a reason to. In all his other dropouts, his perceptions of the world and people and his (limited) interactions with them had remained in sync. When he tripped over Lisa's foot at the top of the stairs, there hadn't been any delay before she tripped over his and fell down the same stairs. Julie hadn't frozen in another time capsule while their romantic tragedy played out. True, the fire at The Cork seemed to have been a glimpse into the past, but even that had been contained, hitting him with the rapid insight of a psychic vision. He hadn't walked, talked and been himself in it.

So, were you so in the zone you couldn't see more than the abandoned house as it had been at some point in the past thirty years, even as your subconscious or some part of your brain in charge of spatial awareness compensated and guided you along? Or did your bubble take you to another time altogether, when the house was empty and none of these things existed? Perhaps the bubble is expanding, blinding me to larger and larger pieces of the world as it blinds the world to me. Either that, or the thirty-year agony of Bryan Simms's soul left one hell of a psychic splatter all over these walls.

He was too tired to dwell on these questions. He wanted to have a quick look around for Julie and go home. Unless he really had jumped back in time, it would be almost five a.m. now. What were these people doing awake at this hour? At a certain point, doesn't the night deal you your final hand? You will either be drunk or not drunk, about to get laid or not even close.

193

Shouldn't everyone have made a decision by now and gotten on with it?

Noel walked into the kitchen. The cabinets and counters were the same mid-century holdovers from before, but the appliances had been updated. The oven was on low, the door cracked open a couple inches. Noel could feel its heat filling the room. He bent to look inside and saw eight cut-open cigars resting on a cookie sheet. The West Coast rapper lifestyle had officially reached Boulder. Someone was baking blunts.

He continued to the back, down the single step into a sunroom. The cold was seeping in from all sides, but someone had turned the space into a makeshift bedroom, with a fold-out futon couch-bed at one end and a dresser at the other. Piles of clothes, stacks of textbooks, the stale smell of athletic socks and wet laundry hanging in the dank cold air.

In the backyard, a tapped keg sat leaning in the snow, beside a circle of lawn chairs occupied by two girls and three guys. All were bundled in heavy coats, knit caps, gloves. They were talking, but he couldn't make out the words. He thought they must be very drunk to sit in the freezing dark like this, but none raised a bottle or cup. Maybe it was drugs. He thought of pushing through the screen door to get closer to them, but he'd just leave tracks and he didn't seem to be missing much. And somehow he knew neither of the two girls was Julie.

The way they sat, the set of their jaw or shoulders. She could be any size by now, her hair any color, but this didn't feel right. She was probably asleep in one of the rooms, if she even lived here.

Noel was half asleep on his feet when one of the guys in the yard stood in slow motion, stretched his arms and mumbled something to the others before heading toward the door. They laughed and wished him goodnight.

Noel backed into the corner of the darkened sun-room. The guy, who was short and chubby with a lock of carrot-red hair hanging from his gray wool ski hat, fumbled the door open, took one step inside and looked around as if sensing someone was here.

The guy eyed the futon with dazed longing, and Noel was sure this was his room and that he was going to fall into bed any second now. But he only swayed on his feet, burped and laughed at himself tiredly before continuing up into the kitchen. Noel heard his feet clap across the linoleum floor, then pause.

'You okay?' the guy said, not overly concerned about whomever he was talking to. 'Hey, you. Hello? Oh, wow. You are gondy with the windy, whoever you are.' The guy laughed again and a few seconds later the front door slammed.

Noel hadn't seen anyone in the kitchen. The music stopped while someone changed the disc or the machine rotated a new one into play. A song Noel had never heard began, first with piercingly simple acoustic guitar chords, then a plaintive voice that sounded like a younger, more innocent version of Sting's. The beat slipped into a soothing progression of drums and was joined by a kindly massaged keyboard and some kind of clopping instruments, like sand blocks, finding the perfect composition of crisp pop longing, reggae leisure and a lyrical pathos that subverted the otherwise pretty song with what struck Noel as grave sadness.

diamond waves through sunglass days go
  byyyyyyy
so beautiful to be here and aliiiiive
though I've built sometimes so hard
did I surviiiive?
Feel us shaaaayyy-kinnn'

He was thinking more about the music than his purpose here when he stepped back up into the kitchen, walked no more than three steps and felt the hairs on the back of his neck prickle hotly as if someone had blown a creeping kiss on him. He turned to his left and saw Julie standing in the corner pantry that had been closed on his first pass. She was staring right at him and his heart boomed thunderously before he remembered she could not see him. He knew immediately it was her because she hadn't changed at all. She was the same rail-thin waif with straight jet-black hair and pale doll skin he had seen five years ago and so often in his memory ever since.

He was frozen with a fear greater than that in finding Bryan Simms on the floor, and he dared not speak.

Backed all the way into the dark pantry, a cardboard can of oats and two bags of tortilla chips on the shelf above her head, Julie was swaying to the music, hands in the air painting with colors only she could see. She wore dark jeans, black sneakers and a thin, camisole-type shirt under her blue denim jacket, but she did not appear the least bit cold. She closed her eyes, lost in the song, and her hands dropped to her sides. It was a lonely dance, private, and a pang of guilt for observing her without permission coursed up from his stomach into his throat.

When the song ended, Julie's mouth pulled into a frown and she squeezed her eyes tight, as if she were trying to reclaim something that had been stolen from her. Then she opened them and stared at him, through him and into the vacant kitchen with childish wonder. Her lips moved but no words came out. Her eyes were solid black but briefly shiny with fleeting starlight reflected from sun to moon to snow off the window over the sink, or perhaps from another source, inside her.

She was on something. He did not have experience with drugs or people on drugs beyond what he had gathered from TV, but he knew she was not really here, even less so than he was. He reminded himself she had been this way before he arrived, and that she didn't appear to be suffering, in pain, or scared, so maybe it was no big deal. Probably she was hallucinating, on mushrooms or LSD or ecstasy, which would also explain the others out back, not drinking but awake and talking in the freezing cold of five a.m.

Julie looked happy, even if it was an artificially generated happiness.

But now that he was here, staring at her, standing less than eight feet from her, he had no idea what to do and in truth gave his next actions no thought at all. He began to move closer, step by tentative step, the better to see her small narrow nose with its rounded tip, the high wide corners of her white cheeks, the full thickness of her black eyebrows, the sweeping fall of her night hair, the thin peach-toned lips he had come so close to kissing once, before his cruel erasure took him away and sent her screaming for help. He was close enough now to catch the sweet herbal tang of her natural perfume, sweat and flowers, the moist peat smoke of her party-soaked clothes, and behind her the dry dust and pasta whiff of the pantry where she had taken shelter. He was three steps away, two, and then towering over her while she watched the psychedelic film playing behind her eyelids, and she lifted her chin just so.

Noel stopped, his heart tolling like a newly formed bell of wet clay.

Julie's eyes came to rest in direct line with his own. If he were solid-state they would be staring into each other, and he could swear, despite his condition, that she really was seeing him and that she was glad for his arrival. What does a blind woman sense when someone enters her sphere, changing the air, breaking the clean surface of her placid aura? Julie closed her eyes again but did not lower her chin. Her bottom lip was moist, and an eternity later fell open with a searching tremor.

'It's you,' she whispered.

Or maybe she said nothing at all.

Noel leaned down and touched his lips to hers, soft as cooling ash settling on torched remains, touching without will, without pressure, but tasting through molecules of breath her sweet wine palate and something stronger with the grainy darkness of dissolved dark chocolate.

Julie pressed to him, the wet corner of her mouth taking his lower lip in, then her tongue, alive and hot-slick against his own, accepting, allowing him to fall into the spell, forgetting what he was doing while simultaneously being here doing nothing else. He cracked his eyes to peek, still kissing her, and hers stayed closed. Was it abstract for her in a way it was not for him, because he was not altogether here and could not be real to her? Or was it that she wasn't here with him, but lost in her chemical high? And if so, was this so wrong, or perfectly right? Fearing not, he began to pull away, but she stayed with him, raising from her toes to keep the connection, and he rode the slide of her lips, edge of teeth, the cold spot of her chin nudging his, and he wanted more than anything to wrap his arms around her, protect her and be protected by her, keep her safe here or anywhere else she would go with him, forever.

And as swiftly as it had began she broke away, lowering and rearing back slowly, a dizzy child stepping down from a parked ferris wheel. She doesn't know what but knows something is not right. Oh God, she was going to panic again. She was coming out of her daze now and seeing nothing where there should have been a stranger, her boyfriend, anyone but no one.

'Are you an angel?' she said, her eyes tracing but missing him.

'Is that what you want?'

'I remember you,' she said with some relief.

'I remember you, too.'

'How did you find me?'

'A ghost showed me the way.'

She smiled wider, if that were possible.

'Are you all right?' he asked. 'Do you need anything?'

'I want to go home.' Her initial playfulness dimmed. 'I'm afraid to try.'

'Isn't this your home?'

She closed her eyes as a bad memory strolled behind them. 'Not any more.'

'Are you sure?'

'I moved. I don't even like it here. I don't know why I keep coming back, but I do.' Her expression drooped and he thought she was about to cry.

'It's okay. We don't have to stay. Do you have a car?' When she didn't answer, he added, 'How did you get here?'

'Don't know.' She leaned toward him as if about to fall, then corrected herself. 'I'm so tired. How am I going to get home?'

'I can walk with you,' Noel said. 'If you want me to.'

'I thought angels could fly.' She spoke this seriously, then laughed.

Maybe she didn't know who he was. Maybe she was so stoned she didn't know angels from boys, Noel Shaker from the Quaker Oats man

200

smiling down at the both of them. In which case he shouldn't have kissed her. A violation. It always would be in some way.

'I can't fly, but I'll get you home safe. Do you have a jacket?'

Julie looked down and tugged at her denim. 'This is a jacket.'

'No, it's freezing out. Here.' He removed the heavy green parka his dad had given him and swirled it around her back, pulling it over her shoulders. She could not see it yet, but she felt its weight, his body warmth captured in its layers.

'Oh, my God,' she said, and shivered. The parka emerged from the bubble as she was reaching for the lapels. She closed the layers around her, folding herself in. 'Wow, that's so fucking cool. How did you do that?'

'Angel trick. Don't overthink it. Let's get you out of here, okay?'

'Okay.'

'Do you want to try and tell me which way to go?'

'I'm scared,' she said.

'I won't hurt you. Take my hand.' He offered it to her.

Julie groped for it, bumped his forearm, clutched it, down, down, until she found his hand. Fingers intertwined, she held him tight.

'There you are,' she said.

'There you are,' he echoed.

Two squeezes, like a pulse. 'Don't let go. Promise you won't let go?'

'I promise,' Noel said, and led Julie from the Funhouse, into the night now turned to dawn.

20

Half an hour or so later they reached Julie's apartment, a ground-floor two-bedroom unit in a three-story stucco building on 30th Street near Arapahoe. The sun was not up yet, but the sky was changing by slow degrees. The walk seemed to have re-energized her if not restored the full array of her sober perceptions. She knew this was home, but couldn't stop commenting on the ozone layer, which had obviously dropped from the atmosphere to swim around their ankles as they walked. The brass numerals on her apartment door looked 'like gold licorice, don't you think?' She'd been making harmless, oddball observations most of the way back, though physically she displayed no signs of inebriation.

And there was the slightly insane fact that she had not questioned his identity or his condition since their conversation in the pantry. She was either chalking the entire situation up to whatever drug she had ingested or actually believed — like a three-year-old believes in Santa Claus — in angels. Angels who talked, walked, could manifest articles of warm clothing, and spoke like a random twenty-year-old guy.

Noel was too cold to be amazed at any of this. Having given her his parka and walked here in a flannel shirt and jeans, his ears felt made of glass and his teeth were literally clicking against each other, at least when he wasn't grinding his jaw with frustration that this endless night (now morning) was still happening.

Julie searched his coat for her keys until he reminded her it was probably in the denim coat underneath, but she didn't find it there either. Fortunately the knob was unlocked.

'Ssshhh,' Julie warned. 'Don't wake Marna.'

'Who's Marna?'

'My roommate. She's a total psycho but she's really nice.'

'Good to know.'

Julie tiptoed into the apartment, towing him by the hand. Noel followed her through the living room, past Marna's closed bedroom door, to the back of the apartment where a kitchen and bathroom sat adjacent to her bedroom. She released him and went to the fridge. She found a half-peeled roll of Nestlé Tollhouse Cookie Dough, scraped the stale end off with a knife, cut a hunk like she was paring a sausage and with the edge of the blade fed a puck of the dough into her small mouth, devouring it with the mechanical thrift of a rabbit working through a carrot. She cut another wedge and did it again. The third she offered to him without turning around.

'No thanks,' he said.

She repaired the cookie dough to the shelf and came back with a carton of milk. Sniffed the top, then swigged heartily, wiping a bead of milk from her chin.

'Okay,' she said, 'Let's go!'

She caught a wad of his shirt and dragged him into her bedroom, shutting the door behind him. She had a bed with a brass spindle frame, the thick mattress dressed with a pink fitted flannel sheet and only one cover — a thick goose-down duvet wrapped in more pilled pink flannel. Julie kicked off her shoes, peeled out of the jackets and launched herself in. She held the duvet up and looked to wherever he might be.

'Hurry, before all the cold gets in!'

Noel bumbled forward and slipped in beside her as the clam closed around them. She shivered and wiggled up against him, side by side. He didn't know what to say, and she didn't say anything for so long, he thought she was falling asleep. The heavy down had settled over their heads and the room was dark enough that almost no light reached through the duvet. The pocket around them warmed with their breath and slowly returning cold-body heat.

'He's still here,' Julie whispered, stifling laughter.

'Who?'

'You.' She elbowed him in the ribs. 'Is this, like, happening?'

Noel sighed. 'Julie.'

'What?'

'How messed up are you?'

'Pretty messed up.' More laughter.

'But you know who I am, right?'

'Of course.'

After a moment he said, 'Who am I?'

'Noel. My mom said you were looking for me, like, a month ago.'

He understood this to be hyperbole. 'But you can't see me, right? You know what my deal is now?'

'A change comes over me,' she said, impersonating him at age fourteen.

'Yes.'

'It's real,' she said. 'You tried to tell me before, but I didn't believe you.'

'Yes.'

'I thought I was losing my mind.'

'Tonight?'

'Back then. Tonight I was just tripping.'

'Are you still?'

'I'm not screaming my head off, so yeah, I'd say so.'

'What did you take?'

'Half a hit of 'cid. And some X. Just two. Wait, no, three.'

'Julie . . . '

'But I'm not, like, seeing things now. I'm coming out of it.'

'Are you okay?'

'I'm trying not to think too much about that. Are you?'

'I'm glad I found you.'

'Do you think when it wears off I'll be able to see you again?'

She pulled his shirt, rolling him on his side so that his arm draped across her stomach, the underside of his elbow soft against her hip.

He said, 'If you can, it won't be because of the drugs.'

'How long have you been this way? This time around.'

'Two, almost three days.'

She digested this. 'That is so messed up. But I knew it was true. When we were younger. Or, I did and I didn't. I couldn't believe it, but nothing else made sense. And then my mom . . .'

'I'm sorry, Julie. I always will be.'

'I know. It was an accident.'

'I shouldn't have been there. I shouldn't be here.'

She ignored that. 'My point is, I remembered the things you told me, and it all fit. And then tonight it was like the past replayed, only I was okay with it, I could feel you there and my mind jumped back, remembering the sensation, only this time I wasn't scared. I thought maybe I was having a flashback or something, so I was like, okay, roll with this. And then you kissed me, and I knew it wasn't the drugs.' She paused, squirming next to him. 'Part of me still believes when I wake up, you won't be here. You'll be gone, because this can't be real, right? I mean, it just can-*not* be real.'

Noel shifted to keep his left arm away from her so that she wouldn't feel the bandages. 'Do you want me to stay? I don't have to, if it's too crazy for you. I just wanted to make sure you got home safe.'

'If you leave now I'll be a wreck, wondering what the hell that was all about.'

'Yeah. Both of us normal. That would be nice.'

Julie didn't respond for a long time. Noel grew warm, then hot, hardly able to breathe under the covers.

'Julie?'

But she was sleeping. A while later she rolled on her side, leaving them spooned. Noel pulled

206

the cover down so that he could breathe. He lay awake long enough to hear Marna get up, make coffee, shower and leave for work or school or whatever Marna did with her days. Then he fell asleep, too.

★ ★ ★

'Oh, my God.'

Noel was on his back, too tired to stir.

'Noel? *Noel.*'

The bed dipped with her movement, then the covers were thrown back and a cool draft roused him a little more. The room was dark again. They'd slept all day?

'Say something,' she said. 'Are you still here?'

'Yes.'

'And you're still . . . ? This isn't a joke?'

'It's not a joke.' He turned to look at her.

Her face was on a pillow beside his. Her eyes were huge, searching.

'Can you see me?' he said, daring to hope.

'No, but those are your legs, right?'

Their legs were tangled together.

'Yes.'

She reared back. 'Did we do anything?'

'Slept.'

'That's all?'

'That's all.'

'Promise?'

'I might be a freak but I'm not a total creep.'

'This is insane,' she said.

'Sorry. Do you want me to leave?'

'Like, what am I supposed to do?'

'Who says you have to do anything?'

Julie laughed with incredulity. 'How do you live like this?'

'Most of the time I don't.'

'Jesus. I thought I had problems. Sorry.'

'It's okay.'

'I can't think about this right now. I'm starving,' she said. 'Are you hungry? I mean, can you eat like this?'

'I can do everything like this, so long as it doesn't attract a lot of attention. Do you have anything here?'

'I can order a pizza,' she said. 'Hey, how did you find me?'

'The parents were worried about you. Should they be?'

Julie scoffed. 'Does he know about you?'

'He thinks it's all in my head.'

'Typical,' she said. 'If that's the case, it's all in my head too now.'

Noel laughed.

'Tell me about it,' Julie said. 'Will you?'

'What do you want to know?'

'Everything.'

She ordered a pizza and they sat in bed, eating Domino's with extra cheese and pepperoni (she couldn't watch; the sight of a slice of pizza dissolving into thin air was too strange for her), and he told her. Everything he could remember, from his earliest memories of the cloak's visitations, through all of the episodes and the things he had done in them, good and bad and meaningless and terrifying.

He told her of his mother's break with reality

and shunning of him, of his fruitless search for an explanation during his late teens, of his own collapse into depression, but did not mention his stitches or the reason for them. Several times she made him stop while she went to get water or use the bathroom, then asked him to resume. Noel felt rescued after being stranded on an island for the past ten years. Julie listened, sometimes turning on the light to stare at him, trying to get used to the invisible dome of bedding, but it was like watching yourselves having sex, too much too soon, and she turned the light off again.

The darkness was better, allowed her to forget for a while what he was. Halfway through, she cuddled beside him, crawling around him, marveling over what she could hear and feel but not see. It was distracting having her so close and he tried to kiss her. She let him, and it seemed for a few minutes that it would lead to everything else, but this frightened her too and she stopped him, asking him to tell her more.

She opened up about herself in ways she never had before, making him laugh over the strangest things, and he was surprised the years had changed her, leaving her scattered yet somehow more alive, messy yet fearless, just as childlike and more beautiful than ever. At one point he broke down crying, with relief that someone was here and believed him, and because there was no one else he would rather this long lost believer be. The night hours passed, and, though his bubble refused to let him go, Noel was content.

They fell asleep holding hands, waking only an hour or two later to talk some more. If he was a wonder and mystery to her, she was a miracle to him. They talked until sunrise.

It was the usual way to fall in love.

21

After Marna showered and left for work on the second morning, Julie launched herself from the bed. She had been restless, tossing and turning in the early hours, in some kind of withdrawal, he assumed. She went to the bathroom, peed, ran the faucet for a minute or two and came back wiping her face with a small towel. Noel had not come back to the spectrum and, upon waking, he was again surprised by how quickly Julie was adapting to his condition. She brushed her teeth as she cracked a window to let some air into the room, rinsed and came back applying lotion to her hands. She rubbed the lotion in faster and faster and then stopped abruptly. Her hands were shaking as she flexed her fingers open and closed.

'Oh, shit,' she said. 'Shit, shit!'

Noel sat up in the bed. 'What's wrong?'

'I just remembered I left my car downtown.'

'What, you think it got towed?'

She started talking too quickly. 'No, it's in the garage on Walnut, I'll have to pay like twenty bucks, but it should be fine, but I left my pills in there. We started out having margaritas at the Rio and I was too fucked up to drive. In my bag in the back. I left them in there but I can't find my keys!'

Her pills. The shaking hands. Her drop in mood. Noel felt something collapse in him. Not hope, exactly, but something like it. She's not just a recreational user.

But then again, what am I?

'Not *drugs*, drugs,' she said, as if reading his silence. 'My prescription. They're for my poles.'

'Your poles?'

'I'm kind of manic. It's not a big deal. But I start to freak out if I go more than one day. And I forgot to take yesterday's.'

'So, we go get them, right? It's okay.'

Julie's lip trembled. 'It's not okay! I'm starting to freak out. This situation isn't helping. I can't . . . I need those pills.'

'That's understandable. I know this is a lot.' He was thinking: *margaritas, acid, ecstasy, a visit by your invisible almost-stepbrother who is sort of becoming your boyfriend. How are you not screaming bloody murder every time I open my mouth?*

'Gee, thanks,' she said, stomping back to the bathroom. 'Glad you approve.'

'Julie, that's not what I meant.'

She slammed the door. Showered faster than a Navy man at sea, came back, said, 'Don't look at me.'

'I'm not.' He pulled the blanket up over his head.

She mumbled, cursing, slamming her dresser around. 'Goddamn it!'

She gave up, sitting on the bed. She was in a big gray sweatshirt and maroon sweatpants, with a knit ski hat crooked on her head, its bright blue pom-pom dangling to the side.

'Hey.' He sat up and pressed a hand to her

back, but she flinched. He removed his hand. 'One thing at a time. What can I do, right now, in this minute?'

'I need my medicine!' She was crying. And not just a little, but was suddenly a wreck. She cried deeply, through heaving breaths. He guessed she needed to, pills or no pills. Probably some of it was coming down off her high, but a lot of it was the stress of him back in her life, his freak condition. How could the world make sense to anyone confronted by him, like this?

She went to the bathroom to blow her nose.

'Okay, I'll go get them,' he said.

She came back and stood with her arms crossed, looking away rather than trying to talk at his approximate location. 'How? How are you going to do that?'

'I'll walk, open your car, grab the meds and walk back. Won't take more than an hour.'

'I can't find my keys!'

He walked to her jeans on the floor, dug around, came up with a small red caribiner with two Honda keys and one regular house key attached.

She softened a bit. 'I can't make you do that.'

He moved to her, resting a hand on her shoulder. 'I'll take care of it, okay?'

'I would do it myself but don't think I can drive,' she said through a runny nose. 'I'm really in a bad place right now.'

'I can't drive your car back, but I'll get your meds. Don't panic. I promise I will come right back, okay? It's going to be okay.'

'Thank you so much.'

'No big deal. I should be thanking you.'

She watched him get dressed, his clothes filling out like blown flags, then blinking out as they were absorbed.

'I don't think I'm ever going to get used to that,' she said.

⋆   ⋆   ⋆

Not yet ten in the morning but already it looked like four in the afternoon, the sky one huge inverted kettle grill filled with charcoal. It was snowing again, albeit gently. If he used the backstreets, he could be downtown in twenty minutes. He walked half a block north on 30th, imagining her alone back in her apartment.

Was she really unraveling? How bad was another hour going to make her? He was antsy, not just about her meds and whatever not having them for the past two days was doing to her. He couldn't help feeling that no matter how fast he made the trip, when he returned she would be . . . not gone, but reverted to her scared self, scared of him, too freaked out by everything to let him stay. Let him stay? What did he think he was going to do with her? Move in? This had to end sometime. Probably she would be depressed or feeling sick, and when he handed her the pills she would take one and then wait for him to leave. She would go back to her life, to reality, and the whole idea of him would be too bizarre to deal with ever again.

He walked faster, scanning the streets, seeing no one, thinking of shortcuts. The intersection of

214

Arapahoe and 30th was coming up. Busy, lots of cars. Right next to the Crossroads Mall. In a way traffic was good. The busier the scene was, the easier it would be to move unnoticed. More distractions. But there were a lot of lights and intersections between here and the parking structure on Walnut and 13th. People stop at the light, what do they do? Look around, see what's happening. What he needed to do was take the Boulder Creek bike path, snaking his way up behind all the homes and businesses, in the trees, where he had more places to hide.

But first he needed to find the path.

Without realizing what he was doing, not even sure the path swerved near here, he cut left across the rolling wide flank of Scott Carpenter Park. It was a popular park in a densely populated part of town. On days when it was covered with snow, the large hill and long runway bottom were often overrun with kids aged three to twelve and their sleds, snowboards, toboggans and anything else that could be ridden for cheap entertainment. Parents liked to stand at the base, a cup of coffee in one hand, nervously watching to make sure the big kids didn't crash into the littler kids, and that none managed to slide all the way into 30th Street.

But today, at not quite eleven a.m., most of the children were at school and most of their parents were at work. A lone mountain biker, probably a dedicated student, was bundled up and pedaling hard toward campus, moving south on 30th, away from the park, but he did not glance in Noel's direction. No one happened to be walking by, and there were no plows or park service employees about.

He focused on making good time. He thought of Julie getting out of the shower. Her naked body that he hadn't peeked at. He'd slept beside her all day. The smell of her bed, the smell of her body when she came back from the shower, all soapy fresh. He hadn't showered in almost three days and was filmy from all the walking. Home. A hot bath. That would be so nice, but he couldn't spare the time. Julie needed her meds.

He watched his invisible feet boost clouds of snow from the perfect sparkling plane stretching before him, plowing for what seemed half an hour to cover only a couple hundred feet, and when he next looked up a police cruiser was parked in the unplowed parking lot beside the park, its exhaust pipe emitting a cyclone of steam.

Noel stopped, his chapped and stinging face flushing with fear. Oh, Jesus. This was very bad. How long had the cop been parked there? What had he or she seen?

For many years Noel had feared that his bubble of invisibility, while absolute in every respect (to the best of his ability to tell during all the early tests he had performed), might, in certain light, caught at the right angle, reveal some kind of human shape. Or the suggestion of a shape, like the thinnest scree of ice melting from a sculpture, or a transparent mannequin sealed in plastic food wrap. Times he had feared projecting even the rainbow effect of a soap bubble blown on a sunny day, seen for a few seconds and gone the next, but in between rendering some feature (his jawline, a shoulder) visible to the chance human eye. Personally he had never recorded such an effect, not in daylight or dusk or night, not with mirrors or magnifying glasses or photos — and he'd tried them all.

But this was different. He was crossing an open field of snow. An error so colossal and lazily committed, he now questioned his sanity. Recent days had wound up his emotions, messed with his head, allowed him to abandon caution. And maybe he was simply, in the manner of dwindling supplies, running out of control.

Staring at the idling police car, his fear came back in a toxic splash, waking him to the severity of his terrible ailment all over again.

The cop car was still there. Noel did not take another step.

Standing perfectly still, he felt them.

Delicate, silent, touching his cheeks like tiny cold bugs.

Snowflakes.

It was one thing to venture out at midnight in a snowstorm, when everyone's visibility was tainted by the darkness and wind, but in daytime? The flakes could be painting him in a connect-the-dots mirage even now, catching on his clothes and face and limbs. Had the cop seen this yet? Or only the ground, the trail in the snow? Even if the falling snow had not given him away, what living thing, what creature, did the cop imagine was making this little path across the park, cutting a line directly toward his idling cruiser? A rabbit? A fox? Noel did not have to turn around and look back to know that his path resembled, more than anything else, a trail of human footsteps.

The cruiser was just sitting there, idling. Which meant someone was in the car. There had been no response. Maybe the cop hadn't even looked this way. Was it possible he had parked for a few minutes to catch a nap before his shift began? Maybe he was sipping coffee, reading the paper, listening to a sports call-in show, or snoring to the static of his walkie-talkie, waiting for a squelch to rouse him and point him toward a crime being committed elsewhere. Hell, the cop might not even be in the car right now, but taking a leak inside that little cinderblock hut of restrooms. Maybe —

The driver's side door opened. A broad-shouldered officer in his winter blues planted a foot on the ground and rose up. He screwed on a flat-topped cop hat, brass badge glinting, and his indistinct face locked on Noel's position. He took a few steps and planted his hands on his hips, projecting his authority into a situation that was so far unexplainable but definitely disturbing his peace.

Any other time, in any other weather, Noel would have simply turned and run. Or walked away, calmly and quietly. But he couldn't do that now. His best move was no move at all. Stand dead still and wait. Let the cop think it was an animal after all, one which had disappeared into a hole in the ground. Let the man grow bored, cold, give up and get back in his car to finish his latte and Danish.

But the officer, who was armed — the shotgun bracketed to the dashboard could be seen through the open door, plus the holster on his hip — and standing at attention, did not look bored at all. In fact his interest seemed only to be on the increase. His right hand casually landing on the holster.

No. Don't you do it, fucker, Noel thought at the cop with such ferocity he almost believed he were capable of invading the man's thoughts. *Not one step more, you hear me? Leave that pistol holstered in good and tight, and never mind the shotgun strapped to the dash. Get back in your car and go jump-start somebody stuck in a snowbank. I don't even exist, you got it?*

For a crazy moment, it actually seemed to work. The cop relaxed his hand from the holster, cuffed his nose and turned away. He looked back toward the baseball diamond and the clubhouse, as if wanting someone else to confirm that, yes, he was being silly.

He walked to the cruiser's rear end and popped the trunk. He bent over, disappearing under the metal lid, and came out fussing with a gray or black plastic block about the size of a heavy-duty flashlight.

It wasn't until the officer marched back to the spot he had been observing from a moment ago, raising the blocky tool like he had stepped into a booth at the precinct firing range, that Noel figured out what he was holding. It was a gun, but not the kind that fired bullets.

Radar. Or a laser version of the same. Used for clocking speeders.

Question was, what was it going to allow the cop to clock?

Back when Noel purchased his used 4-Runner, one of his first stops had been at Soundtrack, the local electronics outlet, to buy a radar detector (he was an extremely careful driver, both in and out of the bubble). The man who had helped him, a short, chatty dude with long sideburns, a skinny piano tie and a Stray Cats hairdo, had introduced himself as 'Dom, like the champagne, only smoother'. After trying and failing to pimp Noel into an Alpine CD player and a Cerwin Vega bass rack, Dom walked Noel through the 'bacon detectors'. You had your radar detector, your LIDAR detector, and the newest thang, which ran about four hundred and detected both. What's the difference, Noel had inquired? Why do I care?

A radar gun, the cop-despising Dom had explained, sends out a cone of microwaves that bounce back and report any disturbance or travel within the cone, registering a doppler shift, which the machine used to calculate speed. A laser-operated gun, or LIDAR (Dom had reeled off the acronym's full name and meaning, but Noel hadn't really cared for the details, just the results) sends out a concentrated beam of infrared light, or actually hundreds of pulses of same, that taken together report a similar discrepancy to confirm movement and calculate the speed of a given object.

All of this information came back to Noel now

in the park, but the big question remained unanswered and he wished Dom were here now to offer an opinion.

I'm not a car and I'm not moving, so what the fuck is this cop's neat little machine going to tell him once he points it at me, Dom? Radar, LIDAR, neither one painted a digital picture of a car, truck, deer, man. But what if the nasty little thing simply bounces its rays off me and confirms what the cop suspects — *it ain't moving, but there's something out there.*

Noel had no idea if the gun could give the cop such information. He had no idea if his bubble would absorb, deflect, reflect or allow the signal to pass through him altogether. He supposed that at this distance of some thirty or forty yards, there was a chance the gun wouldn't be able to find him at all, that its signal would continue across the snowfield unhindered, revealing nothing in its path.

Such optimistic hopes died a few seconds later when Noel imagined he could make out the cop's finger squeezing the trigger and then heard, without having to use his imagination at all, the little machine chirping like a bird.

Tearing his gaze away from whatever screen was positioned on the backside of the gun, the cop looked up with an expression of vague disappointment. He lowered the gun to his side and Noel thought, *that's right, I'm not moving, so your little machine can't help you this time, officer. Now move along.*

The cop turned and lobbed the speed gun into the bucket seat. Then without further hesitation began to march across the snow to have himself a closer look.

Dom? Oh, Dom? What do you make of this bacon right here?

Buddy, I think that gun didn't see shit, but unfortunately for you that only confused him more. You tweezed the copper's nibblets leaving those tracks back there, he's headed your way now, and, basically, yeah buddy, you're fucked.

22

Noel forced himself to keep his body still as his mind snapped and tangled for a way to avoid confrontation, preferably before the cop got close enough to touch. The curious bastard was in no hurry and the virgin snow was making extra work of this short stroll, and that original distance of some forty yards was shrinking with terrifying rapidity. If he continued on this course, in less than a minute the cop would be standing on Noel's toes and things would get very interesting.

The snow dusting down from the gray sky was sparse, but enough for Noel to watch as the occasional flake — large feathery flakes that should have blown by or settled on the ground where he stood — caught on his sleeves, his legs, halting in midair and sticking before they were absorbed into the bubble or simply melted on his clothing. There probably weren't enough of these little 'catchers' to give him away from such a distance, but soon the cop would be close enough to notice the obstruction. An obstruction that, the longer you stared at it, began to resemble an invisible object just about the size and shape of an adult human being.

His options were:

Run. Pray he doesn't give chase or shoot you in the back simply to confirm what he suspects — holy shit, that's a shape-shifting man or alien or some other fucking miracle creature fleeing across the park. Sure, maybe the cop would freeze up, too puzzled to act. More likely, such drastic flight would provoke aggression, bring into question the cop's sanity, and threaten his sense of safety. This was the most appealing option based on sheer primal instinct, but it would only trigger chaos, arrest, serious injury or death.

Thirty yards and closing.

Wait. Do nothing, don't move a wink, don't make a sound. Make the cop go all the way with this, running into you or screaming in your face and arresting your invisible ass on the spot before you give anything away. It will take nerves of steel, but at some point, so long as he doesn't come into contact with you, he might miss you by just enough to grow bored of the game and go home. And if he does bump into you, he might just be too shocked or creeped out to do anything more than back away, skin crawling, and get the hell out of here. This option held less appeal, in that it would require perfect stillness, silence, and willpower.

Even as Noel was considering this option, he noticed a billow of his breath curling from under his nose and realized he would have to stop breathing soon, possibly for minutes while the cop convinced himself he had been mistaken, that there was no one here.

Twenty yards and closing. This wasn't happening. Right? Somebody?

Scare the shit out of him. Wait until the cop gets right up close and then lunge, screaming or growling, making deranged lunatic sounds, using the element of pure surprise to throw the man off stride, trip him up, throw a punch if you have to and then run like a tornado. Insanity, in other words. A level of confirmation sure to force the cop to retaliate.

Fifteen yards.

Close enough for Noel to see his pale cheeks beneath a scrubby, three-day growth of red or brown whiskers, his probing dark brown eyes, the tense caution building beneath the casually inquisitive exterior.

Twenty feet.

Lie. Play ghoul. Talk CIA, National Security. Tell a story, project authority, pull rank, and hope the asshole buys it. Yeah, right.

Ten.

Too late now.

The cop had stopped less than six feet away. He was staring at the precise spot in the snow where the tracks ended and eight or nine inches of undisturbed sugar had accumulated. Noel could smell the nylon and cigarettes and human-ness embedded in the man's jacket, could hear the man's shallow breathing, and it wasn't difficult to stop himself from breathing altogether.

Beneath the fur collar, the engraved gold bar over his breast pocket said M. Sylvester. He looked up slowly, practically sniffing the air, and it was beyond strange and terrifying to watch the policeman study the space where his legs, waist and upper body were hiding in plain sight, until he was simultaneously staring right at him and through him. For a moment they were looking into each other's eyes as surely as if he were a 100 per cent visible person, and at that moment Noel wanted more than anything to speak, to confess, to apologize and give himself up. It was simply unbearable to be stared at by a cop, so close but separated by a secret with the power to change lives, or end them. He felt as though he had already been arrested and was now cuffed to the table in an interrogation room.

A single lazy snowflake dipped and twirled from the gray sky between them, the faintest breeze pulling it toward Noel until it settled on his right cheek, tickling before dissolving to water.

Did M. Sylvester see it? Did he see it? I think he —

The cop blinked, turning his attention back to the ground. What the hell was going through his mind? Was there a war raging behind his watery eyes, logic versus instinct, the fact of the footprints (*Someone just made these!*) versus what his senses were telling him (*And now they're gone!*)?

Pain flared through Noel's lungs. He'd been holding his breath for almost a minute, and he doubted he could last another full minute before he gasped.

Officer M. Sylvester looked to Noel's side, scanning the ground, and then walked in a wide circle around and behind him, out of view. He couldn't see the cop without turning his head, but he dared not move. He was cold and stiff from standing here, and a nervous dizziness clouded his head. He felt perched on a balance beam. Any movement might cause him to lose his equilibrium and shuffle his feet to keep from falling over. Even the slightest shift of his weight would disturb the snow, alert the cop with a delicate wet crunching sound.

The footsteps paused. Leather creaked. M. Sylvester's belt or boots flexing as he . . . what? Knelt? Bent over to inspect the tracks? Crept up behind Noel, gathering courage to shove his nightstick through the air, into Noel's back?

Fire in his lungs.

His heart thudding in protest, demanding more oxygen.

Carefully, silently, Noel released spent breath in a slow and steady stream, and opened his mouth wide to draw deeply, filling himself with fresh cold air, then clamped it shut again.

The swish of clothing. Squeaking boots coming closer, snow crunching, and then the cop was in front of him again, surveying the park with his back to Noel. Hope rose up inside him. Yes, yes, go away now. You had your look, there's nothing more to see.

M. Sylvester turned around once more, facing a few degrees to Noel's right side. He took several tentative steps toward his quarry and stopped, squinting, angling his ear slightly. Listening. What did the cop think he'd heard? Noel's heartbeat? Impossible, but right now it didn't seem impossible at all.

Noel found his own gaze drifting down to the gun. The butt was snapped under a leather cover. If he got close enough . . . no. No way. If he went

227

for the gun, he would only wind up getting himself shot.

'Something else,' the cop mumbled, shaking his head as he backed away a few steps and looked up to the sky.

Snowflakes. Three or four and then ten breaking away from a flock of others, cupped by the breeze, spinning, drawing into the pocket of air between two men.

M. Sylvester's eyes caught on them, following as the cluster spread and met flat resistance at Noel's chest. He blinked, and looked Noel up and down with fascination bordering on disbelief. All but snarling, he took one step forward and slapped at the air, except in this case the air turned out to be Noel's shoulder and the slap of hand against parka echoed dully. The force wasn't much, but the surprise of it caused Noel to stumble, gasping as he fell on his ass, disturbing the snow blanket.

'What the shit!' Officer M. Sylvester ducked back and away, withdrawing his hand as if he had touched fire. 'What in the shit!'

Panic erupted. Noel shuffled back on his elbows, kicking, a flurry of movement flinging the snow in all directions. The cop's eyes bulged and he jumped to the side, hopping in clumsy steps as Noel struggled to his feet, lifting and trailing clods of snow. His breathing was that of a man who has just sprinted the forty-yard dash, and the cop heard it all.

'Don't move! Stay right there! How'd you do that?' M. Sylvester shouted, one hand on his holster, the other jabbing at Noel, palm faced out. 'Who are you? What is this?'

Noel wanted to scream *stop, don't do this, please stop!*, but he knew better than to speak. His experience with Julie and Lisa at age fourteen had taught him that.

Instead, equally unwisely, he continued to scramble away, punching new holes in the snow with his invisible boots, waiting to find out if the cop was actually going to draw the weapon before he turned and ran for his life.

Officer M. Sylvester came at him like a man trying to corner a rattlesnake, unsure whether to trap it or kill it. Leaping forward a few steps, halting, eyes darting up and down, trying to get a mental hold on what he was witnessing.

'I see you, fucker, Jesus Christ, don't move, don't move!'

The holster snapped open and M. Sylvester's thick hand slapped at the butt of the gun, groping for it without taking his eyes off Noel's multiplying tracks.

'No!' Noel finally barked. 'No, no, no!' The gun flipped a switch inside him and he went from scared to furious and flat-out terrified. All he was trying to do was go get her fucking pills, take a fucking walk across town, and now the possibility of the gun equaled the certain end of his life.

The cop froze at the sound of his voice, mouth open, awestruck.

There was no time. Sylvester would not stay frozen for long. Noel saw no other choice, didn't consider but this one.

He ran full-tilt, lowering his shoulder and

screaming just before he slammed into the man's chest. The top of Noel's head connected with M. Sylvester's red-bearded chin, snapping his head back. Noel toppled forward (or was dragged down) as the cop landed on his back. He tried to shove off and run but Sylvester had a hold of his jacket and they fought against each other, a sliding tangle of limbs and shouts.

M. Sylvester's right arm sprang free, waving the gun.

Noel leaped to the side, reaching for the arm, wrestling it like a fire hose. Something hard and strong slammed into his ribs once, twice, slugging him with breathtaking force, and then his right ear went numb as the punches were thrown higher. Ears ringing, dizzy and coughing, he fell on the gun and rolled, pinning the arm for a moment before it sunk deeper into the snow.

M. Sylvester scrambled away empty-handed. Noel felt something hard like a rock against his chest, rolled off to find it was the gun. Things were out of control, he only wanted to stop this before someone got hurt. He clawed into the snow, got the gun in hand, but not its grip. He might have been holding it sideways when the policeman withdrew his baton and lunged, striking the air, then Noel, repeatedly. The wooden club smacked against Noel's back, ribs, a shoulder blade, and Noel heaved himself across the snow, rolling and rolling as the cop knee-walked after him, grunting, shouting, cursing as the black stick came down on Noel's hip with a sharp crack. He screamed in agony and rolled onto his back, preparing to surrender.

He raised his fists to block the next blow, the gun turning on the 'air' of his invisible hands.

Sylvester got one foot under him, and lashed out again, striking Noel in the forearm. The pain was a lightning bolt spearing up his arm, through his neck and jaw, and shot boomed between them.

The cop rocked back on his knees as his neck opened at the throat. A spume of dark blood arced forth, splattering the snow and Noel's legs. After the first few heavy spurts the surge filled the wider wound and drained down the cop's jacket in a sheet. He reached for his throat, choking on his own blood, and the baton fell in his lap. He balanced on his knees for a few seconds, then fell to his side, the blue-clothed body coughing and thrashing violently. The snow piled up into his beard and open mouth as the flowing red melted a small canyon down through the white powder.

By the time Noel threw the gun aside and crawled over to turn the man on his back, removing his parka to use one of the sleeves as a compress, Officer M. Sylvester's teary eyes were glazed over and did not blink as more flakes caught on their lashes, shrinking with the body's evacuating heat until they dripped and flowed into the sockets like reversed tears.

23

'Julie! Open up!' Noel beat an invisible fist against Julie's front door.

A female voice called from the other side, growing louder as she neared. ' . . . are you *still* sleeping? There's a man. He's yelling.'

'Julie! Open the — '

The door was yanked open, but it wasn't Julie who stood glaring at him, then frowning in confusion when she realized there was no 'him' here. This girl was taller, with highlighted brown hair, the bulging lip-jaw orthodontia of a child sucking on a wedge of orange after a soccer game, and blocky black-framed glasses. With the navy skirt, matching blazer, hose and heels, she had the affect of someone's stern mother, and maybe that was the kind of roommate she was. Marna. Probably on her lunch break.

He didn't have time for a proper introduction.

'Julie!' Noel called past her, and Marna yelped in surprise, her glasses slipping down her nose. He pushed past her and she yelped again as he bumped her against the door. 'Where is she?' he bawled, forging on through the living room, into the kitchen.

Julie staggered out of her bedroom, bleary-eyed. 'What? Why are you shouting?'

'Here's your pills,' Noel said, and a small brown prescription bottle with a white cap spun into existence, planting itself in Julie's hand. He released her wrist, took the other and slapped her keys into the other palm. 'I need a ride. Right now.'

Julie said, 'Why'd it take you so long? I was worried — '

'It's an emergency, trust me on that. Can you drive or should I ask Marna?'

Marna had pinned herself to the wall and was fumbling her glasses, these things that might have just played a nasty trick on her. Hearing her name, she gave up and looked to Julie as if a ghost had just tickled her under the chin. Her mouth opened but all that came out was a little squeak.

'It's not what it looks like,' Julie said to Marna. 'I can explain.'

'I . . . I'm late for work.' Marna shimmied over to the coffee table, snatched up her purse and bolted out the door.

Julie stared after her numbly, probably calculating how her next conversation with her roommate might go.

'I'm in deep shit,' Noel said. 'Take your pill and let's go.'

Julie turned toward him, eyes searching.

'Now!' Noel yelled, and she jumped.

'Okay, okay, my coat.' She ran into her room. 'Where's my coat? My keys?'

'I put them in your hand,' Noel said.

'You drove? How did you drive?'

'I took a chance. I couldn't afford to walk all the way back. You needed your pills and I need to get home. The police are looking for me. Or will be soon.'

She came out of her bedroom, hopping on one foot as she pulled the second boot on. 'The police? What are you talking about? What happened?' Booted, she rushed toward the door. He caught her arm, pulled her back into the kitchen.

'Take your medicine first.'

She did. They left.

★ ★ ★

'It's better if you don't know,' he told her in the car. She was driving fast up Baseline, after he told her to go the long route, away from the park. 'And slow down.'

'You told me to hurry.'

'Not so much that we get pulled over or crash.'

She slowed a bit and they barely made it through the yellow light at the 28th Street overpass. 'Where do you live?'

'On Canyon. Between eighteenth and nineteenth, but you're gonna take Broadway down to that little hook that goes by the high school so we can go in the back way.' He doubted they would have any evidence or leads that could point to him so soon, but that didn't matter. He needed to sneak in and get out fast.

Julie focused on the road, hands twitching around the wheel. 'Why can't you tell me? You can trust me.'

'This is bad, Julie. Really fucking bad.'

'Are you hurt?'

'Someone else is.'

She moaned. 'It's my fault. I shouldn't have let you go.'

'I got sloppy, wasn't thinking. I got trapped, and there were other ways I could've handled that. None of this is your fault.'

'I'm so sorry,' she said. 'What are you going to do? You shouldn't be alone, not while you're still . . .'

'I have to be.'

'You can't drive. Let me stay with you, at least until it stops.'

'It's never going to stop,' he said.

'Yes, it will. It will, right? I don't have to know what happened. Just let me help.'

'There's always going to be another — watch the light!'

Julie hit the brakes and the brakes locked up. The road had been plowed but was still covered by half an inch of glossy, compacted snow. They began to slide, the Honda's rear end kicking to the left. The intersection of Broadway and College loomed like a narrow doorway — braking cars on the left, a crosswalk about to be filled with students on the right, and one open but narrow lane in the middle.

'Let up, let up!' he said. 'Just go!'

'Oh, my God!' She traded brakes for gas.

The Honda righted itself. The light turned red. Noel reached across and jammed the horn. Students leaped out of the way as the Honda sailed through and more horns popped off around them. A lumbering dump truck braked in the intersection on Julie's side and they missed being broadsided by several tons of steel and sand, by inches.

'Okay, okay, we're okay,' Noel said.

Julie was too rattled to speak.

'Almost there,' he said. 'Easy does it. I'm sorry.'

A few blocks later she said, 'What do you need at your apartment?'

'Money. My truck.'

'But where are you going?'

'The mountains.'

'"The mountains?"' What, you're going to live off the land?'

'I don't know! I'll figure it out. Staying in Boulder is no longer an option. Not ever again.'

Julie stole a glance his way. 'Did you — is someone . . . ' *dead?*

'Yes.'

She didn't ask him any more questions until they got to the apartment.

★   ★   ★

'You can go now,' he said as she nosed into the rear lot, back by the dumpsters and the tree-lined creek.

'How much money do you have?'

'Enough for a while.'

'How much?'

'I don't need your money, Julie.'

'How much!'

'Sixteen, seventeen thousand.'

'How did you — '

He cut her off. 'I don't have time for this.'

'All right.'

He got out. She turned the engine off and followed.

'No, uh-uh, back in the car.'

'I'll leave in five minutes,' she said. 'Or when you do. Just let me come inside for a minute.'

'What for?'

'I have to pee.' She clenched her knees together.

Noel shook his head, not that she could see it, and let her follow.

★ ★ ★

'Oh, my God,' she said, covering her mouth.

'What?'

He came back from the bathroom, where he had just fished the Ziploc baggie full of cash from the toilet's tank, to find her staring at his re-manifested clothing on the bedroom floor. One sleeve of the parka was streaked with blood. His pants and socks were soaked with it.

Noel said, 'Oh, shit, I almost forgot. I have to take a shower.'

'A shower?'

'If I reappear when someone's around. I'm probably covered with that.'

Julie sat on his bed, dazed.

He came back and crouched, setting his hands on her knees.

'Go home, Julie. Please. If you want to help me, forget what you've seen. I never found you the other night. You know nothing.'

'I want to know what happened to you,' she said.

'What happened to me? Okay. This is what happened to me. It happened a long time ago,

237

it's happening now, and it's going to keep on happening as long as whatever this thing is wants me. I'm a fucking monster, Julie. There's no other word for what I am. I ruin lives.'

'Don't say that. It's not your fault.'

'No? How about, I took a walk through the park this morning and now a police officer is dead. That's his blood, and he's gone. Now you need to leave before someone finds me and you get hurt, because I might be able to live with this, but I can't live with the next one getting hurt or killed being you. Do you understand?'

She didn't respond.

'Your mother is paralyzed because of what I am, and I can't change that. But I can leave before it happens to you, too. I'm going to shower now, then I'm going to put on clean clothes, line my car windows with trash bags, and pray I don't get pulled over before I get into the foothills. Now, be smart and go.'

She was crying again. He started to rise and head for the shower, but she found his hand and squeezed. He tried to pull away, but she wouldn't let go. She stared up at him, touching his face to locate him and speak with him.

'Listen to me,' she said.

'I don't have time — '

'Listen!'

He shut up.

'It's partly my fault you're in this mess. You don't know what this is and you don't have any control over it. It's been that way since you could remember. No one can be expected . . . your family abandoned you. Our family. It's not your fault you never knew how to deal with this. You never meant to hurt anybody. You're just trying to get by and whatever happened today, it was an accident.'

'You don't know that.'

'I know you. I know what you're like. You helped me. You helped me when I needed help so badly.'

'I walked you home, Julie. And now, this? This isn't helping you at all.'

'No, you don't understand. I didn't get a chance to tell you, but I'm finished here,' she said. 'I got kicked out of school. My grades are trashed. What you saw the other night, at the party? That was me. That's what I've been doing. Last week I counted how many different drugs I had taken in the span of five days. Do you know how many? Seven. Not including my stupid prescription. I'm not bi-polar, Noel. Or if I really am, I can't tell because I'm too busy being a stupid party girl who let it all get out of control. If I don't get away from these people soon, if I don't leave Boulder, I'm going to get into something I can't get out of.'

'And I'm the worst drug you could have lying around right now,' he said.

'No. Not at all. You came to me and — don't you laugh, don't you dare laugh when I say this — I thought you were an angel. I really believed that, and then when I sobered up and I saw that it was you, I realized that's exactly what this was. I'm choosing that. I have to choose that.'

'Angels don't kill people, Julie.'

Crack! Her hand slapped him across the face

before he even saw it leave her side.

'Whoa.' His eyes began to water. 'That hurt.'

'Don't ever say that again,' she said. 'All of this is an accident. No one deserves this. God or someone with His powers and His taste for suffering made you this way. You didn't choose this, not the way I chose to throw away my education and start taking every pill and powder I could find. This thing, whatever it is, it isn't *you*. It's a problem and it can be dealt with.'

'There's nothing that can be — '

Julie raised her hand again, and Noel shut up.

'This isn't you,' she said. 'Any more than the drugs and my problems are all me. Because if that's the case, if there's no help, if we are what we do and we can't change that, and there's no one there to help us, Noel, then what's the point?'

He couldn't think of anything.

She stepped forward, reached up and took his face in both hands. 'I remember those two weeks when we were fourteen. The way you used to look at me. Do you know that no one's ever looked at me that way? Not in my whole life. I know why you came looking for me. Well, you found me. We're both pretty fucked up right now, but what if someday we're not? What if we can help each other be better? Get better and find a way to live with it?'

'I can't ask you to do this,' he said.

'You're not asking. I'm telling you. Now get in the shower. Get dressed. I'll pack your clothes and some food and water. I'll drive you wherever you want to go.'

'And then what?'

'And then we'll figure the rest out when we get there.'

Noel ran the water as hot as he could stand it.

★   ★   ★

When he was dressed and his arm was wrapped in fresh gauze, he went downstairs to find Julie in the living room, his backpack and another packed duffel waiting at her feet. She had put the bloody clothes in a trash bag.

'What about the parents?' he said. 'My dad's expecting a call from me about you. He's probably worried sick.'

'I talked to them while you were in the shower.' She smiled. 'It's taken care of.'

She was too calm. He asked, 'How fast does that pill work, anyway?'

'It's not the pill,' Julie said. 'I'm scared out of my mind. Or I guess back into it.'

'Apparently,' Noel said. 'What did you tell them?'

'I apologized for not keeping in touch, thanked them for having my big brother check up on me, and promised them I was going to get some treatment and take night classes until I got readmitted.'

'And they believed you?'

'John said I should use the credit card to buy you dinner. He said I owe you one, and he does, too.'

Noel took the 4-Runner keys from the salad bowl on his counter and dangled them where she could see them. 'Get me as far as Glenwood Springs and we'll be more than even.'

'I thought of some place better.' Julie took the keys and hefted the duffel into his arms. Wearing the backpack and one of his baseball caps she had scrounged from the closet, she looked like a Girl Scout preparing for an overnight. 'Some place where we can both disappear, no matter what condition we're in.'

'Uh-huh.' He held the door open for her. 'Where would that be?'

'You'll know it when you see it.'

Noel didn't bother locking the door behind them. He owned nothing of value besides the truck and the last of his cash reserves. He said goodbye to his apartment and the town he had grown up in, and never saw either of them again.

* * *

Julie had been driving west for a little more than thirteen hours when Noel saw it. He sat up in the passenger seat and said, 'That's your idea? Have you lost your mind?'

'We're still half an hour out.' Julie yawned, staring ahead into the desert darkness. 'Think about it. Really think about the possibilities, and then tell me you have a better idea.'

Noel thought about it for almost five miles. Julie yawned again.

'I know what you're thinking,' he said at last. 'And normally I would agree. The potential is enormous, almost too much to even take seriously.'

'I'm very serious,' she said. 'And you should be, too. This is the best idea I've ever had.'

'There's just one problem.'

'What?'

'I'm not the same person I was when we dropped down out of the Rockies.'

'What do you — '

'Keep your eyes on the road, and whatever you do, don't panic.'

Julie frowned in the glow of the 4-Runner's instrument lights.

'I'm back,' Noel said.

Julie looked at him. Julie saw him. The 4-Runner began to drift over the center line and she slumped, her body giving out. He had to help her steer onto the shoulder, where, after one more look — this one bearing a strong resemblance to a cat that's just been thrown in a bathtub — she bolted from the car.

He had guessed this would be her reaction. She had been lulled into the strangeness of the other version; the real thing was now the frightening thing. She hadn't seen him in five years. The change was too fast, too complete, there was no way to adjust to it. Well, let her have a run, burn off the shock of it. He was too relieved to do much more than sigh and whisper thanks to the mercy of whatever cruel forces had held him captive for the past five days. He turned the hazard blinkers on, got out and stretched, admiring his limbs, his feet, his hands, the cool desert night air that was somehow more real and invigorating for his complete presence in it. He was even pleased to see the bandage on his arm, his own flesh renewed.

He caught up to her in a wash-out of flat sand and brush a couple hundred feet from the highway. Julie was out of breath, bent over, hands on her knees.

'Come on,' he said. 'Aren't you at least a little bit curious?'

She straightened and faced him. He smiled. She started to speak, then only covered her mouth and shook her head, crying but apologetically so. He walked toward her slowly. She took a few steps back.

'I'm still me,' he said.

She nodded. 'I'm sorry, it's just a lot to — '

'I know. No more talking. Just be still.'

He wrapped his arms around her, burying his face in her hair. She flinched, then became still. He cupped her chin and kissed her, kissed her in new ways, because everything was different now. After a minute of holding her and kissing her cheeks and lips, she responded. They sank to their knees in the sand, the soft desert floor that was not warm, and the air was cold, and it did not matter. Everywhere she touched him he became real and his excitement was quick, flooding in. She felt it, too, encouraged it along with her hands and mouth and breath. He shucked her from her jeans, raising her shirt to make sure there were no more layers between them and their warmth formed a seal against the night.

She lay back and he looked into her eyes, watching her look into his own, as he pushed into her wet soft center. They were alone together in the middle of nowhere and though it happened fast and he was not her first, it was more than he had dreamed was possible. All through it she kept her eyes on him, knowing it was the most she could give him, and for this he loved her.

They were less than twenty miles from millions of city lights and ten thousand hotel rooms and billions of dollars for the taking, but Las Vegas was going to have to wait just a little longer before giving itself up to Noel Shaker and his girl.

24

Four years, as it turned out. Love being the cure he had been searching for all along, and then a curse of a different kind. In between, the house took a cut of the action and that cut went deep.

'Jesus Christ. Is that him? It's Shaker, right? Well, wake his ass up.'

Noel was dreaming of guns again when the voice, angry yet bemused, drove him from the heist fantasy playing in the movie theater of his napping brain. Sounded like it was coming from the end of a tunnel, and he knew before he opened his eyes this was not just a voice but the first of the really bad things to come.

'Noel? Noel?' This voice was softer, a woman's, more nervous than angry. A hand wiggled his ankle. 'Please wake up now, Meester Noel.'

'Whossit, what?' Noel sat up, blinking at the white light coming through the window, the desert blast furnace illuminating him on a bed in a room that was at once strange and just like all the others. He couldn't see straight and his mouth was a dust pan. He guessed he'd been asleep for about four hours.

Maria, a heavy but seemingly motorized middle-aged Hispanic woman with her hair pulled back tightly, cute red granny glasses, and a rose in the lapel of her uniform. She'd taught him how to clean a bathtub in under one minute. She was

246

smiling hopefully but not happily.

Beside her was a man Noel had never met but vaguely recalled seeing marching around the lobby and casino floor with a walkie-talkie. Maroon blazer, arms crossed, scratching his cratered nose. Salt and pepper hair sprouting from the ears. Blue tie with a gold clip. Buzzcut, all gray, a hardass. Gently he ushered Maria to the side.

'Thank you, Maria. I'll handle it from here.'

Noel stood quickly and the floor-to-ceiling window overlooking the pools and gardens with their winged lion gargoyles some twelve stories below gave his equilibrium a nasty shove. He lost his balance, and propped himself up again. 'Oh shit,' he said, forcing his eyes wide, as if to prove he had never been asleep.

'Oh shit,' the maroon blazer agreed. 'Noel Shaker. That's you?'

'Yes, sir.'

'And how long have you been with us?'

Noel thought back, wanted to answer with specificity, but it wasn't coming.

'Actually, it's not important.' The man tiredly snatched the badge from Noel's belt fob. 'You're no longer an employee of Caesars Entertainment Corporation. I hope this is not a surprise. It shouldn't be.'

Noel nodded.

'Your keys.'

Noel handed over the master that opened the rooms on this floor, as well as the key to his locker.

'Your check will be mailed within fourteen

days. I'm sorry we couldn't keep you awake, Mr Shaker. Do you want to give me a rash of shit so I can bill you for your little stay in this here Palace Tower suite, or would you like to go without a fuss?'

'No fuss. I'm sorry, Mr, ah . . . have we met?'

'What's your cute malfunction, anyway? Not that it matters, but I'm always curious. A man comes to us, wants a job, is given a job, doesn't do the job he asked for. What's the slide here? Drugs? Booze? Pussy? You're a young guy, decent looking. Don't look like a chicken. You busy screwing your stripper girlfriend's lights out all night, that it?'

'No, sir. I'm just . . . I'm very tired.'

'Right. Okay, sport. Go home and get some rest. I've got to have this bed changed, again, and find someone else to turn the room, again.'

'I'm very sorry,' Noel said. 'If I were in your position, well, yes.'

'Oh, for chrissakes.' Taking pity, the maroon blazer handed Noel a coupon. Beneath the Caesars Palace logo it said ONE FREE BUFFET PASS.

Noel stared at the card and felt like crying. 'Why?'

'I sleep better knowing I gave a man a meal before booting him,' maroon blazer said. 'Knock yourself out. The roast beef's really something.'

'I appreciate the chance to contribute to the . . . ' but he didn't know what he had contributed to.

'Yep.' Maroon blazer ushered Noel toward the door.

'Do you need the, ah, the attire back?'

'Turn in the shirt, cleaned, within three days or we'll have to dock you forty-two dollars. Up to you.'

Noel moved into the hallway, paused. The blazer raised its eyebrows.

'If you need me to leave or if I'm banned,' Noel said. 'Okay. But do you mind — am I allowed to gamble here still?'

Maroon blazer stared at Noel for an extra beat, then sighed with resignation bordering on, then actually crossing over into, disgust.

'By all means, Mr Shaker. Caesars Palace would be delighted to serve your gaming needs.' He smiled icily. 'So long as you don't fall asleep at any of the tables.'

'Thank y — '

But the maroon blazer was already bobbing down the hallway, onto other matters, to things that mattered.

* * *

Royally shit-canned and soon to be drunker than a Roman emperor, Noel took up residence at one of the casino floor watering holes, a dark affair whose bar featured built-in ashtrays and a bank of video poker screens. The flashing faces of jacks and kings and queens minded not at all if he spilled his Cuba Libres on them. He fed another roll of quarters into the slot, ratcheting his credits up to forty. He punched the DEAL/DRAW button, got two tens, the rest low clubs and hearts. Pressed HOLD under both, punched DEAL/DRAW. Got two more tens for four-of-a-kind. Ran up another ten credits.

'There's my little Technotronic bitch,' Noel said to the machine. 'You like that? You like that?'

The machine did not answer.

Tilly, a waitress with amazingly permed crazy high hair the color of macaroni and cheese, sun-freckled Dow-Corning titties, muscle-builder thighs and green eyeliner almost concealed behind the tarantula lashes, set a new Cuba Libre beside his existing half-full Cuba Libre.

'Sorry to hear about your job, Noel,' Tilly said. 'Lou can be a real a dickprick, ya know?'

'No, no, he was really nice. I deserved it.' Noel tinkled a palmful of quarters into Tilly's tray. 'He's letting me stay. To gamble.'

Tilly frowned. 'You poor boy. Want me to bring you a sammich?'

'A sammich? Tilly, baby, in a few days I'm going to own this place. Caesars's got nothing on me. I am a fucking Caesar! Will you be my queen? I want to marry you. Will you marry me, Tilly? Tonight? Now?'

Tilly gave her drink order to the bartender, along with a look that might have said, *give this guy a break, he's one of ours, or was.* The bartender shook his head.

'Tilly-tilly-bo-billy-banana-nana-of-filly,' Noel said.

Tilly laughed despite herself. 'Jesus, you remind me of my son.'

Noel frowned. 'Wanna know a secret, Tilly?'

Tilly cocked her head.

'I'm going to rob this place,' Noel said. 'For millions.'

'Don't talk like that,' Tilly said. 'Not in here.'

'Soon as I change back, it's game on.'

'Change back? Into what?'

Noel grinned. 'A ghost.'

Tilly loaded her drink tray. 'How's Julie doin', hon? Maybe you should go home and spoil her a little bit?'

'Aw, no.' Noel felt wounded by an arrow. 'Nah goin' home to Julie tonight. She can take care of herself.'

'Yeah, I gotta run. Behave, Noel. I'm serious, okay? You don't belong here, sweetie. You never did.'

For some reason known to no one, this was hilarious. Noel brayed and punched DEAL/ DRAW. He got shit. Tossed all the digital cards, drew again. One ace and another pile of shit. He drew again. Got two kings, but tossed them before he realized they were kings. The faces and numbers and suits blurred. His credits, not so high to begin with, dwindled. He tore the paper wrapping from his roll of quarters and they spilled across the bar like orphans running away from a sadistic nun.

Noel surveyed the crowd, the faces like bobbing balloons, until his eyes caught on an ancient Native American man staring at him from the other side of the bar. A figure out of place, in crystal clarity. With his flowing gray hair, deep creases that had aged beyond mere wrinkles into a mosaic of broken shale, and coruscated black eyes, the shaman seemed

251

almost reptilian, a shape-shifting gila monster that had wandered into the casino, and Noel half expected a forked tongue to wag at him as he stared back. His black suit, white shirt and bolo string tie were not the accoutrements of a medicine man; nevertheless he radiated a dark holiness. His solemn gaze cut across the bar and passed through Noel with cliché but no less worrisome omniscience.

As if he were able to communicate with the seer by telepathy, Noel gave himself over, opening his mind to the shaman: *Go ahead. Look inside me, old man, and tell me what's to come of my future. Do you know how I got here? Do you know what my purpose is? If you know what I'm waiting for, can you tell me when it will return?*

The shaman kept perfectly still, the intense connection drowning out the casino's cacophony until they were the last two men in the bar, until the palace was gone and the world was night and Julie lay on the desert floor between them, under the star dome. Noel was certain that the ancient tribesman knew what he was, what horrible secret he carried, and what dark actions he intended to take once the curse returned. More, the shaman peering into his soul knew all that had happened since he and Julie hatched their plans, of the sorrow that had grown like a cancer in their lives since.

This is what you have chosen, the ancient said in Noel's mind, his voice a low rumble, and for the first time since meeting the shaman's eyes Noel wondered if he were being dissected by a dead man. *We are both spirits fated to walk between worlds, among the living and the dead. But instead of abiding the will of your ancestors and seeking your true purpose among your people, you have surrendered to devils.*

If you do not give up this quest for false idols, you will lose the only thing that matters to you and you will be condemned to walk between worlds forever, alone.

Noel blinked, and the shaman was gone. He looked around the surrounding gaming pits and aisles of slot machines, but the ancient was nowhere to be found.

Noel staggered for the exits and entered the cab queue. During the $17-ride home, he watched the hotels and cascading canyons of light stream past, drowning him in the sorrow of wasted time and withering love.

★ ★ ★

The young, dumb and in love trajectory. Also known as, *How we aimed for the stars and wound up one untied shoelace from the gutter:*
Those first few months had been a honeymoon of sorts, the thrill of playing adult. New digs, new clothes, new weather, a new buzz. Staying up all night talking, discussing their private fears and longings, discussing the future. Sleeping late, walking the Strip in search of the charming value buffet. Hugs in the booth, feeding each other pancakes at brunch, sex and a nap and more sex after. Won her a stuffed Pink Panther at Circus Circus. Went to the chapel just

to watch the other couples take a vow in an Elvis suit, a dare, testing the water, giggling all the way home, sex in the elevator, going down on her riding up the tower. Better days to come, coming soon, any day now.

The promising start, now a faded memory you wish had happened to someone else. Nightlife, fun Noel, sexy Julie, party down at the romantically seedy spots, the overpriced clubs, $12 cocktails, celeb-spotting, sneaking into the VIP booth, the delusional charm of being young and feeling the world in your palm. Five grand on the Super Bowl at two-to-one. Boom, it was happening, it was on.

Using the original stake and the Super Bowl haul to run up a lucky streak of twenty-eight thousand. Roulette boogie, forty-two thousand. Feeling blessed, feeling chosen, feeling it would never end. We could make a run at this, make a life here. Julie hitting blackjack, fifty-one thousand. They couldn't walk into a casino without someone handing them money. The Riviera sad sack regulars drooling with envy, Noel buying drinks for all. Wayne Newton. A boxing match. A $1200 handbag for Julie, Armani jeans and sweaters for Noel. A helicopter ride over the Grand Canyon. A white Ford Mustang convert for Julie. New identities, fresh papers from a guy who knew a guy down the street, so they could bounce with impunity once he blinked and the shit went down. We are untouchable. Who needs the bubble, we are our own bubble. Look at the big man, Noel Shaker. He struts. She swoons. They were on their way.

Bright idea number fourteen — kill time learning to become a player, buying the books, watching the videos, mastering the art of when to hit and when to stand. Studying the tells. Counting cards. We're sitting on fifty Gs. Let's put it to work.

They lost it all in nine days. Noel decided to play poker, against men who did this for a living. Lunacy. Idiocy. Tried to stare down a sphinx from New Jersey wearing a sideways Knicks lid. Hey, it happens. Julie cried all night. Noel promised he'd get it back. He said he'd get a job, never believing he'd have to do just that. Swore he wouldn't let her work, never believing he'd have to do just that.

But they were still happy, for a little while. After pawning the 4-Runner they had twenty-two hundred left in the bank, even though the bank was the hotel room safe, then the ceiling tile in the motel room, then Noel's sock, then Julie's coin purse. It will come back, he promised her. Everything's going to come back. We just have to wait it out, be patient. When I ghost back out of this world, we'll own this town. Walk into any casino on Las Vegas Drive and take what's ours. It's not even stealing. It's gamblers' money. We deserve it as much as these crooks, these corporations sucking the life out of working people. We'll plot, plan, execute. Give half to charity, keep karma on our side. We'll find a vault, a count room, a safe. We'll follow an armored truck on its rounds and pounce at the last stop. We'll get what we can take and then we'll get out of Dodge.

He got on with the cleaning crew, the better to case the place while waiting for the bubble to descend. Working the night shift, six nights per week, in a haze of cigarette smoke and dirty floors and blinking musical neon, a nobody in pleated black slacks, a Caesars smock with gold piping, filthy men's nurse's shoes, a drone sponge in one of a dozen cleaning crews at the Palace. Two bucks over minimum wage while long green cash money swam around him, slippery as fish, always out of reach. He longed to risk it all, roll the dice again, but his bank account wouldn't let him, Julie wouldn't let him, his veil wouldn't let him.

Every day a vacation for someone else, everyone else but him, the work never-ending. Popping mini-thins to stay awake, popping Tylenol PM to fall asleep, popping his knees every time he crouched to pluck another condom crepe from under the bed, swab dried cum from another marble floor, plunge another tampon from another toilet overflowing with human desire and waste and this waste of a life.

His plans and schemes and names and protocols forgotten in the mirage of time and dreams of the quick hit, easy money, the big score. His world was dawn and sand glare and air-conditioning bronchial infections. A sore back. Swollen toes. Red eyes. Hot face, smoked out clothes, dirty nails. Metabolized alcohol sweat. General hatred for his fellow man.

Players. A species of which you, Noel Shaker, are not. Texas rodeo boys, riding their own bull market at the hold 'em no-limit stables. There goes another whale from Hong Kong, two hookers and a comped suite, now pick up that lollipop stuck to the carpet, you goon. Noeller Coaster, the Invisible Man himself: invisible to the high-rollers, party girls, cha-chas, flannel club dykes, biker gangs, East Hampton trust-fund ramrods, pop stars, Jack Daniels-swigging frontmen in LA leather, hair metal chicks in paisley bandanas, hip-hop posses, rising white MCs, anorexic models in crusted sunglasses, clean-cut frat boys, Young Life teens handing out brochures for Jesus, sheikhs in flowing robes, porterhouse steak men from the Midwest, rubber sandals and plaid shorts — none see him, now that he is normal. The people look through him, away from him as they check in, drop their Samsonites, chintz on another room service tab, fiz to pay-per-view porn, toss back another Seven-and-7 in the sportsbook, scratch another ticket in the keno parlor, gnaw another Cuban at the Baccarat table.

Walking between resorts at night, feeling the hair on the back of his neck prickling with odd bursts of unwelcome intuition. Sometimes he would turn to find a non-descript sedan trailing behind him, moving too slow even for the choked traffic on the Strip. Other times there would be no car tailing him, but strangers who looked at him briefly before looking away. Once it was a tall skinny guy in a Hawaiian shirt, chinos, and oversized black sunglasses. Once it was a woman with two kids, gawking at him like a zoo exhibit. Was he being followed? Or just being paranoid? There were a lot of weirdos in

Vegas. People-watching was a common pastime.

All his hunches were forgotten amid the sensory rape. How was a working man supposed to think under the constant carnival of video game bleeping, bing-bonging family-friendly slots, the screaming children, the five hundred colors of ten bazillion blinking lights, ring-a-ding-ding, Cock-Eyed-Sammy impersonators singing from the grave, Methamped bus boys, Mexican maids, Arab deliverymen sneering over a pallet of shrimp, red-faced entertainers roasting good sport Jews, racism rampant in the no-boundaries smarm, shock and jive, 24/7 entertainment, it's all just entertainment, stuff to fuck the minutes away until the bank account's empty and the heart attack strikes.

Delay of death.

Time-suck. As in, where did it go? Shit, it's a clockless world here at Caesars Palace, where every man is a king. There is no sun and no moon, no day, no night, only indoor time, bio-dome containment. Bars, casinos, restaurants, strip clubs, musical stages, tiger cages, pirate ship lagoons, drape-drawn rooms, morning noon and night, keep the windows sealed tight. Crush 'em with AC, comp 'em another drink.

What's that smell? The chemical residue of carpet shampoo and floor polish and toilet bowl cleaner a constant tincture in his clothes, his hair, his nostrils. Luiz, his boss, calling him 'you' or 'kid' or 'skinny white boy' and screaming at the terrified illegals, laughing as he brings them to tears, sticking him with the worst of so many awful duties. Someone left a salmon in room 525, take the chisel, Shaker. Y'heard me, a salmon. Clean it up. Clean the shitter, clean the lobby, clean the elevators — but not while anyone's around. Stand aside, get out of the way. You don't exist, got it? Room 786, blood on the mattress, flip it, turn it, make it go away.

The waiting. The Waiting. THE WAITING.

Funny he got fired here. He used to live here. Started in a Centurian Tower suite with powder-smooth pillow cases, got downgraded to the Motel 8, then to a former fuckpad guest house rental on the pawn shop and rubber dick store side of town.

The look in Julie's eyes.

When? When's it going to come back? How much longer do I have to put up with this slave grind? She had stayed sober for the first five of the impoverished months, then it was a glass of wine now and then, then she lost her job as a supervisor working the call center of a travel bureau. Landed at the Mirage as a bartender but somehow, as their mission lost focus, continued to slide into her own fishnets cocktailing at Slots-of-Fun, getting ass-pinched hourly.

He'd long ago stopped trying to convince her to find something administrative, office work, a courier, anything that did not entail hose and garters, the short ruffled skirts, serving drinks and hot dogs to weenies in knock-off Brooks Bros. Knew she was smoking weed on her breaks, on her way home after work. Knew she was drinking during her shifts, in the morning before her shifts. Knew she was lingering at the casinos for an hour, two, sometimes all night instead of home, and why might that be?

At the three-year mark he found her art-school pipe. Tinfoil in the guest house's bathroom trashcan. Chasing the dragon, chasing the dream.

Because this scene, their lives, this shithole guest house in a dirt-floor backyard was too depressing to look at. You could live in it, so long as you didn't see it. A hundred and seven degrees out, a swimming pool everywhere, just not here. Paycheck to paycheck, no one's cooking dinner, can't afford to go out. Room service scraps, you cut off the bite marks and put it in a styrofoam carton, microwave for one minute on HI.

He worked nights, she worked days. Both on the Strip but not in the same building, might as well have been living on other planets. Crossing paths on the way to the bathroom, between drunks, I feel like I used to know you, don't any more, and that hurts too much to really dwell upon, so let's just don't. I have to get up early and go to work. My ankles feel like hammered ore, my spine's still twitching from the dexies and mop work. I think I'm gonna watch some more TV and get my head together, be in soon, night-night.

Three years in, the question becomes not, how much longer can we do this? But what were we doing in the first place? Was that even real? Is this even real? Are you for real? He wished none of it was real.

I could make, like, six hundred a night

dancing. Julie said that. Just a couple months ago. She said that.

He didn't say anything in response.

Now really, Noel. This had gone on longer than Julie was in college. She didn't think it was ever going to come back. She had begun to talk of leaving, making a new plan, starting over somewhere else. Monthly road trips back to Calabasas to see her mother, she said. LA boyfriend, Noel suspected.

Had seen her laughing in the casino one night with a guy holding her up at a blackjack table, handing her chips, whispering in her ear. Clean, conservative, black suit, good hair. A little older, stable, a man drinking a scotch, in command of the table. Double-down, baby. Go ahead, it's only money. Come up to my room later. Maybe she went. Maybe not. But it didn't matter. The road they were on, it was crash and burn. Or the long slow burn before the crash.

Where was his fucking cell? Why couldn't he trigger it? Why was it resisting him this time? Now that he wanted it, why wouldn't it come? Was it because they had been happy or because they wanted it so bad? Did we piss off the muse of the erasure?

The downward spiral continued. They argued, fought like middleweights, she threw a lamp at his head. Make-up sex turned to make-up fighting. He slept on the couch. Dreamed of armed robberies, Reagan and Nixon masks in lieu of a Noel mask.

One day he said, Do you think we should buy a gun?

No, she said, averting her eyes. I don't think we should buy a gun.

But maybe, he thought, I should buy a gun. Pop into one of the pawn shops, buy a piece with the serial numbskis filed off, keep it in the closet beside the bed. In case someone comes for me, for us. In case she brings one of those guys from the casinos home. Keep it under my pillow. In case I need to use a gun.

Yeah, but. Whatever you do, don't tell her about the gun. Don't tell her about the need for a gun. Don't tell her what's eating you, that you no longer believe the bubble is coming back. That it's over. You broke its back and there's no longer anything whatsoever special about you, Noel Shaker. You're just another Vegas shithead who can't look after his girl. A pimp turning her out, turning tricks with her hopes, only there's no money on the nightstand after she goes down on you.

Run away. Tell her you love her, pack your bags, and get her out of the desert.

Save Julie. Save yourself. Get out now.

Tonight.

'Tonight,' he said in the back of a cab that smelled like bean burritos and Pine-Sol, and for the umpteenth time he believed it.

Turned out he was one night too late. Or four years, depending on your perspective.

25

The cab pulled up at the rim of the cul-de-sac. Noel tipped a buck, ignored the scowl.

He walked around the main house where the lights were never on. It was a big Spanish villa, four or five bedrooms and a dried swamp pool, in a neighborhood of a hundred others exactly like it, owned by a video producer they had never met because the video producer, along with his wife and two children, was dead.

At the beginning of year three, Noel and Julie had been driving around looking for cheap rentals, got lost in this better neighborhood, and happened to meet Nora, the realtor who was handling the estate sale. She'd just finished clearing the yellow band of police tape from the front door and a cleaning crew was going in with an industrial strength wet-vac and about two hundred feet of hose.

She hurried over to Julie's Mustang and asked them if she could help them with something, smelling desperation and a possible short-term solution to her client's problem. Namely, that he and the family were dead, the estate was in probate and being contested by various creditors, and in this market was not likely to sell for at least a year. She needed a tenant for the guest house to justify the costs of holding the listing for such a long time. Come have a lookie-loo. Nora gave them a brief tour, offered it for five hundred a month, 'a steal for something so secure and private in this zip code'.

When Julie asked what the catch was, Nora mentioned as off-handedly as possible that the house was still 'unofficially a crime scene'. The producer, who'd dabbled in straight-to-video D-list action knock-offs featuring former wrestling stars and midgets and the like, had actually earned the bulk of his income distributing 'adult cassettes across Las Vegas's many video and novelty emporiums'. The aspiring Zodiac's note suggested a political nutcase who'd taken umbrage with the producer's pervy contributions to the world and believed God had sent him to cleanse the neighborhood.

'The producer was killed?' Noel asked, more intrigued than unnerved. 'In that house?'

'He and his family, yes, a terrible tragedy.' Nora cleared her throat. 'I can let you have the guest house for three-fifty if you don't stir up any problems. I know it's not ideal, but if you help me out on this, water the grass and do a few chores, hold on for at least six months, I can upgrade you to something bigger with less of a, ahem, reputation. What do you say? I'll throw in a free cable install.'

It didn't bother Julie. They'd be living in the guest house after all, not the main house. And they were broke. She wanted something that bore some resemblance to a home, not a temporary place to flop. The by-the-week motels were dangerous, filled with junkies and people knocking on the door at all the wrong hours.

'We'll take it,' Noel told Nora the realtor, and

they'd not seen her since, just mailed the rent checks to the office address she'd given. They'd never even signed a lease, and at the end of the first twelve months, he'd stopped sending the checks. No one, including Nora, had called or stopped by to evict. Noel suspected a lot of the other houses were vacant, too, thanks to the recession and high unemployment.

It was quiet here. They'd never had a problem. Except that their entire lives had become a problem.

Noel walked across the backyard of grass gone brown, then to dust, feeling weirdly guilty about not watering and managing the landscape as he'd promised. In lieu of barbed wire, the cinderblock wall surrounding the property was festooned with decaying cactus. Thinking of a prison pen for coyotes, he let himself into the guest house. The door was unlocked. All lights were off, except for the lamp beside the double bed in their empty bedroom.

The air was dead.

Everything felt dead.

He knew before he found the note.

He walked back to the kitchen and flicked on the stove light. He poured and then nursed a deep glass of tequila. When that was empty, he refilled the glass and went back to the bedroom. She'd left it on the night-stand they'd shared, being able to afford only the one.

But the note is not the real news, he thought. The news is what you were afraid to tell her. That the big change has already happened. Is, in fact happening right now. This is your life, and it doesn't matter who can see you, because you've missed the point and wasted so much of it.

Noel,

I'm sorry I didn't wait for you to come home. I tried, but I couldn't stay a minute longer. This place and waiting for this poisoned dream of ours to come true, it was turning me into someone I don't like. I'm scared, Noel. I'm so scared. I have dreams about death and ghastly inhuman things coming for me, trying to swallow me. I jump at every noise, and there's too much noise here. I carry so much guilt. For what we ran away from, for what we were planning to do. I think we used to love each other but we don't do that much anymore. Maybe we can't. Maybe we never did, except as a solution to each other's problems. But that can't be right, considering where it has led us.

Please don't think any of this is your fault. It was my idea and you were only trying to make me happy. But I need to be alone. I need to grow up and become someone before I can be with someone. And I think I've been the thing keeping you from finding yourself too. When you do, I'd really like to meet him.

I hope you don't stay. I hope you get far

away, and find yourself somewhere else
good and true.

Love,

J

'I'd really like to meet him,' he said to the note.

Noel began to work in earnest on the Don Julio Silver. When only two fingers remained, he carried the bottle out onto the back patio and stared out at the dark outlines of the other houses and rooftops against the softer black sky. He walked to the side of the guest house, until he could see across the bald yard to the main house some hundred feet away. Mature palm trees that had been trucked in and planted around the winding brick path connecting the two abodes obstructed his view. A thicker line of smaller snarling things that could grow in the desert had been planted against the border fence, tracing a jagged shoulder up to the main house's back deck. The house's windows were as dark and lifeless as they had been for the past fourteen months.

He thought back to the comical scene of Nora, a middle-aged realtor in her blazer and business skirt and sensible heels, extracting her agency sign from the trunk of her fancy car and trying to beat it into the hard ground. When was the last time he had seen that For Sale sign, anyway? He couldn't remember, but he was sure it hadn't been there tonight. Soon as someone buys the place, he thought, we will be evicted.

Then he remembered there was no longer a we, just a me. Wouldn't it be funny if Julie left him and he became homeless in a span of twenty-four hours? Yes, hilarious. He took another swing, emptying the bottle, and lobbed it into the weeds.

The main house stood against the night, a shadow that did not seem real in any important way, and now a single window light was on.

Someone had moved in, after all.

Noel stared at the lighted window, thinking about the producer and his wife and their two children. The article he'd found in the paper, just out of a gnawing but harmless curiosity, mind you, said that Ezra, the eight-year-old boy, had been found decapitated.

He stared at the house for a long time, then went to bed and passed out at once.

★ ★ ★

No, we can't stay. We'll leave tonight, together.
This was his first clear thought as he emerged from the placeless swamp of lurid colors and phantom images that constituted his intoxicated dreams. Emerged, like a sea creature washed up onto the shore of wakefulness by a rogue wave, only to be dragged back by the undertow of his exhausted mind and the alcohol flushing through his veins, into a shallow slumber.

The front door creaked and her familiar footsteps came down the hall, into the bedroom, and he felt her.

268

Oh, good. Julie came back. I should wake up now.

He was too tired to move, but not so deep as to resist imagining her stopped in the doorway, watching him sleep, smelling booze fumes, shaking her head. This is what she had come back for? What if she wanted to talk, or better yet take him with her? She might have a speech prepared, a short apology for abandoning him. All he had to do was wake up, then they could get in her car and leave tonight, now. He would drink a quart of convenience store coffee and make the four-hour road trip to Los Angeles, and together they would wake up in the sun, at her mom's house, and John would make them breakfast, give them both another lecture for their foolish waste of four years, but everyone would be happy they had come home. They would start over, humbled, reborn in the glowing light of family.

But not if he continued to lie here like a besotted bum.

Her footsteps, which were the sound of tennis shoes brushing carpet, moved closer to the bed.

Noel shifted his legs, stretching the muscles and pushing his face into the pillow. He was trying to wake up but the process required immense reserves of concentration.

The mattress sagged at one corner and the cheap steel bed frame squeaked. The single blanket he had dragged over himself began to slide along his bare legs, tickling. He couldn't tell if she was pulling it down or up, if she was trying to wake him or slide in with him. Maybe she was tired too, and cold, wanting nothing more than to snuggle and be with him until the new day arrived, sober and bright.

'Mmmm, sorry, baby,' he mouthed into his pillow. He was lying on his stomach, head at a ninety-degree angle, and now his neck and lower back were stiff.

It's coming, she said. Her voice was so soft as to qualify as a whisper, yet was clear, close. *It's coming back soon. I want to help you with it, so we can make the most of it. It's a gift and it shouldn't be wasted.*

Took him a while to decipher the meaning of her words. She was talking about his other blanket. The very thing that, like a get-rich-quick scheme, had ruined them.

'Uhn-uh,' he murmured in protest. Didn't she know by now? He didn't want the shroud to come back, not really. He wanted only her. His girl. A normal life and her love. 'Don't leave.' He used every ounce of his facial muscles to will his eyes open. 'Stay with me.'

The blanket slid away and the cool air drifted over him. The mattress flexed again as she rose. He thought she was leaving him until she leaned over, talking quietly into his ear.

I can help you get it back, she said. *You can have those things, those things you want so much. You can have anything you want. You can have me. I want to feel you again, to have you when you're in the void. I want to feel you inside me, Noel. Touching me. Filling me up until I can't stand it. All of that and our lives back.*

The cool air and his body sliding against the sheets were like skin, waking his nerves before his mind could catch up. His cock slipped against the sheets and his heart thudded through the fog of alcohol and now, at last, he was awake. He rolled over, sure that she was within arm's reach, but his fingers found only air, a pillow, the empty side of the bed where she had slept.

He sat up, nearly trembling with desire and hope. 'Julie . . . '

But she wasn't in the room. The bedroom door was open. The hall light was on. He sighed. She must have gone into the living room or kitchen.

He slid from the bed, taking a few seconds to gain his balance, and smelled the body smell of his own person. His t-shirt was half soaked through with sweat, even though the guest house was almost as cool as the air outside. They never bothered to turn the heat on, he'd stopped paying the bill during the warmer months, and he hadn't noticed until now how chilly it was in the middle of the night.

Below the shirt he wore only a pair of loose boxer shorts, the right leg of which was constraining an erection of the sort he hadn't known since that night in the desert, the first time he had laid down with her and she had given him everything, her hands, her body, her eyes, her love. His hands moving up her back. The way the twin heart-shaped curves of her ass had moved as she turned and looked back, eyes never leaving his, and showed him how to find the way in from behind, hip flesh and the backs of her thighs pale in the moonlight, cold all over except for her center where there was only heat, the uncannily wet depth fitting around him at once tighter and more easily than he had ever imagined. Julie locked against him, both of them coming in clenched waves while the desert cold bristled at his back . . .

Jesus Christ, stop, *stop*. What was he doing here, now, zoning out on sex beside the bed in the middle of the night? His hand had helped itself down into his underwear and he was clutching himself almost painfully. Where was she? She'd come in for him just a minute ago, what was she doing in the kitchen at this hour? He readjusted everything under his waistband and kicked around the floor until he found his jeans, pulled them on, buttoned his fly haphazardly and went down the hall.

'Julie?'

She didn't answer.

'Babe? Where'd you go, Jules?'

The kitchen and living room were one main area, separated only by a small length of coffee tile counter-top and pass-through cupboards. Julie was not in either space. The living room was dark but the kitchen light was on. Had he left it on? He remembered turning on the light above the stove, depressing the metal peg next to the plastic switch for the ventilation fan. But the ceiling light was on now, and he was pretty sure he hadn't turned it on. Had he?

No, he'd read her note, then taken his tequila out onto the patio. Between then and his short trek back to the bedroom, he'd stopped only to urinate and drink a glass of water before slumping down and rolling the blanket over half his body.

Of course he might have forgotten turning the light on, drunk as he had been (and still was, to be honest, but now less dizzily and more dumbfounded).

Another fun fact: the sliding glass door to the patio was open. Had he left it this way? He had no memory of closing it. Maybe she had gone outside.

He hurried through the kitchen, bashing his elbow on the countertop's raised molding at the turn. Whatever was the opposite of the funny bone, that's what he'd hit, sending a deep bolt of pain down to his hand. The pain became a rage. He wanted to find a hammer and smash the ever-loving shit out of the countertops, the windows, the doors, destroy the guest house in a six-hour act of manual labor. Instead he cursed, rubbed the sore area for a moment, stepped out onto the patio.

He almost called her name again, but something about leaving the safety of his familiar living space (it wasn't anything like a real home) and being exposed by the night stopped him short. What if it hadn't been Julie at all but an intruder? And now you've followed them into the yard.

Except this wasn't true, because he'd felt her in the bedroom. She had spoken to him, whispering in his ear.

You can have anything you want. I want to feel you inside me, Noel. Touching me. Filling me up until I can't stand it. All of that and our lives back.

The concrete under his bare feet felt frozen. The hair on his arms stood up and was ruffled by the slight breeze coasting across the desert, winding its way through the subdivision and in broken tendrils that seemed to poke and steal away rather than arriving in a single broadsided gust. He was shivering, no longer mentally aroused at all but worried — for her and for himself. Oddly, though, he *was* still aroused, at least physically. Stupid robot dick. His jeans were buttoned crookedly and the pressure against the front seam bordered on painful.

'Stop it,' he mumbled to himself.

This whole thing was a drunken escapade of the imagination, a near wet dream that hadn't reached its conclusion. What a pathetic shit he'd become. Did he really think Julie had come back for him, hours after she had left him a goodbye note? She was probably pulling into her mother's driveway right —

He saw her. Julie was there, walking up the path toward the main house. She wasn't much more than a shadow of skirt and jacket and her long, blacker than night hair, but it was her. He knew her shape, her walk. He watched her in stunned curiosity for a few seconds as she continued on the path winding through the imported palms, wanting to call out to her or follow, but a kind of regressive shyness made him hesitate. She had, in a way, dumped him. He couldn't take any further rejection.

Julie stopped and looked back at him. He caught a glimpse of her white moonlit face as she raised a hand and waved for him to follow. Then she continued toward the slain producer's house, and Noel obeyed her wishes.

26

As Noel's bare feet moved across the packed dirt and bristly dead grass of the yard stretching up to the main house, he wondered why Julie wanted him to follow her there. What had she discovered? Did she think they could move into the larger abandoned residence? He did not see her reach the back deck or slip inside, but another light was on now, in what was probably the kitchen or a living room.

He tried to recall the producer's family name, as if this still mattered. He had known it at one time, after Nora the realtor had informed them of the tragedy. Later, he'd joked about them with Julie, in the way people will joke about something awful next door if only to diffuse the discomfort. Bindle? Baskins, like the ice cream? Something with a B, that also went with a joke about body bags. See any new body bags today, Jules? Do you think the baggies would mind if we had a campfire in the backyard tonight? Bagley. That was it.

Moments later the sliding door opened and a woman who was not Julie spoke up, her voice bright and clear in the otherwise silent suburb.

'Hi, there? Is that Noel?'

'Oh, hey. Yeah, that'd be me.' A wall of disappointment stopped him on the first step up to the deck. What the hell? Julie had some friend here? Some new tenant she had gotten cozy with? The woman wasn't much more than a head and shoulders leaning out the door and the yard light was either not working or there wasn't one, so he couldn't make out much except for the outline of her hair and a button-up blouse. He felt let down and like a creep. 'I was following Julie.'

'I'm Lucy. Lucy Sapperstein. I guess Nora and Julie didn't warn you.'

'Don't think so. What about?'

'That I moved in.'

'No. Julie didn't mention . . . is she staying here or what's the deal?'

'She was on her way out but changed her mind. We've been up having some much needed girl talk.' Lucy pushed the sliding door open wider and the dining room light added some detail from behind. 'I've been moving stuff around, trying to get settled and, well, come in, come in. It's cold out tonight. I'm having tea. Peppermint. Helps me wind down, you know?'

'Okay,' Noel said, thinking, *that's nice but where the hell is my girlfriend?*

Lucy was already turning away. He crossed the deck and went inside. The house was very warm, was the first thing he noticed. Or maybe he had been cold outside.

'Oh, do you mind?' Lucy Sapperstein said from the kitchen, gesturing at the door. 'I'm a total wimp for the cold. My heating bill's going to be the worst in Las Vegas.'

'Got it.' Noel closed the sliding door. He glanced at the living room and saw piles of moving boxes, some unopened, others overflowing with sweaters, dresses, the neck and head of a lamp shaped like a sunflower. But no sign of Julie.

'I don't think this stove works too well.' Lucy was staring down at a yellow kettle over the heating coil, holding a hand over the lid to check for steam. 'Be just another minute.'

'No problem.'

Noel took a spot in the corner of the kitchen, giving her space. It was a large kitchen with huge squares of clay tile, a center island with a butcher-block top, high-end appliances. Lucy looked like the average business woman as Noel understood the role. Cream silk blouse tucked into a navy skirt, white stockings, her thick brown hair pinned up in a sensible but not unattractive cinnamon roll at the back, but loose and sagging, as if the entire works were about to unspool. Wholesome, fit, a little bouncy, making him think of an aerobics instructor or someone otherwise prone to vigorous movement. He guessed she was somewhere between thirty-five and forty-five. Instead of heels or loafers she had on a pair of scruffy pink running shoes, unlaced, the silver tongues standing upright.

'You must be a night owl like me,' she said, moving to an open cupboard where she had some recently unloaded basic foodstuffs: a box of saltines, jar of peanut butter, a new bottle of generic ketchup. She went back to another box, hovered over it indecisively, and sighed.

'Tonight, anyway. Do you work late?'

'I can't stand all these boxes lying around. I'm

probably obsessive compulsive or something. I have to unpack *right now*, you know?'

'I guess the sooner it feels like home, the better,' Noel said. 'I didn't know the house had been sold.'

'I wish I could afford it. Just renting, so don't worry. I'm not allowed to raise your rent.' Lucy smiled, staring at him intently.

Noel nodded. 'So, did Julie come back or did I miss her on the way out or . . . ?'

'Oh, she's probably still upstairs,' Lucy said, as if this explained everything. 'She was really tired.'

'I barely missed her then.'

Lucy lowered her voice and gave him a conspiratorial look. 'She's still upset. I told her it was probably a bad idea to leave at night. She should get a good night's sleep and wait till morning. Clearer head, safer driving, all that, you know?'

This was something of a relief, but not much. He wanted to see her, talk to her, not stand here with this stranger playing mother hen in the middle of the night. How much did this Lucy know about them? What had Julie told her? How much of it was about what a lousy boyfriend he had been?

'That makes sense,' Noel said. 'I don't want to bother her. I know things have been hard lately. If she needs a little space, I can respect that.'

Lucy gave him an *aw, aren't you cute* look. 'Yeah, I think she needs a little time.'

Noel did not like the sound of this, so added, 'It's kind of funny this happened tonight.

279

Coming home from work I couldn't stop thinking we have to leave now, tonight. I mean, I know she reached her wits end before me, but I think we both want the same things.'

'You do?' Lucy said.

'Definitely. We've stayed too long as it is. I don't care about this place.'

'Really?'

Who did this woman think she was, challenging him? 'Yes, really, Lucy.'

The kettle was not yet steaming. Noel did not want the stupid tea to begin with, and he really didn't want to wait for it to reach a boil.

Lucy puckered her lips and he saw that her lipstick, a barely noticeable pink, was smeared at one corner of her top lip, like a scythe.

'Well, that's good,' Lucy finally answered. 'But I'm not sure Julie knows that.'

Noel nodded some more, his anger rising. 'When did you two meet, anyway? Julie never mentioned you but it sounds like you've become real friends.'

Lucy checked the kettle again. 'Not long ago.'

'I'm surprised I didn't see you.'

'Julie and I met when you were at work. Sorry about that, by the way. But maybe it's for the best.'

'What's that?'

Lucy studied the boxes. 'Your job. At Caesars. I guess it didn't work out, but then it wasn't exactly fulfilling, right?'

'How did you know I lost my job?'

Lucy faced him. She blinked a few times. 'Julie told me, of course. How else would I know?'

Heartburn reached up into Noel's throat. He swallowed what felt like an entire lime marinated in tequila. 'Hate to tell you this, Lucy, but that's not really possible.'

Lucy tilted her head.

'I got fired today. Haven't seen Julie since, so I haven't had time to break the news.'

'Wow, that's weird, huh?' Lucy said. 'How do you think she found out? I assumed you'd told her.'

'I didn't. But I think I can manage that on my own, now.'

Lucy glanced at the stairway, which is exactly what he had been thinking of, though his eyes hadn't gone there yet.

He turned from the kitchen and headed into the living room. 'Upstairs you said. Which room is she in?'

Lucy came around the other side, blocking his path. She put her hands up in a surrender gesture. 'Hold on, Noel.'

He stopped and glared at her.

'I'm not sure it's a good idea for you to go up there right now.'

'Why not?'

'Don't be mad at me. I'm only abiding by her wishes. She said she didn't want to see you yet.'

Noel shifted from foot to foot. 'Then why did she come wake me up?'

'She woke you up?'

'Yes, Lucy, she did.'

'When?'

'Tonight, a few minutes ago. Right before she came back here?'

Lucy looked puzzled for a moment, then nodded. 'Right, but that's when she said she changed her mind. She didn't want you to follow her.'

'She waved at me.' His voice was rising and if this continued for more than another minute he would soon be shouting. 'She wanted me to follow her, obviously. Come on, this is getting ridiculous.'

Lucy tried to smile, to placate him, but he saw anger behind the mask. She said, 'I don't know what happened out there, but when she got in *here*, I asked if she was okay. She said no, she didn't want to do this tonight. Please tell him I'm sleeping and don't want to deal with it.'

'She said that? Those were her exact words?'

'Exact? I don't know about exact, but she wasn't ambivalent, Noel. She needs to rest. Wouldn't it be better if the two of you got a good night's sleep and had this out in the morning?'

Noel laughed in frustration. 'It might. But I just want to see her for a minute to make sure she's all right. If she's sleeping and doesn't want to talk, I'll leave.'

Lucy's eyes narrowed. He was happy to see he was pissing her off. If this woman did not get out of his way in thirty seconds, he was going to shove her aside and dash up the stairs screaming Julie's name.

'Good, then we understand each other,' he said, and set off toward the stairs.

'Wait.' Lucy walked in front of him again and stopped, pushing her hair back, even though it was already in a bun. 'I understand your

282

concern, but I can't let you go up there full of anger like this, in the middle of the night. I can't have a scene between you two that might wake them up. I just can't, so I'd ask you to respect that.'

'Them? Who's them?'

Lucy reared her head back as if he had insulted her. 'My family.'

'What family?'

'My husband and the kids. I might be a night owl, but they're sleeping. They need their sleep, Noel. Julie does, too.'

This news — the idea that he was standing in some family's house, not some single woman's — threw him off track. For the first time since setting foot inside, he felt like a trespasser, the asshole boyfriend sensible people rush to protect a nice young woman from.

'I had the impression you were single.'

'Single?'

'Living here alone.' He looked at the moving boxes. 'You said 'I', when you were talking about moving in. Looking at the place. Earlier.'

Lucy seemed to lose her train of thought, then abruptly turned and walked back into the kitchen to check the kettle. 'Goddamn it, this stove never works.'

Noel wanted to head for the stairs but the idea of her husband and kids sleeping up there gave him pause. Why would Julie want to stay with these people? How had she gotten comfortable with them so soon?

Lucy came back into the living room. She looked at the boxes with a mixture of longing and regret. 'I don't suppose you want to help me? Unpack my boxes?'

'I could, but maybe you want to wait for your husband? In the morning?'

'My husband? He can't unpack the boxes.'

'No?'

'He's sleeping,' Lucy said. Her eyes were flat. Her voice was flat. The bouncy energy was gone, her body had become still, rigid.

The saliva in Noel's mouth disappeared. He couldn't speak. They stared at each other and Noel realized he had walked into an orchestrated situation with no idea who was conducting the music. Get out now, the voice of reason spoke in his head. And immediately after, Lucy's blank expression darkened. She regarded him with an anger that could not be explained by whatever Julie had told her about him. She looked, in this moment, furious.

Very softly she said, 'You know.'

Noel shook his head.

'Yes. Yes, you do. You know everything.'

'I don't.' Noel took a step back, toward the dining room and sliding glass door. He wanted to run but Julie was upstairs. These people were keeping her, he was sure.

'You want to leave now?' Lucy said. 'Is that it?'

'I don't seem welcome.'

'What about Julie? Don't you want to see her?'

'I said I did.'

Her eyes never leaving his, Lucy raised her hands slowly and untied her hair. The bun unfurled and her brown tresses spilled around her shoulders. She shook her head gently, and the layers of her hair separated somewhat.

'Then go find her, Noel. She's upstairs, sleeping in the guest room. Because she is our guest, just like you.'

Noel could not move.

'Go on. Go tell her that you love her. She's upstairs.'

Lucy took one step toward him and Noel responded with half a dozen of his own toward the stairs, but hesitated. He looked back. Lucy had not attempted to follow him but was watching him eagerly. Now she wanted him to go up.

'What's going on here?' His voice cracked.

'You know that too, don't you?' Lucy said. 'Nora told you what happened.'

The producer and his family.

'But you said you just recently . . . ' Oh, God. Oh, God.

'We moved in a little more than four years ago, Noel. We've been here ever since. This is our home. It will always be our home, until you do your job.'

That's not possible, Noel thought. 'Sapperstein,' he said.

'Is my maiden name,' Lucy finished for him.

Their real name was something else. Something to do with body bags.

'Why are you doing this to us?' he said.

Lucy Bagley's hair looked different now. It was darker, shiny. He realized it was dampening in places. As he watched her a drop of blood slid from the ends of her let-down hair and stained her blouse.

'Don't you love her, Noel? Don't you want to be with Julie? We can help you. We can help you be with her, and do what you came here to do.'

The kettle was not steaming because the stove was not on. Lucy couldn't get it to work. He had never seen her touch the boxes or the kettle or move the food into the cupboards. He thought she had opened the sliding glass door, but now he wasn't sure. He might have opened it and let himself in. Or it might have been left open.

It was closed now. He was a full room-span away from the exit. Freedom. But what had they done to Julie?

Lucy took a step toward him and another drop of blood fell onto her blouse.

'It was you,' he said. 'Earlier, in the guest house.'

'I've never been in the guest house, Noel. I thought that was where you and Julie lived.'

'What did you do to her?'

'Are you going to help me unpack all these boxes?'

'Not until I see Julie. Is she even here?'

Lucy smiled and took another step toward him. 'I told you she's upstairs.'

'Julie!' Noel shouted. 'Julie, wake up!'

'Be quiet!' Lucy hissed. 'You're going to wake up my family.' But saying this, she smiled, as if recalling a private joke. 'Or maybe you already did.'

Then he understood. 'That's what you want, isn't it? You want me to wake them up. Or see them. You want me to go upstairs and see them?'

She smiled. Her lipstick was streaked in

several places now and her hair was dripping steadily. Something was different in her eyes, too. They had receded, the color drained. Her face was turning the yellow-white of long-term illness.

'She's upstairs,' Lucy said. 'Waiting for you to become the man we all know you can be.'

He wanted to run away, get out now and never look back. But what if this dead woman and her family had done something to Julie's mind, lured her in here the way they had lured him?

'If you hurt her,' Noel said. But what would he do?

'Yes,' Lucy said. 'Please stay and help us unpack the boxes. I'm making some tea. It's peppermint. It helps me unwind.'

He couldn't stand this any longer. He had to choose. The door or the stairs. Flee into the night and risk the chance that Julie was stuck here, with them, in god knows what condition. Or go up and look for himself.

'Yes, some tea,' he said. 'Could you make me some?'

Lucy turned for the stove and Noel moved at a steady but hurried pace toward the stairs. He made it halfway there before hearing her footsteps behind him, coming with the sound of tennis shoes brushing carpet, the sound that had woken him earlier.

Lucy's footsteps, not Julie's.

Which meant Julie wasn't here, she had never been here, this was all a game to get him into the house.

He had to get out, now.

He stopped at the base of the stairs and turned to break for the sliding glass door, but Lucy was standing in the foyer, blocking his path, and she had changed rapidly for the worse. Her eyes were jaundiced yellow, rolled back in their sockets, and her hair was soaked through with blood. Chips of white bone and small pieces of her brains from the gunshot flecked her blouse. Her mouth was open and her blackened tongue lay loose, the gases inside her coming forth with the breath of an opened coffin.

Noel screamed and backed into the stairs. He tripped and fell as Lucy staggered toward him with renewed urgency, arms reaching for him.

He yelled and kicked at her, connecting with a hip that was as solid as a fence post. Lucy staggered, lunged at him again. Her fingers, moist and bony, scratched at his chest and his throat. He had never believed the dead could touch him but Lucy was touching him now, tearing into his flesh with her nails. He twisted away, thrashing beneath her, and began to crawl up the stairs.

Above him, waiting at the top, were the children.

The girl with her abdominal stab wounds was standing beside her decapitated brother, Ezra, who held her hand as he swayed. The father joined them moments later, at the midway point on the stairs, where working as a family they showed him how they got to be this way.

27

Noel did not know if he woke up or simply got his mind back after spending the past four to eighteen hours without it. He remembered being in a snowstorm, walking through a gigantic field, running from someone or something that wanted to devour him at the same time he was pursuing another entity, this one warm and promising life and rescue from oblivion. Every time he seemed to get close to it, to her, the figure shrank into the horizon and his heart collapsed with the weight of distance he had yet to travel.

This private mirage went on for what felt like days, maybe years, and then in a blink he returned to find himself crouched between a bathtub and toilet. He was on a slate tile floor, with golden rays of sunlight warming his feet from a window above a shower stall. The house was quiet. He did not know which house this was, nor how he got here. The bathroom door was shut and locked. There was blood on the floor, streaks of it, drops that had flung themselves up the wall. He wondered whose blood it was, and what instrument had been used to let it.

He sat arms wrapped around his knees for what seemed like half a day but could have been half an hour. Eventually he realized whatever he had been running from was either gone or waiting for him on the other side of the door, and the only way to find out was to open it.

He stood, every muscle in his body tight with dull pain. Even his jaw muscles ached. He mumbled something and could tell that he had lost most of his voice. He went to the sink for water and seeing his reflection in the mirror thought, cat's cradle. The childhood game played with string. There were dozens of patterns you made with the string, the lines criss-crossing in nets and tangles around your fingers.

The face in the mirror looked like a game of cat's cradle gone haywire, played with red twine. The scratches ran across his forehead, down his nose, at angles across his cheeks, to his chin. His ears were cut along the lobes, in the channels. His neck. Down under his shirt. Thin and shallow in places, deep and caked purple in others. When he leaned over to cup water to his mouth, more stinging lines cracked and itched up and down his back, pinched at his stomach. The shock of it all was such that he did not recall how or why this had happened.

Then he was assaulted by flash memories, the sight of their faces, hissing and screaming above him, dragging him down the stairs, running back up to hide, only to find another in the hallway waiting for him, the little girl with her knife wounds, the boy with the ragged severed neck and no head, their rotting mouths and filmy eyes. The murdered family, swarming him, showing him things . . .

He began to hyperventilate, turned for the door, grasped the knob, hesitated.

What if they were still here? What if it started all over again?

But no, staying was not an option.

He yanked the bathroom door open. A large bedroom, must have been the master. The carpet was stained brown in places, old blood, except in the clean, dust-free square where the bed had been. He ran down the hall and found the stairs, moaning in terror as new memories from the night before — this morning — returned. The little girl biting his ankle. The father pinching the skin under his chin, twisting his head and screaming, *Look at me, look at me!* Noel ran past boxes that had not been unpacked, glanced at the yellow kettle, then he was ripping the sliding glass door open and springing into sunlight. No one chased him, but he ran as if the entire family had woken up again and were on his heels, swooping after him like rabid bat people.

He kicked open the guest house door and rushed to collect his wallet, shoes and a change of clothes. He needed a shower and felt infected by them, but not here. He had to get away from this neighborhood as fast as possible.

*   *   *

At the nearest Wells Fargo branch, the act of opening his wallet hurt his fingers. The joints were swollen stiff, the tips raw, as if he had been handling bricks all day without gloves. Two of his fingernails were cracked and peeled back, the cuticles of all ringed with dried blood. He wondered how they had done this to him, but his ragged fingernails, the soreness, suggested something far more disturbing. That they had worked on him, drove him to it, not as bodies or spirits in the world but as demons of the mind, manipulating him, flooding his brain and jerking his body like a marionette. A family of marionettes with the power to make him scratch himself out of his mind.

'Next? Sir? I can help you down here.'

Noel showed his ID to the teller, a bookish young woman who turned ashen and very quiet when she saw his face up close. With checking and savings, he had $441.29 to his name. The teller seemed relieved he was closing the accounts, taking his meager reserves elsewhere.

Take me, he thought. *Come on, you fucking glass egg bubble shield ultra-violet bitch curse. Take me outta here. I paid you in blood, now it's time for you to wave the magic wand.*

Six blocks later he found the Desert Inn Motorcourt, which might have once been a clean family-friendly place to park your RV and splurge on a room but was now a skid row of impromptu gangbang movie sets and heroin cottages. For $19.99 plus tax he rented a room for one hour. It smelled of wet gerbil shavings. The bathroom had no soap or shampoo, so he returned to the front desk to complain.

The clerk was a woman in the twilight of her middle years, with a purple birthmark stretching from her sun-scorched cleavage to her right ear, wearing a UNLV tank top and polarized sun-blockers. For the bargain rate of $6.00 she sold him a bar of soap the size of a breath mint and a bottle of shampoo made for a Smurf. At his croaking request she threw in a towel with the texture of sandpaper, no extra charge.

The shower was only lukewarm even turned to its hottest setting, but Noel didn't care. He used the towel as a washcloth, scrubbing his body from head to toe three times, until the soap and shampoo were gone and he felt raw. Some of the cuts continued to bleed, but most only turned puffy red. He shook himself as dry as possible, threw out his socks and underwear and put his clothes back on.

The dead always found him, or he them, when he was out of the spectrum, or on his way to the departure gate. But here he was, after spending an entire day and night with them, a solid. He had been waiting four years. He was very hungry.

For food, for an explanation, for his missing ghost.

★   ★   ★

The morning sun warming him as he trekked west on Sahara Avenue, moving closer to the center of energy. Out here at the north end, just a few blocks off the Strip, there were no fancy hotels and casinos, no cinematic waterfalls or lush gardens. There was, however, among the gas stations and warehouses and low ugly industrial buildings and broken glass in the gutters, a sex museum. And a sex toy and video outlet the size of a grocery store. Around the bend were strip clubs, not much more than cinderblock huts, their open doors revealing the darkness of ocean trenches. Noel passed such pits of vice and their lurking denizens; he was after a vice of a different sort.

There were other stragglers like him, a small but colorful class of shattered humanity limping along the wide dirty streets, digging in dumpsters, peeking around corners. In the past four years he'd seen the jet set, the celebrity cling-on set, the card shark set, the bachelor party and girls' night out set. Here was a genus he had never been able to classify but did so now: the styrofoam coffee set. Even though it was well past noon, half the mutants on the prowl had a little cup of coffee.

The terrycloth jumpsuit and rubber sandals lady was clutching hers with both hands, the little plastic lid flap scraping her witch nose at every sip. The shirtless but otherwise clean-cut college kid with the black eye had one in each hand, marching with the injured pride of a legendary debauch. At yet another strip mall, a stoic Vietnamese *papasan* fishing Marlboro butts from the Photo-Mat planters was lighting and enjoying his complete cigarette in increments, one butt and stale drag at a time, then doused each of his recovered treasures in his java receptacle. They were castaways, clinging to the steaming life rafts of sanity even the most offensively brewed coffee afforded.

When he realized they were watching him with as much disdain and repulsion as he experienced in his regard of them, Noel understood, for the

294

first time in many months and perhaps years, his place in the world. These were his brethren, this was his lot. He was *this*, like *them*, no better than *that guy*.

To wit: at the next crosswalk a man with an IV cotton ball taped on the back of each hand, a Panama hat on his sweating melon head, was using a cane to lance imaginary cars passing by. Noel said, 'Hello. Is there anything I can help you with?' but the overture went unredeemed beyond the riposte 'Go fuck yourself'.

He stopped at a twenty-four-hour diner and ate six pancakes, three eggs, a rasher of bacon and three cups of coffee. The tab was $3.29 and in no way a bargain. While he was sitting in his booth, waiting for the caffeine to kick in, he noticed two men in dark suits at the counter, seated beside one another, each reading the newspaper with a slice of pie resting unmolested on the counter. They weren't speaking but he knew they were together, members of some organization. He waited for them to turn and look at him, sure that they would glance his way at any moment, but nearly ten minutes passed and they never did. Eventually, the suit on the right forked the tip of his pie into his mouth and began to chew slowly.

Noel helped himself to a complimentary toothpick on his way out. It tasted of artificial mint.

Calorie-soaked, excited now, he was ready for the tsunami to curl.

★ ★ ★

He crossed through a parking structure to the Strip and another mile or so to Caesars Palace. He walked past the front desk, the sundry store with its t-shirts and novelty ceramic Caesars busts, to the cashier windows. He converted his life's savings, $400, into chips. The casino was slow, with a few early birds trying their luck.

He found the nearest roulette table, empty and brushed clean. He was the only mark. The croupier at attention was a woman named Sable. She had a pleasing almond tan, clean white teeth and hay-colored hair swirled into a small Cleopatra braid. Noel had never met her. If she found his scratched-to-hell appearance disturbing, she didn't show it, and he respected her professionalism. Her job was to keep patrons at the table long enough to empty their pockets, not make them feel like a freak show.

Sable smiled and said, 'Good afternoon.'

He pretended to study the reader board atop the pole, but in truth it didn't matter what had recently hit. He didn't care about winning. He'd come only to ask a question and receive an answer. The question was, Should I stay in Vegas or go look for Julie? He pegged the possible answers this way:

Red means get out now, find her, do whatever it takes to win her back.

Black means stay in Vegas as long as it takes to disappear.

He set $300 on black. Not because he wanted black or because he felt lucky with black, merely because he had to choose one or the other to play.

Sable nodded and nudged the polished spokes atop the wheel's axle. The wheel gained speed. The ball raced around and around. Sable waved her hand across the table — no more bets. Very quickly the ball got restless, dancing and pinging around the number grooves. It flirted with red 30 before dumping into black 8.

'Black is a winner,' Sable said, and doubled Noel's chips to $600.

One half of his fate had been decided. He would not go looking for Julie, yet. He would stay in Vegas until his next change. He did not know whether it would be one day or twenty years, but Vegas was Vegas and he was going to need some money. The more the better. Getting another job was not an option. He'd tried that and it hadn't worked out. Also, he was never going back to the guest house and so had no place to live. He needed a base to work from. Food, shelter, a new wardrobe. Poker was out. Blackjack had never been his thing.

This wheel, though. He liked the randomness of it, the spinning, blurring motion. The variety of bets and contrasting colors. It was the closest thing the casino had to a carnival game. A warmth was building inside him.

'Excuse me, Sable,' Noel said.

'Sir?' The croupier smiled.

'Could you tell me today's date? I forgot to check my calendar this morning.'

'The twenty-ninth.'

This number was pleasing, why he couldn't say. 'Sorry, I've been away for a while. The twenty-ninth of . . . ?'

'February.' Sable winked.

Noel's body began to thrum. His legs nearly buckled. February the 29th was a leap day. Which meant this was also his true birthday.

The number of times Noel had been sure of anything, absolutely dead certain about the result of a given action, could be counted on one hand. This was one of those times. It had to do with his leap-birthday, and it had to do with the slaughtered Bagley family that had assaulted him last night. More than this he did not understand, but he felt that, in this moment, fate was looking out for him and wanted him to play.

'A leap year-leap day,' he said, beaming at Sable. 'I guess I had better play twenty-nine, wouldn't you say?'

'I'm not allowed to say.' Sable tossed him another of her practiced winks.

Noel added the original hundred to the six hundred already on the turf and slid the entire pile onto 29, which was also black.

'Believe it or not, today is my birthday,' he said. 'Only comes every four years, if you want to be technical about it.'

Sable performed a little bow. 'Is it, now? Well then, happy birthday to you, and good luck.'

He expected a pang of last-second doubt, but it didn't come. He felt free, as if he had just been excused from detention. His body felt lighter. His life felt lighter. Somewhere, he was sure, the dark god of his erasure was nodding down at him proudly.

Sable, as if wanting to give him an extra moment to avoid total folly, hesitated. Other than his pile on 29, the board was empty.

Noel forced himself to stop grinning like a maniac and waited her out.

'29 it is.' Sable gave the spokes a smooth shove and the wheel came alive. With an expert finger, its nail painted blood-red, she flicked the little white ball into its polished track. *Ree-ooowwrr — ree-ooowwrr-ree-ooowwrr* . . . The numbers blurred and the white ball made a delicious zipping-buzz in the wooden channel.

Was it his imagination, or did Sable's smile slip for just a moment there? As if she were concerned he had made the wrong choice? No. Sable didn't care whether he won or lost. She had no stake in his financial salvation, his mood, his life. She was an hourly employee. She got paid to do her thing, nothing more.

Sable did the swami wave — no more bets.

Noel gritted his teeth.

No, she didn't care, but he had seen *something* move across her features, tensing her brow, drawing her smile down at the corners. Fear, like an invisible crow feather that had sailed across the table and traced a line between her eyes. Because maybe she wasn't worried that he had chosen wrong or bet too much, but that he had chosen exactly right and bet it all. Maybe he was weirding her out a little here, with his cat's cradle face and four-day stubble. Or maybe she had felt a sliver of what he felt — that something other than dumb luck and blind chance was in the air today, a dark force flitting about, looking for a home, and which had attached itself to this pale young man with hangover eyes.

Noel's heart thundered. His hands clenched the beveled table.

The numbers were no longer blurring but popping with increasing clarity. He saw a 7, then a 21, then the green 00. The ball had stopped meowing and was cruising in a continuous, lazy *zzzuuuzzzzuuuzzzzuuuzzz* . . .

He looked to Sable. Her eyes were locked on the wheel.

Tink-a-dink-dink — and then the ball was hovering in the air, rotating like a tiny white moon before it plunged — *rink-a-dink-CLICK*.

Stuck between gold walls while the wheel coasted, the ball sat in its cradle and above them the screen blinked.

29.

'And a happy birthday it is,' Sable said. She was not smiling.

'Holy shit,' Noel said. 'Sorry, I mean, wow. What are the odds of that?'

He meant it rhetorically, but the croupier answered, 'Straight up on a single number pays thirty-five to one.' She was counting a lot of chips.

Noel couldn't do the math. He tried, but when she shoved the tiers across the felt he simply said, 'How much is that?'

'Twenty-four thousand, five hundred.'

A ventriloquist dummy of a man with a handful of show tickets banded against a detective's leather notebook arrived at Noel's side. 'Congratulations, sir. It's nice to see a winner on such a slow day. Can we offer you a complimentary stay in one of our Centurian Tower suites? Caesars Palace would be honored to have you as a guest.'

A waitress arrived on his heels, a cheerful black woman with chorus line legs and enough cleavage to hide the guest services manager in her corset. 'Something to drink?'

Noel looked from one to the other. 'Thank you, but I've got a couple more bets to place first.'

The waitress curtsied and sauntered away.

The guest services dummy took this news as decidedly welcome. 'We'll hold the offer, then. Enjoy your play.'

But he didn't leave the area. Noel saw him circling the tables, directing the other dealers while keeping one eye on the lacerated rube in need of a $25,000 haircut.

Noel looked at his mountain of chips, then smiled up at Sable. 'I'd like to put all that on one number, but I don't think it will fit in the little rectangle. How do we make that work?'

Sable offered her fourth or fifth type of smile of the day, this one a grimace of the sort one wears when confronted with true insanity. 'I can change those out for chips of a larger denomination. Set them on the table in front of me.'

Noel did, and Sable counted them down quickly, then set him up with twenty-four chips marked $1000, and change. He broke them down into two piles of a dozen and added the hundreds, then carefully ushered the stack onto 29.

'It's still my birthday,' he said, with all the good nature of a man who has just won a down payment on a house.

Sable looked around, craving a witness.

Noel spoke gently. 'Are you going to take my action or not?'

'Of course.'

Perhaps in response to his little jab, Sable snapped into a professional series of movements that set his folly in motion with maximum haste. When her fingers flicked the ball into the groove, Noel nearly levitated from his shoes. His scratches turned to ice. Breath like frost stung the back of his neck. The casino seemed to buckle under tremendous force, as if a fault line had opened beneath Las Vegas Boulevard, and every colored light in the room became a sun, burning his eyes, then was eclipsed by a larger consciousness that shuttered him in darkness.

He was dying a glorious death and saw his life flashing behind his closed lids —

His jellybean self snuggled in the womb as the black veil descended on him for the first time, illuminating and then blackening him like a resident of Hiroshima. His mother's wet areola, enlarged to the size of a movie screen, its nipple spurting milk. His eardrums popped and he was on the street, riding his trike, then watching as Mr Sobretti flew through a rain of glass and ruptured his head against the weeping willow. His parents fighting. His father slamming the door. His mother crying. The Nerf soaring into the April sky. Leaning down to kiss Julie, Lisa's vacant stare through him, racing away on his motorcycle with a bag of jewels, his mother drugged in a therapy circle, his arm opening like a red river, his memories gushing on the tide of adrenaline, the cop in the snow, his neck blood steaming, the dead children on the stairs, their tiny milk teeth, the murder scene they had forced him to relive with them, glimpses of the man who had done it, a chubby older man with crazed hair and voices in his head, butchering and shooting and licking their blood from their faces like a whining dog, Noel saw these things, saw all he had lived through, all he had done.

And more — into the future he had not yet lived, yet knew to be true — he was in a $4000 Italian suit no one could see, lost among the throng of double-breasted warriors on Wall Street, rising in a service elevator, picking a lock, staring at a screen in some executive's corner office, watching information roll on a Bloomberg terminal, his brain plucking numbers from the green shower of encoded numbers he would reference against another file in a safe concerning a pending merger only three men in the world knew about, worth billions. Moving unseen across Union Square, dogs at a rescue pavilion snarling and gnashing at him, bubbled-up and strapped, a gun in his pocket, walking among the pedestrians who flowed through a farmers' market while a faceless man in an Army coat followed him down into a subway station. The shrieking platform, a train car filled with the dead. Rotting corpses, limbs on the tracks, blood-bewhiskered rats, a homeless man screaming his name, he turned to see it was himself, Noel Shaker unwashed and mad in the filth, and in a flickering blink himself again, this same man, Noel Shaker, age thirty-eight, standing in a vast, cavernous penthouse apartment on the sixtieth floor, his palace, a Caesar of his own making hosting a party with three hundred guests while Lehman Brothers sank in the crash of '08, the man without a face in his Army jacket watching from the corner of the party while Noel laughed and poured more champagne. An explosion, a flash of orange over churning clouds below. The cabin of a jetliner gone chaotic, tilting, rocking under the assault of lightning forking across the sky, passengers screaming, overhead bins emptying onto his head as he staggered toward the cockpit, they were going down but he would be saved by a woman who plopped into his lap at the last moment, never knowing she was giving herself up as a human airbag. A hospital, where he stole medical supplies and followed a nurse in black stockings. Graves in Queens, a plot of grass with two freshly turned patches of dirt, one large the other small, with two headstones: one for Julie Wagner and another for her child. A child she had borne and named Colin, the father unknown. All of it flashing before his eyes, here and now as the roulette wheel spun and the ball raced along its circular track, and his heart felt filled with liquid hydrogen and he wanted to —

The dummy was back, the little puppet manager. Sable casting a rictus grin of terror from her boss to Noel. Behind him the endless-legged waitress lost control of her cocktail tray and tumblers shattered on the carpet. Someone at the end of the table screamed, 'Yee-haw! Ain't that a sumbitch!'

Noel blinked. 'What? What? What happened?'

Then he saw it. Blinking up on the board.

29.

Instinctively, Sable reached for his chips, then stopped as it sank in. Her mouth fell open and after the delay she said, 'I don't have that. I don't have that much.'

'The cashier will handle it,' the guest services manager announced calmly, stepping between Sable and the roulette table. 'This table is closed. We're going to have to inspect the wheel.'

Several spectators booed.

Guest services raised his hands to placate. 'Caesars Palace honors all bets, so long as they are not the result of illegitimate malfunctions. Please,' he smiled and his forehead was sweating.

'I can feel it,' Noel said to everyone and no one. 'Do you feel it coming? It's almost here.'

The manager took Sable by the elbow. 'Care to explain this to me? Now.'

'I've never seen him before,' Sable said. 'I didn't touch that wheel.'

He turned to Noel. 'Sir, would you do me the kindness of coming this way?'

'How much?' someone in the peanut gallery hollered. 'What's the payday?'

Noel couldn't get his mind around numbers, their meanings had vanished.

' . . . doesn't just waltz in and call it twice, taking us for almost nine-hundred large,' the Napoleon of guest services was saying to Sable. 'Something happened, and we'll find it, so if you

305

have something to share with us, now is the time to . . . '

The machines and lights on the casino floor became a rivered blur. A crumbling sensation pounded up his legs, through his body, as if he were a building that had just been detonated. Noel covered his mouth to keep from laughing or screaming, he didn't know which, and the little puppet was staring at him, saying to Sable, 'Where did he go? He was just here with us. Where did he go? Did you see him leave?'

A shocked silence fell over them all as they peered this way and that way, dumbstruck. Behind the gaming tables, raised on a wide dais of a watering hole, the ancient lizard king shaman in his bolo tie turned on his barstool and stared at Noel.

I tried to warn you. Now you are home to demons.

Beside the roulette table, standing against the wooden bumper, with one arm stretched over the wheel and two fingers squeezing the round knob at the top of its axle, there stood a middle-aged man in a garish pink Hawaiian shirt, with a cherubic face and a black leather cord pulled so tight around his throat his neck had turned purple and his lips were black. He tapped the knob twice and Noel knew from the look in his bulging eyes that he was happy to lend a hand.

More of them began to appear, blinking into existence around the casino floor. A cleaning woman who had been raped and battered past her body's limits, her uniform skirt torn as if by tigers. A pill suicide dame in a fur coat, the vomit dried to her chin. A black boy in a blue Cripps bandana, his Dodgers jersey perforated with bullet holes. Others, pale as cream and fat with death, simply wandered over, drawn like moths to his dimming flame. Some were rotting, falling apart, others were leaking formaldehyde from cotton-stuffed cheeks and glossed lips. There were dozens of them haunting the casino, the restaurants and bars, and, by implication, the many rooms above. The living died everywhere, after all, but Noel understood now that Las Vegas had more than its share of suicides, homicides, overdoses and heart attacks. They had been here all along, waiting to be seen, and for some reason decided to make his a happy birthday.

'Up in smoke, man!' the cowboy said. 'Up in smoke!'

'He's gone,' Sable said, and cackled at her confused boss. 'What did you do to him, Gene? What did you do?'

Noel closed his eyes and swayed back on his heels. There was no way to claim his winnings, not now, not like this. But he was not bothered by the fact that he had lost $857,500 minutes after winning them. He had been rewarded with something far more valuable and intoxicating.

After spending four years in the hot hell waiting room of the Nevada desert, his number had been called. In the one place on earth where money flowed like the Rivers of Babylon he was now free to roam unobserved by all but the eyes of God.

307

28

Nine weeks later Noel Shaker was a millionaire six times over, and bored.

The secret, he soon discovered, was not the gaming tables. It was not the cashier bays, the stacks and cases of chips, the waterfalls of coins tumbling from the slot machines. It was not the sports book receipts he could have swiped from the lounge tables, the ATM machines or the restaurant cash registers. The secret was not to be found in the countdown rooms and vaults, the keno parlors, the high-stakes poker tournaments. It was not the casinos, the banks, the fortified bunkers below.

It was the people. The gamblers themselves. Particularly the whales from Hong Kong, Saudi Arabia, Tokyo, Sao Paulo, Moscow. It was the men who flew to desert Nevada on their own plane, set up shop in comped penthouse suites, and moved with an entourage of bodyguards and five-grand-per-night escorts. It was the hotshot poker gurus *after* they had cleaned up in a forty-hour Texas Hold 'em death match at Binion's, their velcro saddlebags weighted with chips and — sooner or later — cold hard cash.

Men who considered the house their enemy, and who did not trust the casinos with the money they had just won or were preparing to plunk down. Men who liked the tactile grubbing of cash green money, who used the banded stacks of hundreds as hard-on fuel, who liked to flaunt it, carry it, blow it on luxe goods, screw their girlfriends on it.

These were men who played blackjack at a grand per hand, took poker pots of two, four and sometimes six hundred thousand month in and lost it month out. Men who were used to having a net worth of half a million after the Super Bowl, going broke by March, then up three hundred more by May. Some were hustlers, addicted to the game. Others owned sports teams, oilfields, a chain of two hundred fast food restaurants — men who came to Vegas a millionaire fifty times over and if they left up or down 1 per cent, so what? To such people money was grain fuel, made for burning.

Noel learned to spot them, which wasn't always easy for the simple reason that not all big dogs liked to wear a diamond collar. Many of them dressed in plain suits, or in casual shirts and pleated khakis, with cheap loafers and expensive cigars. They strutted with quiet confidence, their pinky rings emitting power rays. They ordered champagne for their friends and drank soda water. Just as often it was some kamikaze tweaker kid in flannel and Puma sweats who'd flown in from Gainesville or Yale or Mazatlan on his family trust.

Once he learned to spot them, Noel followed them. He learned to hide in their rooms, making himself very calm and silent. He learned to watch over their shoulders as they unlocked their brushed aluminum suitcases and transferred their winnings to the in-room safes, a Gold's

Gym bag bulging at the seams, into the trunks of their limos, to another hotel room where a member of their staff was checked in under a false name. Once he knew where they stayed and where they secreted their winnings, once he learned to be patient, making his fortune back became bafflingly easy.

Under the blinking lights and eye-in-the-sky cameras on the casino floor, everyone and everything was watched, taped, recorded, stored. But in the rooms, under the mattresses, in the rented pool houses, parking lots, and inside the safes and duffel bags and SUVs' removable seat cushions, there were no cameras. In such places where the big money must eventually travel, the adrenaline players, Rain Man geniuses, techno-savants and Lear Jet jocks grew cocky, confident, as relaxed as train robbers who've galloped across the border.

Sometimes they brought their own safes, sometimes they used the safes provided by the hotels and sometimes they entrusted their treasure to private security firms. But wherever and however they stashed their stashes, eventually they and their henchmen turned their backs. Or left the room. Or took a nap. The man who won ninety-two thousand at blackjack called for a pizza, pulled over at McDonald's. The Hollywood ingénue and Turkish heiress who brought four hundred thousand in her Gucci bags and didn't even like to gamble left hers in the six-room suite and left to rent out a nightclub.

At which time the man who had become their

shadow for the past forty-eight hours opened the safe, the box, the suitcase with its digital code and emptied its contents into a hotel-provided pillowcase. He took chips, cash, jewels, credit cards, cash and more cash. Using cleaning carts, trash cans, food trays, laundry hampers, or just carrying the damn thing himself, Noel found ways to migrate the sacks back to whichever of the empty rooms he had staked out as a way station or temporary home.

Funny thing about pillowcases, something he learned from cleaning rooms — you cut your own finger, wipe a good smear of blood across one, fill it with cash and people walking down the hall don't want to go near it. Doesn't matter what's inside. They see a bloody pillowcase in front of a hotel room door, they avert their eyes as soon as possible and keep on movin'. It was the jewelry store all over again, shuffling and kicking his bags of loot down the carpeted corridors, down the stairwells, under the ice machine until the coast was clear.

He stole various passkeys from the maids and from behind the front desk, rotating through them as needed, changing hotels as needed. He used the vacant rooms to shower, to nap, to count his winnings, to lay low until six a.m., when the casino was at its slowest and most understaffed and he could transport his take. Whenever a new guest or a maid tried to enter, all he had to do was speak up with a gruff, 'Not now, please, come back another time', and they would move on. Thinking they had the wrong room, the front desk had made a mistake, they inevitably apologized and tried again later. By the time a manager was summoned, he would be gone.

Sometimes he duct-taped the cash to his body, dressed and muled it out of the hotel. He rented half a dozen storage lockers by phone, the self-service kind. He used lockers in the employee rooms, the casino gyms.

Before his first week in the blink had ended, he had amassed almost half a million dollars in cash plus other valuables. A single, two-day bender run against a sloppy Greek who'd made his fortune in olive plantations netted him so much cash his arms got tired. Soon he needed a larger receptacle and a more efficient way to transport the money. He stole a suitcase from a pharmaceutical salesman who was sleeping off a bachelor party, but soon this was overflowing and too much to kick down the road. Using a room phone and a stolen credit card, he called the front desk and asked them to transfer him to a local courier service. He gave the dispatcher clear instructions, promised a large tip for a successful delivery and had the suitcase shipped to his former address at the guest house.

He followed the courier from pick-up to the elevators, all the way down to the lobby and out into the courier's van. The courier was a goofy kid in his early twenties, probably a student, and he listened to the same Tupac track three times on the way out to the suburbs. As instructed, he dropped the case on the front porch and knocked on the door. Noel walked around the back, let himself in the sliding glass door and answered, standing out of sight, just behind the front door. He told the kid to set the slip on the floor, he had a disability. He closed the door, signed for his delivery, added a $100 tip and the kid went happily on his way.

He used the same system with two other courier companies a total of twenty-three times.

Counting one hundred paces off the northeast corner of the Bagley's property wall, he found a one-armed saguaro cactus and dug a deep hole. Wrapped the suitcase and additional duffels in Hefty bags, and dragged a large rock over to cover the turned earth. When his present blinding run came to an end, he would rent a car, dig up his treasure and split town. He would set up a new life in a new city, buying a humble house and average American car and hide the remainder of his life savings in various safety deposit boxes, attic boxes, home safes and new holes in the ground.

He started at Caesars because he was familiar with the layout and felt the casino owed him for the winnings he had been forced to abandon at the roulette table. But soon he moved onto the newer resorts, where the uber-rich tended to mine lady luck. MGM Grand, Bellagio, Mirage, Mandalay Bay, Luxor, Rio, the Venetian. It was like fishing. You just had to learn where to cast your net, find the hidden sharks under the reef. Sometimes days would pass without a nibble, other times he netted two or three great whites in a single night. He followed them to their condos, to their second (third, fourth, their fifteenth) homes in the gated communities. He followed some to McCarran International Airport and hit their luggage before they ever set foot inside the terminals. He waited until they had parked, and sometimes he used a short length of pipe or rope to put them out.

Timing and luck were not always on his side. But when the risk was too great, he simply walked away. When the prospect woke up at the wrong time, returned to his room because he had forgotten his lucky inhaler, when anything threatened to trap him, all Noel had to do was freeze, step quietly behind a door, step onto an elevator, or blend into the crowd. On the few occasions when the victim or his people realized something was missing, every visible human in the vicinity became suspect. But Noel blended in everywhere he stood.

Sin City opened its doors for him, and he sinned repeatedly. The constant movement took its toll, his paranoia went up and down like one of the elevators, but in truth there were no close calls or brushes with death. Hunting and foraging, employing his superior evolutionary advantages to survive, to thrive, to break the weaker links in the chain. It was human nature in all its glory, the biggest game on earth. He felt no more guilt than the CEOs of the billions-earning corporations who sucked the lifeblood out of their guests. Like the house itself, he was a force, he was risk, he was fate and luck. Sometimes the money you brought to Vegas stayed in Vegas. Sometimes you went home a loser, and pointing a fingers at the unfairness of it all might have meant something if they knew who to point it at.

Most of the responsible parties — the greedy house, the rigged machines, your own addictions, the God who had turned his back on you — were faceless, impossible to see let alone argue with. Noel Shaker was just another of the invisible predators, the ones you didn't realize had turned your pockets out until it was too late.

★ ★ ★

The dead, for their part, had decided to leave him alone. Based on previous experience, he should be seeing them everywhere he looked now. But he wasn't. Since the lingering rabble of them had appeared in the casino amidst his roulette triumph, he had not seen a single ghost, spirit, or psychic reverberation — whatever they were. And whatever they had to do with his disappearances, however they were provoked and stirred to animation before him, something had changed. Either they had grown bored with him, or he them, and the borderland that once existed between his invisibility and the revenants was paved over by something else. The mental blockade of his acceptance of the curse? The defensive energy of his newfound confidence? Some higher power or referee that controlled the playing field, a law of physics rewarding him for surrendering to it? Maybe they were a symptom of the transition in and out, powerless to heckle him now that he was in full immersion.

He didn't know the reasons. He was only grateful for the reprieve.

Prior to the blinding run that began on his birthday at the roulette table, Noel's longest stint had been four and a half days. Back in Boulder, with Julie. Then he'd dried up for four years, the pressure and misery of his existence mounting until he had shed all other concerns, including Julie. Indeed, he had felt it shift gears the moment he read Julie's goodbye note. His encounter with the dead family had only poured fuel on the fire. It had led him to roulette table, and when he insisted on playing 29 not once but twice, the leviathan finally tossed the seas and swallowed him like Pinocchio. He knew at once it was going to be an epic jaunt. His first estimates were triple his previous record, or about two weeks, and he welcomed the possibility.

But he hadn't expected this. Nine weeks in the bubble, Noel was scared he might never come out again.

He was wealthy enough to spend the rest of his life living like a senator, but he was bored with the taking. He was mentally fried, physically exhausted, and repulsed by Las Vegas itself. The smoke, the food, the noise, the lights and the never-ending parade of debauchery and delusion. He was surrounded by people and he had never felt lonelier. Living on room service and sleeping in anonymous beds, sneaking from hotel to hotel, he longed for peace, quiet, security, a home. But he could not leave like this, transparent as air. He didn't want to squander his best chance at a secure future by blowing town in a stolen car, losing it all in a hot pursuit across the Mojave. He needed to wind down, get away from the resorts and clear his mind so that when he was restored he would have a plan in place.

Which is why at the eight-week mark he stopped stealing so much as a pillow chocolate. Not to atone with karma, for he knew that if karma existed he was quite screwed for life. He stopped because he had enough and needed to consolidate his resources. He spent three days rounding up his money from the various employee locker bays, storage units and patched-up walls inside the guest house, relocating everything to the hole in the sand out beside the saguaro. He didn't like being at the guest house, knowing what mind-altering, self-inflicting nightmare visions awaited him in the main house. But like those in the casino, they'd not shown themselves again, as if the horror had been ventilated through the psychic mine-shaft he had dug for them. Still, he knew he was pushing his luck by even remaining in the city, in the state where he had committed so much larceny.

He kept off the Strip, touring pawn shops until he found one with an open cabinet and sleepy clerk, then stole a gun and a box of shells. He slept for sixteen hours, the filed down .38 under his pillow.

He took long hot baths and debated calling Julie. Things were very different now. He was no longer Noel the minimum-wage bum and basket

317

of anxiety. He was a man with resources. But he couldn't sell her on the new life he planned to offer her over the phone. He had to see her in person, and to do that he needed to be whole again. She'd accepted him this way once before, of course, but the past four years had changed all that. She'd run away from his problems, from him, and if she wasn't half insane by now, he needed to approach her in the sober light of his own body and earn back some trust before announcing he happened to be filthy rich.

Week eight in the void turned to week nine, and he grew restless. He was drowning in memories of her, the good times and bad, but he clung to the good. He remembered a night they had spent together at Caesars, not long after their arrival, when the future had seemed so bright. They'd had some minor luck gambling, but were not yet consumed by the promise of more more more.

They decided to take a night off from gaming and enjoyed a simple but romantic dinner at, of all places, In N Out Burger. The renowned fast-food chain was a few blocks off the Strip, and with the line of more than a dozen cars at the drive-thru it had cost them a $30 cab ride on top of the eighteen bucks spent on Double-Doubles, fries and shakes. Almost $50 for a fast-food dinner. But feeding each other their wrapped burgers with grilled onions and dripping cheese in the back of the cab, he'd never felt so at home with her, humbled by her acceptance of him. That they could have fun on a date like this, that this was enough, that he was enough, just him, no superpowers or fortunes — it was his only memory of true happiness since they'd left Boulder.

They'd finished their burgers and shakes in their room, watched an hour of TV, cuddling on the bed but too lethargic for sex, and then headed down to one of the quieter lounges for a beer or two. Noel couldn't remember the name of the bar, or if it even had one, but he recalled sitting there with Julie, watching the people stroll by, making up false histories for the strangers, laughing, studying people.

After an hour or two she wanted to go back to their room and sleep. They'd turned around to pay their bill and Julie fell into a trance, staring at something behind the bar with an intense longing he'd never seen on her before. He followed her gaze.

Sitting on a small glass shelf raised above the cash register was a set of what he first mistook as figurines but were actually toys. Little plastic action figures with a safari or circus theme, arranged as if on display in a toy store window. Julie explained that they were the Adventure People; she'd gotten the same set for Christmas when she was eight or nine. There was a bearded man in macho boots and zookeeper shirt. On the other end was a woman, a fierce gal with cute legs and khaki shorts, a bandana tied at her throat, her hair tied back in a ponytail, a toy whip raised in her plastic fist. Between them was a caravan — cage-like train cars on rubber wheels, a real canvas pop-up tent where the couple slept, and of course an assortment of wild animals they kept and, presumably, trained for the circus or whatever traveling show they put on around the world. A pair of lions, a tiger, a gorilla, a bear, chimp, alligator and so forth.

'That's who I wanted to be,' Julie said, eyes glinting. 'When I grew up, I was going to be that woman, strong and adventurous and free, taking care of all those wild animals, living with a handsome man in a little red tent. We'd go to Africa and Asia and South America, meeting new animals and dazzling crowds everywhere with our amazing shows. Look how strong she is, standing there with her whip. She's not afraid of anything and even the lions love her. Doesn't she look happy?'

'Yes.'

She didn't speak for a long time, only stared at the Adventure People.

'We could still do that,' Noel told her. 'If that's what you want, I'll live in a tent with you. We can travel, go on safari, buy some tiger cubs and a zebra, all of it.'

'No, it wouldn't be the same,' Julie said. 'Look at them. This isn't a vacation for them. This is their life. They are fearless and this is what they do.'

When the bartender came back with their tab, Noel asked him why there happened to be a set of twenty-year-old safari toys sitting in a place normally reserved for old photos of Frank Sinatra and Dean Martin. The bartender said he didn't know the whole story, but it involved a vintage toy collector who'd come through the casino one night. The toy collector, an old man with a drinking problem, had run some con and tried to skip out on a tab, but the manager busted his ass and started to lead him off to security. The old man had pleaded for mercy and offered some toys in lieu of payment, promising they would be worth a lot someday. The manager, who was a nut for model cars and boats and dolls, had taken pity and set the old booze hound free, and now there was a set of Adventure People sitting behind the bar, collecting dust until the manager decided enough time had passed for them to be worth real money.

Noel had promptly stood and counted everything in his wallet. 'I'll give you three hundred and six dollars for the whole set.'

'Sorry,' the bartender demurred. 'The manager's holding out for a couple grand.'

Noel was incredulous. 'Some old man toy collector drank two thousand dollars' worth of booze?'

'No, but the manager's gotten attached to the little guys. Especially that dude with the beard. Don't ask me why. He's a weirdo. Likes to go home and make sculptures out of melted Barbie dolls.'

'I want to talk to him,' Noel said. 'Call him at home.'

'Forget it,' Julie said, leading him away. 'That's crazy. We're not spending two thousand dollars on some old toys.'

'I'm getting you those Adventure People,' Noel promised her. 'Soon as we strike it big, I'm coming back.'

'Aw, Noel.'

But he never did. In the heady rush of their rise and fall, he'd forgotten about Julie's Adventure People. Now he wondered if they were still there. Probably not. Probably the hotel had remodeled and the entire bar was gone, replaced by one of those ridiculous slushy machine places, where waitresses in halter tops served thirty-two-ounce blue and orange frozen margarita and hurricane concoctions that poured out of transparent volcanoes and came with a glow-in-the-dark straw.

But damned if he wasn't going to find out. If the set was there, he'd steal the Adventure People for her, or leave two grand on the register with a thank-you note. Either way, it would make a nice gift, one he hoped would convey all the right things about their future. We can go anywhere and do anything, baby. We can be whoever we want. All we need is a tent and each other.

That, and maybe a couple of lions to guard the $6.3 million I stole for you.

* * *

He woke early on a warm May morning and set out for the Strip one final time. He made it to the hotel's main entrance and paused in the lobby to read the signs. Funny, he'd spent so much time here and couldn't remember behind which bar Julie's souvenir was kept. It had been set deep in the Palace, tucked back somewhere between the sportsbook and the newer mall that

322

led to the Forum Shops. The kind of place you could walk by three times and never even notice.

Noel veered right, into the casino, past the noodle restaurant with its large tanks of bright orange goldfish. Business had picked up with the warmer weather and the solids swarmed all around him. He knew there was a short cut through Cleopatra's Barge, and he followed the signs and arrows in that direction. He took his time, careful to avoid bumping into anyone. He watched the people, families and a gaggle of businessmen, a beautiful young couple sharing a waffle cone filled with pistachio gelato. Good people, average people, happy people.

Less than ten paces later Noel forgot about Julie's Adventure People.

It was amazing to look back, once it had all gone down, just how remote the odds were. Astronomical, really, and heart-stopping to behold. That the two of them should ever cross paths, that the two of them should be able to see each other at all.

A middle-aged man whose tweed sport coat, wavy brown beard and slightly befuddled demeanor suggested something along the lines of a dealer in antiques or a professor of philosophy. He was alone when he vanished under the sign for the sunglasses store. Two minutes later, donning a new pair of white Oakley shades with fire-orange iridescent lenses, he re-manifested just three doors down, on the other side of the walkway near the coffee and dessert bar, where he took out his wallet and paid for a crêpe smothered in blueberries.

Following, heart jackhammering, Noel did not believe what he had seen. He must have imagined it. He trailed cautiously as the man took a bite of his crêpe, wiped compote from his beard and stepped into one of the Palace Tower's eight elevators.

Inside, just before he vanished for the second time in less than five minutes, the professor faced the open elevator doors, raised his obnoxious white sunglasses, and *winked* at him, mouthing three words that shattered almost every illusion Noel had come to hold about his condition and his very place in the world.

I see you.

There was another and, whoever he was, his veiling was an instrument of his will.

29

When the stranger vanished, the white sunglass frames with their fire-orange lenses fell down to his invisible nose and hung suspended 'in the air' for an extra second or two, then they, too, were absorbed into the man's bubble, and the elevator doors began to close. Dumbstruck, Noel lunged but did not arrive in time to get his hand between the rubber safety bumpers.

A hand. My own hand.

Noel saw it reach out and slap the elevator's brushed aluminum fascia. He looked down. His arm, his legs, clothes, shoes, bridge of his nose, a lock of hair dangling near the corner of his eye. Everything, him. Just like that, his ten-week spell was over and he was back amongst the solids.

Why? How? Had the stranger done something to him? Surely it wasn't a coincidence. For a crazy moment Noel wondered if the man had stolen the thing from him, as if there were but one bubble for all mankind and somehow the oddball had usurped the power with a passing glance. No matter. It was just one more thing he needed to ask the guy about *everything*. His world had been rocked. Something huge was happening here and his mind was reeling.

Noel stabbed at the buttons in vain; the elevator was already rising. He watched the row of floor numbers above, each glowing as the elevator ascended. There was no way to guess which floor the man would exit onto, of course, but when the number 13 glowed orange and stayed there for at least thirty seconds, Noel couldn't stand it any longer and took the next available elevator, pressing 13 as he stepped on.

He had the cage to himself but at the last moment someone yelled, 'Hold it, hold it!' and loped in, jostling the doors back open. Noel cursed under his breath as a father with curly black hair and his wife and two daughters trundled aboard with a mass of shopping bags. He had been gone so long, he wasn't used to people seeing him and his instincts for self-preservation drove him back into the corner. The possibility of attention left him ill at ease, reminding him that he was now visible not just to people but to the eyes in the sky, to the Caesars Palace security team. Suddenly being here did not seem like a good idea. He should be leaving town, now, taking his money and getting as far away from Vegas as possible.

The family paid him no mind. At the sixth floor they exited and mercifully no one else stepped on, which would only mean more stops, more time for the stranger (Noel kept thinking of him as the professor, even though he had no idea if the schlub was one) to get away.

Noel jabbed 13 again. 'Come on, come on.'

The elevator lifted. Dinged. He hopped off, eyes already surveying every corner, every hall. He took a right and walked fast, looking over his shoulder every few seconds. The odds of finding the professor were not good even if the man were roaming in a solid state, and they dropped to nil if he didn't want to be seen or had already shut himself in one of the hundreds of rooms.

Noel hit a dead-end hall and reversed course. His mind was racing, alternately joyous and dying of curiosity for having spotted another like him, going in and out at moments of his choosing. That couldn't be, could it? But how else to explain the timing, the casual theft of the sunglasses, that knowing wink? And to top it all off, the man had somehow allowed the sunglasses to linger, a clever magic trick that said, *Look what I can do*.

Who was he? Where did he come from? What did he know about it and what could Noel learn from him? The prospect of answers to the questions that Noel had been wrestling with his entire life made it difficult to keep from running down the halls, pounding every door, shouting for the man to come back, reveal himself.

He passed a sign which read USE STAIRS IN CASE OF AN EMERGENCY and his heart sank. What if the man had taken the stairs? But then, why would he? If he wanted to hide, he could hide anywhere. If he wanted to be seen, he would have —

Wait. At first the man's casual blink in and out had seemed a random thing, or a trick to help him steal the sunglasses (sunglasses which looked flatly ridiculous on a middle-aged fellow in a tweed coat and cushioned loafers). Noel realized now the whole thing had been staged for his benefit. The man had showed himself to Noel on purpose.

He found me when I was bubbled-up, so

327

obviously he knows what I am. What if he knows who I am? How long has he been watching me? What if he had a front-row seat to half the things I've done? To all of it?

Which raised the most troubling question — how had he seen Noel to begin with? It had happened so fast, Noel had almost forgotten he himself was invisible. Was it possible the man had the ability to see what the rest of the solids could not? What kind of power was the professor wired into?

He was sweating now, racing up and down the halls. He took another elevator to the twelfth floor and checked every hall. He did the same with the eleventh. This was crazy. He could do this all day and night and get nowhere.

Calm down, you idiot. Use your head. Pick a spot and wait.

The stranger had gone up to one of the floors in this tower, the Palace Tower. Logic mandated he had to come back down. At some point he would want food, drink, a game, a girl, whatever he was into here. Noel didn't like the idea of standing in the hall or parking his ass at one of the bars or restaurants for what could be hours or days, but he had to find this guy. The information such a creature might provide could prove far more valuable than the millions Noel had buried in the desert.

Noel rode another elevator down to the lobby. He needed to find a perch as close to the source as possible. The bell dinged and the doors opened. Noel took his first step and a warm breath of faintly sour milk passed before him.

'Giving up so soon?' The low, playful voice was already moving away.

Noel flinched, then froze up. The stranger had been in the elevator with him on the way down. The doors began to close and Noel jumped off.

'Hey! Get back here!' he called.

Into the thoroughfare, looking both ways. To the right was a narrower hall of shops, to the left were the restaurants and the widening mouth of the main casino floor. He started toward the narrower passage but glanced back once more, just in time to see the professor walking backwards, solid-state, shaking his head with condescending disappointment. Incredibly, a group of young guys in various basketball jerseys over their white tees and baggy jeans passed the professor as he vanished again, and none slowed or gave the expected double-take.

Shit. Noel darted back toward the casino, weaving between tourists and a security guy in a black and gold windbreaker. He made it as far as the noodle restaurant with the high tanks of goldfish when the voice came from behind him and to the right.

'Why always in such a hurry?'

Noel turned and the professor was nowhere to be seen, but seconds later a short woman with a cropped black hair and a black paper ALDO shopping bag in one hand yelped, turning to swat whatever had just pinched her butt.

Noel walked toward her and twenty or thirty paces beyond her the professor left another breadcrumb for him, this time in the form of a cocktail glass filled with ice. One second it was sitting at the edge of the banister wrapping around a bank of oversized slots, the next it was soaring, drumming the carpet with ice cubes. One or two people saw it land but no one seemed to question who was responsible. Thus did the professor create a trail for him to follow through the winding circle of casino rooms, daring in his disruptions, flagrant in his offenses, keeping far enough ahead and weaving side to side so that Noel could track him without ever coming within arm's reach.

In one aisle of cheapie slots, a silver fox griped 'Hey, now!' as her plastic bucket of nickels crashed to the floor. On the rear perimeter of the sportsbook, a padded armchair fell on its back. One, two, three, four glass ashtrays were flipped like coins. The sound of a large bell being rung sounded to Noel's left and he turned in time to see the life-sized statue of Joe Louis wobbling on its foundation. On and on, deeper into the bowels of the resort the professor led him, taunting and teasing.

Noel shouted, 'You proved your point! Talk to me!'

And soon after, the breadcrumb disruptions tapered off. Noel reached the entrance to the Forum Shops and the trail had gone cold. But he was sure the stranger wouldn't leave him. This was a game to him. He wanted something, must be enjoying this. Even if he knew more about the trait that bound them and had known others who were hostage to it, he must have been at least a little intrigued by a new player in his midst. The professor wouldn't give up now, but, if he really didn't want to be seen or talked to, chasing him was a waste of time. Either way, Noel wasn't going to let the man jerk him around all day.

With that, he turned and headed back through the casino, toward the front desk, into a deli where he purchased an iced tea. He sat on a stool in front of a video gaming pod shaped like a spacecraft and sipped his drink, trying to appear bored. Twenty-five minutes later there was no sign of the professor or his mischief.

Okay, you win. I'm leaving. I can't leave the money out in the desert, not with you running around, watching my every move the way you probably have been for days, weeks . . . I want answers, but not if they cost six million.

Noel tossed his tea and went through the main lobby, through the revolving doors, past the cab line and down the wide sidewalk toward the main drag. He'd almost reached Las Vegas Boulevard when a sedan yellow cab sidled up to the curb and kept pace with him.

'You can't even find the light switch, can you?' the same low voice said, this time without the playfulness. Noel turned to see the frumpy solid-state professor staring at him from the back seat. 'I was trying to find out what you've learned to do with yours. The answer, obviously, is nothing.'

Noel cast a nervous glance at the driver, a man of indeterminate age with skanky rat's tail of hair looped down to his shoulder, bobbing his head despite there being no radio on or music playing in the vicinity.

'Don't worry,' the professor said. 'These guys see more imaginary people and hear more voices than you and I put together, but I'll restrain myself.'

Noel smirked.

'Hop in. I'll take you to my place and show you my collection.' The door opened and the professor scooted back to make room.

Noel shook his head. 'Aren't you supposed to offer me some candy first?'

'God, you're wound tight. That was a joke.' The professor rolled his eyes. 'I'm hungry. Let's get some lunch and swap war stories.'

'Did you do something to me? Back in there, when I snapped back?'

The professor smiled. 'Well, that's something we can talk about. But not here.'

There is always a choice in life. Give him your phone number, accept the job offer, get in the vehicle with the complete stranger. But there wasn't a choice this time. Not for Noel. He had to know what this man knew, consequences be damned.

Noel got in the cab and shut the door.

'To Pink's,' the professor told the driver, and the car jerked away from the curb. He turned to Noel and offered a small, dry hand. 'Theodore Dalton. Good to finally meet you, Noel.'

'Where'd you get my name?'

'Please. I'm surprised you're still here. If I were you, I'd have socked away my winnings and skipped town a long, long time ago.'

Noel had lost the capacity for speech. The bastard knew it all.

The professor slapped him on the shoulder. 'Loosen up, my friend. I'm not going to turn you in. I want to help. We have so much in common we might as well be brothers.'

This sentiment turned out to be true in many ways. In others, not at all.

30

Theodore Dalton was one of those men who, after a particularly satisfying bite of his meal, made little wiggling motions of childlike pleasure with his fingers. He chewed with his mouth open. Bits of whatever he was shoving into his face tumbled down the bib of his shirt. He emptied entire napkin canisters, littering the table with a new one after each wipe, and smacked his lips at every sip of soda. All of this was bad enough on its own but was made worse by the fact that his lunch of choice was two chili dogs with cheese and onions and a large Diet Pepsi, the straw of which he offered to Noel as if they were on a date.

Noel looked at the straw. 'Thank you, no.'

'You hardly touched your food. Such a waste. These are the best hot dogs in the world.' Now that their game of cloak and dagger had concluded, Dalton was not lively company. Though he had the vocabulary of an adult, something in him seemed to have been stunted at age thirteen.

'I don't have much of an appetite.' Noel looked around the restaurant Dalton had chosen for their meeting, Pink's Hot Dogs, near the entrance to the Miracle Mile Shops attached to the Paris resort. It was a busy spot — with foot traffic on the open mall side and a crowd of Pink's true believers inside — but the public meeting place did not put Noel at ease. He couldn't shake the feeling that someone was watching them. He didn't believe Dalton when he said he was 'a former elementary school teacher and pastor, lifelong bachelor, presently unaffiliated with any company, group, or branded sect of society. I have hobbies and interests and I am not out to partner up with my fellow man, I am merely a lone wolf.' Noel had no reason to trust Dalton. He could be anything. A government asset. A member of a cult. The aging pervert who finds himself lacking the vigor to play out his designs and seeks a surrogate.

'Oh, but you do have quite the appetite,' Dalton countered. 'You've been gorging for weeks. What *do* you intend to do with all that money?'

'Retire. How did you find me?'

'You cleaned my room.'

'Excuse me?'

'I spotted you a couple years ago. I come to Las Vegas for a few months every winter. I'm from Wisconsin originally, but with every passing year the cold becomes more intolerable. You used to work at Caesars. You were changing the linens as I was checking out. I stuck around for another day or two hoping to see you turn more than a hotel room, but you didn't. I figured you'd give yourself a promotion sooner or later. Vegas has a little something for everyone like us, ha!'

'But how did you know?' Noel leaned forward, lowering his voice. 'Two years ago I wasn't in the bubble.'

Dalton licked his thumb. 'The bubble? I never thought of it that way. More of a net. Better yet, an eraser at the end of a very long pencil. Sometimes a great big ol' handful of them.'

Noel was not interested in metaphors. 'You didn't answer the question.'

Dalton met his gaze. 'I can feel it. You learn to see it in their eyes.'

'There are more like us?'

'Of course. Just like there are more with seven toes, psychic hotlines in their foreheads, blue skin disorder like that family in Kentucky.'

'How many do you know about?'

'Not many, but more than you might think. There are probably forty or fifty currently practicing in the States, maybe a hundred times that who haven't tapped it yet and probably never will. Are you telling me I'm the first you've met?'

Noel's silence was answer enough.

Dalton sighed. 'How old are you?'

'Twenty-four.'

'But it feels like fifty. Living with this, it ages you, kid. Some days I feel like a cat stuck on my eighth life. You need a hobby, something to keep you vital.'

Noel scoffed. 'Because I have so much time on my hands.'

'What *have* you been doing all this time? You really haven't figured it out?'

Noel threw up his hands. 'Who am I supposed to ask? A doctor? Mine didn't come with the owner's manual.'

'When did you break your cherry?'

Noel was starting to feel interrogated, when he wanted to be the one asking the questions. 'My mom used to talk about it. Things that happened when I was a toddler, when I was nursing. I really don't know.'

Dalton regarded Noel with his bizarrely childlike curiosity once again. His pupils were different sizes — one normal, the other consuming all but the thinnest margin of its bordering green iris — and Noel thought the man was either ill with something or had a glass eye, though he wouldn't have been able to say which was real. The gaze was unsettling and Noel looked away.

'It's a lonely life,' Dalton said. 'Do you have anyone? Family? Friends? Someone you can trust?'

The truth was no, but that would sound pathetic. 'When I need them.'

Dalton took this with skepticism, pursing his lips around the straw until the soft drink gurgled on empty. 'I used to be just like you. Wandering around the country, looking for something to do, somewhere to call home. But eventually I learned how to fill the void.'

'I'm not looking for anything except answers,' Noel said.

Dalton seemed not to have heard him. He was in a minor reverie. 'That's what the weaker ones are for, of course. To pass the time, keep us company.'

'Weaker ones.'

Dalton smiled. 'I envy you, I really do. So much of the discovery ahead of you. All the things you have left to do, to learn. There is nothing like the flowering.'

Noel shifted in his chair.

'Waking up to the possibilities,' Dalton added. 'For you, right now it's money, but I think you will find that a passing charm. There is so much more to life than money. The things we acquire, they become us. Which is why it's so important to choose carefully.'

All of this airy discussion was frustrating Noel, and making him a little queasy.

'Look, Mr Dalton — '

'Theo, please.'

'Theo. I need to know what it is. If I don't get a handle on that, I'll never — '

'No,' Dalton said. 'You don't *need* to know what it is. That part is easy and you're probably on the cusp of it. You *want* that very badly, I can see. But what you *need* to know is who you are, what to do with yourself. Isn't that the eternal question for all of us? For them?' He gestured at the other patrons, the people entering and exiting the mall. 'What is my purpose in life? What is my place in the world? The fading means nothing without that. In this regard we are no different than them.'

'Okay, I get that,' Noel said. 'But can't you just tell me — '

'It's a gift,' Dalton cut him off, turning pious. 'The greatest gift in the world. One that must be put to exceptional use or not used at all.'

Now they were getting somewhere. 'Turning it on and off, can you show me how to do that?'

'I can.' Dalton squinted. 'But the question

— and it's a serious one, I'm not being coy for the sake of entertainment — is why should I?'

Noel stared at the former teacher, this rumpled boy-man in his thready tweed jacket. 'I can pay you. I have a lot — '

'Money I have no use for.'

'What do you want, then? Why wouldn't you tell me? If you've lived with this for half as long as I have, then you have to know how badly . . . I mean, come on.'

'But can I trust you? Because the things you can do with it, we're talking about power now.' Dalton's eyes blazed with an appetite that had not been sated by the two chili dogs. 'This is not a power of the sort you see thrown around by politicians, bankers, randy athletes with eleven children and their own brand of sneaker. This is a power only the gods once knew. And I don't know if you're ready for that. I think — yes, I think it would be better if you proved to me first that you are up to the task. The mission. Or maybe it's a calling, I don't know. But it is a matter of a higher purpose and dedication counts. It counts for so very much.'

'What do you want me to do?'

Dalton grinned in the manner of a prisoner who's finally found the leverage he needs to dominate his whimpering new cell mate. 'This is sensitive stuff. There are things, things I haven't shared with anyone. I see signs of worthiness in you, but this isn't a clubhouse, you understand? There are no rules and some people can't handle that. Some people need boundaries, discipline, religion. They come unhinged without it. Others need to be set free.'

'I understand,' Noel said, struggling to maintain his patience. 'What am I going to do? Call the FBI? I'm like you. I don't want attention. I just want some answers.'

'So you keep saying. But the mentor-disciple relationship is a very delicate thing. The knowledge I pass on to you, it's part of me. You ask me to help you manage your condition, you're asking me to share something that is sacred. How do I know you won't hop on an airplane and do some real damage? Topple some head of state, igniting another sand war? For that matter, how do I know you won't use it against me?'

'I won't. Why would I? You know enough about me, if you've been following me. You could call the police and I'd be just as screwed.'

'Pffft.' Dalton waved a hand. 'You act like this stealing business is something of consequence. What if you find yourself up against the wall and you are forced to make a sacrifice? Do you have the mettle to do whatever it takes to protect yourself, to protect the secret at all costs?'

Noel tried to make sense of such questions. 'All I know is, I want to live a normal life. I'm prepared to — '

'Wrong. See, that's your first mistake. There is no normal life, not in this. You should have learned that much by now. This thing of ours, it runs on your emotions. If you run around hot and agitated and crying every time someone gets hurt or gets in your way, it will rule you. Cold. Absolute zero. That is what you want to achieve.

That is the only way to make it work for you. It must be governed with the remorselessness of a hangman.'

Runs on your emotions. 'Are you telling me this comes from us? From something inside us?'

Dalton giggled. 'Where else could it come from? Outer space? Do you own a special suit? I don't. How do you think I was able to see you when no one else could? It's the mind, my young friend. Mine happens to be stronger than yours.'

Noel's thoughts were spinning off in ten directions. 'Wait, wait . . . '

Dalton continued, 'All this time you've been in Las Vegas waiting for it to come back. Did it never occur to you maybe it was here all along? Well, don't beat yourself up. Maybe you just weren't strong enough. All these people coming and going, everywhere you turn, it's no wonder. But you're still growing, I can see that. You've survived this long and that's no small feat. Someday you'll be able to walk on the field during Game Seven of the World Series and wipe out the entire fan base just before the winning pitch. Imagine what kind of curtain that's going to take. Fifty thousand people, blinded. Now that would be something, though of course the viewers at home wouldn't be affected — my point is, you're not ready. And until I know I can trust you won't lose control of your bladder when the, ah, let us say the authorities come down on you, why should I give you the keys to the big machine?'

Curtain. Machine. Earlier he'd said something about an eraser at the end of a pencil. Now he was talking about emotions, blinding people. Noel thought about his mother's weak mind. His father's strong one. A few kids on the playground, then Julie, then half a dozen people inside a jewelry store. Gestation, pressure, the casino floor. Something clicked inside of Noel, lighting him up with epiphany.

'We don't disappear.'

Dalton raised his eyebrows but said nothing.

'We don't go anywhere, or change at all,' Noel said. 'It's them. The witnesses, observers, whoever they are. My mother. I did it to her first because I could, because I was closest to her, and maybe . . . she was weaker, afraid of losing me. Then some kids on the playground when I was angry, scared. When I was a teenager it ran out of control like a hormonal rage. That's it, isn't it? We don't vanish. We blind them.'

Dalton winced. 'Eh, 'blind' is a wee bit of hyperbole. They don't lose their vision.'

'No, no, not everything,' Noel said. 'Just us, to us. We make them blind to us. Holy shit! This explains so much. The reason it works on our clothes, stuff in our pockets. That's us, we see that as part of us, right? But it has to make sense, or, or, no, it's like we have to *believe* it. We can't take something with us unless we know we can take it with us! We have to factor that in and *assume* — '

'Calm down. If you learn how to get a grip on this, a grip on yourself, I can show you how to take a lot more than what will fit in your pockets.'

'Like what?'

342

Dalton leaned back to enjoy the fawning. 'Oh, I don't know. A pair of sunglasses, a suitcase, a car. Maybe a house in an empty neighborhood.'

Noel thought of the Funhouse, where he had found Julie. The way his time with Bryan Simms had kicked things to another level, walling him off from the party, screening death from thirty years ago by way of a haunting while all around him the furniture was hidden. He thought of Julie.

'What about people, another person?' Noel said.

Dalton grinned, nodded. 'If they don't fight it, sure. But there are limits. Remember that the observers are always compensating, whether they know it or not. Their eyes continue to see us, but somewhere behind the eyes, in the visual cortex, the portion of the brain which translates visual sensory input, our eraser swipes. The body doesn't like it when the brain does not respond to its office memos, so it works harder to relay the message, panics, sends out an SOS. The brain doesn't know what to do with that blinking red light on the dashboard, or, in our case, the vacancy in its field of vision. If we blot out too much, there can be an equal toll on the gray matter. Some of my overtaxed witnesses have reported black spots, dizzy spells, crawling bugs of negative space in the broad daylight where I was standing. Plenty have simply fainted while I worked. Or worse. I believe I gave my father a stroke when I was sixteen.'

Noel was aghast. 'How did you learn all this?'

'Experience. Once you get it under control

343

and realize you don't have to run like the Gingerbread Man every time you want to go out for a coffee and newspaper, you notice things. And I've, ah, interviewed some of my quote-unquote victims, but I fear we're getting ahead of ourselves.'

Noel rubbed his eyes and laughed with relief. 'All this time. The way people get uncomfortable around me. It's like they can feel it. And they do, because it's in me. It's so obvious. How could I not see it?'

'People are usually blind to what's sitting right in front of them,' Dalton said. 'Many of them are grateful, because who wants to look at the problem? Who wants to deal with the unpleasantness? See no evil? That's our want ad. We just push their own desires to ignore the problem. We tidy up the messy scene. I like to think of it as a sponge. A clean little sponge that I can slip beneath their skulls and smear away the stupid pictures on their television-rotted brains.'

'My God. My God.' Noel was lost in a string of memories. Seeing himself change so many times over the years, making himself vanish not *before their very eyes*, but in their minds. In the mirror, in his own mind, from himself. Hiding from his problems, then unable to do it for Julie because he wanted to be with her, not lost. But to himself? That didn't fit Dalton's explanation.

'One thing,' Noel said.

Dalton sipped more Pepsi.

'If what you're saying is true, this works on us too, on the self. When I blinded others, I blinded myself. I could not see my own face in the mirror, the clothes on my body. How do you explain that?'

Dalton parried with a sly smile. 'Are we not as others see us? Do we not construct our models of ourselves on the reactions of those closest to us, on the lingering glances of strangers passing by, on the face in the mirror? Why is it that some people see a green shirt and call it blue? A blue shirt green? We call this colorblindness, but all it really implies is that reality is not fixed, is not ultimate, is nothing more than the collective perceptions of a family, a society. There was a time when automobiles didn't exist, computer chips, the Bible. A thing has to be imagined — seen by the mind — before it can be born. Whatever is in us that allows us to do what we do, it must be wired into the imagination, literally where things, including the self, are imagined so that they may become real. Or, in our case, real but invisible.'

Noel laughed. 'You know something crazy? I think I can feel it. Just knowing all this makes it feel more . . . accessible. Is that possible?'

'Confidence matters. You see this in the arts. With musicians, painters, writers, and in sports, where winning breeds winning. A man who believes he has control of his talents is much more likely to execute his passions. Doubt is the killer. Hesitation doesn't keep twenty spinning plates from crashing to the floor.'

'But is this really, what's the word? Innate? Natural?' Noel said. 'I was born this way? Or did I grow into it? How do we know it's not environmental?'

345

Dalton yawned. 'Maybe it's both. Nature and nurture. I have to believe that at some point the seed, whatever kernel of it is there to begin with, finds its reactive property for germination.'

Noel continued to nod, drinking it all in. Something big was missing, though. Something he wanted to know but was afraid to ask. It would sound crazy, but then so did everything they were discussing.

'What about the dead?' he said. 'The lost ones. Spirits.'

Dalton became very still. 'What about them?'

Noel took a deep breath. 'They appear before or during for me. Do you see them? When you are in the bub — when you are, whatever you called it, faded? Do you see the dead?'

Dalton seemed to melt in his seat a little. 'Noel, I do. I see them.'

'I thought I was losing my mind.'

'Yes, I get headaches.'

'It's fucked up, isn't it?' Noel said, wound up and glancing around in all directions as if vengeful spirits would at any moment spew forth from the stores and Dalton would show him the trick to vanquish them. 'I didn't know what they were, not for a long time. I saw them when I was a kid. I thought they were my imaginary friends. People from TV. Actually, one was.'

Dalton chuckled. 'Oh, yes. Just like on TV. They aren't really human, are they? Another trick of the mind. It's easier to see them that way.'

'My scratches,' Noel said, turning his arm over to reveal a faint pink welt. 'Ten weeks ago I

346

looked like a cat's scratching post. They did this to me. Or maybe they made me do it.'

''They made me do it.'' Dalton repeated, his eyes full of wonder. Admiration. 'My, you are a special one, aren't you? They want to be released. They sense we have the power to set them free.'

'That is exactly what it feels like,' Noel said. 'I hate them.'

'I'm just amazed . . . it's incredible that you understand all this, Noel. I might have underestimated you.'

Noel did not understand why this seemed to please Theo so much, but he was relieved there was one more thing that was not his burden alone.

Dalton stood abruptly, excitedly patting his pockets, sat back down. He looked at his watch and removed a pen and a small spiral notebook from his jacket's inner pocket. He jotted something with a flourish, tore a slip from his pad and handed it over as he rose once more.

'Where are you going?' Noel said.

'Stop by that address this evening, around six or seven.'

Noel was unable to mask his disappointment. 'Is this your house?'

'One of them.'

'But — '

'All this talk,' Dalton said with a wink. 'It's easier if I show you.'

Noel sat a while and wondered what else there was to see.

31

If Dalton was a slob in public, he became fastidiously composed at home. After a light dinner of curry skewers he'd grilled with a small kettle on his ninth floor terrace, served with a dry white wine and a large salad rich with avocados, the professor was at the sink, his blue striped shirt cuffs folded crisply to the elbows, washing dishes with nary a splash. Noel remained at the small but elegant dining table set beyond the alcove holding a plaster statue, a copy of something he'd seen in a book before: the woman with no arms or legs, reduced to a turning bust with a wreath at her curls, flat white eyes undefined, cast downward as if in modesty or shame.

The rest of the condominium, one of several Dalton 'kept around the country' for when he tired of hotels and 'felt the need to repair to a habitat of my own making', had been appointed with thick brown drapes and white crown molding above the fibrous beige wallpaper. The place was tidy, the furnishings spare but soft, with lots of extra throw pillows and folded blankets tossed around the armchairs and small sofas. Track lighting beamed warm cones of light into all the right spaces without becoming intrusive. A tower shelf had been stocked with oversized art books and a few small, meticulously tended plants, and a discreet Bose system that suffused the apartment with classical music.

Noel had to admit he had been expecting something weird and dismal out in the desert, the kind of place where one expected to find abandoned cars in the front yard, a dungeon basement outfitted with shackles, chains and glory holes. So he was relieved when the taxi driver took one look at the address and delivered him just five blocks west of the Strip, to this clean white stone and black glass plaza among commuter traffic, amid grocery stores and what appeared to be mild-mannered business executives and well-dressed young couples with nice hair and normal lives.

'Put it in real estate,' Dalton said at the sink, pausing to sip more wine between soap bubbles. They had been discussing money, how to maintain an income between fades, during the ups and downs of the lifestyle. 'Tangible assets, preferably of the sort that can be lived in or rented. Hire a property manager. I get rent checks in the mail every week, at half a dozen PO boxes. Oh, you need those too. Use the little strip mall kind, the ones that provide other services. They can forward your mail, fax you things, run a new passport photo. Quite handy.'

'Good advice,' Noel said. He raised his wine glass, sniffed it for the third time, and set it back down. He didn't care much for wine. He was growing restless again. In addition to finances, they'd talked about Colorado, Noel's parents, Dalton's short-lived marriage to a woman in Tacoma, Washington (it ended when she came home to find him singing in the shower and peeked around the curtain to discover there was no 'there' to Theodore Dalton). Dalton had talked of his travels through Europe and even threatened to haul out the slide projector, but so far they'd discussed nothing more of the strange talent they had in common. How to manipulate it, turn it on and off.

Dalton paused in his humming. 'More wine?'

'I'm good,' Noel said. 'Mind if I use your bathroom?'

Dalton turned and appraised him, wiping his hands with a waffle-textured towel tucked into his tubby waistline. 'Second door down the hall.'

'Thanks.'

Noel headed through the living room, past the small foyer, down the hall floor of what looked like lacquered bamboo, until he came upon the second white door. He flipped the switch and shut the door behind him. He urinated briefly, but stood there over the toilet longer than was necessary. He hadn't needed to go that bad, but something about sitting in Dalton's presence made it difficult to think, to steer his own thoughts, to focus on the more serious business at hand. The condo was on some kind of climate control, but Noel had felt a chill during dinner. Echoes from another apartment that sounded too close. The subtle impression that someone else was watching them, or listening to them, or maybe had left the condo just minutes before Dalton opened the door with a smile and declared, 'You found it. Welcome to *Chez Dalton!*' in a terrible French accent.

Yes, something was a little off here, but Noel

couldn't figure out what.

Maybe it was simply the man himself. Dalton was . . . odd.

Earlier today at the hot dog stand, the professor had shifted from goofy to cryptic, controlling to enchanted. But tonight he seemed content to offer nothing more than the polite but smothering company of a lonely middle-aged man. Did Dalton really think they were going to become friends? Partners in the calling, the mission, whatever he had called it? The sense that Dalton was lonely and wanting of a . . . companion of some sort, this was stronger than ever. Noel did not know or care whether the man was gay. He only wanted to avoid implying that he was open to whatever kind of budding apprenticeship Dalton had in mind.

Noel flushed the toilet and moved to the sink to wash his hands.

No, we're not going to be friends, Noel decided. I need information. He's excited to play teacher. I'm humoring him with my company, but if he wants to keep doling out the instruction manual in tidbits, I'm skating town tonight, taking my money to California, to Julie. The hell of it was, the more time that passed without Dalton bringing it up, the harder it was for Noel to interrupt the fuddy-duddy and ask a direct question for fear of coming off rude.

Noel dabbed his hands with the towel beside the sink. On a whim, he flipped open the medicine cabinet's mirrored door. Inside were three glass shelves, stocked with an assortment of the usual over-the-counter reliefs: Aspirin,

Excedrine, Vicks Cold & Flu. A pair of nail clippers. No prescription bottles from which he might color in Dalton's mental health profile. There was one odd item, a bright blue plastic box in the shape of a horseshoe. Noel took it down, inspected the seam around it. There was weight to it, something inside.

He thumbed the latch and got a pair of dentures smiling back up at him. Not clean ones, either. These were old, the fake gums gone to a milky shade of brown in places, the white teeth slightly yellowed and dry. The antiseptic yet stale scent of their last bath found its way up into his nose and Noel closed the lid, feeling the need to rinse his hands once more. Well, Dalton was not elderly but he was no spring chicken either. He probably had a set of chompers just like these in every one of his apartments around the country, the poor gummy bastard.

When Noel came out of the bathroom, the lights seemed to have been dimmed. Outside the terrace window, which faced away from the Strip, twilight had passed and the desert was fully dark but for the speckled chain of street lamps and car lights scattered below. A piano concerto tinkled whimsically at low volume. Dalton was seated in the armchair furthest from the kitchen, slouching, his shirt cuffs loose, his eyes sunken and gazing tiredly at his nearly empty wine glass. Noel stood at the edge of the centered rug, hands on his hips, waiting for Dalton to notice him.

After what might have been half a minute or more, the professor sniffed and looked up with a weak smile. 'You don't have to linger,' he said. 'I appreciate the chance to entertain you. It's been a long time since I've had anyone over for a meal. I've missed cooking.'

'Dinner was great. This is a nice place.' Noel felt rude standing but wasn't sure if this was his cue to leave or just a turn of self-pity.

Dalton surveyed the condo, shrugging. 'It's a place, but we really don't get to make a lasting home, people like us. You try to get a foothold here and there, but . . . ' Dalton sipped his wine, the opinion either not worth finishing or obvious enough.

Noel shifted on his feet. 'It's getting late. I should be going soon.'

Dalton nodded. 'Back to California, I presume. Before somebody decides to mount up a posse in search of the invisible bandit.'

'Right. Something like that. I wanted to thank you again for everything you told me. About how it works. It's a huge relief to have some idea.'

Dalton finished his wine. 'You would have figured it all out on your own. I'm sure of that. I wish I could help you with the rest, but in this, as in all of life, we are alone. That's the real shitty of it, Noel. There isn't anyone who can die of cancer with you, not really. Visiting hours always end and eventually it's time to fade away.'

Okay, this was descending into something too maudlin for Noel to deal with right now. He tried to think of something positive to add, something uplifting, but nothing came to him and all he could think about was how to make a graceful exit.

'Listen to me go on,' Dalton said with a snort. 'Better yet, don't. You have time, my young friend. You can do whatever you like to do.'

'I think things will be easier now,' Noel said. 'Now that I have a grasp of it. I wish I knew how to practice it. Get better at using it, controlling it.'

'I wish you luck,' Dalton said. 'But I fear it controls us. Such is often the case with one's most dominant characteristics, is it not?'

Noel patted his pockets as if to search for car keys he did not own. 'I guess I'll see you around, then.'

'Maybe so.'

Noel stood there, waiting for something more from his superior, but Dalton only stared off at the ceiling. He was about to take his leave when something deeper in the apartment thumped on the floor, heavy and muffled, like a book fallen from a shelf.

Dalton cleared his throat. He looked at Noel.

Noel raised his eyebrows.

'Well, yes,' Dalton said with a sigh. 'We were speaking of the others. The side effects, our necessary visitors.'

Noel's skin began to crawl. Something was indeed happening here. Had Dalton been leading up to this?

'Right,' Noel said again, his voice cracking slightly. 'We never finished that. It sounds ridiculous now, but, well, I don't know who else to ask.'

Dalton straightened himself in the chair. 'Do you want me to help you learn how to dispatch them? These souls who continue to haunt you?'

'Actually, they haven't lately. I don't understand why, but it seems to have stopped. I haven't had to deal with them for the past ten weeks. Do you see them every time?'

'Every time?'

'Every time you're in it, or using it? With me it was just before, or during sometimes. But my episodes were spread over longer intervals. I thought maybe for you it would happened inside, like, all the time.'

Dalton's eyes widened. 'Oh, that would be exhausting. Heavens, no. Only once a month or so. More when I'm feeling strong, but it's getting harder the older I get.'

'Harder?'

'To find the right ones,' Dalton said. 'To . . . how did you put it? To release them, so they can't make you do it again? I liked that. But the hunt grows tiring. Exhausting.'

The thumping at the back of the condo came again, this time in a rapid series. *Thump-tha-thump-bump*. Dalton glanced toward the hall, then smiled at Noel.

'What was that?' Noel said.

'What could it be? Isn't this the point of our inquiry this evening?'

It's easier if I show you, the professor had said earlier today.

No, Noel thought. Not here. He can't have one here.

But then, hadn't he felt *something* off in the

355

condo all through dinner? The strange suspicion they were not alone? The feeling of being watched?

'That's not possible,' Noel said. 'You can't just plan that, right? Keep them around?'

'I can, and I do,' Dalton said. Before Noel could ask how, he added, 'Go have a look. See for yourself. It's a harmless one. I promise.'

Noel found himself stepping back, toward the front door. 'This is a joke, right? What is that in there?'

'Part of the deal, Noel. They come with the territory. If you don't learn how to tame them, to control your visions and exorcise your demons, they will rule you and then they will ruin you.'

Noel choked out a laugh. 'You're insane. I'm not going back there.'

'You will,' Dalton said. 'If you want to take control of your life. If you want to harness the power you were born with. Don't you want that? I thought you wanted that very badly.'

Noel stepped into the foyer and peered down the hall. At the end, another white door faced him. It was closed, but the light in the room behind it showed at the seam near the floor.

He turned back to Dalton. 'How does it work? What am I supposed to do?'

Dalton remained seated. 'There's no great secret about it. You stand before it and let go of your fear. Let them know who is master and who is dog. The rest will come to you.'

'The last ones I got close to scratched my face. They fucked me up, man. I think they got inside my head.'

356

'It's *all* in your head,' Dalton countered. 'That's why the power is in your hands. We are superior to them. We have nothing to fear. They can't hurt us unless we allow them to stay.'

Noel was curious, no doubt, but he didn't trust Theodore Dalton and he didn't trust himself to resist whatever it was they could do to him.

'You have to go now,' Dalton said.

'Why?'

'Because I've opened my home to you and you now share the burden.'

'If something happens to me — ' Noel began.

'I will come to your aid,' Dalton finished.

Sweating now, heart racing, Noel took several deep breaths and walked with as much confidence as he could muster to the end of the hall and, without pausing, opened the door.

32

Behind the white door was a bedroom without a bed.

A wide dark dresser stood against the far wall, adjacent to a set of windows with the shades drawn. Closer, against the nearest wall, was a smaller table with a short lamp (the source of the glow under the door and the only lighting in the room). A manila floor mat of some six by ten feet lay spread across the center of the lacquered wood floor. The space was quiet, as bare and tranquil as a Japanese tea room.

There were no bookshelves, nothing lying on the floor to explain the thumps from a minute ago. Whatever he had been expecting — and he was prepared to find just about anything — it wasn't here. He stood still a moment, waiting for the obvious sign, a voice, an apparition to ooze from the walls. Nothing happened.

He realized he had been holding his breath since entering and now almost coughed with the sudden need for air. His lips parted and he drew several deep breaths, blinking, waiting, his tension subsiding.

There was a smell, or maybe a scent. One so subtle he had not noticed it until now. Soft, faintly woody, and perhaps a bit sweet, like moist cedar decking after a rainstorm. It was a nice smell, clean and pure.

He thought of turning around and calling back

to Dalton, to call the man's bluff or inform him that his pet ghost or whatever was supposed to be waiting in here had decided to move on. But he didn't turn and he didn't speak. Something like constrictive boredom prevented him from doing anything at all. He felt tired, dulled. The possibility that Dalton would drug him had crossed his mind earlier in the evening, but he had dismissed that by now. And anyway, he hadn't had more than a courtesy sip of the wine.

This wasn't like being drugged or drunk. Noel's thoughts were lucid, if a bit slow. His body felt late in responding, but to prove nothing was wrong, he waved a hand before his own face, flexed his fingers, and everything was working fine. Emboldened, he walked a few steps deeper into the room, crossing the mat with the steady but patient gait of a real estate prospect who doesn't wish to appear too eager. He was looking toward the blinds over the window, thinking of the view from here, when the air stirred behind him and a warm draft brushed the side of his arm.

Noel pivoted, tilting off balance a moment before regaining his position. He peered from left to right, to the floor and up into the corners of the room, even though the current had shifted less than two steps from where he now stood.

Nothing had changed. The room was still empty.

Had there been a sound, too? Something like a sigh? Maybe it had been the exhale of the air-conditioning unit. Climate control.

Don't be afraid, he reminded himself. It's all

in your head, according to Dalton. Maybe if he refused to give in and be afraid of what was in here — *it was nothing, nothing was in here* — his conviction would assert its own reality to keep it this way.

Hmmm-hhhmmmeeeemmmhhh.

The whimper came from his right, a few paces in front of him. Sounded like someone breathing into a pillow, a half-moan against sealed lips.

Noel backed into the window shades, rattling them slightly, the noise making him jump. The muffled sound came again, this time with greater urgency, distress. It was human. It had reacted to his collision with the blinds, which meant it was aware of his presence in the room.

'I'm not afraid of you,' Noel said in the calmest voice he was capable of. 'You can't bother me now. I have my own hands and I'm not falling for it, okay? If you want to scratch something, go scratch yourself.'

Silence followed, lasting perhaps a minute.

Then a different sound began to fill the room, a trickling, almost drumming sound of falling beads or sand. Noel looked up at the ceiling, half expecting to find a water stain spreading and leaking through the drywall. He scanned the walls, and then the floor, and then —

The floor. A dark stain was spreading on the floor, about four feet in front of him. Colorless but for the darkening in the manila floor mat as it absorbed some type of liquid, like a water stain on carpet. The spot was blossoming, then elongating like a small river, following the lower grade of the flooring.

A new smell. This the acrid smell of urine.

'What the . . . ' Noel whispered, feeling somehow duped and primally alert.

'Therein lies your ghost,' Dalton said from the hall. 'Are you ready to set it free?'

Noel turned to see the professor standing a few feet back from the doorway. His shirt sleeves had been rolled to the elbows again and he was wearing some kind of gloves. Noel could not make them out in the dim hallway, but they were too thick to be dishwashing gloves.

'What's going on?' Noel said, edging toward the door. 'What is it?'

'Some of us think of them more as demons. But that's beside the point. Are you ready?'

'Ready for what?'

The whimpering came again, along with heavy breathing. The breaths were stifled still, plunging and sucking in quick bursts of panic.

Noel turned from Dalton to the room, back to Dalton, back to the room. He couldn't see anything yet, only the stains.

'You wanted to know if it worked on other things,' Dalton said, stepping closer to the doorway. The gloves were leather, fuzzy. Suede work gloves. 'Do you understand now? Do you see the potential?'

Noel's heart was galloping in place. His temples began to throb. He felt on the verge of unlocking something he no longer wished to unlock.

Dalton took another step. 'The ability to take away their sight is the ultimate power, Noel. If they don't see it, it doesn't exist.'

'What are you doing?' Noel said, but some part deep inside of him knew the answer already. 'This isn't a vision. This isn't what I meant.'

'We tell ourselves the things we need to in order to live with what we have done,' Dalton said. 'Behaviour adjusts attitude and belief. It's okay. He can't hurt you.'

He?

Noel stared into the empty air inside the bedroom.

'Concentrate loosely,' Dalton said. 'It's like an optical illusion. It's difficult to see, but once you see it, you won't be able to unsee it.'

Noel didn't want to see it, but he could not look away. His mind raced for an answer to Dalton's riddle — what was this? what could it be? — until he realized the answer was Dalton himself. What he was. What he could do.

They made me do it.

The hunt grows tiring. Exhausting.

Only once a month or so. More when I'm feeling strong, but it's getting harder the older I get.

Noel understood. Dalton was in command of his fade. He had the power to blind others. He had been living with this for a long time. He had developed odd tastes.

He's blinding me right now.

With that thought, the pressure in Noel's mind relented. The pain in his temples, the sluggishness of his thoughts, his heavy body, and something intangible — all unknotted itself and released him. It did so without a fight, as if this too had been planned, and the full scale of what

Dalton had done tonight sent waves of terror through him as the professor withdrew his blinding shroud as swiftly as a magician yanking a tablecloth from beneath the setting.

I once was blind but now I can see.

The young man was somewhere between his late teens and early twenties, pale skinned and well muscled, with shorn stubbly black hair. He was sleepy-eyed, only now rousing from whatever Dalton had given him to render him pliable and willing enough to follow the professor home. He was bound with black rope or rubber cord, arms at his sides, feet together, constricting him nearly everywhere to a wooden post bolted to the ceiling and through the floor mat. His white Adidas track pants were stained with piss, his bare feet wet. His eyes opened wide and lowered sleepily before widening again, and Noel knew the guy was waging some kind of war to regain full consciousness.

'Are you fucking sick?' Noel said, turning to his host in the hall. 'Let him go!'

Dalton frowned, shucked off his leather work gloves and walked to Noel, shoving the gloves into his hands. 'Hold these.'

Before Noel could respond, Dalton turned to the roped man, removed something from a front pocket Noel could not see, and, with all the fuss of a child dabbing paint onto a canvas, proceeded to poke the hostage in the stomach, once, twice, three four five, pecking here and there without hurry. His movements were so deliberate and patient, Noel didn't understand that Dalton was stabbing the man with a knife until the sixth or seventh strike, when the blood began to pour from his wounds and the man began to scream against the tape.

'Stop!' Noel shouted, lunging at Dalton.

'See that?' Dalton said, turning and jabbing the knife at Noel.

Noel stopped, the wet red blade inches from his own belly.

'See how easy it is? You never even knew he was here. I could have kept you in the dark all night. That's power.'

'What did you do?' Noel groaned, wanting to be sick. 'What did you do? Why are you doing this?'

'Because I can.' Dalton grabbed Noel by the wrist and slapped the handle of the knife into his palm. 'Now finish him.'

The man tied to the post was writhing, moaning against the gag, sweat bursting from his forehead as blood surged from nearly a dozen wounds in his belly, his chest, his pelvic region.

Later he would have time to be ashamed of his inaction, but now, in this moment, Noel felt as though he were having an out of body experience. His mouth fell slack. He stared at the knife in his hands. It was an arched flat wooden thing with a silver blade that tapered to a nasty point. A Buck knife or something similar, greasy with warm blood.

'You did it to me,' he mumbled, unable to look up, wishing he never had to look up again. 'You do this out there, to others, the witnesses, so you can take people? So you can hurt them and kill them?'

'I told you of my roots,' Dalton said.

I was once a pastor in the town of Black Earth, Wisconsin, and before that I was a dairy farmer's son. When I was nine I fell from the back of my father's tractor and cracked my skull open on a knob of fieldstone. I spent two days in a coma and did not speak for almost a year, but I survived and in my heart I know that was when the gift was handed down to me.

Noel wanted to throw the knife away in disgust, but he didn't. Couldn't.

' . . . what I didn't tell you about was the creatures.' Dalton was still talking. ' . . . all kinds of the smaller living things, how they responded to me after that. I took what I needed on the farm in order to feed it, and for my efforts it repaid me tenfold. First there were baby chicks, then two of the meanest roosters you'd ever hope to meet, and that vicious German shepherd from the Orlanski farm next door. Hogs in need of cleansing. You do what you can to resist, but eventually the fade demands a sacrifice.'

'I'm not like you,' Noel said.

Dalton inched closer to him and clutched his wrist, rolling it so that the knife blade turned before them.

He said, 'In high school there was a girl, a very dirty girl. Do you want to know her name?'

'No, I . . . '

'Shirley. Shirley Minturn. She smelled like dirty socks.'

'Stop,' Noel said, wresting his arm from Dalton's grip. 'Get the fuck away from me!'

The professor was undeterred. 'You can find

365

her in the news archives, though they never did find her. She drowned. In a river. A dirty river, but one that flowed cleaner than she did.'

Noel was having trouble breathing. His vision was spotty. Was Dalton still doing it to him, or was he merely about to faint?

'It's all right, Noel. Don't be frightened. This is something we both understand. You can trust me. We're just talking. What is it they say? What happens in Vegas stays in Vegas?'

Noel stared up at the bleeding man strapped to the post. The man was there, then not there, there again, then blurring like melting film.

'I'm not part of this.'

'Oh, Noel. I can see it in you. I can smell it like perfume.'

'I never hurt anyone,' Noel said, his breath escaping in one long shudder. *The policeman in the snow* . . . 'Not like that. I never — '

'You're lying.' Dalton's tongue waved across his upper lip. 'But you're a good boy. You fought it, but what's the use when it's so easy for us? Your first was clumsy. Perhaps you told yourself it was an accident. It is not an easy task to complete, but I can show you how to make it the easiest thing in the world. Like flicking the heads from dandelion stems.'

Hop in, Dalton had said from the back of the cab. *I'll take you to my place and show you my collection.*

'Get out,' Noel said.

Dalton smiled.

He's not just some fuddy-duddy professor, a very rational and strangely calm part of Noel's

366

mind asserted now. *He's a serial killer. An honest to fucking God serial killer. This is what he's chosen to do with his fading. Or maybe he was always going to be one, and one year his Christmas stocking came packed with an extra special gift to make it easier.*

'Get out!' Noel screamed, and threatened Dalton with the knife.

Dalton retreated, giggling, and began to circle the room. He ducked behind his bound and bleeding victim, then popped up on the other side.

'Calm down, Noel. You're going to get hurt.'

'Get the fuck out!' Noel shrieked, and ran for Dalton.

The professor darted to toward the door and Noel brought the knife down in the back of his shoulder, stubbing the blade into bone before withdrawing it. Dalton released a high-pitched squeal and ran into the hall. Noel followed for several steps, but when Dalton slammed the bathroom door behind him, he stopped.

He returned to the bedroom and found the roped hostage no longer struggling. His head was hanging low, chin against chest. Noel put a hand against the stained shirt to feel for a heartbeat. At first there wasn't one, then something, but it was faint.

Noel began to saw at the ropes. When he'd cut through two strands, he was able to pull the rest away and the guy crumpled before Noel had time to toss the knife and catch him. He kneeled, rolling the man to his back. What was he supposed to do? He didn't know how to perform

CPR. There were too many wounds. The man was bleeding to death. He needed to call for an ambulance.

He got to his feet and ran into the hall.

Dalton emerged from the bathroom and stopped, blocking the exit.

Noel raised the knife.

'That's your choice?' Dalton said. 'Are you sure? Think very carefully, now. Because there's no coming back from this one.'

'Get out of my way, you fucking psycho, or I will take you down.'

The professor hesitated. Considered. Something was twisting behind Dalton's face, anguish and fear and whatever demons lurked in his soul.

'Don't be like this,' he said at last. 'We can be friends. We have to be friends. We need each other, don't you see that?'

Noel stepped forward and jabbed the knife at Dalton. 'I'm calling nine-one-one. You're fucked.'

Dalton backed away, his face changing as swiftly as a flipped coin, this side showing seething hatred. 'Don't be naive. It's too late for the police. Now that you know, we have no choice but to be friends.'

'Move now,' Noel said, walking forward, backing the man into the living room.

Dalton laughed, but there was panic in it. 'Soon as you learn to hate them for their ability to lead normal lives, you won't be able to help yourself. Let me save you the heartbreak. We can start tonight. You don't like boys? That's all right. I know a ranch. In the desert, where they keep the girls. You can choose your own and, trust me, it will be a love like no other. Once you feel that, you won't ever have to love again. Your precious Julie will have all the sentimental value of a baseball card.'

Noel stopped, his ears ringing with violence. *Julie?* Did this piece of shit just say her name? He came forward and took Dalton by the collar and shook him once, hard enough to sprain his neck. He pressed the blade against the professor's nose lengthwise, ready to swipe it off.

'If you go near her, I will bury you alive.'

Dalton raised his hands in surrender. Noel threw him to the floor and Dalton landed hard on his tailbone, gasping. He made no effort to stand.

Noel went to the kitchen and took the cordless phone from its cradle. There was a dial tone. He punched 9-1-1, never taking his eyes off Dalton, knife held up like a crucifix.

'Nine-one-one, what is your emergency?' a woman said.

'This is Theodore Dalton,' Noel said. 'I've just killed a man in my apartment. Please send help now.'

Dalton cackled on the floor. 'I love it! Now we have a real shooting match!'

The woman was asking questions but Noel couldn't understand them. He was pacing in a circle as Dalton began to rise. The professor stood, rubbing his back, and slowly walked around the living room, into the hall, to the front door.

'Get back here!' Noel said.

'You will never see me coming,' Dalton said.

Then, as he opened the front door, he looked back at Noel and wiggled his fingers goodbye, vanishing before his footsteps began to echo down the hall.

He was gone. And Noel couldn't stay. The dispatchers would have the address. Emergency responders were already on the way.

He ran to the bedroom and checked the bound man on the floor for a pulse. He attempted mouth-to-mouth. He clasped his hands together and pumped the breastplate. He used paper towels from the kitchen and hand towels from the bathroom to try and stop the bleeding.

But the young man who wore sandalwood cologne was gone.

The sirens grew louder, and everything was moving too fast.

33

Footsteps, real and imaginary, roaming the hall. The dying sound of a muffled cough from the next room over. Low voices that fell silent as they passed his door, the intermittent burr of the ice machine drowning out an attempt on the doorknob. The thin blade of light at the threshold, blinking with foot shadows. It could be happening even now: a tentacle-like probing of his mind from the stairwells and elevator shafts, breaching the walls, swirling overhead like invisible smoke, clouding his eyes and blinding him to the evil slug dragging itself within toward its nutrients.

I see you. I'm coming for you. I'm here now. Let me in.

Solid, unable to flip the switch, Noel lay awake in a vacant room on the Palace Tower's ninth floor at Caesars, knowing sleep would not come tonight, tomorrow and possibly for days. The moon-gray screen of the alarm clock on the nightstand between the two beds taunting him, daring him to sleep. 3.48 a.m. He sat up, popping his ears to catch the telltale click of a lock being picked. Minutes passed and he felt a draft, air circulating in the room, even though he'd turned the thermostat down to keep the air conditioning in slumber. The idea of invisible molecules parting for an invisible body propelled him from bed to the window. He scooped the curtain to peer down to the pool area and gardens with their stoic winged lion gargoyles that could not protect him.

Not so much as a lone security patrol walking about, but what did it matter? When Dalton came for him, he would not arrive in his visible element. He would come the way he had come for the others lining the graves in his forty-year serial spree. One minute the coast would be clear, the next Noel would feel a piano wire sinking into his throat, the ice pick gliding into a kidney. Or maybe only a single inhalation through the ether-soaked rag, then darkness . . . until he awoke in a much smaller room, six feet long, constructed of pine.

He padded to the bathroom. Checked behind the door, the shower curtain. Stared into the mirror. The reflection was that of a man in the foment of breakdown. A sheen of sweat on his face, neck lined with road grit, puffy gray streaks under his bloodshot eyes, five days of stubble turning into a rash. He was afraid to run the water, to shower, to flush the toilet. Any sound could give him away.

He'd been trapped in here for almost twenty-four hours. Door dead-bolted, chain in the slot, chair wedged under the handle. Excessive? He might have thought so yesterday, even after the horror of Dalton's revelation.

But things had changed.

★　★　★

After running from Dalton's condominium, he'd holed up at the same nameless motorcourt motel where he'd taken his shower after his mind-rape in the Bagley residence. Too frightened to do anything other than shower again, washing away the young man's blood, he'd spent the longest night of his life trying to wrap his mind around what he'd gotten himself into. The guilt of what he hadn't seen coming, what he could have prevented had he acted sooner. The sheer terror of realizing his fingerprints were on the knife, the young man, all over Dalton's condo. He'd wanted to curl into a ball and die.

Eventually daylight returned and he knew he had to move. After hailing a cab at the aging Stardust, his first stop was the guest house. Figured he would pack a small bag, take the shovel back to the saguaro and dig up his cash. He was visible now, ten weeks of missing mobility options slamming back into the realm of possible, easy. He would suitcase as much of the cash as he could carry to the nearest cab line, pay a fare to the rental car agencies at McCarran International, pay cash for something nondescript and drive for two days straight. Florida, West Virginia, Canada, Mexico. It didn't matter, so long as it was far from Las Vegas and Theodore Dalton. Somewhere along the way he would call Julie from the road, tip off the police, convince them to send her round-the-clock protection.

He told the driver to leave him at the corner, two blocks away. When he reached the cul-de-sac on foot, the scene before him zoom-leaped and distorted with its own Hitchcock score. Three police units — two sedans in the driveway and a

373

hulking SUV slanting across the lawn. Sirens and cherries off, but no fewer than four officers circling the premises — windbreakers on, evidence bags in gloved hands. And who might that woman be? Why, it's Nora the Missing Realtor, a lady he hadn't seen since she had rented the place to him and Julie almost two years ago. But here she was, summoned for a matter far more serious than a delinquent rent check, standing beside a deep green BMW, pacing with a cellphone stuck to her ear.

Dalton had called them.

Want to locate millions of dollars in missing funds from that spate of casino muggings? Want to know who killed the guy in my condo last night? I know the address and he's a bad, bad boy.

LVPD scouring his residence, taking fingerprints, dusting his toothbrush and flipping through his sock drawer, sifting through trash.

And yet they were still working on the house. What if they hadn't yet found exactly where X marks the spot?

Noel backed off casually, as if he had been waiting for a ride who hadn't showed, glanced at his imaginary watch, and walked away. Four blocks north through the subdivision, another six east, into the desert, circling in a wide arc, shuffling low to the sand and scrub. He got lost for twenty minutes, so frightened was he of walking up on uniforms with shovels. He doubled back, closed in. The backyard was clear, no sign of the police. Hope — Dalton had known where he lived, but maybe he hadn't been there to see Noel burying his stolen funds. It took him another ten minutes to find the courage to creep up and locate the saguaro, his marker.

At its base was a raw hole more than seven feet deep and four feet wide. Empty as vampire's grave. They'd already found it. Six million and point-three change, the future he'd risked his life for, was at this minute bouncing downtown to an evidence locker. He was flat busted, poorer than he had been on the morning of his birthday. The gutting horror of it was so grand and complete, there was nothing to feel. His entire nervous system had been surgically removed in one swift yank. Dalton could be following him right now, he realized, and it mattered not at all.

Noel turned and wandered deeper into the desert, a mortar blast victim. He got lost for three hours before the sun's descent finally scared him back toward civilization.

Julie.

Dalton had struck back with one anonymous phone call, but would it be enough? Would tattle-telling about the money satisfy someone as deranged and compulsive as Theodore Dalton? No, not even close. Because this wasn't about anger, hurt feelings, or even the fact that Noel knew what Dalton was. This was how the former teacher and minister from Wisconsin had his fun. This was sport to him, his calling. If he'd wanted to merely to kill Noel, he could have faded at the condo and found a way. But instead he had run, so that the game could continue. Dalton would go after Julie next because that would inflict the most pain on his rebellious almost-disciple, and because he could, because using his power to take inferior life forms made him feel like a god.

Noel needed to find a phone. He needed to call Julie at her mother's house, hear her voice, warn her of what was coming. Then he needed to get to Calabasas, California, as soon as possible, because, against a killer with Dalton's powers, Julie would never stand a chance. The police might have just become an option out of necessity, meaning discovery and capture for Noel. But that was of minor concern when weighed against the possibility of Dalton. His father John, her mother Lisa — they couldn't protect her. Julie first, everything else later.

But the Strip was blown for him, he realized within the first two blocks. Looking for a payphone, scanning the streets and sidewalks for his enemy, Noel realized he wasn't safe out here. Dalton could be anywhere. In this car, in that cab, inside that store, around the next corner, right behind him, one hand over his grinning mouth. The far bigger problem was almost laughable — Noel didn't have any change in his pockets. He'd left his wallet in the guest house, a habit whenever he went out during one of his spells. The risk of blinking back, in the presence of others, of being trapped and ID'd, was not worth the value he got from carrying an ID, cash, credit cards. These were things he couldn't very well use while faded anyway.

Once again he was forced to return to the only other environment that afforded him the advantage of familiarity — Caesars Palace. That it was the one and same place where Dalton had found him to begin with only seemed to confirm the crazy logic of the choice. It was a move the killer might very well least expect.

Only when he strolled through the revolving doors and spotted the front desk did he remember that stealing a key and checking himself into a stolen room would not prove so easy now that he was just like everybody else. Dalton knew how to control it. In time Noel might learn to, but it wasn't working now. He'd tried a hundred times today, concentrating, wishing it so, trying to bounce it off random strangers, but his Goddess of Light was on hiatus. He needed a room, the phone, a tab he could run up for as long as it took to reach Julie. To hell with it, I'll follow a maid on her rounds and slip in when she's not looking. But when he was only a few paces from the casino parlor, a woman called his name.

'Noel Shaker! Hey, hey you!'

He cringed, but the voice was friendly enough. He turned to see Tilly, his former cocktail waitress milf crush, standing behind the front desk. Gone were the ruffle skirt and stockings and push-up bra. At some point in the past ten weeks the woman had gone corporate, with a new fashionably chopped hairdo, the blazer, white blouse and tie. She'd even ditched the clown paint in favor of clean make-up that showed her true age but made her look more beautiful than ever.

Noel approached the front desk sheepishly. 'Tilly? Wow, I love what you've done with your . . . '

'Career. I'm an assistant manager,' Tilly beamed. 'I have a 401K.'

'You look amazing.'

'Thanks. You don't. What are you doing here? I thought you got smart and moved away.'

'I'm leaving soon. Just have one or two more things to take care of.'

Tilly cocked her head with condescending sympathy. 'How is Julie?'

'Back to California. Staying with her parents. But I'm going after her. In fact, I need to call her. Something important came up and I lost my cell.'

'Do you want to use one of our phones?' Tilly gestured to her right.

'I do, but a little privacy would go a long way. We need to have one of those talks, you know?'

'Okay. Sure. Want me to check you in?'

Dalton couldn't return to the condo now. He'd stayed at Caesars before.

Noel inhaled, glanced around. 'Tilly. I need a favor. Two, actually. One is small, the other, well, I don't want to get you in trouble.'

'I don't want you to get me in trouble either.'

'I won't. But I need to know about a guest. He's a creep. He's been following her, and me, and he's dangerous. Extremely.'

'Oh, shit. Not again. Is his name Randall?'

'No. Why?'

'We get a lot of stalkers here. Complaints you wouldn't believe. Last week it was Randall from Missouri, shooting upskirt footage. They raided his room and found, like, hundreds of hours' worth.'

'Awful,' Noel said.

'Yeah, he's going to get something worse than a camera up his skirt in prison.'

'My guy's worse,' Noel said. 'Way worse. Can you poke around in your system, see if he's checked in or out recently?'

Tilly bit her lip. 'I'm really not supposed to.'

But in the end she did. Because Tilly had been a cocktail waitress for nine years and she had been forced to rebuff her share of creeps.

'Nothing under Theodore,' Tilly said, and Noel didn't know whether to be disappointed or relieved. 'But we've had two Daltons in the past week.'

Noel perked up.

'One is a woman, so I'm not giving you her name. No offense.'

'None taken.'

Tilly drummed her nails on the keyboard. 'Hmmm.'

'What?'

'The other is just an initial. T.'

It seemed crazy the professor would use his real name, even an initial. But, then, Dalton would be that smug, cocky in his abilities.

'That's him. His room number?'

Tilly stared at him.

'I'm not going to cause trouble, I swear.'

'That's what everyone says.'

'Tell me this. Is he still here?'

'He's listed as checked in since the first of May, checking out . . . let's see . . . well, he was booked for another week, but his reservation was changed this afternoon. He's checking out tomorrow.'

'Tilly, it's for Julie.'

'But you said Julie's gone, right? If he's here and she's not . . . maybe you should leave whatever this is alone?'

'He threatened to kill her. He's broken into our place. He's got a track record.'

Tilly's eyes widened. 'Well, Jesus, Noel. Call the cops.'

'I can't.'

'Why not — oh, Noel. What did you do?'

'Nothing.' Tilly crossed her arms. 'Okay, I shoved him. I knocked him down after he threatened her, and me. That's it, I swear to God.'

'You swear to Julie? Swear on her life?'

Noel crossed his heart and pleaded with his eyes.

'If shit goes down,' Tilly said. 'You didn't get this from me.'

'Absolutely, I promise.'

She gave him the room number. 'Go away now.'

'Wait. The other favor.'

Tilly rolled her eyes.

'I have to call her,' Noel said. 'I need a room. For thirty minutes. In and out.'

Tilly sighed. Noel begged. She slipped him a key in an envelope, jotting the number at the top.

'If you make me regret this, Noel. If I lose my job? I'll hunt you down and kill you myself.'

'You just saved a life, Tilly.'

She shooed him away. He restrained himself from sprinting to the elevators. This was good, this was better. After burning Noel at the guest house, Dalton would expect him to be on the run by now. If Noel could stop him from leaving Las Vegas, Julie would be safe.

But even though Dalton was still here, the smart thing to do would be to call Julie first, prepare her in the event Noel did not make it out of here alive. He meant to go to his room first, to make the call. But the one Tilly had left open for him was on the fourteenth floor and the number she had given for Dalton's was on six. Riding in the elevator, watching the numbers light up, the temptation was too strong.

Dalton first.

Confirm he's here, then you'll know Julie's in a different state, safe.

Noel got off on six and walked quietly to room 622, which was just around the first corner, almost within view of the elevator bank. He leaned his ear to the door. The television was on. He idled a few minutes, acting like he was waiting on a friend. A couple who appeared to have retired while still in platinum health, decked out in their in tennis-club whites, exited the room across the hall. Noel nodded hello and they smiled, trailing Mentholatum fumes. Noel wandered to the end of the wing, dallied around the soda machine, came back when the coast was clear.

When he pressed his ear to the door a second time, the TV volume was lower and a man was speaking. To someone on the phone, most likely, because there were no responses during the pauses. He couldn't make out the words but he knew the obsequious tone. Theodore Dalton.

Noel had the killer cornered.

34

Shall we knock? Play room service?

No, Dalton would sniff out the ruse, check the peephole, drop out if he hadn't already, and the advantage would be lost. Better to wait for the door to open, then pounce. All that money, gone. Noel could taste it now. He wanted to deliver Dalton an equally shocking blow. One hard shot to the throat, subdue, overcome before the fucker knew what hit him. Hell, maybe disable both knees, poke an eye out, blind him for life, canceling the threat for good and leave him bleeding on the ground for the police.

For Julie. To keep her safe.

Forty minutes passed, then an hour, and Dalton did not exit his room. People came and went, and Noel kept up his charade of whistling along like any other dumb tourist, fumbling for his key in the little envelope Tilly had provided, hovering near the elevators. Ducking under the peephole every time he passed the door.

Patience, patience.

Another half-hour later a maintenance man lumbered in, making his rounds with an extended dustpan and sweeper, a canvas trash dolly. He was taller than Noel and twice as heavy, bald with a pencil mustache, three neck rolls and the largest pair of green Doc Martens Noel had ever seen. Knuckle tatts, an eagle with a snake in its beak on one forearm. Military or a skinhead, but in either case a friendly one, giving Noel a smile and a knowing nod. Noel had never seen the guy before today and prayed the reverse was also true.

'How the tables treatin' you, boss?' the bald hulk asked as he smoothed the sand with a tiny rake.

'Hm? Oh, my gambling days are over,' Noel said. 'Luck went bad years ago.'

'I hear ya. Man's gotta have some kinda game, though. Especially in this town.'

Okay, I'll play along. Act normal, nothing to hide. 'I might throw a few bucks down on a ballgame, but park me down by the pool with a few drinks, that's about enough excitement for me.'

Big dude was also a lonely dude, or a bored dude. 'Pool here's okay. But the really nice ass doesn't show up till the therms go above ninety, know what I'm sayin'?'

'Yeah?' Noel pretended to look at his watch again. 'Shit, my girlfriend's late.'

'You wanna see some real talent, try the pools at the Hard Rock, Palms. Most of the chicks here are broken.'

Noel forced a smile. 'Good to know.'

Apparently, ensuring that all of the ashtrays in Caesars Palace were as pristinely groomed as a trap on Pebble Beach was not high on the man's list of priorities, only this one. He finished and stood about fifteen feet from Dalton's door, using his dustbin as a cane. A gleam in his eye, a big dumb grin.

'Women,' Noel said.

'You're telling me. Had myself a game-changer a couple weeks ago, though. Buddy of mine was out for his bachelor party. I hooked him up with a room, he hooked me up with something else.' The giant made a bored, jerk-off motion with his right hand, then mimed the act of snorting cocaine from a straw. 'After about three days of yee-haw, we're sitting down by the pool bar, just sucking eggs, hungover as fuck. Couldn't been more than seventy-five out, no pussy within a hundred yards. We're talking major drought.'

'Uh-huh,' Noel chipped in. He glanced at Dalton's door, leaned against the wall, rubbed his eyes. Leave, please leave.

But the maintenance man continued, 'We're just about to get out of the water, 'cause our fingers are starting to look like fuckin' prunes, and all the sudden this real piece of work comes out — Indian or Iraqish or one of those from those places where they're supposed to be covered up from their eyes to ankles, you know? Habib or some shit? She's wearing a white Caesars robe, the ones they sell in the gift shop. She's alone. Long black hair, with those giant movie star bitch sunglasses. So, okay, there's like two hundred empty chairs, but she takes one right across the pool from us, facing right at us, less than twenty feet away. We're like, helloooo. She drops the robe.'

'Let me guess,' Noel cut in, wanting to get to the punchline. 'She's naked.'

'Not even, bro. This is an order of magnitude beyond naked. She's wearing a swimsuit, just a perfect white bikini. Bang, like snow against all

384

that dark skin and I actually caught myself reaching for my goddamn sunglasses only to realize they're still sitting on my face just like I wish she was.'

Noel glanced at Dalton's door. Still closed. TV murmuring. The bald white Scheherazade of the maintenance staff was inching closer and closer to it as he attempted to keep his audience rapt.

'Her shit was tight. Off the charts, okay? Perfect body, big ol' naturals, but we can't even begin to lift our eyes above her waist because — are you ready for this? I shit you not — she's got the hugest blackest squirreliest goddamn bush you have ever seen. Crawling out of her bikini like wild vines, man. Up to her navel, down the legs. You could have put this one in front of the fireplace and sipped Moët on it.'

'That's terrif — '

'Your first thought is, okay, she doesn't get it. She maybe was in a hurry and didn't check the mirror, because *how does she not know*, right? But this wasn't a case of 'oopsey, I missed a spot shaving'. This gal might as well have strapped a couple of black sheep to her hips. She knew. This was on-purpose bush. And then it finally dawns on me, damned if she wasn't proud. She was! Think about it. Some girls, it's the tramp stamp above the ass, the smokin' cleavage, one of those lil' ankle bracelets from Tiffany, whatever. For her, it was the natural splendor of God's untamed mammal. And you know something?'

'No, I really don't,' Noel said.

'All my life, or at least since I saw my first porno mag in the fourth fucking grade, I thought there was something shameful about that. I thought bald was, like, the standard. 'Cause who needs it? What's its purpose? But this broad, I don't know if she was Arab or whatnot, but she changed all that. Converted me in a blink. I ran straight home that night and told my gal, I said, yo, Leslie, no more trips to Brazil. No more spa wax. I want the Black Forest. You start growing that shit out right now or we're through. And you better believe I meant it.'

Noel blinked at the man. Why was this stranger telling him this? What was the response here?

'So push comes to shove, and Leslie, well, she fucking split,' the huge man said. 'Do you believe that shit? Here I am ready to accept her as God made her, and she tells me I'm the creep! I guess she just wasn't up to the task, huh?'

Around the corner, the elevators dinged. A door opened. Noel couldn't see it, but he knew the sound by now.

'No, really, can you believe that?'

Noel glared at the janitor. 'Yeah, okay, I guess I can. I'm happy for you, all right?'

'Happy?' The guy laughed. 'You don't look so happy. What's wrong, bro? You think maybe your gal left you? What do you think's taking her so long?'

What in the name of God was going on here? Enough. Noel put his hands up. 'Look, I'm in the middle of something, so no offense, but can you give me a little space here? I don't want to hear your stories, okay? Jesus.'

If anyone had exited the elevator, they would have taken one of the halls by now. Noel was sweating. Something was wrong here.

The bald man made a clicking sound of disapproval. 'No problem, guy. So, what's the deal, is this a stakeout?'

'Excuse me?'

The janitor shrugged. 'Guy paid me a hundred bucks to keep you on your post. I figured — '

'What?' Noel's sweat ran cold. 'Who? When was this?'

The elevator door swished closed. Noel headed toward it, bracing himself, and from behind him, on the other side of the hall, there came a delicate *click*.

Noel stopped, turned back and looked at Dalton's door. It was ajar. Just about one inch, but rebounding . . .

Noel's eyes darted from the door to the maintenance man and back. 'Get away. Get out of here right now, you stupid fuck.'

The maintenance man took a step toward him. 'Sure, soon as we're through. Guy said there'd be another hundred if I kept you here for — '

But he didn't finish that sentence. For a moment his mouth froze half open, then he took another step and then he gagged. A bright line of red appeared under his chin, widening from ear to ear, and then he fell to his knees and the blood came out of him in a pressurized fan. He hovered upright, and another line opened vertically from his throat down to his belt. His shirt split open and fatty tissue and another torrent of blood slopped out.

Noel stared in mute shock and he might have heard two soft steps on the carpet before he felt the air before him *stir.*

He backed down the hall, eyes wide, arms out and patting in a shield to defend against what he could not see.

The giant fell on his face and his blood pumped onto the carpet, pooling over the dense fibers. The heavy green boots drummed the floor and one hand reached out for someone — maybe Leslie, maybe the hirsute princess from the pool — to take it.

Noel could not remember if he was backing into a dead end. He decided to break a sharp left for the elevators, made three steps and froze.

What happened next was as detailed as high-definition video run in slow motion, but spliced in and out of Noel's reality in less than two seconds.

Theodore Dalton manifested from thin air, blocking the path to the elevators. What little hair he had was mussed, and his mouth and beard were running red as if he'd drunk from the fountain he'd just opened. The professor's outfit had been replaced by a blue jogging suit, the crotch tented with a violence erection, and in his stocking feet he moved in total silence. His eyes were glossy and wild blue, rolling in his skull as he made a wiping motion against his pant leg and two big strides later raised his right arm above his head. A sickle of hotel light gleamed from the stout serrated blade, and in a less-than-blink he exited the spectrum.

After that, the swoosh of the knife arcing past Noel's ear was the only evidence Dalton was real and this was happening.

35

Dalton's blade passed Noel's ear close enough to leave a feather-tickle of air and the fabric of Noel's t-shirt ripped from chest to navel. Leaping away just in time, Noel fell, rolled in a panic, and scrambled to his feet before feeling the first of the stinging. Then he felt the warm wetness and knew Dalton's blade had got him.

'Oh, good boy,' Dalton's seemingly disembodied voice announced, and in those few words Noel heard all the bloodlust of a man who has had decades to refine his tastes. 'I love this part. I call it the three blind mice.'

In this situation there was only one option and it matched Noel's most primitive instincts. He bolted, running down the hall as fast as he could. He didn't know how fast Dalton could run, or if there was an exit this way, but if he stayed in the hall and tried to fight his way to the elevators, the blade would find him and finish him.

The room doors blurred. It seemed to take no more than six great strides before the hall ended. To the right was another USE STAIRS IN CASE OF AN EMERGENCY sign and Noel braced the door, blowing through with a slam that echoed four stories up and down. No choice about which way to go; his momentum simply threw him against the door and bounced him to the right, toward the stairs going up. He caught a handrail and took the steps three at a time, rounding the landing and launching himself halfway up the next flight. The door slammed again.

Below and behind him, Dalton was breathing hard but coming for him.

Noel thought any floor would do. All he needed was another hall, a long corridor that would give him the space to build a solid lead, grab an elevator and head back down, leaving the casino and Theodore Dalton behind forever. But there were other elevators, other stops, people who might delay his exit. He had no idea when or where Dalton would reappear, and once he was out in the world he would never know how close Dalton might be. He needed a shell.

In his pocket was the key for the room Tilly had assigned him, on the thirteenth floor. A room, a door between them, a phone to call for help. They'd started on the sixth floor. Noel had already run up three flights, two per floor, which meant he was coming up fast on the eighth floor. Five floors to go, ten flights of stairs. Footsteps slapped the concrete and squeaked. His own heavy breathing echoed and mixed with the killer's. No way could the fatter, older man catch him on the stairs.

Three big strides and another flight was gone. Using the rail to swing himself around as fast as possible, the fear of the knife digging into his heels propelling him on, up, around, faster and faster. Knees pumping, blood racing.

Tenth floor.

Eleventh.

Halfway up the twelfth, Noel lost his grip on the handrail and slipped at the turn. The velocity flung him into the outside wall and the foot he kicked out to reach for the second step went high, snagging on the edge of the stair. His ankle rolled his foot to the inside until the sole of his shoe was vertical. He went down, shin slamming into the stairs, elbow into the wall, the entire hard face of the flight stopping him like a fence made of granite.

'Agh, sonofabitch, Jesus!' The pain raced around inside him from four points of contact and made his head swim. Acidic pain taste in the back of his throat.

Wham wham wham, gulping breath, *wham wham slap slap slap* . . .

Dalton was at least two stories below, but he hadn't given up.

Noel reached for the rail and his elbow throbbed electrically. A dry gash under his forearm, skin opened, probably a bruised bone. The ankle was worse. When he set his weight on his right foot, the pain was glorious.

Slap slap slap, a string of coughing, hacking, deep breaths. *Stomp . . . stomp . . .*

Dalton tiring but still catching up.

Noel hopped on his left foot, using the rail as a life rope, and hopped again, but this would not do. He needed both feet. If he didn't swallow the pain and run up two and a half more flights, he would be gutted in the stairwell like a hog in its pen, and Julie would be next. Tonight, tomorrow, six months down the road. As long as Dalton was at large, she would not be safe.

Noel unleashed a banzai scream and hammered the stairs.

Dalton laughed and shrieked and bumbled after him.

At the top of next flight there was door 13. Noel shoved through and broke left into the hall, his ankle throbbing so bad the foot below it no longer wanted to respond at all. It was numb, clumsy, like dragging a boot filled with sand. He scanned the numbers on the doors, realized he had no idea which room Tilly had assigned him. Reached in his pocket, hobbling, slapping the wall for support, waiting for the door behind him to slam open, releasing the monster back into the maze.

A folded slip of paper. He flipped it open. Thank God Tilly had remembered to jot the number on it. 1334.

Noel hopped and limped to the next door. 1348. But did that mean 1334 was up ahead or had he already passed it?

Behind him, the stairwell door swung open with a bang.

Too late now. Only one way to go. Straight ahead, pray he hadn't passed 1334 yet. If he couldn't find it, he'd have to try his luck with the elevators. And if those were tied up, he'd be a dead man.

Dalton was breathing hard, breathing bad. Sounded like a man who'd been underwater for the past two minutes. Good, I hope you have a heart attack, you fucking slug. Noel figured he had a ten-second lead, no more.

The next door, on his left, read 1344. The numbers were going down. His room was just a little ways up ahead. Encouraged, he forced his right foot down and soldiered on. One big step off his left, then a softer, nearly crippling hobble with his right. Step, hobble. Step, hobble. He was loping down the hall at a good clip when he bashed a small display table and a vase of flowers to the floor.

1342.

1341.

1340.

And then a blank wall on one side, the wide berth for the elevators on the other. He calculated the distance to go. Fifty feet at most.

'I'm going to eat her parts . . . eat her sunny fucking face,' Dalton said behind him. He sounded ragged but very close. ' . . . taking the next flight . . . to Los Angeles . . . suck her milk . . . '

Noel grunted and stomped ahead.

1338 . . . 37 . . . 36 . . . 1335 . . . one more and he would be home free.

He fumbled the key from its paper sleeve.

' . . . staying?' Dalton said. ' . . . play with me?'

His ugly choking laughter.

Noel jabbed the plastic key at the slot.

Too high.

Too low.

In.

The little red light stayed red. He jerked the handle.

'Motherfucker!'

Red.

He removed the card, wiggled the knob to clear the mechanism, slammed the card in.

'You're going to . . . die here.' Dalton was steps away.

Blinking red.

Solid green.

The tumbler clicked. Noel wrenched the handle, flung himself inside, snagged his foot on the carpet — his bad foot — and his leg buckled.

Dalton hit the door.

Noel screamed and slammed it back. The door stopped three inches from the latch and Dalton howled in agony. At that moment the arm re-imaged — Dalton was inside up to his elbow — and the knife fell to the floor, on Noel's side.

Noel brought the door back as far as he dared, then rammed it home again.

Dalton moaned like a trapped bear cub.

Noel brought the door back one more time and flung it hard. Dalton's arm was withdrawing when the door smashed his fingers into the frame. Noel drove his shoulder into the door over and over, grinding Dalton's fingers with whatever strength he had left. The professor gasped in a series a great big whoops of surrender.

'Let go, let go, lemme go!'

Noel did not release the hand, its shattered bones and bulbous swelling fingers. He kept the door planted as he crouched for the knife. Caught it in his right hand and swept it up, raking all four of Dalton's fingertips. The knife bounced over speed bumps of bone and blood spurted high. This time there was no scream, only three knobs of reddened flesh that fell to the floor as the rest of Dalton's appendage slithered out into the hall.

Noel thumbed the lock, slipped the chain and

backed away, holding the knife out as if Dalton really were about to turn into smoke and filter in through the threshold. But he didn't. A series of shouts and curses rebounded off the door, and stopped abruptly. Noel forced his breathing down, down and under control, waiting for the assault to resume, but there was only silence. He wedged the desk chair under the knob.

He was locked in now. Dalton was free but wounded. Bleeding profusely by now. Unless the man had truly lost his mind and all sense of self-preservation, he would have to go away. Find something to wrap his hand in, escape. It was a miracle they hadn't set off a series of alarms and screams, but as far as Noel could recall, on this floor, there had been no witnesses.

The dead man bleeding all over the sixth floor would be a problem. Someone had to have seen that by now. Police would be summoned. Soon there would be sirens, a dozen cops rapping on hotel room doors, cornering witnesses. Would they bother with the thirteenth floor? For a murder, yes, they would scour the place. Faded or not, Dalton was in no condition to stick around.

Noel was safe for now, but he could not afford to stay.

He backed deeper into the room and drew the curtains, shutting out the sunlight. He went to the bathroom, tore off a wad of toilet paper, picked up the fingertips and flushed them down. He rinsed the knife and washed his hands. He was bleeding into his torn black shirt, from the long but shallow cut Dalton had made across his chest. He washed that, too, and hesitated to use any of the clean towels to wipe away his own blood. More evidence he had been here. Noel was the victim, Dalton was the killer, but Noel's crimes — the theft, and, more to the point, what he was, what they both were — essentially rendered them both monsters.

Noel sat on the bed, picked up the phone. Julie did not own a cellphone — they each had at one time, but had been forced to cancel the service to save money.

He did not know Lisa's and his father's home number because Julie had been the one to make the calls over the past couple years. He called information — a risk but one he had to take. After seven rings, he got the home voice mailbox. Heard his father's voice. He did not leave a message. He tried again, then again every five minutes, a dozen times, then hourly. He could not think of a message that wouldn't sound like lunacy. He didn't want John or Lisa to hear it. He wanted to talk to Julie.

He leaned back against the high faux-leather head-board, trying to still his mind. He had no idea what he would tell her even if she had answered. A warning would only bring more questions. What had he gotten mixed up in? What did he expect her to do? What was he going to do now?

He waited for the sirens to come, for the knocking to begin. But as the afternoon light bled from the sky and night fell over the desert, there were no sirens a hundred and thirty feet below. Tilly did not send a maroon blazer to kick him out.

He checked the peephole every half-hour, but of course there was nothing to see.

You're being a coward. You have to get out sooner or later. Go now while you can, because when morning comes it's only going to get worse.

★ ★ ★

When the gray moon of the alarm clock showed 5.55 a.m., Noel rose from the bed and checked the peephole one last time. He opened the door and scanned the empty hall. Dalton did not come for him, but he'd left a souvenir.

On the floor just outside his door was a standard-sized manila envelope with his name written on one side, in blood. Noel shoed it back into the room, shut and locked the door. He opened the envelope and a series of twelve or more large glossy color photos sifted into his free hand. Together they told a story, one that Noel was already familiar with.

In the first, Lucy Bagley's face confronted him with wide-open eyes, her mascara running, her teeth bared and clamped on the barrel of a large shiny silver pistol.

In the second, her husband. Garroted with pantyhose, another pair pulled down over his face, a spray of blood recently erupted from his left ear where the head of a golf club now lay broken off and resting on the carpet.

The daughter blindfolded, the knife being put

to use in her midsection.

The son before, alive, pale with what was coming.

The son after, minus his head.

The framed family photographs on the fireplace mantle, beside Ezra's severed head. An arm and hand above it, combing the hair.

There were a dozen more capturing them in their final repose, the mess the killer had made of them some four years ago, but Noel had seen enough. He dropped them in disgust. The man who'd slain the producer and his family was one and the same hunting him, his disappointing protégé. This could not be a coincidence. But the Bagleys had been murdered before Noel and Julie ever found the guest house. How could Dalton have known they would choose that guest house?

He hadn't known, of course.

I knew. I felt it. I was drawn to the scene of his crime the way I was drawn back to Bryan Simms in the Funhouse. I resisted it for four years, almost like Julie was protecting me, keeping me out of trouble, but eventually the fading pulled me in. I had to look inside, to feed it. Because Dalton and I are alike. The fading brought us together. The fading demands a sacrifice.

He took the envelope with his name and Dalton's blood on it, and when he shuffled the photos to stuff them inside the last in the stack fell out, face down on the floor. Noel turned it over.

Julie stared up at him from a restaurant booth he could not recall. She was smiling, a red circle finger-drawn around her head.

He dialed the home number again, but she didn't answer.

No one did.

36

The resorts never close, never sleep. Middle of winter, sweltering summer, the deadest seasons, when no major conventions are in town. Four a.m., six a.m. It doesn't matter. Someone's always awake, always up, always on the move, eating, drinking, cruising for sex, trying their hand at one of the gaming tables, using the gym, waking for a red-eye breakfast, crawling out of a cab, staggering to a room to pull the blinds and sleep off another night better forgotten. A night when the beast snapped its chains, the kraken was released. When normal folks from Plano, Texas, discovered something dark and vicious they never imagined had been living inside them all along. And there was always a dealer to serve these walking wounded, the revved-up table bangers. Cleaning staff, front desk, concierge, security. Even the aging resorts have something going on. This morning, at a little past six o'clock, Caesars Palace was no exception. Business was a long way from full swing, but solids were on the move.

Noel Shaker walked among them, taking an uneventful ride down the elevator with no stops until the cage bobbed once and the doors opened on L for lobby. Curiosity urged him to have a peek at 6, check out the crime-scene tape, the bloodstained floor, but he couldn't risk that.

He exited, vowing to maintain a balance of

vigilance and continual motion. Down the marble corridor, past the coffee and pastry shop (open but vacant save for a lone Latina in chef whites), past the sunglasses store (closed), the luggage store (closed), into the wider mouth at the front of the casino. The Italian restaurant was closed, ditto the noodle joint, though a slender Chinese woman in heels and a dress was at the hostess stand beside the high aquariums with their hundreds of now-dimmed goldfish, writing something on a clipboard. No one watched him, no one cared who he was.

And that was good, because while he had been lucky to avoid getting blood on his jeans or shoes, his black t-shirt had some spots and streaks on it. He didn't think the stains would be visible to anyone who wasn't standing within arm's reach, and he had no plans to let anyone get that close.

Behind him was the larger maze of the casino with its dozens of tables and hundreds of slots, dinging and bleeping and *loom-loom-looming* their electrical music in sleepy fashion. He passed the cashier's counter with its imitation gold jail bars and the maroon-blazered cashier on duty, a black woman with braids and bright red lipstick, did not look up as he passed.

Then it was an easy hook into the front lobby, with the wide arcing front desk to his right and freedom — the revolving doors and cab lines and fresh air — to his left. There were two people working check-ins for the three or four early arrivals, an older man with presidential hair and a younger woman who was not Tilly but might be in another ten years. The vast room was quiet and another maintenance man was running a floor polisher around, jigging to it in a private lullaby. Noel wanted to run but his ankle, while no longer throbbing in a siren of pain, was still sending hot tendrils up his leg that flared every time he came down on that foot. His back ached, his head ached. Bright lights overhead. The gray-blue of sunrise just beyond the windows.

Noel crossed an arm over the tear in his shirt and pretended to fuss with an itch at his ear, concentrating on walking in fluid steps, burying the limp and paying for it, gritting his teeth. Any moment now he expected someone to shout, 'Stop! You, hold it right there!' but no one did.

He was less than a dozen paces from the revolving doors when he saw the policemen. They were standing outside, facing each other, one on each side of the central revolving door. His heart sank. He'd begun to wonder if Dalton had somehow cleaned up the mess on sixth before anyone reported the dead man, but clearly that had been wishful thinking. Noel slowed but continued his forward progress so as not to draw attention. Ahead of him, a perky middle-aged lady with a large turquoise purse was exiting the revolving door to the right. She was scooted right up to the door, waiting for the automatic turnstile to release her, and when the gap opened she set off at a clip close to running.

The cop on her side whistled loud and darted back to stop her. She reared back and gawked at the officer. He waved a hand in apology and said something that got her to cough up her ID. He nodded and sent her on her way.

They were looking for somebody. Had they connected this crime scene to the condo? They might not be onto Dalton yet, who left no witnesses by virtue of his talent, but if they were, then they were onto Noel too. His fingerprints taken from the condo. They probably would not have the name Noel Shaker, but would be happy to stop anyone who appeared suspicious. Someone, say, who looked like he hadn't slept or bathed in five days, and by the way, what's this stain on your torn-up shirt, sir?

The front exits were not going to work.

Noel changed course and continued through the lobby, into another hall decorated as a temporary art gallery whose theme might have been The Wild West and Sleepy Cowboys Who Lived There. There had to be more exits, plenty of them. But, then again, this was a casino and they practiced a school of feng shui that funneled you away from the exits for the same reason they didn't want you to see a clock.

Soft carpet, high ceilings, the quiet calm pregnant with imminent crisis. He passed a throng of Japanese teens who looked like an ad for energy drinks and portable musical devices, then was winding around a Harley-Davidson store (closed), and came to a four-way intersection. A hall leading toward what he guessed were conference rooms on the right, to his left a grand staircase with marble banisters that rose one story and split two ways, and straight ahead more unknown. He continued straight for another hundred feet or so and now his ankle was warning him not to push it if he ever wanted to walk right again.

Doors, doors everywhere, but none were exits. The signs overhead directed him toward restrooms, the athletic center, more shops, and of course there was always a new route to get back to the casino. Noel knew he was only wading deeper into the resort and he doubted he would find another exit all the way on the backside. But the Forum Shops' east entrance was coming up, and he knew there was a way to exit onto the street from there. Or some kind of passage into the next resort . . .

He picked up his pace, angling right as the next curve approached. When he turned that corner, the mall's first leg came into view. The fashion boutiques were closed but the mall's main center lane was open. Huge potted plants that were really small trees were positioned beside quaint park benches for resting, and it was on the third of these benches that he spotted Theodore Dalton, seated with his legs crossed, right hand bandaged thick as a boxing glove, sucking on the straw of a rather large paper cup with a Mrs Field's Cookies logo. He was eight or ten retail storefronts away, but there was no mistaking him.

'Piece of shit,' Noel whispered.

The cameras are going to nail us both.

This little mind-wipe trick of ours might work on human beings, but if what you told me was true, we can't fool the cameras. They've been recording us all along. How are you not in jail right now, fat slug?

Noel took two steps back and Dalton turned his head slowly, casually, until the two men were once again staring at each other. Dalton had changed yet again, from the blue warm-ups into a pair of white drawstring pants and a loose-fitting, almost flowing dress shirt of navy linen. Seeing Noel, he lobbed his drink to the floor, slapped his healthy palm on his thigh and heaved himself up. He stretched theatrically, his entire body rippling with shimmering light, going chameleon with the backdrop of mall and store signs before slowly, teasingly, filling in again. The bastard was showing off. He went solid again, yawned, and took up a stroll in Noel's direction.

He was in no hurry, but the sight of his flat eyes and swinging thick arms and that tireless pot belly were enough to turn Noel around and send him back toward the front entrance at a fast jog. Just before Noel turned the corner, he glanced over his shoulder.

Dalton had vanished, and Noel had never wished so badly for the power to follow him into the void. This simply wasn't fair.

It was going to end here, he realized. In Caesars' arena they would wage their final battle, until one man was showered in roses, the other walking in the fields of Elysium.

37

Noel chose the grand staircase. It was a kind of torture that went against the Geneva Conventions on self-abuse, but, short of running into the arms of the police out front, it was the only choice. There probably weren't more than twenty-five stairs on the first riser but they felt like three hundred. At the landing he made a U-turn to the right and climbed another twenty or more, cresting into a hall that pointed him to the spa and fitness center.

As for the invisible Mr Dalton, there were no shouts or cries this time, no wagging knives. Here on the second floor, away from the sparse morning foot traffic and far from the casino, there was only a hushed silence. He could not hear the predator's footsteps and he had no plan for where to go, what to do. But soon enough he was gimping his way through the unattended and open-walled spa shop, where one could purchase all manner of soaps, powders, lotions, swimsuits and fancy robes for the upcoming steam and whirlpool experience. He knew he was headed toward another dead end of some sort, but there was no one around at this hour and if they were going to have it out, better here than in view of the solids.

The hall to the spa itself stretched on for another hundred feet, at least. He came upon a barbershop where he might have found a pair of scissors or a straight razor, but the door was locked and the sign said that JOEY G., BARBER TO THE STARS would not be in until ten. The air grew humid and scented with chlorine and other stimulating aromatics as he reached the end of the hall and spa entrance. The small door was open and as Noel approached the front counter, a young man in a light green polo and black slacks appeared with a stack of folded towels in one arm. The soft brown eyes beneath their delicate brows were slow to register Noel's shaggy appearance, the disappointment in them translating as *oh no, not another one, it's too early for vagrants.*

'I'm sorry, sir, but the spa doesn't open until seven.'

'I have to use the bathroom,' Noel said without slowing. 'It's an emergency.'

'Unfortunately, you'll have to use the ones back that way — '

'There's no time.'

The young man stepped around the counter and tried to block the way in. Noel put his hands up and smiled, noting the nametag.

'Relax, Hector, I'm an employee. I've been on the maintenance team for two years and this won't take but a few minutes, I promise.'

Hector smiled crookedly, maybe buying it, probably not. 'What's your name?'

'Noel Shaker. Call Tilly at the front desk. She'll vouch for me.'

Hector sighed. 'Make it quick, man. And don't use anything other than the toilets.'

Noel carried on, then paused. This wasn't

right. He came back. 'Hector?'

'Yeah?'

'I lied. I used to work here but now I'm just running from a very sick man with a knife. He's following me right now and if you get in the way I guarantee he's going to kill you.'

'Say what? The hell you talking about, man?'

Noel opened his shirt for Hector, revealing the cut from yesterday. 'He did this. The man following me is the man who killed the maintenance guy on the sixth floor yesterday afternoon.'

'Yo what? Somebody got killed?'

'The tall bald guy with the tattoos, wears those green Docs? You remember him?'

Hector's eyes widened.

'Well, he's dead. Got his throat and belly filleted yesterday afternoon. You need to hide now, in a closet, an office, or better yet find a way out that doesn't involve that hall right there. Now, Hector. I am not fucking with you.'

Hector glanced down the hall. 'You want me to call the police?'

'Sure, but get the hell out of here first.'

Hector grabbed a set of keys from under the counter and disappeared behind a door to the side. There was a locking sound and Noel hoped it would be enough. He didn't need anyone else getting hurt in this.

He shut the door to the main entrance but the knob was a dummy and the lock was a key-deadbolt only. He didn't have time to bring Hector back out with the keys.

He turned back to the counter to search for a

weapon. Oh, if he only had thought to carry his gun when he left home two days ago. But he'd only been heading out to steal a stupid toy set for Julie. He hadn't planned on meeting a serial killer with superior blinding skills and becoming mortal enemies with same in less than twenty-four hours. There were no weapons here unless a ballpoint pen was a weapon. And with nothing else at hand, why not? Noel took the pen and shambled into the spa.

It would have been nice if at some point in the past two years Noel had bothered to become familiar with this charming hotel feature, but this entire wing of the resort and the spa were foreign territory. A confusing maze of small rooms and tiled corridors. He passed a lounge with padded armchairs and ottomans, the day's ironed newspapers laid out for guests, along with a selection of fresh fruits, coffee urns, bagels, carafes of fresh orange and pineapple juice sitting in a tub of ice, and a flatscreen television mounted to one wall, turned to *SportsCenter*, the volume down very low.

The backside of the lounge opened into the locker room, with a carpeted floor, wooden lockers and benches, a pyramid of clean white towels stacked inside a huge wicker hamper. Towels everywhere he looked, in shelves along the walls, in every room. He moved through the next section, a rectangular space with sinks and shaving creams and lotions set out. Q-tips. On the other side of the wall to his left were the urinals and toilets. Beyond those, a bay of shower stalls, their glass doors open and waiting, white robes everywhere. More clean towels, and another wicker hamper for spent ones.

Exiting the bathrooms he came to an elevated platform which held the largest whirlpool, steaming but not yet bubbling, and a little ways past that, in a right-turn alcove, were three steam rooms — herbal, regular and a cold room blowing artificial snow. Everything was on, running, ready for the early birds. More towels. A large tub of ice with dozens of short bottled waters. Tightly rolled washrags in ice, for cooling down after the steam. Noel took one and rubbed his face, threw it in the hamper.

How was he going to defend himself in here? There were no exits — only the front hall and whatever else lay behind the room Hector had locked himself into. Hector'd be calling someone right now. Front desk, the police, security. That was probably for the best. Noel would have a lot of explaining to do, might get in some serious shit if Dalton told them about the muggings, the six million they'd found in the desert, but he would rather go to prison than be murdered. How long could prison hold him anyway? Eventually he would blind his way out.

There was one more room, separate from the others, which he found at the end of a longer cement corridor. Larger and darker, with a rainforest feel to it, a thundering downpour sound emanating as he approached. Elevated from the main floor, on a platform of tile, were three pools — very hot tub, warm tub, cold tub. A hard running deluge shower in the middle, televisions on the walls, and heated S-shaped

410

lounge chairs on the left perimeter. More bottled water, more towels, a bowl of miniature oranges.

But in all of this there was no place to hide. Only walls and water. What could he do with water? Nothing while he was solid. He might be able to make something of the deluge or the pools if he were in Dalton's state. At least then they would be on something of a level playing field. He could —

Wait a minute. Water. Steam. Showers. Pools.

Noel couldn't hide in any of these elements, but neither could Dalton.

The water would give him away, even while he was faded. He would register in outline, in the water he disturbed, the way the snow had given Noel away in Boulder. It wasn't much but it was his only chance, to level the playing field somewhat. But what was the best way to inch himself closer to Dalton's state? What could he use to blend in? The water, the towels? Everywhere Noel looked there were towels. Thick white towels and white walls and light colored tile. Anything, every little bit, would help.

Noel stripped off his clothes and threw them in the nearest hamper, thought better of it, and pulled them back out. He spread them on the floor, as if hastily shucked, near the entrance to this main room with the three pools and deluge, right where Dalton would see them and, if Noel were lucky, assume he had gone into hiding here. The truth would be easy enough to discover, but the clothes might buy him an extra minute or two.

Dick and balls naked, holding only the ballpoint pen, Noel doubled back toward the steam rooms, teeth clenching every time he turned the corner in anticipation of whatever cute weapon Dalton had brought to the show this time around. Passing the bathrooms, he looped around the corner and risked checking the door near Hector's front counter. It was still closed, but unless Dalton had fallen far behind on the stairs or taken a wrong turn outside the spa, he would be close.

Or was already inside.

Thank you, Hector, Noel thought when he noted for the second time the steam rooms were already cooking, even warmer than just a few minutes ago. Noel wrapped himself in a towel and carried the bucket of water bottles to the herbal room. The tub was heavy. Maybe twenty small bottles of water sitting in two or three gallons of melting ice. He propped the glass door open and lugged the tub in, placing it on the top seating level at the back of the white tiled room, in the corner where from the door visibility would be at its poorest. He sat down beside the tub, took in the view.

He could see the door.

This wasn't going to work. The room wasn't hot enough. The steam hadn't been on long enough, was too thin. Noel would be exposed. All he needed was a five-second advantage, the delay between Dalton entering the steam room and then making him out on the other side. That would give Noel enough time to come down on him, but only if the steam was thunderstorm thick. Otherwise Dalton would spot him in the second he opened the door, or even looked through it. And what was he going to do with the water bottles? Throw them at the slug?

Noel got up, exited the steam room carrying the tub, but left two bottles on the highest tile bench seat. He realized he was no longer holding the pen. No idea where he'd dropped it. Excellent. What else was there?

Towels. Enough towels to dry off a small nation. Rolled. Stacked.

Stackable.

If he could arrange enough of them to look like a body . . . in the steam room . . . and the steam room continued heating up, filling up, then maybe . . .

Noel limped to the nearest wall and took two armfuls of rolled towels, carried them into the herbal room, eucalyptus cleaning out his sinuses as he worked. Hurried back into the row of shower stalls and grabbed another dozen towels, carrying them like cord wood. After three such trips he had enough and he wanted nothing more than to lie down and soak his ankle in the ice tub. Instead he built a crude humanoid shape on the top tier, in the corner beside the bottles of water, and shut the glass door, noting that the glass walls around it had been drilled and outfitted with steel plates at the bottom.

The glass door could only be opened outward, not into the steam room.

Running now, to hell with the pain, still naked and having no idea if Dalton was watching him put on this charade, he cut back into the locker bays. He threw a dozen or so towels into the huge wicker basket for spent towels, messed them up and climbed in. He buried himself, crouching until his knees touched his chin. He needed to stay on his feet, in case he needed to leap. His ankle throbbed and he forced himself to ignore the pain, put it away somewhere in the trap of his mind, talked to his ankle and told it to be patient, this would all be over one way or another very soon. Hang with me for another fifteen minutes, dear ankle, and I promise I will ice you for a month.

Now he closed his eyes, asking his ears to reach out, stay vigilant for any noise. No, not noise, any *change* in the noise that was already here. Very faintly, from behind at least three walls, came the dull drone of the deluge shower thundering the tile in the elevated room. The deluge was a constant benchmark, just enough to give a background to the otherwise silent spa. What he wanted now was to listen ever so closely for an interruption in the pattern. Would he be able to hear a difference, a change in the acoustics, if someone walked down the hall, between the source of that noise and Noel's basket?

Probably not, but it was his last hope.

He waited. His knees were cramping and he'd only been crouched this way for a couple of minutes. Dalton had to be in the spa by now. He might have wasted a few minutes checking the other halls, looking behind the counter in the spa store, peeking through the barbershop's glass door. But he would be drawn here, as Noel had been, lulled by the hidden location and relative calm. More, Dalton would know Noel had chosen this space for the privacy and opportunities to hide, or fight. Knowing Noel was not able to drop out at will, Dalton would guess that he would choose the next best thing, the steam room. At least, that was the prayer.

Five minutes passed. Probably not even that, because hiding and waiting in a situation like this, from a murderer no less, dragged the minutes out like hours. Noel's knees ached and his left foot, the good one, began to tingle from lack of circulation. He shuffled side to side, but refrained from too much movement that might stir the towels piled over his head and shoulders.

Where were the police? Security? Someone should have crashed the spa by now.

Either Hector hadn't called them or Hector was dead.

Noel decided not to think about that. He had to stay sharp, not count on help. He was going to have to do this alone.

How long now? Ten minutes? He hadn't heard anything new.

He kept his eyes closed and tried to think of nothing except himself as a sponge for sound. I am a blind man, I can hear anything, he told himself. Listen, listen for the faintest change in the droning water.

His back was stiffening. His thighs burned. He couldn't do this much longer.

A memory came back, with the sharpness of a vision granted by his heightened senses and scorched raw nerves. He was two or three years old, playing hide and seek with his mother. Rebecca had fed him waffles, he remembered the smell of syrup on his fingers, on his nose. She'd flicked soap bubbles at him and turned back to the sink, and he'd disappeared. He remembered it now as if it had happened yesterday, his first true jump where he'd been conscious of the opportunities it afforded. He hadn't known then what it was, that he was doing it to her. That he hadn't disappeared at all, only erased his presence from some part of her mind. Taking his body and clothes right out of the junction where the eyes meet the brain, blotting himself from the nexus of her perceptions and the organs, melting a few synapses, tricking her beautiful loving mother eyes. How cruel, what an awful thing for a boy to do to his mother. No wonder she'd gone insane. He'd done it to her hundreds of times in the years that followed.

My mind. My mind over hers. Stronger than my own mother's.

I couldn't do it to my dad, but I pulled the veil over Julie's eyes once, never again. So many people I blinded . . .

Why can't I do it to him? To Dalton? He's not strong, he's sick. I'm younger, healthier, better. He doesn't deserve it. I do. I don't kill people for sport, he does. I should own him. Where is the God in this? Confidence matters, *Dalton had said over lunch.* It's the mind. Mine was stronger than yours. *He's grown confident, powerful on his crimes. He thinks he's invincible and that I am a rookie, a scared little boy. And why shouldn't he? What have I done to prove otherwise? Nothing but run and hide.*

He's dominated me from the first moment I saw him.

No more. Whether he comes with a knife or a gun, I own him. I can take him down. I will drop out and I will corner him. I will because I can, because I deserve it, because that motherfucker will never get within a hundred miles of my Julie.

I own him.

I own him.

I OWN HIM.

And with that, Noel opened his eyes, sure to find himself gone, a mass of air tenting the pile of towels.

But no. There were his feet, turning purple and white with lack of blood flow. His hairy knees. His sad prick, shriveled with fear inside a wicker hamper. His sharp nose, his arms, his long useless body. It hadn't worked. He was still here.

I don't care. I'm taking him down. It's now or never.

I will own him.

Noel took three deep breaths and began to rise. The towels slid from him like leaves from a native creature in a primeval forest. His legs tingled, his ankle screamed, but he ignored the pain. The locker room was empty. Dalton wasn't here, he could feel that much. He walked calmly to the row of toilets and backed against the wall, peering around the corner, into the central hall. He saw nothing, withdrew. He closed his eyes, listening. The drone of the deluge was louder now that he was not covered in towels, but still steady, constant, the sound of someone showering in the apartment overhead. He wanted desperately to look, to search the rooms, but looking wouldn't help. If he relied on his eyes, he wouldn't see Dalton until Dalton had cut him open and tasted his blood. He had to trust his ears.

His closed his eyes, breathed in and out. He listened.

A minute passed this way, Noel naked, blind and vulnerable as a newborn, trusting his ears alone.

Another minute, maybe two.

And then it came. The blip. No, not even a blip. A one-second, tiny, almost imperceptible flattening in the droning sound wave. As if someone had passed a hand over Noel's ear without fully cupping it. As if someone in another room had flushed the toilet and caused the shower in the next apartment to hiccup. A tiny, perfect, audible fade. Here in a mental blink, gone just as fast. It might have been anything, a door closing somewhere, the churn of a ventilation fan kicking on. But it was all he had, and if he was going to trust it, now was the time.

Noel opened his eyes and stepped off the wall, rounding into the corridor of shower stalls. He walked calmly to the other end, into the main hall. If his ears had been correct, this was the hall Dalton had just passed through, dimpling the sound wave.

At the end, in the leg of the L, were the steam

rooms. He walked toward them, hewing close to the right side wall, slowing as he reached the turn. He leaned forward, cheek against the wall, until he could see around the corner with his left eye.

In front of the three glass doors to the steam rooms, in the small concrete space with its white robes hanging on the pegs, there was nothing. No body, no motion, no disturbance of the stacked towels, no doors opening or closing, no sound . . .

The rubber mat. It was wide, a blue runner that stretched in front of each glass door. Maybe an inch thick, with hundreds of small holes cut into the material for water to run through. The surface was pebbled for extra traction, and the whole of it sloped toward the center, under which was drain.

Noel stared at the mat, focusing, and saw a depression near the far edge. It was not foot-shaped, but it was a dent, rounded, maybe two and a half inches in diameter. A heel print. While he was staring at that, another one appeared about eighteen inches behind the first. Motion, weight, a body.

Dalton.

Noel's heart boomed. The steps were moving toward him and he almost screamed. But Dalton wasn't coming at him, he realized a second later, because the door to the first steam room was opening. Dalton had simply backed up a pace, turned, and opened the first glass door in the row, slightly to his left.

Noel wanted to storm the bastard now, but he

forced himself to keep still. If this was going to work, he needed the added element of the towels buying him an extra second or two. He waited, holding his breath, retreating so that Dalton would not see him when he realized Noel wasn't in the first steam room and exited.

Dalton needed to check the other rooms. If he only checked door number one before heading back into the hall, he would walk right into Noel and it would be over. If he checked door number two, the herbal steam room . . .

Noel counted to ten, listening for the squeak of the door, the hiss of steam jets when the door was open. Neither came. How long does it take to check a steam room that's hardly larger than your average rich man's walk-in closet? Five seconds? Ten? No more than that.

Noel counted to five. When he got to three, a draft pulled by him and the hissing got louder for a moment, then quieted. Dalton had just exited door number one.

He waited for Dalton to round the corner and run right into him, but he didn't.

Another draft, this one softer, with the same escalation of hissing steam. This time the steam stayed louder longer and he knew Dalton was holding door number two open. Which meant he was looking in, with his back to Noel's position, cautiously trying to decide what was in here as his hackles registered something amiss.

A three-count later Noel turned the corner and saw, for a period of two or three seconds only, the outline of Dalton's head and shoulders and half of his torso cutting into the wall of rolling herbal-infused steam. Moving forward, deeper into the room. It was like seeing a ghost and it chilled Noel in a way that seeing the other ghosts never had, terrifying him and exciting him in equal measure.

I got you, slug. I own you.

Then the door was closing and Dalton was inside.

Inside, stirring the clouds with his arms and hands and probably his blade, on his way to stab a dummy fashioned from towels.

Noel leaped forward and planted himself to one side of the steam room door. He braced his feet as best he could and peered through the glass. The steam was chaotic, swirling, and then the white towels were flying. A water bottle smacked the wall. Dalton's voice, spewing anger, and then the slapping of his feet as he came back.

Noel spun and braced the glass door with all his strength, both legs, his back to the glass for maximum surface and leg leverage. Dalton slammed into it, shoved hard, making Noel's bare feet slip on the rubber mat. Noel set his right foot forward, the good one, making it the anchor. The door had no latch or lock, and for the first minute Dalton managed to jar it open an inch or two, but no more than that. The steam was thick now, much stronger than when Noel had first entered, and there was no rubber mat for traction inside. Only slick tile, wet with condensation.

Noel prayed the glass would not break, that Dalton had not brought a gun. He didn't think a gun would be Dalton's style. The glass was at least an inch thick and safety regulations would require that it be tempered and extremely strong.

Dalton roared, slamming into the door, but the harder he threw himself at it, the worse he rebounded. Noel took the jarring twice, three times, and on the fourth of the blows he pulled the door toward him, opening it just enough to throw Dalton off stride. He hesitated only a moment before slamming back in place, by which time Dalton's face was in reach. Dalton crashed into the door with a surprised grunt, then howled and crashed backward into the tiled riser.

Though Noel couldn't see him stand, spots of bright red bubbled into existence within the steam and fell from head height, as if the clouds were beginning to drizzle blood.

He had broken Dalton's nose.

Now the real panic set in and Dalton went wild. Noel braced the door with all he had, used his long frame to lever and focus his mass. Shoe sole prints slammed into the glass, outlined in water beads and trickling condensation. Then his fists or something round and duller thudded, pummeling the glass one inch from Noel's turned face. Dalton's bandaged hand, invisible but soaked through, smeared the glass in wide patches, streaked it with more blood as his severed fingertips reopened.

'Sonofabitch I'm going to kill you fucking dead!' Dalton screamed. 'Little fucking rat cocksucker I'm going to cut your balls off and rape your girlfriend do you hear me I'm going to destroy you and your family and everyone you've ever known!'

Dalton screamed and yelled and beat against the door, but after three or four minutes the blows were coming softer and Noel was growing stronger, boosted by the taste of victory, by the knowledge that Dalton was doing everything wrong. He was too stupid to stay calm and wait it out. He had discovered he'd been outsmarted, trapped, and now was throwing a hissy fit. And the angrier he became, the calmer Noel was.

Good. Perfect. Go crazy in there, old man. Run yourself out of breath and hurt yourself. The sooner you expend your energy, the sooner you're going to collapse.

Noel didn't want Hector to come now. He didn't want the police or security to get involved. He wanted to watch Dalton suffer and go down like the rabid animal he was.

At what must have been the seven- to nine-minute mark Dalton stopped battering the door. The cursing and screaming stopped. The room went silent but for the hissing steam. Noel couldn't be sure, but he thought the slug was on his knees, or sitting on one of the benches, lungs heaving and choking on the humidity. Noel was tempted to open the door, but he didn't trust that enough time had passed. Dalton might have fainted, but could just as easily be hoarding his reserves, mustering one last stand, waiting for Noel to walk into his blade.

He waited. Keeping his shoulder to the door, adjusting his footing, watching the roiling clouds of steam for any sign of movement. He didn't like sitting on the other side of the glass, knowing Dalton was probably watching him, studying him, planning. He felt almost as trapped, and, worse, examined like a specimen on a slide. He was an open target. But if Dalton had a gun, he would have used it by now.

More minutes passed, and Noel thought Dalton had been trapped inside the steam room, fully clothed, for at least fifteen and maybe as many as twenty minutes. How long could a clothed, out-of-shape man survive in a steam room? Surely half an hour or an hour, though he would be severely dehydrated and weakened, possibly on the verge of a stroke. Noel did not want to stay here for an hour, but he knew that he would. If that's what it took to end this, he would stay all day.

Noel watched as the last of Dalton's blood washed down the glass, pushed by smaller beads of condensed steam to the tile floor. He counted off another minute, two, three, and when he was ten seconds short of five, a piercing scream tore through the clouds.

Noel redoubled his stance and the screaming went higher and higher, and higher still. It was a woman's scream, then a teen horror movie vixen's shattering peal, then something sexless and inhuman, a demon being torn apart at the limbs. It almost convinced Noel the man was dying of something new in the room and he was tempted to cover his ears, but just then a tremendous force crashed the door, the hardest one yet, as if Dalton had launched himself from the top riser like a steroidal wrestler.

The force of it knocked Noel back on his bad foot, and his ankle gave way again. Something inside cracked and Noel growled in agony. He fell to the slick mat and the door swung wide as Dalton tumbled out in a gasping hot sweaty ball. Noel rolled, tried to sit up, but his hands slipped and a terrible weight fell on his chest.

He was under Dalton, waiting for the blade to plunge, but the killer came equipped with only his fists. The blows started in, cracking into his jaw and neck and temples with frantic energy. The wet bandaged hand pawed at his face and Noel shoved back, using his longer arms to push Dalton away as he lashed out in a series of kicks, one of which struck the killer's gut or groin.

Dalton grunted hard and the weight lifted. Noel scrambled across the mat, twisting and shuffling on his knees. As he was rising, another blow caught him in the hamstring, then another in the lower back. Noel allowed himself to fall with the blows and flung himself forward, reaching for the counter as he went down. His right hand caught on the pile of rolled towels and he clenched one before slamming to the floor.

He spun to his right, rolling like a log two times, until he was looking up again. Something hard stabbed into his sternum — a foot, a stomping foot — and Dalton screamed above him.

'Take it!' Dalton screeched. 'Take it, take it, what you get for fucking with me!'

Noel caught the fucker's ankle in his left hand and twisted, jerking back and forth as he flapped the towel open with his right. He roped the towel around the limb. He yanked toward his chest until the other foot slipped and the weight left the leg and Dalton was falling.

The slug crashed to the floor and Noel crawled up onto his attacker, until he was straddling Dalton's belly. The towel was still clenched in his right hand and he whipped it around now, spread it, smothering the man's face. Noel saw the shape of the mouth in white cotton a split second before he felt the bite on his knuckles.

He yelled and punched down with his left fist, striking something hard, maybe Dalton's forehead, and the mouth released his fingers. Noel punched again, three times with his right, until more red appeared in the towel. Dalton's head floated off the floor a moment, dazed, and Noel used the towel to render the head shape fully, mapping it, striking the center repeatedly before twisting and looping the towel into a thick cord around the back of Dalton's neck. He crossed the strands, yanking the towel as tight as it would go. Dalton gagged and Noel slammed the back of his head against the floor. If they had not been on the rubber mat, this would have ended it, but they were and it was not over because the old professor had gone wolverine with survival rage.

Dalton kicked and thrashed and tried to buck Noel off, and Noel rode him down like a cowboy grinding a steer into the sod. He jerked the neck, slamming the head into the mat, raising and then dropping his full weight on Dalton's chest, pulling the towel ends until his arms screamed and burned.

Dalton's legs jimmied and the man choked and choked and Noel pulled the towel ends tighter still, his arms filling with flaming nitroglycerine. He had been winded a moment ago but now was in a surge and his arms passed through pain into an ecstasy. He intended to pull the towel until Dalton's head popped off like a dandelion stem.

'I own you,' Noel whispered. 'I own you. I own you. I own you . . . '

He said it over and over, calmly, staring into the invisible mask beneath the now visible runners of blood pouring from Dalton's nose and the flecks of white spittle ejecting from the invisible mouth. Noel pulled the towel ends with all he had and leaned down close, until his face was in the seizing sprinkler of blood.

'I see you, fucker, I see you now. Are you listening, Theodore? Can you hear me inside your prison cell? You don't see me, you don't ever see me. I see you. I see you now and I own you.'

Slowly, resolving in a time-lapse reel, stage by stage, no more than a shadow at first, then a colorless shape, then as skin seen through a sun-warmed bed sheet, and finally into wet living color, Dalton exited his fading. He was losing his control, his strength, his ability, and Shaker was the force relieving him of it.

Fascinated, never relenting, Noel stared down in wonder as Dalton filled in, became whole, and with eerie coordinated timing, as if one

427

man's color and life and life force were flowing into the other's, Noel's throbbing arms and clenched hands began to seep away with the lingering liquid retreat of a sunset sky, with the slow ballet of camouflaging octopus arms sliding into the coral den. In all his other turns, for twenty-four years, at the beginning and end of every episode, there had been no graceful transition, no sense of easing into the pool where light could not go. He had only ever blinked, been flipped, shut out, locked out of his life and the world. Or snapped back and paroled into the larger prison of his life with the cruelty of a heart attack. For Noel there had never been a fading, only a switch, a brute shock, a life sentence.

But this time was different, this one was unique. He rode it, accepted it, let it come slowly and took the reins atop it, telling it not yet, not yet, a little more, a little more, I own you. You are mine, sweet precious thing. I am your source, I am your power, I am your Lord. You listen to me now. I am your father, you are my child, we are one. The color was him. The light was him. The dark was him. He chose it, he chose how much, he chose when. He chose now, on his own terms, and he knew that from this moment on, for all the reaming days of his life, the fading would serve him.

He released the towel and roared.

'*I OWN YOU!*'

By the time he had vanished in total, Noel Shaker was standing free of all his pains, and the killer beneath him was nothing more than a

428

ruined old man with burst eyes, piss-stained trousers and the bloodied pig face of an errant playground bully.

Dead as dead could be done.

38

Hector was in the spa supply closet, crunched down in the corner beneath vats of laundry soap and stacks of toilet paper, clutching the handle of a broom whose whiskers bristled against the door when Noel entered. His belly and lap were soaked with blood. He had been stabbed at least three times, twice in the stomach and once under the sternum to puncture the heart. Noel checked for a pulse and any sign of breathing.

Hector was not coming back.

The door's two locks appeared intact, which meant Dalton had talked his way in, or that Hector chose the wrong moment to attempt an escape. Noel took the keys from Hector's pocket, leaving the body as he had found it. He locked the main entrance and returned to the spa.

The clock in the lounge read 6.52 a.m. In less than ten minutes the spa would be officially open for guests. They would linger for a few minutes, then pound on the door, then call the front desk to complain.

Keeping himself in the bubble, which was no longer a bubble but a wide array of tentacles he visualized and used to snake the walls and doors in a thousand directions, until he had spun a web that would blind anyone who walked into it, at least to him, Noel showered in one of the stalls, using the body wash dispenser to fill his palms and rid himself of Theodore Dalton. He looked at his fingers, thought of prints, then remembered something important.

He went back to the steam room and found what he was looking for on the blood-smeared floor. Dalton's knife. Had the professor, in his panic, lost it in here? Could he really have been so sloppy? Or had he given it up? Why would he forgo such an advantage? Was it possible that some part of the man, even on a subconscious level, was ready for the game to end? *The hunt grows tiring. Sometimes I feel like a cat stuck on my eighth life.* Is this what he had wanted from Noel? Someone to take his place? Relieve him of duty?

Noel carried the knife out and wrapped it in the dead man's hand, using the fingers to smudge the handle, and left it where it belonged.

At the row of sinks in the long vanity, he used a disposable razor and the cream provided to clean up six days' worth of stubble. He gargled and rinsed with the mouthwash and helped himself to a cold bottle of water. He wrapped a towel around his waist, faded it and walked back to the rain shower room.

He collected his clothes and shoes and carried them out, confident nothing would slip and reveal itself as he pushed a shield ahead and behind and to each side of himself as he exited and strolled back to the grand staircase. He walked barefoot, limping slightly, through the halls, past the front desk, into the casino among dozens of people and he thought, *all of you.*

He slipped the clothing into a random trash receptacle.

Still wearing nothing more than the towel, shivering in the resort's climate control, he wound his way back to the twenty-four-hour sundry shop and waited until the clerk turned around to restock the shelf behind her counter with more cigarettes. He pulled a green Caesars Palace t-shirt and black drawstring vacation pants from the rack, absorbed them, and spotted a peg hung with cheap flip-flops. He took a guess at the size and quietly carried his new outfit back to the casino and into the nearest restroom. He dropped the towel in one of the stalls, put on his new clothes and re-entered the visible world by thinking, *OK, now*.

He reached for the bathroom stall door, realized he needed money, and thought, *not yet*. He was veiled again before finishing the thought, his mind working like a hyperactive mirror that absorbed light as fast as he could think it, as fast as light could travel, as fast as perception could be manipulated. In the wake of the killing and with the rush of his newfound confidence, he was not concerned with numbers, crowds. He felt ready to blind all of Las Vegas.

He walked onto the casino floor and studied the tables. A grizzled couple in Western shirts, hats and cowboy boots were having a decent run at roulette. Noel watched them for a moment, walked behind the croupier, waited for the woman to lean forward to flick the ball and grabbed a tall stack of lavender chips marked $100. He put them in his pants pocket, waited a moment for her to bend over again to rake the losing chips from the felt and took another stack.

432

He repeated this method at six more tables, spreading the take among roulette, blackjack and craps.

He returned to the bathroom, dropped his shield and carried the mass of chips to the cashier cage in his full personage. The black woman with braids and red lipstick he had seen earlier this morning smiled and counted him out. He thanked her and walked away with $9000 and change.

He walked back to the gift shop and bought a Caesars beach tote. He made sure no one was watching at the moment he turned it on again, taking the bag with him.

At the bar that had been his original destination yesterday morning, he waited until no one was looking in his direction and flipped the switch. The safari man, the brave lion-taming lady, their little red pup tent and the Jeep. Julie's Adventure People set was looking a little dusty up on the glass shelf above the register, but it was still here, even the monkeys. He climbed over the bar — it was closed and no one was on duty, though this wouldn't have stopped him — and delivered the toy set into his bag, and climbed back out.

Into the bathroom, to reappear, so that he might dine in peace.

He killed an hour at the breakfast buffet, most of it spent chewing and swallowing and groaning with pleasure. He could not remember the last time he had eaten. When he had his fill of bacon and waffles and two bagels stacked with onions and lox, he blinded the mall workers and patrons inside the Forum Shops, which were now open.

He exited Caesars Palace a little more than an hour later to find more than a dozen police officers clustered around the front desk, running back and forth between the lobby and the hallway leading to the spa. Several were plain-clothes detectives, taking notes, eyeing the lobby coolly. Others were checking IDs and taping off doors to control the crowd flow. No one entered or exited without being carded. If the police had been able to see him, they would have stopped the man dressed in a new indigo-colored Emporio Armani suit, the white tapered dress shirt, gold silk boxers, $2000-TAG Heuer timepiece, and crocodile-skin loafers, but the matching crocodile-skin Armani billfold in his breast pocket would have revealed no ID, only a thick fold of cash.

Noel repopped in the cab queue and five minutes later was stepping into an orange and white minivan that smelled of roasted almonds and stale air-conditioning. The driver was a kind-faced woman of sixty or so, unseasonably bundled in a thick plaid hunting thermal and a red UNLV baseball cap.

'Where to?' she asked.

'McCarran International.'

'On your way home?'

'Yep.'

'Had enough fun for one weekend?'

'Or a lifetime.'

A cardboard can tinkled as the woman fist-popped almonds en route. When the rental car lots came into view, he thought how much more practical it would be to drive. Safer, with a few hours of cruising through the desert to clear his mind and think about what he was going to say to her when he got to Calabasas.

But the truth was, he was anxious to see Julie, to tell her everything was going to be all right — he had control of it now. Not to mention he'd never been on an airplane before and he really wanted to know what it was like to fly.

★ ★ ★

It must have been a Monday, occasion for the exodus from Sin City. The line of three or four hundred people waiting to get through security stretched down the mezzanine and around a corner. After using the restroom to drop out and secure his bag with Julie's toys he confronted the line and thought, *a tunnel, a tunnel over all of you.*

He walked to the cordoned area where the long single line fed into six chutes with their luggage scanners and metal detectors. He ducked under the rope and walked through an empty lane not currently in service. A grating beeping sound erupted overhead. One of the toys must have triggered the metal detector. Many heads turned but no eyes found. He kept walking.

An hour and forty minutes later he had found what he was looking for, in the terminal for Southwest flights. Judging by the number of people waiting at the gate, this would be a light load heading for Los Angeles. He counted just twenty-three passengers and boarded last. On the plane were more than sixty open seats and nine unoccupied rows from the tail up.

Twice he got halfway down the aisle before having to double back as someone got up to dig out a newspaper or a book from luggage that had already been stowed, and a third time to avoid a flight attendant who turned abruptly from the rear galley and came marching forward with a fresh stack of pillows. A female passenger in a brown velour tracksuit chose the wrong moment to lean across the aisle and whisper something to her friend, making contact with him. Fortunately it was only the back of her elbow and when she turned to say excuse me and saw no one hovering behind her seat, she only paused in confusion, shook her head and went on with her gossiping.

Planes are crowded, anonymous, he reminded himself. They are all too busy nervously suppressing their frail mortality to worry about the invisible shoulder bump, the coughing empty seat.

To be safe, Noel stepped into the galley storage bay beside one of the rear lavatories and killed another ten minutes, until everyone was seated and buckled in. No point in sitting down, only to get boxed in or sat upon by some last-minute straggler. When it was obvious no one else would be boarding, he chose the third to last row, which — along with the two behind him and six in front — he had all to himself. He chose the window seat, for the view.

Another flight attendant went through the

safety announcement and, this being his first time, Noel paid her his full attention.

Then the turbines were winding up, the plane lurched back from the jetway, and they taxied around to the main runway. The engines began to roar and Noel felt the need to tighten his apparently floating seat belt as the nose lifted and his body made a transparent depression into the seat back. Aloft, he stared through the window and watched Las Vegas become another kind of Adventure People play set, with its plastic model buildings, twinkling lights stabbing into the merciless desert glare, and seeing the traffic coasting silently up and down the Strip he could not help but think of the Matchbox cars he used to play with in his tree house, watching them vanish in his innocent young hands.

Goodbye, Las Vegas. If you ever saw me, you won't ever again.

* * *

Despite his inner warnings not to succumb, Noel nodded off before the beverage service began. The hum of the jets and gentle bobbing of the flight lulled him down inside himself, into a maze of corridors and hotel rooms where he was frantic, searching for Julie, knowing that her life depended on him finding her before it was too late.

Something evil was coming for her, something infinitely worse than Theodore Dalton, and only he had the power to stop it. The building — a sort of mutated, nightmarish version of Caesars

Palace with black stone walls and floors wet with blood and long filaments of black algae that bore a strong resemblance to Julie's hair — trembled as the entity pursued her. Noel followed, shouting after her. She turned and looked back, hearing his voice, but could not find him, could not see him. There was a howling noise beneath him and the deep, undiluted anger of the beast reverberating through the floor bounced him off his feet. He was thrown over a stone ledge, falling down the center of an endless stairwell that spiraled into the abyss, passing porthole windows lighted with flickering candles inside rooms where people from his life — his mother, his father, Lisa, his friend Trevor and the short goblin Dimples — suffered individual agonies as he fell. Then he was slammed into a chair, strapped down, and he could not breathe through the clouds of steam choking his lungs.

A bell dinged loudly from the overhead speaker and Noel woke to discern the source of his dream. A flashing seat belt sign. Turbulence. The jet was jostling and rocking severely. Sitting so far back, he felt the tail of the plane swinging in greasy, rudderless abandon as the pilots fought to stabilize it. Though he had never flown before, he was pretty sure this was not normal, and this suspicion was confirmed a moment later when a broad plank of air seemed to slap the plane's belly, throwing them high and slamming them back into their seats with teeth-clacking force. At least three women screamed and the contents of several purses and carry-ons launched around the cabin as if they were all trapped inside the guts of a donkey pinata under assault.

All of this happened before he'd even had time to check himself and make sure the veil had held. It had, even while he slept.

The nose pitched down and Noel's stomach sprang up into his chest as they began to lose altitude with the velocity of a dropped bomb. Yellow oxygen masks on their clear plastic cords plunged from the ceiling trapdoors like an armada of spiders. The captain was stating matters of some importance over the public address and the flight attendants were clutching the tops of the seats as they staggered down the aisle, pantomime-ordering the passengers to bring their seat backs up, install the masks over their faces, put away all sharp objects. Desperate conversations, mouths opening and closing, but Noel couldn't understand a word being spoken.

Under the shrieking of the plane's descent and the blood rushing behind his ears, he couldn't hear a thing.

39

Noel resisted the urge to follow the herd and don his oxygen mask. He didn't want to black out or suffocate, but pulling the mask over his head would force him to reveal himself. This might not be a problem given the current panic, with everyone so distracted even the flight crew might figure they had simply overlooked the well-dressed man who suddenly appeared in the back, or that he'd been seated in another row and moved during the chaos. But if all of this resulted in some sort of emergency landing where people would be cataloged, medically examined and identified, he did not want to give himself up until it was absolutely necessary.

Of course, if they were really going down, not in the conventional 'emergency landing' sense but to crash, then staying unmasked (in both senses) would be a wasted effort. It wouldn't matter who he was or what he had done — he'd simply be dead.

Did he need the mask? He felt light-headed, and, for that matter, light-bodied, but probably everyone felt this way now. The plane was still traveling at a disturbing downward angle and the fuselage was quaking and Noel wondered, if he kept himself faded through the termination of the flight and its passengers, what would the rescue teams and clean-up crews find? Would they stumble onto an invisible corpse? Or would he lose control of it at the moment of his collapsed mortality, the way Dalton had?

He reached for the mask, fumbled the flimsy elastic straps, debated and debated, but decided to let it go. Another minute, just another minute, and then if things are still looking like doomsday, I'll put it on. Because deep down he really did not believe he was going to die. Not here, not now. Not after all he had survived. Surely fate couldn't be so moronically cheap as to let him get this far only to end his journey by way of a random airplane disaster. Could it? No, of course not. But this, too, was probably something the rest of them were thinking. This can't be happening to me. It's not my time.

Maybe it is our time. Maybe it will never feel like our time, even when it is.

He flashed back to his big win at the roulette table, on his birthday. When he had felt the universe, or at least his own small bubble in it, buckle under the exploding pressure of his oncoming ten-week blow-out. His life had flashed before his eyes then, and it did so now, in a capsule of that capsule moment, returning him to the vision he had experienced then now as a hastily edited rerun. He had seen his past episodes, the worst moments, the turning points, and then the eye of his mind had cast itself into the future, allowing him a glimpse of the life he would lead.

It might have been out of order then, and it was definitely out of order now, but somewhere in the flurry of images, impressions and touchstones to come he had seen himself wealthy in New York, hosting a cocktail party in a penthouse apartment. He had seen the liquid waterfall of green on a financial services terminal, where as a witness to privileged information he stood to make a fortune. And before or after those things he had experienced this moment, this life-threatening now, himself trapped on an airplane, the world on the verge of turning upside down just outside his window while passengers screamed and —

But would you look at *this*. They *weren't* screaming now. The plane was groaning and shaking in its descent, but in all other ways the cabin had gone quiet. The other passengers seated ahead of him were not making a sound. Their heads were bowed, the tubes of their masks stretched down tautly, supplying them with oxygen. But no one was moving, looking around, phoning loved ones.

He thought he must be mistaken, but when he unfastened his seat belt to rise up and get a better view of them, he saw that he wasn't. A chill rippled through him as he surveyed the cabin, the passengers, the flight attendant in her jump seat at the front of the plane. She was halfway out of view behind the bulkhead, but he could see her legs folded loosely, one knee fallen open despite the fact she was wearing a skirt, and her head lolling limply with the plane's rocking, chin against her chest, the yellow mask crooked around her mouth but hiding her nose.

She was out, they were all passed out.

So why wasn't he?

Noel sat down and rubbed his hands over his

face, knuckling his eyes, trying to keep himself awake. He was awake, yes? Alert? Not sleepy? Yes, he was fine. Scared shitless but otherwise fine.

The next thing he noticed was that the plane had begun to level off. The endless shuddering had lessened, and over the next minute stopped altogether, the sky suddenly as smooth as a down feather bed. The side-to-side pitching of the tail had ceased. Noel looked around hopefully, skeptical but already hurrying into relief. Maybe we're not going to die! It's under control, the captain has control of the plane!

But no one said so. No one else was celebrating, talking, raising their heads. The flight attendant up in the jump seat was still zonked. Neither the captain nor his co-pilots provided an update over the PA.

The plane was just flying smoothly, level and steady on its course, and everyone was asleep. Oh, Jesus, this was wrong. What if the pilot and his crew were sleeping, too?

No, no. Don't think about that. Everyone else panicked, the blood rushed to their feet, they went under from lack of oxygen, that's all. They're going to wake up any moment now. The captain will apologize for the scare any moment now.

But several minutes passed and no one woke up.

The flight crew made no announcement.

Noel unbuckled his seat belt again and stood, looking over his shoulder before wading into the aisle. No one was behind him, and everyone

443

ahead of him appeared to have been euthanized. A strong urge to shake one of them came over him, if only to make sure they weren't dead. What in the name of God was this? What was he supposed to do? How long was he supposed to stand there and watch this before he started screaming at them, pounding on the cockpit door?

He was standing in the center of the aisle, looking from the back of one head to another, waiting for something to happen, when a man in the front row stood up. He was tall, wearing a black suit, and the back of his head showed graying blond hair cut close, with curls on top, and a toughened neck of angry sunburned skin.

As this man was edging into the aisle, a second rose beside him, and then a third. The other two were younger and shorter, but dressed in black suits, white dress shirts and dark ties that matched the larger man's. The big guy turned in profile and gestured toward the exits. His underlings split — one to stand post at the front door for boarding, the other at the emergency exit over the wing. The latter was a short stocky guy with a tight face, black crew cut, and unhappy eyes, just eight rows ahead of Noel.

Noel edged back into his row and sat quietly, his stomach doing barrel rolls of a different nature from when he had been sure they were going to crash.

The tall man strode around the corner of the bulkhead and applied a short, shiny silver instrument to the jump-seated flight attendant's neck, held it there while he looked at his watch for a few seconds, then returned to the center of the aisle, pocketing whatever device he'd just used on her.

His two henchmen each withdrew a silver pistol with an oversized sight of some kind attached to the top and braced themselves, backs to the doors they were guarding. Noel thought it strange and not a good sign they weren't surveying the cabin or its passengers, but merely staring straight ahead, guns held across their chests.

Terrorism? A hijacking of some sort? Is this something averted or something happening?

The answer came soon after the apparent superior of the threesome headed down the aisle toward Noel, when his haggard, squint-eyed features came into view, and Noel's gaze fell to the hands. The man, who went six-five and could have hidden small children in his slacks, had the largest hands Noel had ever seen. The fingers were thick as drainpipes and as abrasive as cast iron, chapped pink and gray from some kind of exposure. It was the hands — one holding the shiny silver gauge at his side, the other now casually drawing a shiny silver pistol like the others from a shoulder holster inside his suit — that placed him in Noel's memory.

It was the man who'd been talking to the snow shoveler outside Noel's apartment, arguing with the guy in his headphones while pretending they weren't casing his ass more than four years earlier. Noel remembered thinking the older man was a former basketball player, watching those pink bananas jab the decoy in the chest before they sensed they, too, were being watched and moved on.

Which meant he really should have rented a car and driven to Los Angeles, because this airplane was not malfunctioning. It had been commandeered and used to trap the thief, killer and possible threat to national security known as Noel Shaker.

'I'll start with the facts,' the big man said, then paused to clear his throat before continuing evenly. His eyes passed over the empty rows and seats without fixing on any one position, and he seemed curious but not especially concerned. 'My name is Wade Anlun and I am a senior asset within an agency of the United States government that does not hand out titles. My colleagues and I have taken control of the aircraft. No one on board has been harmed and we are here to ensure that doesn't change between now and landing. I am one of twelve men in the employ of this Great Republic who know who and what you are, Noel Shaker. I have been following you and studying you and at times chasing you, for seven years. I know most of what you have done during that time. With respect to your actions in Las Vegas, Nevada, I know everything. We have enough film to screen a mini-series.

'More facts: I do not give two shits that you have stolen millions or taken human life, deserved or undeserved. It is not my goal to arrest you and punish you for your crimes, though both are well within my authority and jurisdiction. My interests may shift in these directions if you attempt to run, hide, harm me or any of my men, several of whom you cannot see right now any better than we can see you. Understand now, you cannot run or hide, because you have been contained. We know you are on board. We have simple technology that has told us so. We have you, and you will deplane with us, willingly. Between now and touchdown, we have much to discuss. You may resist my overtures but doing so will not help you or the people you love, some of whom are also in our custody.'

No one answering the home phone.

'Final facts: you and I will speak now, face to face. You will show yourself and engage me as a gentleman of goodwill until our arrival, at which time we will conclude our business at a secure location of my choosing. I will personally guarantee your safety as long as you honor mine. We will discuss a certain responsibility of yours that I hope you will see as an opportunity to save yourself from imprisonment, physical and psychological dissection, and more than likely an early and needless death.

'You have sixty seconds to show your agreement to these terms by revealing yourself. If the minute ends and I cannot see you, hands raised, you will be considered a treasonous hostile enemy of the United States of America and of me personally, and you will never see Julie Wagner alive for so long as you live, which, I promise, won't be through the end of the week. Proceed.'

Non-Agent Wade Anlun stowed his firearm

and raised a cuff to look at his watch.

The other two guards or bagmen or whatever they were pivoted from the door and trained their guns down the aisle in a crossing pattern, their expressions betraying no emotion whatsoever.

Noel stood up in his row and dropped his blinding web, manifesting before them in the amount of time required to unfasten a seat belt. He raised his open palms.

Anlun looked up and met his eyes with a tired, unimpressed nod. He walked to Noel's row and sat in the aisle seat, boxing the obvious line of escape. He gestured to the window seat and Noel complied. The big man said nothing for a minute or two as the plane cruised and Noel entertained visions of hi-tech prison cells, needles in the forehead, surgeries, a bunker in a mountain where he would spend the rest of his life.

'Well, I guess congratulations are in order,' Anlun said at last.

Noel swallowed and unfastened the top button of his shirt. 'For?'

Anlun turned and smiled at him. 'You've graduated into the big leagues.'

Then, while the rest of the passengers slept off their sedative gas, he explained what he had in mind.

40

The jet touched down at Los Angeles International with only the faintest of bumps and all but the three operational people in the cockpit — plus Noel, Anlun and his personnel — slept through it. The pilot taxied them to a leg at the southernmost end of the airport's U-shaped terminals and into a maintenance hangar. Anlun did not wait for the seatbelt sign to change before standing. His agents had stood guard, guns drawn, all through the flight and landing, but had not pointed their weapons in Noel's direction since the boss finished his speech.

When the plane rocked to a halt, Anlun stepped back to clear Noel's row and gestured. 'After you.'

Noel stood and walked up the aisle, averting his eyes from the sleeping passengers, but was unable to keep himself from looking down at the sleeping flight attendant in the jump seat. She was drooling and would probably wake with a very sore neck, but otherwise seemed to be fine. The door was closed and the agent guarding it stared through Noel without expression. Noel turned to Anlun, awaiting instructions.

Anlun said, 'The door, Stieglitz.'

'Sir.' The agent stowed his firearm and unlocked the hatch.

A rolling stepladder was already in place.

Stieglitz went first, scanning the empty building as he descended. Noel took his cue and went next, with Anlun bringing up the rear. Noel did not see the one who'd been guarding the emergency door over the wing exit the plane. He imagined someone was going to stay, to take care of the sleepers.

'What's going to happen to them?' Noel asked when they reached the tarmac.

Anlun walked to his left and slightly behind him. 'They'll wake up in about fifteen minutes and be given a speech by the pilot as medical personnel board to help them off in a smooth, orderly fashion. Everyone will be examined in the portable triage tents and trucks on their way now. The risks and details of their ordeal, the ventilation malfunction, will be explained. Then they'll be sent to their destinations. Don't concern yourself with them. We've done this a few times.'

Anlun steered Noel toward a large black SUV that had pulled up, the center vehicle in a trio of the same. Another agent exited the passenger side and held the second door open for them.

'You're not worried they'll talk?' Noel said.

Anlun was sucking from a bottle of water he'd acquired sometime between landing and thirty seconds ago. 'Of course they'll talk. They'll tell everyone they know, the media, their lawyers. Some of them will make a little money from it, the airline will settle out of court, Uncle Sam will pick up the tab. The pilot and his crew are under non-disclosures from the Attorney General and they will honor that if they ever want to

450

fly again. And, seeing as how pilots hate nothing more than being grounded, none of this will mean a thing. It was a ventilation malfunction. Now, hop in.'

Noel got into the truck. Anlun sank into the leather beside him. Stieglitz took the passenger seat and the driver, another drone with oiled blond hair, led them out of the hangar as a convoy of half a dozen ambulances and a dozen supply trucks, their sirens off, wheeled around the corner. They left the terminals for a service road and within five minutes were on public streets moving away from the airport. Noel watched as the palm trees clicked by down the center median until they looped right and around up onto the massive 405 Freeway with four or five more lanes of traffic that never got above forty miles per hour.

'I still don't understand,' he said, facing Anlun beside him. 'If you kept track of me using the cameras, why didn't casino security grab me sooner?'

Stieglitz handed Anlun a small case of black leather. Anlun unzipped the case and flipped through half a dozen DVDs stored in the transparent pages, then removed one.

'I'll show you.' He inserted the disc into the overhead player and the monitors in the seat backs flickered to life, screening the same footage.

The view was black and white, as on closed-circuit, shot from the eye or eyes in the sky at Caesars Palace. After jumping from one camera to another, bouncing from gaming tables

451

to a hall to the front lobby, it settled on a bar raised on a dais, then roved and zoomed in until Noel saw his old friend Tilly arriving with a tray of empty glasses. No sound accompanied the feed.

'There's you getting shit-faced,' Anlun said without a trace of merriment.

Indeed, Noel was hanging onto the bar beside her, looking up at her, his mouth moving through the conversation they'd shared the night he was fired. This went on for a few minutes before Tilly left and he went back to his video poker.

'We could have taken you now or at any time leading up to this,' Anlun said. 'But we were waiting for Dalton to find you.'

'You knew about Dalton?' Noel said, incredulous.

Anlun gave him a look.

'Why didn't you stop him?'

Anlun paused the video. 'He was on hiatus and we needed to see how you would respond to his overtures. If he would guide you to a higher level of control, which he apparently did, though not in the way we had predicted. We also needed to know if you would go far enough without going too far. As you have gathered, this little talent of yours has certain properties corrosive to the average society's notion of acceptable morality. On a scale of one to ten, one being Mother Teresa, ten being a total poisoned psychopath who eats his victims out of sheer boredom or gases political opposition with all the bother of my wife making a bowl of microwave popcorn, Dalton was a solid eight-point-seven. We needed to see how far you pushed the needle on the scale.'

'What's my number?' Noel said.

Anlun shrugged. 'If we were concerned with that, you'd be dead right now.'

Noel shook his head in disgust.

'Here,' Anlun said, pressing play.

The footage switched locations and times. Now Noel was standing at the roulette table on his birthday, by himself except for the croupier, Sable. He won the first bet of three hundred, then the second on black 29 for over twenty-five thousand. The short guest services manager and the Amazonian waitress arrived. A small group of strollers gathered to watch. He played again, hitting the monster score on black 29. Commotion broke out, people crowded in, the guest services manager took Sable aside. The peanut gallery shouted and booed the manager as he shut the table down. Then everyone froze and looked around in shock, confusion, heads turning this way and that. Noel didn't understand what was happening until he saw himself, a random body, walking away from the table with his arms raised in victory. No one saw him leaving. He'd just 'vanished'.

'They couldn't see me,' he said. 'But the cameras got me.'

'Which is to be expected, knowing what we know about the nature of your psychic abilities.' Anlun pressed pause again.

'I'm not psychic,' Noel said. 'I can't tell the future.' *Although I have communed with the*

453

dead from time to time.

'Psychic, medium, paratalent,' Anlun said with a smirk. 'You're all mindfuckers to me.'

Maybe that's it, Noel thought. Psychics, mediums, paratalents, faders . . . what do all of us 'mindfuckers' have in common? We tap into something on the other side. Or deep inside. In the place where time bends like a pretzel, showing us past and future, where perception and reality blur into the same warped movie, where the restless dead can still reach an audience. Maybe the fading is but one road on a great big map of highways and rail lines, impossible to travel without glimpsing some of the roadside carnage. We become conduits, flypaper for all kinds of —

'Am I boring you?' Anlun said.

Noel rubbed his eyes. 'You all? How many of us do you know?'

Anlun took another book of discs from the agent up front and fanned the pages at Noel. 'This is about five hundred hours of footage from your spree of muggings. We have you in seven different casinos committing forty-six acts. There's a lot more where you're not stealing but watching, following, shadowing victims.'

'But why didn't security stop me? You control them, too?'

'We pulled a few strings,' Anlun said. 'But mostly we let them try. We could have let them get you, if and when you manifested, and taken you into custody by pulling rank. But most of the time they never got close to you.'

Anlun fast-forwarded through some boring

casino traffic, then paused just as an entourage of Chinese men in suits lost something valuable and spread out in a panic. Noel saw himself breaking away from the rearguard, a thick padded envelope under one arm, for only half a dozen steps before he bent and slipped it, unnoticed, under the carriage of a passing baby stroller pushed by a couple who were busy watching the Chinese men curse and run around like chickens with their heads cut off. Noel was visible to the camera and it all looked ludicrously obvious he'd stolen the packet, but of course no one on the floor could see him. Less than a minute later hotel security flocked in but Noel had already stepped out of frame, following the baby stroller. He remembered that one now, reclaiming his parcel in the elevator just as the couple shoved the stroller onto their floor.

'The camera has you there,' Anlun said. 'But when security descended upon the scene, 'you' weren't where you were supposed to be, or anywhere to be seen. The eyes in the sky had you, the human eyes couldn't keep you.'

'They never thought to communicate with the guys in the control room?' Noel said. 'In real time, tracking and spotting me? How hard could it have been?'

Anlun frowned. 'Are you telling me you didn't have this worked out on your own? That you were counting on dumb luck?'

Noel's face colored.

'Or maybe you knew you would be safe in either event,' Anlun said.

'What do you mean?'

'Think about that for a minute. It wasn't just the people on the ground. You started burning the others.'

Noel seized upon it. 'The eyes in the sky. I fooled the cameras? That's not possible, is it?'

'No, not the cameras,' Anlun said. 'Technology is cold, inanimate. It's not sentient and it doesn't lie. Your juju doesn't work on mechanical recording devices, so far as we know. You took out the people watching the monitors. The entire staff, the guests. Frankly we still don't know how hard you pushed and how far you reached out.'

'Okay. So, they never found me because they didn't think to look for me,' Noel said. 'They didn't see me onscreen at all, so they had no idea what or who they were looking for.'

Anlun said, 'Yes.'

'But couldn't they go back and watch the tapes? I mean, the cameras had me. They record this stuff, keep it on file for weeks or months, right? Are you telling me they never bothered to look back, even after the number of muggings went up?'

'They did go back,' Anlun said. 'We screened it for them, and it still didn't work. The ones who were in the building when you did your thing could not pick you out on screen.'

'I don't understand.'

'You didn't just disappear. You erased these people's perception of you, their ability to see you at all, permanently.'

'How does that work?' Noel said.

'You tell me,' Anlun said.

Noel's head ached.

'It's not the eyes,' Anlun said. 'It's the brain. You've gone into memory somehow, in a way that not only wipes you from their minds and eyes, but takes away the possibility of them ever recognizing — of remembering — you ever again. At least, unless you want them to. Unless they see you again, in the flesh, memory-stamping you at a later time and place, and so on.'

Noel said nothing. He was thinking of his mother, the damage done.

'After Dalton's body was found, we set up a perimeter around the resort. You were spotted in the cab line, then we kept finding you and losing you at the airport, when it became evident you had control over it. On and off, whenever it suited you. We knew you were heading for Los Angeles, so we canceled as many tickets as time permitted and placed our bet.' Anlun stretched his long legs and adjusted his belt. 'Imagine the applications of that, Noel. Casting a defensive cone against all witnesses within your given perimeter, through walls, up and down several floors, clearing the building, a city block, leaving no evidence where it matters most. In the minds of the ones who were there. If I can control the access to the scene and who sees the evidence after, and you can control the witnesses from inside, well, whatever it is, it's like it never happened.'

'No,' Noel said. 'It happened. But no one will ever be able to connect me to it.'

'Yes.'

'You've been on this for a while,' Noel said.

'You know more about it than you're telling me. How many others are there? What else do you have them doing?'

Anlun handed the DVD case up front in exchange for a single disc. 'There aren't any others, not any more. We've come close to a few, but not like you, not like this.'

'Dalton said there are dozens more. Maybe hundreds.'

Anlun thought about this. 'Maybe. People are strange, you know. When they have something, a talent like yours, a power, they tend to get very cagey. It tends to ruin them very quickly. They go into hiding, fall into drug and alcohol addiction, commit suicide. Until someone comes forward or we get lucky the way I got lucky finding you in Boulder, you're our best hope. And, frankly, your shelf life's probably not much better than a car battery's.'

Noel did not think any of this was good news. 'Best hope for what?'

'I told you that on the plane,' Anlun said.

'You said you needed me to find something precious for you in Bolivia. You didn't tell me what or why or anything else about it.'

Anlun eyed him up and down. His face gave nothing away, but his eyes were deep with sadness, and more, some kind of personal failure.

'Would I be correct in assuming you haven't been following the news much lately?' he said at last.

'I've been preoccupied.'

'There's a lot of eyes on this one now, but they

don't know what's going on inside, how bad it really is. The potential for a public relations disaster has become enormous. This makes our job difficult. A lot more difficult.'

Anlun inserted the last disc. This time he did not turn and face the screen when Noel did. He simply sat sideways, watching Noel. Reading him, his reactions to what was unfolding on the monitor.

It was very boring for almost seven minutes, then disturbing without being clear what was going on, who these people were, or why they all looked so miserable. The footage was grainy, sloppily captured, in and out of daylight and nighttime. Then there were a lot of people, white and black and brown, men and women and children, filing down a trail in some sort of woods or sparse jungle, all dressed alike in plain gray clothes, walking toward a tent with stadium lights raised up on poles.

There was a jarring cut, then static, then they were standing in rows in a large room, like a gymnasium or auditorium of some sort, though it might have been open air, the sky too dark to tell. There were bleachers. Then a man stepped on stage before them and began to talk. Calmly and jovially for a few minutes, then with increasing energy. Soon he was pacing, winding up like a motivational speaker, then thundering with anger, and the audience was no longer miserable but animated and, with alarming and unnatural speed, becoming rapt.

They cheered and smiled and clapped, but their eyes were dull, vacant, lost.

The footage jump-cut to a smaller room. There were fewer people in this one, and the same man, who was handsome but chubby, his face sweating, his hair mussed. He wore different clothes from the others, a suit of sleek black cloth that seemed to be all of one piece, some kind of holy garment that might have been homemade. He wore large-framed glasses and pointed at the gathered ones, with hands clad in leather work gloves.

Then some people were standing but others were down on the ground, crawling over one another, crawling toward him only to be pushed back from the shorter stage he prowled. He stepped down into 'the pit' (as Noel was coming to think of it) and two other men, both enormous in size, closed in beside him. And then he — the speaker — and he alone was doing things Noel did not believe one human being could do to another. Then he did another thing, and another, to someone else. The people changed in ways that should not be possible. They became animals and anarchy erupted and when they turned on one another barehanded and baring teeth, Noel looked away.

'Stop,' he said. 'Turn it off, now.'

Anlun reached across the console between them and took Noel by the back of the neck. His enormous rough hand felt like a barbell with the strength of a shop vice. Anlun squeezed his neck and drove his face downward, within inches of the screen. Noel glanced from the corner of his eye and what he saw terrified him more than what was unfolding on screen.

Anlun's lips were pulled back, his teeth grinding. His eyes were inflamed and the veins beneath the skin of his forehead were pulsing like small rivers.

'Not me,' Anlun growled. 'Them. You look at them and see what's happening down there. You two-bit carnival freak, you watch that until the very end and then you can look at me, not one second before. Do I make myself clear?'

Noel tried to nod but he could not move his neck. Anlun felt him try. He released, and Noel's neck began to refill with blood that had been dammed up.

Onscreen, the motivational speaker man from before was back. He had something long in his hand, a steel rod of some sort. It wasn't until after he began to use it and the subjects began to jump that Noel realized it was a cattle prod. A cattle prod with something pronged and sharp attached to the end.

'One other thing you should know,' Anlun said. 'And this was news to me just two months ago.'

Noel covered his mouth and fought to keep from throwing up.

'My former son-in-law, who earlier this year lost what few brains he ever had, he's in there. With them. With that. He's part of it now. He came back to the States once to empty his bank accounts for the cause, and on the way back decided to take my granddaughter with him.'

Noel jerked away from the screen and stared at the non-agent. Anlun raised his eyebrows, daring him to say anything else.

461

41

The rest of the fifty-minute ride to Calabasas passed in silence. Noel was too stunned by the implications of what Anlun had shown him to notice where they were going until the agent driver swung the SUV into the driveway of the large Mediterranean home and Noel saw his father's old restored Saab in one of the three open garage bays.

'Why do you have to involve my family?' Noel said.

'We're not involving them,' Anlun said. 'This is where you get off.'

'Aren't you staying? Coming back for me? What is this, my last day of R&R before we hump out?'

Anlun shook his head. 'We're not coming back. You're free to do as you please, Mr Shaker.'

Noel would have scoffed if he didn't think doing so would have pissed off the non-agent again. His expression must have been enough.

'If you're going to run, you'll run,' Anlun said. 'I can't make you do anything. Fritz, do we have any more coffee up there?'

The driver produced a thermos. Before taking it, Anlun said, 'Is it hot?'

'Iced,' Fritz said.

'Then what the fuck did you put it in a thermos for?'

Fritz did not reply for a moment. 'To keep it cold?'

Anlun waved him off and looked at Noel. From his suit pocket he removed a business card and Noel took it. No name or address. Only a phone number.

'Call me if you have any thoughts.'

'You can't be serious,' Noel said. 'This isn't . . . does my family know?'

'About what?'

'This. About me, you, Vegas, everything.'

'Not unless you tell them,' Anlun said. 'Which I doubt is a good idea.'

Noel fell back in his seat. 'I don't believe you.'

'I'm a man of my word. We talked. You listened. You're free to go.'

'No,' Noel said. 'I'm not free to do anything. You're going to track me, you'll be there, you'll always be there. It doesn't work this way.'

'No? How does it work?' Anlun looked at his watch.

Noel looked up through the windshield, to the house. He thought he saw a curtain move.

'Go see your family,' Anlun said. 'They're probably worried about you.'

'What about Julie?' Noel asked. 'On the plane, you said if I ever wanted to see her again. You said they were in custody.'

'I wanted to make sure I had your attention.'

'Unbelievable.'

'The world is full of unbelievable, Shaker. But it's still just the same old stupid world. Now get out of my car. I'm late for a meeting.'

Noel could not help looking back after he opened the door and slipped halfway out. He was sure they were going to grab him and

463

tranquilize him at any moment. But the three men only sat staring forward, waiting for the door to close.

'Look,' he said, leaning in to address Anlun. 'I wish I could help you, but I have to stay here. I have some things I need to put right with my girl. My father . . . I can't do the things you want me to do. I just . . . there's not a chance in hell.'

Anlun glanced at him. 'Understood. Thanks for hearing us out.'

Noel backed away and shut the door softly. The big black rig reversed from the driveway, straightened and shot off through the neighborhood.

'That didn't happen,' Noel said, shifting his lone tote bag from one hand to another. 'There's no way.'

His father stepped out onto the porch and set a hand over his brow to shield his eyes from the sun.

'Can I help you?'

'It's me, Dad. Noel.'

John Shaker lowered his hand. 'What do you want?'

Noel walked up onto the porch and stopped a few feet from his father. 'I was hoping we could talk for a few minutes.'

'Julie's not here.'

'All right. Does that mean you and I can't have a conversation?'

'You disappear for four years, doing God knows what in Las Vegas. You take our daughter to Las Vegas?'

'Julie's an adult, Dad. I didn't kidnap her.'

464

John's face was filling with pressure as if air were being pumped into it. 'Yes, and she's finally sorted you out. She's trying to get herself back on track, and I have no intention of allowing you to — '

'Stop it, both of you,' Julie said. She was standing in the doorway.

At the sound of her voice, Noel's heart skipped and then churned double-time. He looked past his father to her and began to smile, but she wasn't smiling at him.

John did not turn around, only glared at his son.

Noel said, 'I didn't come here to create a problem or argue with either of you.'

'And yet you always do,' John said. 'Please, Noel. Lisa's not well. This is not a good time.'

'I'm sorry to hear that,' Noel said, watching Julie. 'I have something that belongs to Julie, that's all. I want to give it to her, then I'll leave.'

She stared at him for a moment, then stepped down onto the porch.

John turned on her. 'You have to be at work in an hour.'

'I won't be late,' she told him as she walked by, taking Noel by the arm. 'Come on. I need to eat before my shift.'

She walked him to a used Honda sedan parked on the street. She got in and Noel opened his door, set the bag on the floor.

'Give me one second,' he told her.

'Don't push it,' she said.

'I won't.'

He walked back up the driveway. John was still

staring at him, lips compressed into a flat seam, hands on his hips, gut sucked in, chest inflated.

'I'm sorry for all of the problems I've caused you and our family, Dad. I don't expect you to forgive me.'

John allowed no quarter.

'But whatever you think of me, of Mom, it's important for you to know that we may be a lot of things, a lot of things you don't like. But we're not liars.'

John shook his head. 'I'm way past this, Noel.'

'No, not yet. But you will be. Look at me, Dad. Look at me, now.'

John stared at his son. With contempt. With disappointment.

'Watch me now, Dad. Don't blink. Are you watching me now?'

'For chrissakes.'

'Are you watching me?'

'God knows why, but yes, I am watching you, Noel.'

'Thank you.'

He faded over a period of ten seconds, until he was all the way inside. He stepped forward. He hugged his father tightly, holding him for a while. John did not move. Noel released him, stepped back, and showed himself, coloring in a smooth incoming tide. He turned his hands over, craned his neck this way and that. He smiled.

John blinked several times.

'Thank you for being my dad,' Noel said. 'That's all I wanted to say.'

John frowned, looked at Julie's car, the houses across the street. He looked at Noel and opened his mouth, but the words didn't come.

'It's okay, Dad.'

John coughed and pulled himself together. 'Well, don't keep her late. She has a job, and homework after.'

'I won't.'

John turned and stepped back inside.

In the car Julie said, 'How'd it go?'

'You weren't watching?'

'I thought it was between the two of you.'

'Yeah, it was.'

'So? Is everything all right?'

'Maybe,' Noel said. 'Maybe not.'

42

They sat on the hood of her car, a loaded cardboard carton of Double-Doubles and fries between them. Noel was sucking on a strawberry shake, Julie a chocolate. In front of them were the main runways to LAX. Every few minutes another jet floated down, wings tilting this way and that, flaps braking against the air as the engines roared and shook the palm trees lining the In N Out Burger parking lot off Sepulveda Avenue.

'How far away is work?' Noel said.

'Back in Studio City, on the Valley side.'

'I'm sorry I brought you all the way down here,' Noel said, plucking a clump of melted cheese and grilled onions from the paper wrapper and cleaning his fingers. 'You're going to be late.'

Julie shrugged. 'I'm a waitress at the Mexacali Cafe. I can always find another one of those. It's a job, not a career.'

'Is there something else you're working on?'

Julie threw a fry out onto the grass where a pigeon treated it like a worm. 'I'm finishing my degree in art history at UCLA I only have a year and a half to go, then we'll see.'

'Maybe the MBA and travel,' Noel said. 'Combine the two, live in London and work in the art world.'

Julie laughed. 'I don't think I can leave my

mom again. I want to be close, I need a home.'

'And this feels like home.'

'Some days. More than anything else ever did,' she said.

'That's good. I'm glad.' He wasn't even sure what he'd brought her here for. If he'd had a speech prepared, it had been rewritten so many times it was now just a mess of disappearing ink.

Julie elbowed him in the ribs. 'What'd you bring me?'

'I don't know. Nothing special.'

'Come on.'

'I'm not sure if it matters any more,' he said. 'Everything's different. It was just some dumb thing.'

'It's not dumb if you thought it was important. Give it to me, or else I'm going to be pissed.'

He looked at her, in her black dress shirt and the jean skirt and her black wedge heels. Her hair was shorter. Her skin was brown and looked as smooth as a seal's. He could tell she had been sober for weeks, probably from the first night she left Las Vegas.

'What's wrong?' she said.

'Nothing. Nothing at all. You look like an angel.'

She groaned and shoved him away. Noel walked around to the car door and leaned in for the bag. He came back and used the hood as a stage. He set up the traveling show, with the caged boxcars, the safari jeep, the lions and elephants and rhinos, the monkeys and the red canvas pop-tent. When he had arranged them all, he removed the mustached man in his hat and macho boots and placed him beside the tent. Lastly, he took the brave woman with her sexy khaki shorts and her plastic whip raised in one arm, and set her on the other side of the tent.

Watching Julie, he shifted the woman closer to the man. 'There?' he asked.

Julie laughed.

'Maybe too close,' he said, and moved the woman a few paces away from the tent. 'I don't think they're ready to share a tent yet.'

'Aw, Noel.' Julie slid down from the hood and hugged him, holding him with her small arms until he was against her and with her from knees to shoulders. She set her cheek against his chest and he ran his palm down the back of her hair, slowly, making it last as long as he could.

She looked up, searching his eyes. 'What happened to you out there?'

Noel shook his head. 'Nothing important.'

She knew better. 'I don't want to know. Except for one thing.'

'What's that?'

'Did it come back? It did, didn't it?' She held his face in her hands, staring into his eyes. 'I can see it in you.'

'I'm the same,' he said with no strength.

'No. Not at all. I've never seen you like this.' She released him and stepped back, crossing her arms. 'You got control of it. I know you did.'

'I don't know what you're talking about.'

Julie looked at her feet. 'Are you going to stay?'

'Do you want me to?'

Another plane fluttered down, tearing the sky in half with sound.

'I want you to do what you want to do,' Julie said. 'Because anything else won't work.'

'Yeah. I don't think I'm welcome here.'

'Your dad misses you, Noel. He always has. He just needs some time to get to know you.'

'Do you miss me?'

Julie thought it over, grinning. 'Sometimes. Sometimes not.'

'I miss you every day, Julie.'

'No, you don't. Besides, I'm not that hard to find.'

'Then I will find you again,' he said. 'Soon.'

Julie looked frightened, and he saw her guard going up. 'Where are you going?'

'The important thing,' Noel said, closing the distance, taking her hands, raising them, kissing her fingers, 'is that you know. Whatever we do next, wherever we go, whoever you're with, whoever we are to each other. If you need anything, anything in the world, I will help you get it. I will do anything for you, Jules. I promise.'

She seemed confused, trying to smile but sad despite it all.

He kissed her cheek and whispered in her ear. 'Thanks for the ride.'

She was crying. Whispered back. 'I'm sorry I left you there. I'm sorry, Noel. It was the worst thing I could have done to you and I hate myself for it.'

He clutched her, held her face and looked into her watering eyes.

'You saved my life, Julie Wagner. Believe it.'

He backed away from her. She watched him

go, shaking her head, reaching a hand out, then letting it fall. When he got to the curb near the street, he turned and trotted across the road, onto the median, and further, looking back every few steps.

She waited, watching him, arms crossed as another plane screamed down to earth.

Noel jogged across the field for a few hundred feet and looked back. Julie was climbing onto the hood to watch him. She stood up and shouted something but he couldn't make out her words.

He jumped and caught the fence, digging the toes of his crocodile-skin shoes into the chain link, and when he was straddling the top, he paused, looking back at her. Julie had a hand over her mouth and she was standing on her toes.

He made it last for her, the coming sunset over the Pacific lighting him like a torch before he gathered the rays into himself and quenched the flame with a final burst of color going black as nuclear ash, then only his silhouette, and then nothing more than a blown kiss he hoped would reach her in due time.

When he hit the ground, his ankle held. He jogged toward the terminals as another plane thundered down and caressed him with its jet wash, and this time he did not look back.

43

At a bank of payphones inside the international terminal, Noel used a calling card from the newsstand to dial a number he had never written down but had committed to memory. The line rang through eight times and he didn't think she was going to answer until she did.

'Hello?' She sounded somehow annoyed and aloof at the same time.

'Rebecca?'

'Yes?'

'Hey, Mom.'

'Who is this?'

'It's me, your son. Noel.'

The line was quiet for a few seconds and he thought she was going to hang up.

'Noel? Is that you?'

'It's me, Mom. I'm sorry to bother you. I was just thinking about you and it's been a long time. Too long. How are you?'

'Well, for Pete's sake, Noel. Where are you?'

'I'm in Los Angeles, Mom.'

'How old are you now?'

Noel laughed. 'Depends on how you count it. I think I've only had five or six birthdays, so I guess I'm still just a kid.'

This made her happy. He knew her sigh. 'Honey, are you okay? Do you need money? Are you in jail?'

'I'm fine, Mom. Safe. I'm happy.'

'I miss your face,' she said. 'Isn't that funny? Sometimes I think I miss your face more than I miss you. What a terrible mother I turned out to be.'

'No, Mom. Don't ever think that. That's what I wanted to tell you. You were right. You did everything right and you were never wrong. Do you understand?'

'What are you talking about?'

'You believed in me when no one else did. You always knew, and you never let go of that. You weren't wrong about any of it. Don't ever let anybody tell you otherwise, okay?'

'Oh, Noel.' Her voice changed. When she spoke again she sounded like an enchanted girl in a fairy tale, not at all like any mother should sound. 'Always going away. Where no one can find you. Hm, my boy? Where do you go? What do you do?'

'I'm here. I'm right here, Mom.' Noel swallowed, closing his eyes. 'You just can't see me when it happens. No one can. But I'm always here, and you're always with me.'

She giggled and began to hum with delight.

Noel wiped his eyes with his thumb.

'What it's like?' she said with dreamy longing. 'Tell me, Noeller Coaster. What's it like to disappear?'

Noel swallowed. 'It's beautiful, Mom.' He bit his fist. 'The most beautiful thing in the world.'

'Yeeessssss. I'm so proud of you. My miracle boy.'

'Thank you, Mom. I'm proud of you, too. I love you. I have to go now, okay?'

474

'Be careful, Noel. There's monsters out there, and in here, too.'

'I know. I will.'

'Promise?'

'I promise.'

'You know, for such a tall drink of water you're a good kid.'

'You should know,' he said. 'You made me.'

She sighed again, breathed heavily for a few seconds, then was quiet. Noel held the receiver until the monotone beeping signaled for him to put it down.

Behind him, in one of the gate lounges, dozens of people were staring up at the two televisions where one of the twenty-four-hour news channels was reporting on an escalation in the situation that had 'captivated the nation'. A blonde reporter was standing on a ridge near a canopy of foliage with rolling emerald hills in the background. The sky was a tropical heavy gray and a slight breeze was forcing her to hold her adorable black felt beret under a sheaf of papers to keep it from flying away.

Noel walked closer to hear, but the sound was off and he could only read the scrolling, descending captions of white text for the hearing impaired.

It said:

. . . according to reports coming in from two former members who remain anonymous and who recently risked their lives to escape the community, which federal officials are now call-ing a religious cult with possible mass suicidal

tendencies, including some seven hundred and
fifty-eight or more members and devotees,
including as many as sixty-two children inside
what has been coined by the media, The Alexander Brighton Crew in reference to the 1978
tragedy in Jonestown, Guyana, and which
others are calling The Brighton Beach Club,
though we should note we are some two hundred or more miles inland from any beach,
where members who have spent the past two
years living inside the compound where reports
of physical and sexual abuse, psychological torture and forced indoctrination, and even, if you
can believe it, Robert, executions and the consumption of human flesh, yes, reports now of
cannibalism have surfaced, shocking the world
as the former businessman from St Petersburg,
Florida, who served as a missionary for several
churches in the late nineteen eighties appears to
have now, wait a minute — incoming reports
now suggesting 'the moment of final ascen-
dency', as it's being called by survivors in
protection of Interpol and the Federal Bureau of
Investigations, Alcohol, Tobacco, and Firearms,
who have surrounded the compound, believed
to be heavily armed, as protests and international cries for non-violent confrontation alike
threaten the stability and likelihood of a safe
rescue, we are told we may be just days or even
hours away from unimaginable tragedy . . .

Half of the screen filled with a photo of the
primary suspect behind all this good fun. He was
one and the same glossy-faced slug with geek

476

glasses Noel had seen on a car TV earlier today. Alexander Brighton, forty-eight.

Noel stared into the man's pixilated eyes and mouthed three words.

I see you.

★ ★ ★

Six hours later he boarded the 747, fully faded, only to find all but a dozen of the seats empty and no Continental personnel preparing the cabin for take-off.

Anlun had his own row. The rest of his colleagues were several rows back, seated, reading reports and conversing on cellphones.

Holding himself, the passengers and most of the terminal in his blinding grip, Noel took the empty seat next to Anlun.

'Nice to see you again,' Anlun said.

'You can't see me,' the empty seat responded.

'You would be surprised what I can see.' The non-agent retrieved a dossier from the briefcase between his legs and handed it to Noel by dropping it over his lap.

Noel stopped it from sliding to the floor. 'How did you know?'

'I told you on the last flight,' Anlun said. 'You've graduated to the big leagues. You'll never be happy playing farm ball again.'

'This isn't play. I'm not doing this for me.'

Anlun sipped from his bottle of water.

'Did you hear me?' Noel said. 'This is your fault. If you hadn't showed me that video, I — I'm not promising anything. I'm your scout, a

477

pair of binoculars. Nothing more. This is one time and one time only.'

Anlun looked toward the eyes he could not see, squinting, as if by concentrating he could read them. He gave up.

Said, 'I was the fourth man on the crime scene, you know. In the steam bay where you left Dalton.'

'Your point?'

Anlun blew air from his cheeks. 'Six-point-three million. That must have hurt.'

The seat belt halves undulated from beneath the armrests and rose up like a pair of curious cobras which kissed briefly before merging as one.

Noel slipped Anlun's water bottle from his monstrous hand, savoring the surprise of the deed a moment before drinking his fill. He swallowed.

'The things I've lost,' Noel said, handing over the last of the water, 'cost so much more than I ever took.'

The jet taxied away from the terminal. The engines gulped vast amounts of air and fuel to hurtle them down the runway. The nose of the aircraft was up before he knew it, the landing gear was shuddering, and for a moment, between sky and ground, heaven and hell, womb and grave, Noel Shaker weighed less than the molecules of air he breathed and disturbed.

Acknowledgements

I'd like to thank my editor Daniel Mallory for basically saying, 'Yes, go write that' after I emailed him three or four rough sentences describing how I woke up one morning thinking about the emotional horror of invisibility and the ways in which the condition had not yet been addressed in popular fiction and films. I doubt many authors have an editor who makes the leftovers from their nightmares seem brilliant, but Dan is one, and his early and consistent support for my work makes a huge difference in the pleasure I take from this job.

★　★　★

Major thanks are also due to my agent, Scott Miller, who had several keen insights into how I could further develop the relationship between Noel and Theodore Dalton, and for his astute inquiries into the nature of the deceased characters throughout the novel.

★　★　★

My friends and fellow scribes Eric Miller, Bob Lagier, and Craig Wolf also read the manuscript and provided a little ass-kicking in the precise areas I most needed one, reminding me time and again how the little things are also the big things.

*   *   *

I appreciate the ongoing dialogues, both online and over burgers and tacos, with all of you guys. You are all serious readers and writers in your own right, and I am lucky to have your time and brain power to augment what little I have of my own.

Other titles published by
The House of Ulverscroft:

THE PEOPLE NEXT DOOR

Christopher Ransom

Mick and Amy Nash are an ordinary couple leading ordinary lives. And then, into the house next door, their new neighbours arrive — the Renders. They are beautiful, charming, perfect . . . and not at all what they pretend to be. Too late Mick learns that something is deeply, darkly wrong with the neighbours. Who are these people? Where did they come from? And what are they hiding in the basement? As death and darkness descend on the neighbourhood, only Mick can save his family and expose the horrifying truth about the people next door.

DARK WATERS

Robin Blake

Preston, 1741. When drunken publican Antony Egan is drowned, coroner Titus Cragg is not surprised. But he does his duty to the letter and the inquest's verdict is accidental death. Meanwhile, with the General Election imminent, the town is agog with rumour and faction: two local seats are to be contested by four rival candidates. Then Cragg's friend, Dr Luke Fidelis, finds evidence casting doubt on the circumstances of Egan's demise. Further suspicions are roused when a prosperous farmer, in town on political business, collapses. Is there a conspiracy afoot? The Mayor and Council have their own way of imposing order. However Cragg, determined not to be swayed by their pressure, and assisted by Fidelis's scientific ingenuity, sets about bringing the true criminals to light . . .

THE PAINTED BRIDGE

Wendy Wallace

Lake House is a private asylum for genteel women of a delicate nature. In the winter of 1859, Anna Palmer becomes its newest patient, tricked by her husband and incarcerated against her will. Anna sets out to prove her sanity, but her freedom will not be won easily. As the weeks pass, she finds some surprising allies: Lucas St Clair, a physician who believes the new medium of photography may reveal the state of a patient's mind; Talitha Batt, a longtime inhabitant who appears as sane as she is; and the proprietor's highly strung daughter. Yet the longer Anna remains at Lake House, the more she realises that — like the ethereal bridge over the asylum's lake — no one and nothing is quite as it appears . . .

THE BURNING SOUL

John Connolly

Randall Haight has a secret: when he was a teenager he and his friend killed a fourteen-year-old girl. Randall did his time and built a new life in the small Maine town of Pastor's Bay, but somebody has discovered the truth about Randall. He is being tormented by anonymous messages, haunting reminders of his past crime, and he wants private detective Charlie Parker to make it stop. But another fourteen-year-old girl has gone missing, this time from Pastor's Bay, and her family has its own secrets to protect. Now Parker must unravel a web of deceit involving the police, the FBI, a doomed mobster named Tommy Morris, and Randall Haight himself . . . because Randall Haight is telling lies . . .

WHEN SHE WOKE

Hillary Jordan

Hannah Payne's life has been devoted to church and family. But after she's convicted of murder, she awakens in a new body to a nightmarish new life. She finds herself lying on a table in a bare room, covered only by a paper gown. Cameras broadcast her every move to millions at home, for whom observing new Chromes — criminals whose skin colour has been genetically altered to match the class of their crime — is a sinister form of entertainment. Hannah is a Red for the crime of murder. The victim, says the State of Texas, was her unborn child, and Hannah is determined to protect the identity of the father, a public figure with whom she shared a fierce and forbidden love.